THE Elegant Gathering OF WHITE SNOWS

The Elegant Gathering of White Snows

KRIS RADISH

Spinsters Ink Books
Denver, Colorado
USA

The Elegant Gathering of White Snows © 2002 by Kris Radish
All rights reserved

First edition published June 2002
10-9-8-7-6-5-4-3-2-1

Spinsters Ink Books
P. O. Box 22005
Denver, CO 80222
USA
Cover Design by Lightsource Images
Interior Design by Gilsvik Book Production
Library of Congress Cataloging-in-Publication Data

Radish, Kris.
    The Elegant Gathering of White Snows/Kris Radish.--1st ed.
      p. cm.
    ISBN 1-883523-42-7
    1. Women-- Wisconsin--Fiction. 2. Female friendship--Fiction. 3. Wisconsin--
Fiction.
    I. Title.

PS3618.A35 E44 2002
813'.6--dc21   2002021077

Printed in Canada

AUTHOR'S NOTES

SOMETIMES A STORY FORMS in a writer's mind that will not her sleep, rest, breath or stop to change her clothes. This is what happened with *The Elegant Gathering of White Snows*. This story, all these women, their lives, their sorrows, joys, losses—it all came to rest in my mind, heart, and soul and this story came alive. These women became my friends. I talked with them. They whispered in my ears when I fainted above my computer keys. I felt their hands on my shoulders.

Their voices became the voices of all women. I truly believe that but there are some distinct voices that need to be thanked. No one writes a book alone. It is impossible.

From the beginning it was my mother who formed my feelings on female friendship and for that I am grateful every day of my life. The way she talked with her women friends, loved them, spread them into her world. It was a fine example. My Auntie Barbara also held my hand as a young girl and then as a young women taught me the joys of sharing laughter, secrets, and a "what the hell" attitude that has steered me through more than one blind alley. My Girl Scout leader, Mary Baker, gave me the fine gift of adult friendship and she inspired me to be myself—no matter how tough that might be. I will always love her.

There are dozens of female musicians who worked as artistic muses while I formed the words to tell this tale. Nanci Griffith and Laura Nyro were the strongest voices and their music was an inspiration.

Bev Siligmueller told me a wonderful story about a tea and she became the source for the title and the main thread in this book. Todd & Holland Tea Merchants in Illinois deserves credit for helping me understand the scared rituals of tea and for keeping my own tea bin full. My cup runneth over.

When everyone else grew sick of the sadness, sorrow and joy in the very real lives of these women walkers my dear friends, Carolyn Sorensen Balling, Coni Thorn, Kristine Klewin, Lauryn Axelrod, Pat Steuer and Jean McGoff, Vickie Radish, Audrey Limbert, Marie Dorothy Finegan and Betty Fowler kept pace with each step of this story.

My editor, Vicki McConnell, made the words in this book that were humming—sing very loudly. Vicki, I kiss your face. Nina Miranda, Spinster's Ink woman extraordinaire, pushed and pulled in the right places against enormous odds. Nina—you are a treasure. My photographer, Lisa Witte, who has tremendous talents not only captured my image but helped me through a particularly difficult time during my own Elegant Gathering. Lisa—you are a gift.

My daughter, Rachel Ann Carpenter, and all the daughters of the world, also need to know about the glorious spiritual connection that all women hold and the power women have to change and charge the world. This book is real. A movement—one foot first—it can inspire and change the world.

My fondest wish is that every woman in the world would have the chance to experience their own Elegant Gathering.

This book is for all the women I love, have loved, will always love, have yet to love. Most of you know who you are—the rest—get ready. It is especially for my mother. She was my first girlfriend and remains the best.

CHAPTER ONE

J UST A GLASS. Balanced for a moment as brief as a breath. Like a confused dancer undecided about a direction here on the edge of the ancient yellow Formica counter. A speck of light filters through the crystal etchings on this last, best glass, one of three remaining after years and years of life following the goddamned wedding.

Susan watches the glass, her hand stretched out in a flat welcome, her stomach moving in waves as the glass falls and Susan, always anticipating the next movement of everything, moves with it.

"Shit!" She screams as the glass punches through the soft skin in the folds of her fingers. "Shit! Shit! Shit!" The blood gushes, covering the spot where she used to wear a ring and then down onto wrists that are as thin as the stem of the broken glass. Before a drop of blood hits the floor, before Susan can raise her hand, before a thought can form, the women come running.

There is a concert of unrehearsed movement on the kitchen floor. Alice runs for the dish cloth; Chris is on the floor cradling Susan in her arms; Sandy is looking to make certain the good bottle of wine has not spilled. Joanne and Janice are crouched like frogs close by, their hands dangling between their legs; Gail guards the small door between the kitchen and the living room, and Mary is poised to grab more towels and maybe, if the cuts are deep enough, those big bandages she knows Susan keeps on the shelf behind the kitchen sink.

"Is it deep?" Chris asks, extending her fingers around the tiny bloody wrist where a red colored stream begins moving over her own fingers.

Everyone waits. There is a silence that reaches toward Susan who answers by pushing herself into Chris's chest, bending her head so she can lie against her friend. Then there is the unspoken gesture of Alice slipping the stained dish cloth into Chris's free hand, and Chris placing it around the bloody wrist once and then twice like she is wrapping a holiday gift.

"Hey," Susan stutters, a whimper visibly rising from her stomach through her chest and towards any opening it can find. "I'm fucking pregnant, fucking, fucking, pregnant."

There it is, suddenly as plain as the long splinters of glass. Forget the blood, forget the crystal glass, forget every damn thing. Everyone moves closer, except Sandy who reaches for the bottle of wine, grabs the plastic cups off the side of the table and then sets them down in a circle around the bottle of wine.

"Oh honey," Alice says, reaching without thinking to run her fingers, already bent with arthritis, into the edges of Susan's incredibly short hair. "It's okay, sweetie, we're here now, we're here."

Susan weeps into Chris as if she is a giant Kleenex and although Chris has never rocked her own babies, she rocks Susan.

Back and forth, back and forth, while the other women slide closer, reaching first for a glass of wine until the eight women are touching, breathing, drinking, sitting in a mass that has quickly surrounded Susan and Chris.

"How pregnant?" asks Gail.

"Just barely," whispers Susan. "I found out yesterday."

"I take it this isn't the best news you ever had?" Chris already knows the answer. "Oh, you poor, poor girl."

Everyone knows right away. They know without Susan saying a thing, without looking into anyone else's eyes, without a single movement in the room. Susan knows they know. These women have seen the lining of her soul, the secrets of her heart, the insides of her mistakes and faults. When they walked into her house 30 minutes ago under the pretense of one of their charmed female gatherings and saw the circles under her darting eyes, saw her hair matted to one side, saw the newspapers stacked on the living room table, saw only one car in the driveway, they knew.

"It's not John's baby. Oh Christ, it's not John's baby."

While it is impossible for the women to sit any closer to each other, they quickly try, tucking under legs, clasping their plastic cups, scooting sideways, brushing shoulders and pushing their rear ends just another inch closer to Susan and Chris.

"Does John know?" Mary asks quietly knowing already that the one thing John is ever in and out of is a hell of a lot of trouble, and definitely not a wife he most likely hasn't had sex with in 20 years.

"I don't even know where John is," Susan answers. "A clinic in Milwaukee knows, but that's it. John hasn't been here for a long time. He's gone, he's always gone, he's always been gone."

Now there are a thousand things to say and the women are restless, tapping the plastic cups with nervous fingers, holding back questions, wanting to skip over the obvious and find a solution, solve a problem, help their friend, a woman they love. But they wait, because they know this has to happen slowly, and they want it to be perfect and right and cautious, just a little bit cautious, because Susan has never been like this, and it's important, so important.

"Let's pull the glass out of that hand before we go any further," Alice says. "Here, just open your fingers, and let me clean this up."

Alice, with her bent fingers, is the one who knows about babies born and unborn, alive and dead, and when she touches Susan, picking the little shards of glass out one at a time and dropping them into Janice's outstretched hand, she tries hard to think only of that. "There now. We'll just put a few Band-Aids on those fingers, and I think you'll be fine."

The Band-Aids are passed over, more wine is poured, and Sandy and Mary quickly pick up the remains of the glass and drop the pieces onto the shelf where Susan keeps her recipe boxes and cookbooks.

Susan shifts, turning to face the women who surround her, but Chris won't let go of her and pushes in her legs to hold the tiny woman against the full frame of her body. The women talk then, the same easy conversation they might have had in the living room, without a broken glass, where Susan would have eventually told them in greater detail about the boyfriend who has been standing in the wings for years, more—always more—about John, the missing husband, about the risks of a baby when you are past 40 and tired and angry and sad and don't want any more babies anyway.

Another bottle of wine comes off the top of the counter, and this sad circle of friends becomes lost in remembering and talking and simply being there together on Susan's kitchen floor. An hour passes, and the voices rise and fall and rise and fall like a wave moving from one wall to the next and then back again.

The women talk about abortion, and they talk about what bastards half of the men they have married and loved and slept with are and always will be. There is a chorus of sorrow that floats from one woman to the next, and these women who have spent time together for years and shared their loves and who have talked about lust and hate and crime and passion don't see that the early evening has passed, and that there is a half moon rising outside of the high kitchen window.

They talk with great sincerity and kindness about helping Susan and driving her to the clinic and helping her to get that damn attorney to file the divorce papers and getting off the fence with the jackass she's been screwing for 12 years. The women talk about these things mostly without anger, but that rises from them too, in an unseen layer of life's tragedies and sorrows that always seems to hover close.

As the women talk, they don't see themselves as separate entities even though they are each as different from one another as the proverbial fish is to the bicycle. They are grandmothers and career women, housewives, a secretary. They are divorced, married, grieving, wildly happy, conservative, liberal and a combination of every sad tale in the universe. But those differences are overshadowed by the fact that they are all women and friends, and because they have shared their secrets and because now they are lying on the floor in Susan's kitchen and they have made the world stand still.

When their words begin to slide into each other after the fourth bottle of wine, Sandy decides they must eat. No one rises from the floor though, and the time or the place doesn't seem to matter. It becomes clear first to one and then to the next that they matter, just them, and nothing else matters for these hours, not another person or thing or problem.

"Well," Sandy finally says, "I'm just thinking, 'Thank God that Susan threw that glass on the floor.' I haven't done anything like this since the last time I got stoned in college."

"Oh, Sandy," laughs Chris, leaning back to shift her weight, "the last time you got stoned was probably this afternoon. Isn't this the day that kid drives through from Madison?"

No one looks shocked or stunned, especially because it is Sandy who has always had a hard time remembering it is no longer 1968, and they are once again and always talking about the unspeakable, about what really happens in a life, about what really matters most. There is shifting, the flush of a toilet, bowls of red Jell-o and a tuna salad, and chips and salsa, and whatever else Sandy can reach by crawling to the refrigerator and then shoving the plastic containers across the ten feet of space from the open fridge door to the pile of women on the floor.

Something else is happening during the sharing of food. There is the flow of erotic energy that has the scent of people in love in those first months when there are hours of talk and always a communication with bodies and eyes. Women especially know about this phenomenon. Women who cling to each other and who flock to female friends and say everything and anything with such ease it is often embarrassing to watch. It is like the magic moment of discovery when something finally makes sense, when someone finally says the right thing, when the pieces of life finally flow in the correct line. It is bright and sexual and the release of a thousand demons when a simple idea begins to grow until nothing can stop it, and then something that just an hour ago was unbelievable and unthinkable makes perfect sense.

Chris gets the idea first, and it comes to her just as quick as every other wonderful thought that has helped her escape death a hundred times and tackle life in every conceivable fashion. The idea is hers because she has missed this the most, this love affair women can have with each other. These hours where women talk and hold each other and pass on whatever bits of courage they need to get on with it; the times when they can become emotionally naked and turn themselves inside out and continue to love what they see anyway; and a moment just now, when you can tell someone you are pregnant and don't want the baby and hate your life and your husband and the man who made this the baby with you and "could you please, right now, tell me what in the hell I am going to do about this mess of my life?"

The others, often sidetracked by the very things that they now discuss, have missed it too. It has come to them sporadically in their lives, and not often enough because there is never enough time. Luckily, during these last months these women together have become an electric charge. There is a current of life running among them, and somehow a spark of magic has risen up and the women have become powerful and invincible and now they can do anything they want.

"What time is it?" Chris begins, and the question startles everyone because they don't care what time it is and they think with great joy that they may never care again.

"Geez," Janice says, rolling over on top of a pile of potato chips, "it's probably late, but screw it, let's just stay up all night and have a slumber party."

Mary rolls towards her with outstretched arms. "Let's make it a party that lasts ten years, and we'll just live on the floor and eat and drink and talk and never let anyone else in the house."

"Oh God," remembers Joanne, moaning as if she has just had an incredibly personal physical experience. "Once when I was living in Chicago, I did that for three days but it wasn't with a room full of middle-aged women."

Everybody smiles and Chris knows that her simple question, like the broken glass, has changed everything. She smiles. "Quick, tell me something you have always wanted to do but never did, everybody think of something, just tell us all whatever pops into your mind."

Everyone begins dreaming. The women slide around on the floor, roll their eyes, and their thoughts come to a mutual conclusion. In unison they dream of leaving. Simply walking out the door and moving on from something or someone. The magic of friendship has spoken to each one of them so they are dreaming the same dream.

Chris says what will happen next is just for them and absolutely no one else. "No one," she emphasizes with a half scream, because she has done this in her life a thousand times and she knows that to do it, even once, is necessary for survival, for change, for forgetting and moving on. To do it together would be a miraculous occurrence.

"We could do it, you know," she tells them, becoming the teacher they are waiting for. "None of us have babies, hell, half of us don't even have a uterus anymore. Imagine it, just imagine it and don't think about anyone else but yourself. That's the secret here."

The women are thinking and Chris urges them on. She reminds them of the months and months they have tried to talk away everything from menopause to rape. She tells them that sometimes a simple movement, a simple act, can be more therapeutic than a million meetings around a living room coffee table listening to old records from the 60's and drinking wine that isn't quite as good as you'd like it to be.

"Are you trying to convince yourself too?" Sandy asks her, leaning across a set of legs to bring herself closer to Chris. "Where are your demons, dear friend? You've been everywhere and done everything. We have to be in this together."

Chris is the only one who has never cried during all these

months of meetings and shared secrets, and when Sandy sees that her question has made Chris weep, she is momentarily startled. When she reaches beyond Susan to wipe Chris's cheek, she doesn't say anything else but waits. Everyone waits.

"I've never had real friends," Chris tells them as softly as they have ever heard her speak. "My life has been so different from yours, but I would have given my left tit or any one of my adventures to have had an hour like this just once 10, 20 or 30 years ago. I could never be careless with any of you, with all of the things you have told me and being with you like this or wherever we choose to go, would just mean so much to me."

No one is stunned by this confession or by the tears or by Susan's unborn baby. Among themselves they have seen and heard and felt so much and now they are tired, so damned tired. It is the tiredness that somehow gives them strength.

"Of course," Chris adds, not as an afterthought but as part of her confession. "I've never been much of a friend myself, it was always too frightening for me. So I didn't quite know how to do it until I met all of you."

There is nothing else to say then as the women bend to touch Chris as a silent way of thanking her. Susan moves out of her arms and without realizing it at first, all eight of the women—wearing glasses and stretch pants, old tennis shoes, loafers, mostly jeans and socks that are too thin at the heel and toe, find they are sitting in a perfect circle.

Everyone is anxious, ready, pensive about what will come next. They feel it coming but for minutes they can't move, and then Alice—of all people—starts them out. Alice who has a hole in her heart the size of Miami is the one to bring them up and out of their woman circle one at a time, reaching first for one hand and then the next, then pulling with such a fierceness it's a wonder her back doesn't go out. Even in this extraordinary moment she is still Alice—kind, gentle and firm all the way.

"We'll go," she said. "I think we'll all go. Enough with all of this suffering and sacrifice and waiting for something to change. Just enough is what I say."

Alice pauses to shift her thoughts back towards the direction they usually travel. It's a worn path of practical things like coats and warm soup and keeping your head covered in the wind, but even Alice feels a change in that wind. She shudders with pure excitement as she adds what she hopes will be the last perfect thing she ever utters. "It won't be cold even if we stay out at night because I've been watching the weather, and it's not supposed to get below 50 at night. Let's try and do the best we can for clothing with whatever Susan has around here.

No one has exactly said what is going to happen next or what they are about to do, and that is the wild beauty of all the sudden movements, of the giggling, of the not-at-all frightened looks the women exchange.

There is a quick raid of socks and only one shoe exchange because Susan is so small that no one but Susan can wear any of her shoes, although Sandy puts on a pair of John's hiking boots. She can't bring herself to leave them on for more than a few seconds because the thought of anything that is his makes her want to vomit. "We should throw these right out the window," she says, flinging the boots down the basement steps. They bounce into the side of the dryer and leave a two-inch dent.

Alice makes everyone take a coat or a sweater. When they are ready, they huddle by the door waiting for the right moment to push it open and walk out into the night.

"What an unlikely marvelous mix of womanhood," Susan shouts as she kicks open her own front door with her size four feet, forgetting about the baby and John and her throbbing hand. She screams, "Let's walk!"

In the darkest part of the night, just after midnight, the women crush the dewy grass without hesitation, heading north down a highway that is as black as hell, but as inviting as anything they have ever seen.

Associated Press, April 26, 2002
—For immediate release.
Wilkins County, Wisconsin

WOMEN WALKERS SHAKE-UP LOCALS

Police report that a group of eight women are walking through this remote county on a "pilgrimage" and refuse to talk to authorities or to relatives who have tried to stop them.

It's the craziest thing I have ever seen," said Sheriff Barnes Holden. "They are out there just walking and they won't talk to anyone."

Holden said he received numerous calls from people who have passed the women in the middle of the night and wonder if there is something wrong.

"Apparently they are on some kind of pilgrimage, and they won't talk to anyone but each other until they are finished," said Holden. "I tried to stop them but there's no law against walking down the side of the road if you want to."

He said he met early this morning with a husband of one of the women who said he thinks a study group the women have been attending may have gotten out of hand.

"The husband told me these women have been meeting for several years every Thursday night. He thinks they just got carried away and started walking and praying," said Barnes.

Jeanette Sponder, 68, who lives near Granton where the women have been meeting, said county residents who have heard about the women walkers have been leaving food and water for them along the highway.

"Obviously this is something important to them," said Sponder, who said she knows all of the women. "If they are smart, they'll keep walking and get the heck out of this county."

Paul Ridby, of Granton, said his wife is one of the walkers and he has no idea what is going on.

"I thought these meetings were just some excuse for the women to get together and eat and gossip," he said. "I suppose they will just stop when they get tired, but I hope it's soon because I'm kind of lost here."

The women are now heading south on Wittenberg Road and refuse to talk with anyone.

—30—

The Elegant Gathering: Walking Women

The women popped into Walter Schmidt's headlights a good two miles East of the Timberline Bar and Grill out on Highway K, where he had spent the past four hours drinking tap beer, eating pickled eggs, and playing Michigan rummey with his pals, Poker and Hal. "What the hell," shouted Walter as he slammed his truck to a halt and shook his head to make certain he was not hallucinating.

Walter had the window open for a number of reasons. First of all, it was late Spring and one of those clear, soft, warm nights that brings all the scents, sounds, and sights of a season right inside of a person. Second, he was as drunk as a skunk, and being 82 years old, he needed all the extra air he could swallow to get himself and his '87-Chevy shortbed back inside of his banged-up garage.

This was not the first time Walter had driven home from the Timberline with his head hanging out the window. When his wife Gracie died 15 years ago, Walter started going to the Timberline on a regular basis—regular meaning every night of the week, every week of the year.

During those long drives home, Walter had swerved to hit countless numbers of deer, run over at least eight good-sized raccoons and ground squirrels, forced his truck into every ditch on both sides of the road, and crushed about a billion moths, flies, and night bugs on his front grille. More than once, he simply pulled over, threw his jacket over his rounded shoulders and slept until the morning shift dairy herder stopped to wake him before the cops drove by.

In all those years, Walter had never once seen a line of women walking slowly up the side of the road. He was fairly flabbergasted and still not certain he was sober enough to actually know if he wasn't making the whole damn thing up.

The women heard him slam his truck to a stop, and he watched as they halted for a moment to look into the cab. Walter was immediately struck by the peaceful looks on their faces. He ran his eyes up and down the line, counting eight women in all, and searched their eyes for something, anything, that might give him a clue as to why they were walking on this remote country road in the middle of the night. All he saw were soft smiling eyes, lips turned up in half smiles, and heads tipped to the side to look at him.

He didn't quite know what to say, which was a miracle in itself. Walter spent his nights at the bar because he was afraid of silence. He was afraid of the empty rooms in his 100-year-old farmhouse, afraid of the empty bed, afraid of the long fields that rolled out from each side of his house. The few hours each day that Walter did manage to stay inside of his house were filled with his constant whistling, the endless drone of the television, and his gnarly fingers tapping on chairs, counters and tables. He missed Gracie so much that the sight of all the women walking, apparently happy, was overwhelming. Walter began to cry.

One of the women walked over to his truck and asked him the question he knew he should have asked them.

"Sir, are you okay?"

Walter reached across the steering wheel with his shaking hand and touched the woman's arm she had placed across the edge of his window. She had dark eyes and lines that stretched out from the edges of her mouth and didn't disappear until they turned the corner at her jaw line. Walter had all he could do to keep himself inside the truck. He wanted to get out and stand in the road and have this woman put her arms around him. He wanted to cry and cry into her shoulder, and then have her drive him home and sit by the bed while he slept off his beer. He wanted to wake up and hear her singing in the kitchen, just like

Gracie sang every morning as she fried up bacon and scrambled the hell out of his three eggs.

When Joanne saw that he was crying, she reached up and wiped the tears from his eyes. Walter closed his eyes when her fingers touched him. Joanne's touch left a warm path down the side of his face, and he put his hand right where hers had been and looked into her eyes.

"What are you all doing out here?" he asked. "Where are you going?"

"We are just walking," she said, as if this was something they did every day. "Just walking."

Walter didn't think what the woman said was strange. He could see they were walking, but he wondered where in the hell they were going.

"Do you need anything?" he asked next.

"You could say a prayer for us," she told him, stepping away from the truck.

Walter didn't want her to leave, so he quickly formulated another question. "Do you want to stay at my place tonight?" he asked. I've got plenty of rooms and the house is empty, except for me."

"That's kind, but we can't stop. Not just yet. We have to keep going."

"All right then," he said, nodding into the night, wishing he was young enough to snatch this one away and turn her into Gracie. "You be careful and stay off to the side, especially towards morning when the milk trucks spin by here."

Joanne was back in line by then and Walter saw them all move ahead. He lurched his truck forward and drove down the highway, watching the women in his rearview mirror. They got smaller and smaller, and as that happened, he drove slower and slower until the highway was empty except for him and the dark night.

Four miles down the road, he turned into his long driveway and thought about stopping and waiting for them to come by so he could see them again. Then he thought about rushing in to make coffee and getting out some bread for sandwiches. But instead he pulled ahead, put the truck in the garage, and walked into his empty house.

Walter had left the television set on, he always left the television set on. He had blown out three expensive sets since Gracie died because these new sets weren't made to be left on 24-hours a day. When he came into the house, without thinking about it, Walter went into his cluttered living room and turned off the television set. Then he went to the bathroom, brushed his teeth, splashed some water on his face, and went into the bedroom.

After he pushed open the window facing the highway, Walter took off his pants and socks and shirt and shoes and he crawled into his bed. Then he turned to face the window and he waited to see if he could hear their footsteps on the highway.

Walter fell asleep in about five seconds so he never heard the footsteps. But in those brief moments before he began dreaming he did hear something rustling in the tree below the window and then a plane flew over. He heard the house crack and sway when a single gust of wind blew out of the woods.

OBITUARY

The three-week-old baby daughter of Alice and Chester Jessup was taken back to Jesus on Jan. 3. Annie Marie Jessup was born January 2, 1947 at County General Hospital. Baby Annie died in the arms of her mother. The little girl was born with a hole in her heart and doctors were unable to save her.

Survivors include her parents of rural Granton; one brother, Richard, one-year-old; grandparents Bruno and Lucille Jessup and Frances and Frank Hildenbrand, all of Wilkins County. Numerous aunts, uncles and cousins also survive.

Funeral services will be held January 7 at 10 a.m. at St. Mary's Catholic Church, 359 Sawville Road, Granton. There will be no visitation and the burial will be private. Friends who can help are asked to donate money to the parents.

—30—

The Elegant Gathering: Alice

With each step, I think of my baby. She would be a grown woman now, and as we pull up out of the spot here where the cars like to spin around and the gravel hits my ankles, that makes me think of her. She would be like me—with thin legs and hips that never moved back after those babies—and hair that was gray long before the age of 30. But I hope she would not have this burden of sorrow and this missing inside of her that has eaten a hole right through my heart. Fifty years grown she would be, and there has not been a minute that has passed all these years when I have not thought of her.

My name is Alice Marie Jessup, and I am walking for my baby. The baby who died in my arms when I was but a child myself. The burden of this loss I have kept nestled inside of me year after year without telling anyone about it, without letting on to Chester that he might just as well have shot me in the head the night she died because without that baby girl my life has been a life of sorrow. Only when I met these women and I could sense that they had sorrows and burdens to share did I tell them about Annie, my beautiful Annie. Only when I told them week after week and year after year until finally this walk, did I feel my heart lift and know that my baby was truly in the arms of Jesus.

I can remember every single thing about the day my baby died, and about the night she was conceived and about the hell my heart has entered into.

Chester for sure did not want this baby girl, and that is what hardened my heart against him since I knew Annie came into me straight from heaven. Chester worried about food and money and if the plant would lay him off, which it did over and over again. We had just had our son the year before when I was only 19, not thinking about food and clothes but about the touch of those little hands on my face.

When Annie came into me, it was as if a light went on behind my eyes and I saw her face and I knew that she was my beautiful baby girl. But Chester stomped and raged and said he knew a doctor down in the city. I swear to God that I could have killed him right then when he suggested such a sick and terrible thing. I have held that back until this walking time, I have held back my anger and hate and my sorrow and every mean thought that came and went all these long, hard, horrible years.

For Chester did this to me the night he came home from the Lakewoods Bar smelling like smoke and bourbon and pushing me first against the side of the hard wall and then on the cold floor without consideration of what that felt like. He was drunk, and in a million years could never remember the single act that took away my heart.

We were poor with the war ending and no jobs and the economy zig-zagging up and down, and neither of us had more than a country high school diploma. Chester with his bad leg from his uncle's combine was the boy who never went to war and stayed home to wonder what his life could have been like if he had.

Oh, I loved Chester then. He had sad eyes and a way that was soft and made me want to tuck him under my breast and tell him that there are many ways to be a man. When we married, it was no different than anyone else, I suppose. A simple street dress for me, a borrowed suit for him, and nothing after that but the groping in the Manchester Hotel for one night before we started this long life that has brought me to this road.

Richard came along so fast, it was as if he moved from my loins before I could sit down. He was a fine boy, serious though, and I remember that one time when he put his hand on my belly to feel his sister growing inside. A smile crossed his face that was as bright as the sky and he said, "Sister, mommie, sister."

Things were so much simpler then and I wanted babies, that's all, just babies. When my girlfriends Gloria and Pat went to secretarial school, I never thought once about doing that. I wanted a house filled with diapers and toys on the steps and a clothesline that stretched across the yard and was never empty. Is that so bad? Now people might say that was bad, but in my heart, all along there was never room for anything else but all the babies I never had. All those little fingers that never touched my eyes to see if they would blink, as if the magic was in the simple touch of a hand.

My mother tried so hard to let me know that it was okay to regret this. To grieve the loss of a beautiful daughter. Three times this had happened to her. Three dead babies had slipped from her insides into a blanket, and then they were burned out on the wood pile by my Daddy, who stood in the smoke and cried. There was no hospital then, only Grandma Jansky who would come and try to pull the dead babies from a womb that was as hard as a rock.

I never knew something was wrong. That is what I can think of as we walk past the Spring corn that is just shooting up. All I felt was Annie's heart beating so close to mine and this wonderful feeling of having a baby inside of me. The days passed, and we always managed to eat and we had shoes and Chester went back to work for a time and I would say, "See, now, we are all fine, Chester, just fine."

I had my Richard then, too. His weight on my hips as I hauled him back and forth from the garden to the house and out to the line was never a burden for me, even though he was such a big boy. He loved to pretend to be a bucking pony, have me bounce him on my hip, then he'd gallop way and back, for another bounce under the pines by the edge of the house.

I remember the sky towards the end of that winter. We didn't have much snow that year, and when it finally came down as if a dam had burst, Richard and I went out right away. The sky would always be gray and the clouds dropping so low, we tried to catch them. Once when the temperature dipped below zero for days, and we went out anyway and the sky was just the same, as if time had stood still. Richard pulled on a long sheet that was frozen solid on the line and part of it cracked off in his hand. I always kept that side of the sheet where I slept after that and when my legs would get cold because of that missing piece, I could remember the sky and Richard's startled face when he came to me with the sheet, white and solid in his hand.

The winter passed, and Annie grew and grew and then Chester was laid off again. We had to go on the County Relief but our folks helped too when they could with a bit of food and baby clothes, though Chester hated anything like that and I told him to shush and take what we needed so that we would do the same for our own children. He sulked and pounded through our tiny house until I asked him to leave. Then he would stroll through the yard until he figured out he could get in the old truck and drive downtown. When he pulled out of the long driveway during those days, my heart would often twitch and move inside of my chest because as mean as he could get, I knew that Chester loved me and I did love him back.

Richard had been so perfect and easy to carry and deliver, I never thought about possible troubles and heartaches. I hauled the wood and kept up the house and planned what it would be like to have this baby girl. Never, ever did I think that anything would go wrong.

Annie wanted to see our fine winter skies and not wait for the Spring rains. Chester was in the shed working on Joe Dobbyn's truck. The pains started quickly, there was no warning like with Richard. It was just after Christmas, too early for this baby that barely filled the extra tucks I had let out of my single dress. The Christmas tree was standing against the wall next to the kitchen and when the first pain shot through me, I grabbed for the tree and tumbled backwards, spreading those little loops Richard and I had made with old newspaper all over the kitchen floor. Later, much later, I found one of those loops stuck in the edge of the heat register. I held it to my breast as if it were a precious gem.

I called to Richard first, and he ran to get his daddy. Chester came flying into the house with a wrench in his hand and grease stretched from one side of his face to the other and I laughed at that. "Chester," I told him, "we have rags you can use, honey. You don't have to wipe your hands on your face." Chester didn't laugh. He fell to the floor right by me and asked if we needed to go and I said, "Yes, Chester our little girl is coming now."

Driving to the hospital then, I didn't know what was going to happen in the next few hours. I didn't know that I would never, ever have another baby. That I would never be able to enjoy having Chester brush his hand across my breasts or make love to me. That my heart would shatter into a million pieces and that the days and nights of my life would be a relentless struggle. I didn't know that Annie would have the most perfect face, and eyes that shined like the stars. I didn't know then that I would hate God for such a long time. Driving to my mother's to drop off Richard, all I knew was that Chester should hurry because my water was about to pop and fill up the space on the floor where Chester kept his spare engine parts.

Richard ran into Mama's house oblivious to the swirl of confusion that was building around us. He was running towards cookies and fun and the arms of a grandma that loved to lift him up and swing him about the kitchen. He was just a baby himself, barely walking, and when he turned on the steps to throw me a kiss, I caught it in my hand and held it to my lips.

23

Chester drove on like a mad man. He never looked at me or said a word. The bottom of the truck rumbled as if it had never been quite bolted in place and once, when he hit a rut and it felt as if my bottom had been ripped open, I shouted for him to be careful.

These days when I go to the hospital I am amazed at how it all works. There are couches and soft lights and bedsheets that offer the colors of the rainbows. In my day, it was cold and steel and the curt words of a doctor and nurse who made me want to run and hide. They could have been kind at least. They could have held my hands while Chester paced in the halls leaving a trail of grease on the solid white floor. But they were all business, and I had to calm myself, which somehow just never seemed quite right.

What had started out so fast quickly seemed to take forever. Annie took her sweet time moving herself down inside of me, and when I thought the pain of it all would make me pass out, I imagined her face and then I counted again. I would never tell another woman that she will forget the pain of childbirth. There is no way to forget the pain of childbirth. Years later the remembrance of the pain would wake me from the dead of sleep, and I could feel sweat running down the insides of my legs and the pillow would be soaked. It is a beautiful, wonderful miracle to have a baby but the pain, the pain can make me wince even now when I have suddenly never felt so free and happy.

The birthing hours passed like years in that big room. Once I heard another woman come through the doors and they put her on the other side of the curtain for a while. She was crying softly and when I turned on my side, I could see the curve of her belly. I wanted everyone to go away so I could talk to her. I planned how they could move our beds together and we could lie on our sides, face to face, and hold hands. I pictured her face and made up a story about her life. I saw her later with a baby bundled in her arms, and I could not bear to see the baby or to let them come near me. I am ashamed to say that now, but only ashamed since I have started this walk. With each step something new is pushed through me, something terrible from that time and the more I walk, the less there is left.

Chester is one of those men who would not have been able to be with me even if they let him. He is strong about many things and has seen more than his share of life and death and blood and guts while working on the farm, but he could not bear to be in the same room with me and see the arch of pain cross my face. When I finally tired of hearing his footsteps outside of the delivery room, I asked the nurse to please make him sit down.

"Sir," I heard her whisper to him. "Your pacing is bothering your wife. She needs to concentrate now, so please take a seat out in the waiting room and don't come back here until someone comes to get you."

That's not quite how I would have said it but this nurse was no Florence Nightingale. Chester must have turned immediately, because I heard his boot heels hitting the floor and then there was no sound except for my own heavy breath and the nurse fooling around with some towels and more metal objects in the corner.

This is when I started to talk to Annie. I thought if she could hear my voice that maybe she would want to come out and see what I looked like. I talked to her at first like I would to any baby. You know what I mean. Sweet baby talk and whispers and I called her "my sweet baby girl." I told her over and over again how much I loved her and when I wanted to bite down and right through my own lip because of the pain, I talked even more.

Once, just after I started talking to Annie, I noticed the nurse lifted up her head and looked at me. In that moment I wondered if she was a mother and if she thought about her own delivery each and every time they wheeled a crying woman through the doors of the room. But that is the only time she ever met my gaze, and then I ignored her for the rest of time and focused on my baby girl, only my baby girl.

"Sweet baby, please come out now and let your mama hold you in her arms," I said to her in the softest whisper. "Let me tell you what Richard is like, and what it will be like when Springtime comes and we walk through the grass at the edge of the corn-fields."

I must have talked liked this to her for hours. The talking helped me leave the pain and go to wherever it was I was talking about. I could actually see the tattered brown baby carriage and a sea of tiny green corn shoots poking through the rich, brown, muddy soil. I could bend down and smell Spring in the grass and that musty cool smell that hangs across the yard each summer morning before the heat consumes everything.

Chester told me later that the doctor came in several times to tell me to push and that if I didn't, the baby would never come out but I never have been able to remember that. I tell you I can remember that the old kitchen rags were on the line and that once I tipped the carriage towards the sun so my baby girl could feel it on her face, and then I sat down and rested my head against the side of the wicker carriage, so scratchy it reminded me of lying in the August hayfields.

The time finally came and it felt as if my hips would explode. I wanted to see Chester so bad and to have him put his hand across my face like he did sometimes but I never said that because I knew it wouldn't happen. There was a commotion, and the nurse dropped a metal pan, which made made me jump. Maybe that's what really brought Annie into this world.

I pushed and I saw the top of the doctor's head disappear under the sheet across my legs as if he had been swallowed up into a deep and endless cave. I saw him next just as a series of contractions moved through my body like an ocean wave and I could feel the placenta push itself out.

The time then stretched out until each second seemed like a minute and each minute like an hour. When I had Richard, the doctor tossed him into the air and shouted, "Hey, Chester has a big boy!" and I waited for that or for anything but there was only silence.

"Tell me, please tell me," I finally asked, my voice sounding pathetic and frightened.

This is when the nurse could have touched me or reached out her hand or what I would have done is to have given me the baby no matter what was wrong, because that is all a mother wants, to touch and see her own baby.

But everyone waited. Finally I rose up and screamed, "Damn it, show me my baby!"

The doctor got up and gestured to the nurse and she quickly handed him a blanket. The doctor wrapped my baby girl up, and then came up beside me. This is when I shouted for the second time. "Show me the baby, now, just show me the baby."

The doctor's arms moved out, and I watched his mouth open and words came spilling out, but what he was saying did not register in my mind. I only wanted that baby in my arms. It was when she came to me then that I knew she was ill because her lips were the color of the blue summer sky and her ears as red as the sky in early winter when Fall will not surrender. I took her to my breast and heard the doctor whisper, "It's a girl." That second I named her Annie Marie because that is what we'd been calling our baby girl all these months. Annie Marie. Annie Marie.

If my baby girl would have been born any time but then, she would have lived and I would not be walking down this highway for hours and hours. They would have patched up that tiny hole in her heart, the hole that sucked out all the days and nights and years of life that she might have had. How many years now have I thought about that? Sweet Jesus, my life has passed and I have mourned a lifetime of might-have-beens. I have rocked in front of the window and thought about those hours when I felt her quiet heart thumping against the palm of my hand. There is no way to measure a loss like that, not every human heart can understand what it is like, only another mother, another woman who needs to walk away from such grief and loss.

After I had Annie in my arms, I asked the doctor to tell me about her condition. She had a hole in her heart, an opening that you could put your pinkie finger right inside of. I made him show it to me, and I could see right inside of my girl where she was pink and beautiful, that is all I could think, how beautiful she is on both sides.

"How long?" I asked him and I knew by the dip of his head, and the way he had his hands pressed against the side of my bed that there was nothing he could do.

"Hard to say but it won't be long, I'm sorry Alice, not long at all."

"I will not leave her, and you will not take her from my arms until it is time."

"But Alice . . ."

"Tell Chester," I commanded him. "Then someone help me so I can sit in the chair, just put a chair by a window. Is there a room where we can sit with a window? I want a window so we can look outside."

The doctor shook his head and then shuffled off, and I heard Chester scream out in the hospital hallway. I called to the nurse and asked her to hold Annie for just a moment while I used the bathroom. She told me I could not get up yet, but I pushed myself off the bed without acknowledging her and with each step to the bathroom, I left a spot of blood on the floor. I left the door open so I could see that she was holding Annie. When I came back, I found she had set out some sanitary napkins and underwear for me. I took Annie again as the nurse pushed a wheelchair over.

Someone found us an old rocking chair and a room that looked out across the parking lot to a grove of oak trees. I noticed right away that there was one clump of trees that had red and orange leaves still clinging to their tops from the long past Fall, and I took great comfort in seeing that.

While I waited for Chester, I pulled open my gown and I pushed Annie towards my breast. I thought if I could make her eat that maybe some kind of miracle would happen and she would be healed. My God, my God, my God she looked so normal and beautiful when she turned to take my breast. Her lips parted and her eyes were closed and her skin was as clear and bright as the snow falling across the lights on a December morning.

Annie's sucking was pure reflex and natural instinct, but I imagine her body knew there was no time or hope because she didn't suck for long. When she pulled away I stretched her out across my lap and unwrapped her blanket. I touched every part of her: Her tiny legs and her long eyelashes and the insides of her ears. That's how Chester found us; I never heard his feet pounding down the hall, and only when he touched my shoulder and I turned to see his tear-stained face did I know that he was in the room.

It took the rest of that day and one night and then a morning before she died. These were hours so long and so painful that I wished a thousand times over for my own death. In those hours, everything I loved or could love, even Chester and Richard, was eclipsed by the silent form of my dying daughter.

My only comfort then, and every moment in the days and

years that followed, and up until this walk was knowing that my Annie did not suffer. I pulled her blankets and sleeper off of her when the doctor told me it would not be long, and I held her naked against my own chest. Her heart was thumping wildly but Annie looked like the angel that she is even when I knew she had taken her last breath. She simply stopped breathing and then her little fists that were clenched into balls unraveled and her legs dangled from her knees and I knew that it was over.

Everything after that is a blur inside of my mind. I know I would only let Chester take her, and what happened after that I never knew or cared about. I stayed in the hospital, curled up into a little ball for another day until Chester beseeched me that Richard was crying and could I please come home and what about the funeral?

Life swirled around me, I acknowledged it but never joined in. No one but a few know that I never went to the church or the cemetery for the burial. Not even Richard remembers that I spent the day rocking by the window and holding Annie's blanket against my face. When Chester and Richard came home, I rose from the chair and ate with them and then I stepped back into their lives. But the truth is I never really lived again.

It has taken me fifty years to come to this point. Fifty years before I could empty my heart of the sorrow that has choked off my soul. I watched my husband grow old and learn how to walk with his head bowed to the winds of the world. Not once in these years did we sit and talk about the pain and the missing and how we should somehow be able to go on. It was as if nothing else mattered after Annie, and I know now that it was wrong to let my life, my husband's life and the life of my wandering son pass me by. But I was helpless, so helpless I felt like a woman without limbs rocking on the edge of a wide cliff, unafraid to look down, to do something as simple as to open my eyes.

Richard never remembered anything about Annie. We told him as he grew older, and when he asked us why the other kids had brothers and sisters but he didn't. Somehow Richard did just fine, and I like to think that he never knew about my deep well of sadness, about the wall of anguish that separated me from his father.

He became a bright shining star for me, went off to college, and traveled the world with his geology hammers and trucks filled with rocks. When I saw his first child, a daughter no bigger than half of my short arm, I could barely bring myself to touch her because her face had the same soft lines and tiny nose of Annie Marie. Now they all live so far away, just so far away.

Today on the highway the weather has been warm. By noon I could feel the heat rising out of the asphalt as it pushed against my hands. When I put one foot in front of the other hour after hour, I have a feeling that I could almost fly, that I could lift my arms and soar the rest of my life as if I have never been troubled or burdened by anything.

Somehow this feeling is familiar and I keep seeing myself lying in the brown, Fall grass 50 years ago with my hands on my swollen belly watching the hawks circle above the fields and thinking then that I could fly because I was so happy.

I'm closer now to that long absent feeling, closer with each step, and although we are walking forward together, I feel as if I am stepping back. Stepping back so that I can start over, from that time in the grass when I was happy and my heart flew with the birds.

Chapter Two

MAYBE IT WAS THE SIGHT of Walter that threw Mary off course.

He was the first living thing the women encountered as they not-so-silently moved up the highway from one telephone pole to another. They were counting stars, relishing the dark night that surrounded them and laughing heartily at the sight of an unused Tampax they discovered lying alongside the highway—as if someone had placed it there as a marker for them.

"Oh my God, look!" shouted Sandy pushing at the feminine hygiene product with the toe of her dark tennis shoes. "This is a sign from heaven that we are on the correct highway."

Mary didn't laugh as the women gathered together, stopping simply because they wanted to, because they could, because now anything was possible. She stood back, hands on hips, eyes on the horizon, her heart beating like a wild drum.

Sandy queried, "Don't you all remember a thousand stories

about the female reproductive system, cramps and babies, and the course and crimes of the uterus? How many of you have ever thrown a Tampax, used or unused, out of a car window?"

"Dear," Alice answered immediately, in a voice as proper and calm as the sky above them. "Women my age would never throw sanitary articles out of car windows. Didn't your mother and grandmother ever talk to you ladies about rags and wringer washing machines?" Alice had her hands locked behind her, and she talked in a voice that her friends knew was not-so-serious, but they knew too that Alice has seen a side of life that they could barely comprehend. They knew as much of Alice as there is to know, and these women would drag her from a burning car, take a bullet for her, jump off a cliff if they thought that any such actions would make Alice's life happier or easier. Despite their assorted miseries, the women see Alice as standing alone because she is the oldest and she has seen the most and she has been poor and constantly sad. She has lived through a time when women would never ever consider walking down a long highway in the middle of a black, cool, spring night to exorcise their demons and flick their middle fingers at the world.

In the hours since the women have left Susan's house, since they have moved from one field to the next and walked dozens of miles, the world has already pulled on a new face, and the women are part of that changing landscape. They are determined, gleeful, thinking and sorting through thoughts and feelings as deep as the Earth they stand upon. But there is Mary, slowing her pace as they leave the side of the road and bowing her head and lifting her arms to circle herself in a kind of hug as they move ahead.

Chris, the observer of the world saw Mary falter, and her mind flew in several directions at once. Because of her work as a journalist, Chris has known and interviewed 100 Marys but it was only in that moment as she looked off into the nothing, that she had an inkling of what it might be like to be a Mary, unsure of everything, always needing someone to affirm her actions, to give permission for living and walking and breathing.

The Marys of the world, thought Chris, start out in high school creeping from one boy to the next because the idea of not having a boyfriend, or just somebody always there, is so terrifying they cannot even imagine it. In her own school, there were a good dozen Marys and their weekly dramas of breakups and new romances made her laugh and provided hours of free entertainment.

The college Marys were the same girls with different faces, and even in the days of burning bras and groping for personal sexual satisfaction, she was amazed at how many Marys made it through those years with their needs intact and strong as hell. There was no time then or need or desire to figure these women out. Chris simply had no time for the man pleasers, for the women who seemed to abandon themselves for someone else, for the Marys of the world who could never quite bring themselves to walk away from or toward anything.

Her last editor had been a Mary to beat all Marys. Married and divorced three times and anxious immediately to fill the empty space next to her with someone, anyone who had a penis and shaved something besides his legs. This editor was as complex as Chris's own heart. One minute she was making decisions that could change the course of lives, and the next she was canceling her entire life for the chance to be with someone she barely knew.

Then there is Mary Valkeen, mother of three, wife of Boyce, struggling up this highway with her arms embracing her own heart as if trying to keep it from falling outside of her chest. Chris suddenly saw in Mary's face the struggle it had been to walk just a few miles, and what a struggle it will be to turn away from her friends. When she slowed her pace to stay even with Mary, Chris wanted to cry out when she saw the veil of agony that had crossed her friend's face.

"Mary," whispered Chris as they dropped back from the rest of the women and Chris laced her arm through Mary's crooked elbow. "Are you having a hard time?"

Mary looked up quickly, not surprised that someone had noticed her lack of enthusiasm. She didn't think she had the heart for it. That's what Mary wanted to say. "I'm embarrassed by my lack of commitment to my friends," she wanted to admit. "I just don't need this," she could add and then, "Oh God, I wish I could be like you, I just can't do this, because I already have what I need."

What Mary wanted was to go home and crawl into bed next to Boyce and his thick, rambling arms. She wanted to lie there warm in her own bed with the sound of the cracked alarm clock humming next to her left ear, and then wake up in just a few hours so she could hand her boys an apple and a granola bar before they race off for early basketball practice. "I'm not strong like you."

"We're not that strong," Chris responded, inching over to push as close to Mary as she could. "You know only a few of us would do this alone, but together, well, together it's different."

"I can't do it." Mary clenched her fists, began to cry as they moved slower and slower behind the other women. "Don't hate me."

"Hate you? Oh sweetie, we love you," Chris said with love and warmth. "You don't have to stay with us if you don't want to. No one has to stay, but some of us, we just have to do this. It might seem ridiculous or goofy in a week or next year or maybe never, but right now this is the most important thing in the world to some of us."

There was a second and then another of silence, and Chris

could see that everyone was looking down the dark highway with eyes focused somewhere else. She guessed they were thinking of everything and anything, and in a lifetime there would never be enough walking time to capture all their thoughts.

"Listen," Chris finally told Mary. "You know it's fine to want to go home and be who you are. We'll all do that eventually too, but this walking is going to make some of us even more than who we are now. Can you understand that, Mary? You know some of us have these pains and heartaches that might only get worse if we don't do this."

"I've never needed much," Mary said, looking off into the night like the rest of her friends. "I used to wonder if there was something wrong with me because I wasn't like half of the other women I knew. I hate to work, hate to travel, hate to be away from the kids and Boyce. I love being in the house when the kids come home, knowing the schedules, what will happen from one day to the next. It's a comfort to me."

Chris wished Mary would stay then so she could just prove to her that it would matter if she stayed. She wished she could show her with her words that there was something so absolutely fabulous about connecting with other women on a grand adventure, that the insides of her kitchen cabinets could be blown to hell and back again and she wouldn't have to leave the next intersection, where there might be a phone at the gas station.

One and then two cars passed by them, and when the women turned to look they were blinded, like unsuspecting deer paralyzed by headlights.

"Damn!" shouted Sandy. "Those cars scared the hell out of me."

"How do you think they feel?" Joanne laughed. "My God, they must think we've fallen off a bus or something."

That's when Chris told everyone they needed to get off the

highway for a few minutes. She walked them through a row of bushes and not knowing what she might step on next, sat down fast on a fallen tree where she expected to tell them about Mary and other practical matters.

"First of all," she began. "This is a good place to rest, and secondly Mary wants to stop."

"Mary?" Everyone said her name at once, turning in the dark for an explanation that was totally unnecessary. Mary has been a good listener all these months, holding hands and tilting her head when someone has needed her attention. She has come to the meetings and bought the best wine and made it clear that she loves each of them and the time they all spend together. As the women sat on logs and piles of damp leaves at the edge of a rolling field, they already knew that a dramatic movement, a surge into the night, a walk away from troubles of the heart could be a powerful force and they were feeling the power of what they were doing.

When Sandy got back from the bushes and Gail finally decided to squat instead of sit so she wouldn't get her pants wet, it was Sandy who made them think of heartaches, losses, regrets, the hand of a lost lover right there, of all the weight of the world that they were dragging among them.

"I think Mary knows she can do what she wants, but we'd better talk about what we're going to do when dawn cracks and our husbands wake up and discover that we are missing and walking down some county highway in nothing more than our slippers and spring jackets."

Alice laughed, and that sound at the edge of the highway was as startling and clear as the car headlights.

"Alice?" asked Joanne, who loves to be called J.J.

"Oh, I'm just thinking about Chester waking up and not knowing for a week or two that I'm even missing."

"Shit," bemoaned Gail, "My kids will miss me the minute they run out of milk or can't find clean underwear."

Everyone smiled because they would at least be missed, except Susan who has left a trail of tears from her front yard to this very spot. "Listen," Chris began, steering them back on course. "We have to agree on some things, those of us who are going on, and Mary, you can help too."

Mary rose just a bit when she heard this, maybe because she wanted to redeem herself. She wanted to do something that would keep her with the women walkers even though she was going to part from them, wouldn't be with them physically, pounding up the road. Mary leaned forward like a bird waiting for breakfast, her mouth open just a little to form an O, round and exact as a single Cheerio.

While the stars shifted and the moon dropped lower, the women made their plans. Mary would call her husband from the next gas station to come and get her, and once back at home, she would call the other husbands and tell them about this journey. No one else wanted to stop. No one blamed Mary. No one else, though, could begin to think of stopping.

Chris sighed loudly. "Someone will eventually call the newspapers, and people will try to figure out what we're doing, and they will say we're all lesbians or that we belong to a cult and have buried six babies in the back yard."

"I've always wanted to be a lesbian," Sandy mused.

"I've buried one baby," Alice blurted out.

"I think the Catholic Church is a cult," added J.J.

"There you have it," Chris concluded. "We shouldn't talk to anyone. We should just walk and play it by ear. Do what we feel we should do, but we shouldn't talk. I think if we're hungry, then we'll eat. It seems like we shouldn't worry about, well, you know, normal things. We should worry about us, just us. Do you agree?"

As she spoke, Chris had been waving her arms around like a preacher. She had gestured in circles and moved her hands so her fingers pointed into the air, and she had no idea where the words or thoughts or movements were coming from exactly.

No one wanted to talk. They wanted to think and imagine and they wanted to walk until they forgot things. No one was tired. No one was cold, and food and drink were about as far from the thoughts of the women walkers as attending a Tupperware party. They wished it would stay dark until they are finished so that they could hide from the world for as long as they wanted to.

"Is everyone okay with this?" Sandy looked from one face to the next as another car whizzed by.

"Does anyone think we're nuts?"

Susan asked this question, thinking to herself that if she had half a brain, she would have hit the highway 27 years ago, just a week after she married John. She wished she would have had the guts to do something with her life besides screw her brother's boss. She was thinking that disappearing from her own life in the middle of the night with a bunch of women who love her could possibly be the smartest thing she has ever done in her life.

"Oh come on," said Janice as if she had just been lied to and knew all about it. "If I stopped now, if the rest of us who really want to do this stopped now, we'd never be able to look at each other again for the rest of our lives." She continued, stopping long enough to suck in some air. "The one thing I know is that even if most of my life doesn't change, even if the shitty parts are still the shitty parts, I will still have done this. I will have walked."

Before they rose to their feet and returned to the highway, J.J. made everyone stay where they were for another moment. She had this idea, this picture in her mind that she wanted to keep safe. A picture of them, just sitting there gazing out into the night as if it is something they do every Thursday night of their lives.

"I love to take a moment like this and freeze it in a sacred part of my mind," J.J. explained. "I can remember the last time I breast-fed each one of my kids, what chair I was sitting in, what time it was, what I had on, what they had on. I remember where Tim and I first made love and how he smelled, and I remember the first time we met at Sandy's house and how the candles burned in the window and how it felt when I walked in and saw you all smile and my heart, my damn heart seemed to stop. Those are the things I remember."

"That's remarkable," Alice told her. "Remarkable."

"Well, I think if you don't just stop once in awhile that everything important, every moment that seems big just then when you are doing it or having it, gets lost and rendered meaningless."

"That's profound," Chris said, imagining all of them, just as J.J. wanted her to, sitting and twitching in the dark.

"I don't mean it to be, it's just something I've always done and this, just these minutes, seem like something I don't ever want to forget because we'll stop eventually. Then we'll have to make dinner and someone will get the flu and at least one of us is bound to get pregnant again and well, we might forget that this walking and talking and sharing was important. We might forget that we cried on Susan's floor and then got pissed off about every horrible thing that has ever happened to us, and started walking."

"I won't forget," said Sandy.

"Me either," said Janice.

"I'll remember," Susan declared. "I'll always remember."

"Me, too," added Chris and then Alice.

"I'm in," said Gail.

They each formed a permanent memory then of each other, of the way the dark hides some parts of their faces and not others. They looked around at the buds on the trees and smelled the damp grass and watched as the moon dipped lower. The women moved as close to one another as they could, tipped back their heads so they could feel the night air brush against their smiles. They breathed slowly and then uncrossed their legs and then one by one, they rose up from the ground and started walking again.

Associated Press, April 27, 2002
—For immediate release.
Wilkins County, Wisconsin

SEVEN WOMEN CONTINUE WALKING

The women walking through this county on what local residents say is a "pilgrimage" have stopped at a rural farmhouse for rest and food.

Although one of the women has apparently left the walk, the remaining seven are into their second day of walking and have refused to talk to reporters, police officers, or relatives who have followed them to find out what they are doing.

Sheriff Barnes Holden said the women are all good friends who apparently started walking during a weekly study group. "I don't know how much studying was going on," he said. "I think they spent a lot of time talking and my wife said things like that are usually just an excuse to get together and talk."

The women, who walk at a steady pace, often change positions and sometimes hold hands. When approached with questions they smile, raise their hands as if to say "stop," and keep walking.

Friday afternoon they walked off of Highway D at the intersection of Wittenberg Rd. and into the yard of a small farm. The women were greeted by the farm's owner, Lenny Sorensen, and quickly ushered into the house.

Neighbors said that Sorensen, 46, has been separated from her husband, Jackson, for the past several months.

Reporters who approached Sorensen were told to leave the property.

—30—

The Women Walker Effect: Lenny

Lenny heard about the women walkers when she turned on the radio Friday morning. "What the hell?" she said to herself because there was no one else to talk to. Lenny, whose God given name was Elenora, had been called Lenny her entire life, talked to herself so much that she often felt as if Jackson had never left and she hadn't been alone for three months. "That son-of-a-bitch," she said every time his face popped into her head.

Just after the short radio report, when Lenny was imagining what the women would look like when they paraded past her front yard, the first call came in. She knew it was Jackson. He called her five times a day at least, and after that first week, she never bothered to answer the phone again. She considered having the line disconnected but thought about robbers, like those idiots from Racine who held some poor woman captive because they needed a truck, and she decided to just let the damn thing ring.

Jackson sent her mail too, long letters with the address of his cheap motel sprawled across the envelope. He apologized, told her he worshipped the ground she walked on, begged her to answer the phone, anything so that he could come back home. The letters were all stacked up inside of a brown paper bag in the corner of the kitchen.

After the first two weeks he was gone, Jackson sent his buddy Pat over to make sure everything was okay. Lenny was out in the barn when he came, doing the same thing she had done everyday for the past 26 years—hauling feed for a barn full of hogs.

"Hey, Lenny," Pat hollered from the door.

"Well, shit, Patty boy, did that son-of-a-bitch send you to check on his little wife?"

"Come on, will ya," Pat said, swaggering a bit in his big boots and ripped-out barn jacket. "Yeah, he called, so shut up and let me help you."

"Patty, do you know what? I shut up for 26 years while that bastard ran all around the county with Melinda, and Grace, and whoever in the hell else happened to have a set of jugs bigger than mine. I'm not shutting up again."

"I know he loves ya."

"Loves me?" This cracked Lenny up. "Love for him is a hard on. Just grab a bag and shut up yourself."

After that, Pat showed up every night to help her, and he was smart enough not to mention anything about love or Jackson again. Lenny almost started looking forward to the sight of him bending over in the barn, but she managed to stop short of that because she never wanted to look forward to anything that had to do with a man again.

Lenny was 46 years old, not bad looking for a woman who had lived with a son-of-a-bitch, raised two fairly decent kids, and hauled hog feed for most of her life. Her biggest problem now was trying to figure out what to do next.

What she really wanted to do was go back in time and graduate from college. She wanted to whack herself upside the head for having run off to marry Jackson at the end of her junior year at Iowa State University. She wanted to stop crying half the night. She wanted to press a magic button and be the kind of woman everyone thought she was—a real hardass.

Lenny wasn't a hardass. That's why she put up with Jackson for 26 years, thinking day after day that tomorrow would be the day she would boot him out. But the excuses were always there. First it was the kids, then he broke his leg, then she had to have a hysterectomy, then the hogs got a virus. Then finally, there wasn't anything else, just the long nights and the begging and the stains on his clothes when she pulled them from the hamper.

The morning she kicked Jackson out was the coldest day of

the year. She pulled her father's old double barrel shotgun on him while he was heaving his guts out in the barn. She pushed a suitcase toward him with the tip of her work boot, threw the keys to the old car at his bad leg, and told him he was moving.

"What?" He wiped his mouth with the sleeve of his shirt.

"I've had it, you big fucking jackass."

"Jesus, honey, put that thing down."

"You call me honey again, touch me, even look at me and I'll blow your balls clear to hell."

"Okay, okay," he said stepping back and into the stacks of hay after he saw her eyes narrow to a slit as she brought the gun to her cheek, ready to fire, ready for anything. "What do you want?"

"I'm taking everything, and you get the suitcase and the old car. Go, go fuck your way through the rest of this county but don't ever come back here or I swear to God, I will kill you."

Jackson left with his tail between his legs, and Lenny managed to fire a round into the air just before he got into the car, hoping the entire time that he might shit in his pants. That was the strongest moment of her life, and she had spent the last three months trying to figure out how to get back to that place.

When she heard about the women walking, Lenny stopped dead in her tracks and closed her eyes. She pictured each one of them strutting down the highway. This vision gave her a moment of joy. She walked with them for a minute, felt the spring air brush across her face and through her long dark hair. Her arms propelled her along—back and forth as if they were on fire. The sun tanned her arms, her feet flew, she was free and happy and smiling, always smiling.

Lenny picked up the phone to call Sue, a friend who lived down on Wittenberg Road. She wanted to know if the walkers had turned or were still heading her way.

"What do you think about them?" Sue asked her.

"It sounds pretty damn wonderful to me, walking like that, not talking to anyone, being with your friends."

"Should we run out and join them?" Sue laughed at what she thought was the absurdity of her own question.

"The thought has crossed my mind, but I just want to see them. Maybe that's what I need."

"What you need is a good screw," Sue told her.

Sue wanted to keep talking but Lenny suddenly had an idea. She wanted to do the chores, throw a big dinner in the oven, get some wine out of the garage, take a shower, and get those women to come into the house.

The chores were like a zillion pounds of weight around her waist that kept her tied to the farm. There had been plenty of times when Lenny had thought about shooting each one of the hogs in the head and burying them in the pit behind the fence. But she knew the hogs would eventually save her when she sold the whole damn place—lock, stock and barrel. When that would happen or how it would happen, she had no idea.

All she could think of now was the walking women. She fairly flew through the chores after she called Pat and told him that a friend was visiting and would help her for a few weeks. "Don't come back until I call," she told him.

Lenny hadn't bothered to cook a big meal for months. She ate frozen burritos, salads, vegetarian pizzas—all the foods she loved but Jackson had hated. For the women, she hauled up two turkey breasts from the freezer, peeled a bag of potatoes, washed off some broccoli, got out her mother's homemade cranberry sauce, whipped up some rolls, and breathed a sigh of relief when she found a perfectly good cherry pie lurking in the back of the freezer.

After she set up the dining room table, she showered so long the water turned cold. Then she dressed for the special occasion.

Put on her silver Indian bracelet from college, the ring her grandmother gave her when she graduated from high school, the one pair of jeans that had managed to fit her for five years in a row, a red flannel shirt that highlighted her dark skin, and the black cowboy boots with the thin, fine bottoms.

At 5:25 p.m., with the smell of turkey floating like invisible bubbles throughout the house and out into the front yard, Lenny took the phone off the hook and set it under a pillow on her bed, grabbed a bottle of wine and a glass and went out to sit on the edge of the front porch.

Lenny knew in her heart that she could get the women to stop. She knew if she walked out to the edge of the yard when she saw them turn the corner, if she went out onto the road and started walking towards them that they would simply follow her into the house.

It was 6:20 p.m. when she finally saw them. Like a desert mirage: first one and then the next woman popped into view, shimmering under the sun as they walked through what was left of the almost hot spring day.

Lenny finished her second glass of wine in one quick gulp, set it down gently on the step and started walking out onto the highway. If the women saw her, they didn't act like it, but for sure the few cars following them must have spotted her. Lenny ignored them, figuring they were bored local kids or some of those damn reporters.

Something magical happened to Lenny on the road, like someone reached inside of her and fluffed up her heart as if it was nothing more than a goose down pillow. She was 19 again and happy, and the entire world stretched out in front of her and glimmered, just like these women walkers glimmering on the road.

When she got close to them, Lenny smiled. She laughed too,

a soft chuckle that moved up from the soles of her feet through her legs, past her thighs and stomach, through her soaring heart and into her fine white throat.

There was a woman about her age walking in front. She was over six feet tall, and she wore Nike tennis shoes, black jogging tights, a blue shirt and carried a white sweatshirt over her shoulder. When Lenny met up with her, the woman smiled and locked her arm inside of Lenny's. Together they strolled down the highway and into the front yard of the hog farm.

"Please come in." Lenny held open the door. "The wine is on the kitchen table, the bathroom is upstairs and I've set out towels by the shower."

When the women were all inside of the house, Lenny went back out by herself to talk to the people in the cars. What she said was fairly simple. "Leave us the hell alone." She said this with her hands on her hips and one foot slightly in front of the other.

Two reporters hopped out of their car anyway, and Lenny bent down to pick up a stick, then headed towards them. "This is private, that's all," she told them pointing the stick towards the car doors.

The reporters saw the look in Lenny's eye, that same look Jackson had once seen, and they quickly returned to their cars and backed down the driveway.

Lenny threw the stick into the air then and stood for a moment by herself right in the spot where she would put the *For Sale* sign, then she turned and walked into the house, wondering the entire time if her feet were really touching the Earth.

The Milwaukee Journal, May 4, 1970
Waukesha, Wisconsin

HAMMES AWARDED SCHOLARSHIP

Jeffrey G. Hammes, 18, a senior at Johnson Hill High
School, was awarded a full athletic scholarship to Notre
Dame University where he will play middle linebacker
for the Irish football team.

Hammes, an all star player for the Hill team during
the past four years, was heavily recruited by numerous
colleges and universities including the University of
Wisconsin, Stanford, and Northwestern.

"I can't believe it," said Hammes, the oldest son of
John and Carol Hammes. "This is just the greatest thing
that could ever happen to me, and I'm really excited."

Bill Stoughten, Hammes' coach throughout his high
school career, said Hammes is not only a superb athlete
but also an outstanding student and team leader. "This
scholarship comes as no surprise to me," said Stoughten.
"If I had more guys like Jeff, we'd probably win the state
championship every year."

Hammes won the Singelton Award for sportsman-
like conduct this year and was chosen by his teammates
as team captain the last two years. He was also on the
Journal's All-Conference team the last three years and was
selected by his school to represent them at the National
Sports Convention in Toledo last January.

Hammes plans to study Business at the University
and said he might consider a professional football career.

—30—

The Elegant Gathering: J.J.

This morning I could not take my eyes off of the skyline. I have never been out here like this to watch the sun rise, and now I am thinking that I may never, ever miss another one the rest of my life. When I watched the sky open up and change from dark to light, I felt as if I was exploding on the inside, like something burst open and I could feel whatever it was running through the veins in my body.

The girls call me J.J. because my name is Joanne Johnson, and this is the first nickname that I have ever had. I like it. When this is over, that's what I am going to make everyone call me.

This morning after my experience with the sun, I walked for a long time with Susan. She was crying, and I did something that I have never done before out like this, I reached down and took hold of her hand. I don't know why people get so riled up about holding hands because it's just so nice to be able to touch someone that you care about. All this focus on sex, everyone thinking about it all the time. It's pathetic, that's what it is. You should be able to touch someone if you care about them.

Susan cries a lot, and I always want to be able to do something to make her feel better. When I felt how warm her hand was, I put it up to my face and turned to look at her. She smiled and said, "Thank you, J.J.," and I knew that it was okay for me to keep holding her hand.

Holding someone's hand helps me too. I have spent a great deal of my life feeling lonely and fairly frightened of everything. These women here, behind me, around me, in front of me, they have given me such great comfort and strength that I can hardly think about it without crying. For the first time in my life I have feel truly safe. I know that these women would do anything in the world for me and I would do the same for them.

When we started out like this, we never bothered to think about anything else. Now that I am thinking about it, I concluded this was very wise because we are all women who have always thought about everyone else and now it's finally time, for just a while anyway—for us to think just of ourselves.

These past few days I've felt truly relaxed and not worried about anything except putting one foot in front of the other. If I can manage to even say the word happy, then that is what I am right now. There is nothing to hold up, no one to smile at, no more secrets that can come flying out of a mouth that is tired and finally needs to stay closed.

It is so unlikely for me to be here, because what happened to me when I was 17 years old has spun a web inside of me that has kept me from letting go of those terrible moments when the web was born.

Before befriending these women, I told only one person what had happened to me. I told my mother, and I'm sure she told only my father because she is the one who came back to me pleading that I do nothing. So that is what I did for all these years, until these women. My husband does not know, my two daughters do not know, but Jeff Hammes knows.

When I read in *Sports Illustrated* about his bad knee injury and his addiction to painkillers ending his NFL career years ago, I can honestly say that I was glad. I can honestly say I feel he deserves nothing good, and the people who raised him and coached him and knew about the blackness in his heart deserve the same.

My own mother should have helped me. She should have sent me to talk to someone, but I never even saw a doctor. In 1970 the world was not as accepting and open as it is now. Even though we were all supposed to be liberated from the Sixties, Waunego was not so liberated—at least not in my neighborhood, where nearly every house had a two-car garage and large lawn and a father who drove to work in the city.

What I think about most is my own teenage daughters. I have always wanted to tell them what Jeff did to me, but somehow I have never been able to say the words. Would it help them? Would they shrink back and give me that big-eyed look I have come to know as, "What's wrong with you, Mother?" Maybe I needed to do this walking first, or maybe I needed to wait until they were just a bit older. Surely Jess and Sarah are stronger and smarter than I ever was. That is why I have not blurted it out when we have had our talks about sex and being careful and being in control of your own body.

But there isn't a day or a second when I don't think about something terrible happening to them. Oh, I know all mothers worry like this. All mothers creep through the house at night when their babies are sleeping, just to watch them breathe, just to know that for those few minutes their babies are alive and safe. All mothers wonder each time a door closes behind a baby how long it will be before they hear the door slam again and then those feet pounding across the kitchen floor. When a siren wails and we are home alone, we expect tiny pieces of our stomachs to pass into our throats. There is endless worry.

I hate to admit my special worry, the one that I carry within me when I watch them pulling down the edges of their bras, playing with eye shadow in the hall bathroom, or pouring over the photos of the senior boys in the high school year book. That worry borders on becoming a consuming fear that is dangerously close to an illness.

I have no sons. No young man on testosterone overload to guide through these years. Maybe just that, the fact that I am a mother of daughters, has brought me finally to this place of walking women with our no-name tennis shoes from the sales rack at

Kohl's. I think that only in the telling and the sharing of this story with the people I love the most, only then will this deep dark hole in my heart be filled with the light from the sun that I am knowing so well these days.

Of course there's Tim. My wonderful husband Tim. I have imagined telling him about Jeff so many times that there could not be a number that high. We would be in the car holding hands or sitting on the couch with our backs pushed up against the middle cushion, and I would want to say, "Tim, there's something I have always wanted to tell you." But words would never come, and I would turn to look at him in his old sweatsuit, with his forehead that seems to slant toward the attic, and I would think about how much he loved me and how my telling might change something. Maybe he would love me less. Maybe everything that I had would change. Maybe the secret had become such a part of me, I couldn't live without it.

I would always talk myself out of revealing my secret, and then it would feel as if that old place of terror would grow just a little bit larger and then I would say to myself that Tim is looking at me and he loves me, but he really doesn't know this one thing about me that has moved through my life like an attached shadow. And I would cry in the bathroom for betraying him with this secret, with the one thing that I have never been able to find the courage to tell him.

Something wonderful did happen to me when I first told my best friends the secret. It kinda felt as if something vile had busted loose and filtered itself out through my mouth. Like the top of a huge wall or a dam broke, and the water seeped through and the weight of the world rushed slowly off of my head, then my neck, then my shoulders until finally even breathing became easier. I can remember the moment as if it happened this morning.

When it actually happened was December 12, not quite two

years ago, and all eight of us were drinking wine at Janice Ridby's house. Her husband was out of town on one of those cross country truck runs, and we used that as an excuse to have a get-together. We did start out to talk about books or the economy the first time or two that we held these meetings, but that never lasted long. It was so much fun just to get together and to not be making crafts or something like that, which none of us like to do anyway. I had to have three glasses of wine before I even brought the rape up, and it wasn't even something that I had thought about. Maybe the reason was because Janice had already told us about her uncle, but suddenly right when the bowl of chips and salsa passed through my hands and into Susan's, I blurted it out.

"Hey," I said fairly softly. "There's something I never told anyone that I want to tell you. Something that happened to me a long time ago."

This announcement pretty much stopped everyone in their tracks because I hadn't ever shared much before this night. Well, some things like how I hate it when Tim walks around in his boxer shorts after his shower but nothing ever like this.

"Whatever it is, it's okay to tell us," said Susan, who was just trying so hard to get over that horrible mess with her husband.

"Well," I started out again, hesitating because suddenly this huge swell of emotion washed over me and made me start crying. "Oh hell, I don't know why I'm doing this but I've always wanted to tell someone and you're all like sisters to me."

Alice was next to me, she's the "Mom" of the group, and she put her short little arm around my neck and held me close. "Get it out, honey," she encouraged me. "Tell us, get it out of there so it won't eat you up."

"All right," I said. "It's just hard because this was so horrible, and no one helped me, and I guess, I guess I never, ever talked about it."

"You were raped, weren't ya?" This question came from Sandy, who is about the most direct person I have ever met in my life.

I just nodded and felt Alice's arm tighten around my neck.

"High school or college?" was Sandy's next question.

"High school," I answered.

"Well, you're still cute so you were probably really cute in high school so my guess is that it was one of those jock bastards and everyone begged you to keep it quiet because it would ruin his pathetic little life."

"Something like that," I mumbled, surprised at all that Susan seemed to know and trying hard to get the images of Jeff Hammes out of my mind that were dangerously close to making me scream.

"Honey, just tell us about it. It's not good that you never talked about it. Joyce is right about that, keeping things in can always keep them lurking on the tip of your tongue waiting to jump out of your mouth. I can't believe you never told anyone. But then again, we all have our secrets."

I told them the whole story, from the beginning through to the end, which is exactly what I thought the telling would be—the end.

The images come in jagged pieces—prom night, tuxedos, the proud look in my father's eye as he ushered me into the foyer where Jeff was waiting with a pink corsage. The ride in Jeff's brother's convertible, the bottle of whiskey in the back seat, and me not wanting any, and him drinking all the way to the dance, during the dance, after the dance.

Now I wonder if there were other girls watching me that night who had been through the same thing. Did he throw each of them on the back seat, put a hand around their neck, rip holes in their clothes, thrust himself into them so quick and hard that it felt as if they were ripping open?

"I was a virgin, you know," I told the girls. "I was one of those popular girls who also happened to be good, and I was caught totally off guard. I'm not certain I even tried to fight back. I think I might have been in shock."

Gail, Mary and Chris were so angry when I was telling my story that they got up and moved around Janice's small living room as if they were pacing in a cage.

"I hate this," Chris finally said. "The same thing happened to my sister's best friend, to my college roommate, to the woman whose desk faces mine at work. Sometimes I get so angry about this shit that I could blow in half." She hesitated for just a second and then went on. "I bet nothing happened to him, did it?" She didn't wait for an answer. "What gets me is how many of these guys are trying to raise daughters. I bet they dance a whole different way now."

"Chris, sit down," Alice said softly. "We are all angry about this, but let J.J. finish. She needs to tell us."

There wasn't much more to say. Just being able to say what happened, that's what I needed to do. Still, I told them the rest. About coming home and running to the bathroom and stripping off my clothes, then ripping them into shreds while my mother stood outside of the bathroom door and pounded to get in.

"What's the matter, Joanne? Let me in. Please let me in."

I did let her in because I was in such shock I could not remember how to turn on the shower. I was standing by the door, naked. She saw the marks on my throat, up and down my legs, and my ruined clothes in a pile on the floor.

"Mommie, please, please help me." I fell to the floor, sobbing.

My mother was a good mother. She loved me and took care of me and was always home when I needed her, but this time when I needed her to do something, to make Jeffrey pay somehow, to stand up to the world for me, she could not do it. "Don't tell anyone about this, Joanne. Just let me talk to your father about this."

When my first daughter was born, sliding so easily from inside of me I knew for sure that birth was a miracle, I held Jess tightly, so close, I could not imagine anything or anyone ever coming between us. I promised her that second, the first time she looked into my eyes, that I would never let anyone hurt her, and if someone ever tried, they would pay a high price. They would have to face me. A mother. Her mother. Now my daughters are women themselves. Jess is 17, beautiful and wise, and Sarah, at 15, has a glow of confidence and life that makes me stand back in amazement. They have made my story more demanding, more urgent.

Maybe you can guess the next part of my story. After I was sedated with a white pill and lying in my bed, Mother went to tell my father what happened. My father was an executive in a large manufacturing plant in Milwaukee who relied heavily on his community contacts. I don't know what his reaction was exactly, but I can imagine—I know my father's work was more important to him than anything, even than me. I found that out when my mother came back to me an hour later. She was crying as she got into bed next to me. She whispered, as if she were the child, "Your father believes we should just pray that you don't get pregnant. He told me, this will pass and you'll feel better."

My mother was right about the feeling better part, but not about things exactly passing. This treacherous event in my life never passed. The rest of my high school days I spent in a shell, counting the seconds until I could graduate and leave everyone and everything behind me.

In college, I had a chance to forget at least temporarily what had happened to me. I found new friends, people who didn't know me in high school, who would never guess that part of my recent past. I dated, though it was fairly impossible for me to let anyone get physically close. I could never explain why. While the rest of my friends were sleeping with each other pretty much all the time, I was hovering in the background wondering how I would ever be able to let anyone touch me. One night I simply picked out the nicest guy I knew, consumed a large amount of alcohol and let him take me to bed. From what I can remember, he was gentle and kind but there was nothing remarkable about the sex. He didn't hurt me, so I could joke to myself that I'd saved several thousand dollars in therapy costs.

I remained cautious after that. It was so difficult for me to trust men that I could barely stand to go out with anyone more than once. In a different world I probably would have chosen the company of women. My friends then gave me great comfort without even knowing that I had this tragic shadow sleeping behind my eyelids. All those girlfriends who shared my dorm rooms, came home with me on the weekends, studied with me all night and shared the secrets of their hearts and souls gave me hope. Somehow their support and love kept me kept me from falling completely off my center.

Loving one of my girlfriends romantically might have been a natural thing to do, but it really never dawned on me. Still I did love them. I loved Sharon when she let me put my head in her lap to comfort me without asking questions. I loved Meg for talking to me one night for six straight hours when I told her I was afraid of the dark. I loved Debbie for letting me go home with her two Christmases in a row so I wouldn't have to face my own parents.

I loved those girls like I love the girls right now who are walking with me, who have shown me how to feel the power of my own legs moving me down a highway that is as new and wonderful as anything I have ever seen.

If I only could have known the magic and power in this

personal performance of ours, the knowledge could have saved me so much trouble all these years. I have spent countless hours reading books and articles about the lasting effects of rape on its victims. I have scanned the television listings for all those goofy talk shows where women come on and talk about their own rape experiences, and I have spent a thousand nights looking off into the dark night, wondering if I would ever feel the power of my own healing.

Once I read somewhere that the agonies of life never disappear. The pain may splinter, and parts of it might dissolve but the anger and the struggle always remain inside of us. In some cases, they become so much a part of us that we can never get rid of it. A few people even learn how to treasure the traumatic experience that has settled inside of them.

That is a powerful thing, I think, and maybe what has happened to me. The simple telling of my trauma—to my sisters here —has seemed to set me free in a way that I never thought possible. I imagine when I tell my daughters and my husband, I will become even more empowered than I could ever have dreamed.

Then too I have come to know because of these walking women, that I need to be an example for my own daughters. How different my life would have been, Chris told me, if my own mother had risen up with a whip in her hand to defend me and to right the wrongs. These steps along the highway are giving me back something powerful that was taken away from me a long time ago. I know with all my heart that I must pass this power on to my own beautiful girls.

Another thing that I know is that Tim will enfold me in his arms and surround me with his love just as he always has. Somehow I finally feel confident that when I do tell him, he will not shrink away from me or even be angry. I have been lucky to have him love me all these years, and that has been the single gift that has kept me moving ahead, slowly at times, but I have moved ahead.

When the telling is over, I know that I must go back to my mother, too. She has never been able to look me in the eye all these years and it is only now, this second when I see the legs of my friends moving like powerful pistons, that I know her life must have been filled with anguish and loss and anger too. I know she loved me. When this walk is over, I'm pretty sure I will be able to go to her and tell her that I forgive her. I will try. At least I will try.

I will try to forgive her for everything and everyone that she could not control. Forgive her for being able to hold me for only an hour or so in my tiny single bed that rocked and swayed with her own well of tears. Forgive her for all the long nights when she sat on one side of the upstairs bedroom, and I sat on the other, both of us so alone, so sad, and so scared. Forgive her for what she could not do to make my life sweet again.

But first, before I go back to them all, there is this walking that seems to be lifting up the very soul that holds my bones together. I have to be careful these days not to wish myself swept away into the eternities on this wave of happiness. I need to go back to my daughters, my mother, my Tim and finish this incredible journey.

CHAPTER THREE

IT WAS ALMOST IMPOSSIBLE to get Alice out of Lenny Sorensen's bathtub. "Girls!" shouted Alice, who left the bathroom door open so she could talk to the other women, "This is wonderful, I haven't felt anything this wonderful, well," she said, stumbling over her own words, "well, just never mind."

Everyone else was sitting around Lenny's house wrapped up in a towel or an old bathrobe or one of the few oversized shirts of Jackson's that Lenny hadn't thrown into the hog pen. Lenny ushered them into the house, pointed them towards the refrigerator and bathroom, and then ordered them to strip so she could wash their clothes.

"My God!" shouted Sandy, as she waltzed through the kitchen sipping wine in a red towel that barely covered her rear end. "This is about the most hilarious thing I have ever seen in my life. Lenny, go put a towel on, you're overdressed."

Lenny didn't say much as she gathered up underwear and

socks to throw into the old green washing machine at the back of the kitchen. She was surprised that she didn't know any of the women who had marched up her yard and into her life, but she told herself that was most likely because she had spent way too much time feeding pigs and driving a tractor instead of going out in public and actually acting like a human being. She watched the women move through the house talking, helping each other pull off pants, and pour glasses of wine with such ease she considered for a moment stripping off her own clothes and joining them.

"What's so funny?" Sandy leaned against the washing machine. "You've got the biggest grin on your face."

"I was just thinking how natural you all seem around each other, and I thought I should take off my clothes and join you." Lenny settled next to Sandy as the 34 year old washing machine kicked in, sounding like a helicopter landing in the living room. The noise forced them to raise their voices.

"Well, you've probably got the best looking ass here, especially if you work the farm. Why'd you let us in?"

"Why'd you come in?" Lenny fired back, wanting just a few more minutes before she opened up her heart, before she exposed her admiration, before she told this unknown half-naked wild woman drinking wine in her kitchen that the women's footsteps had already changed her life.

"You're a woman for starters," answered Sandy. "You know," she said honestly, turning to look out the kitchen window. "I'm not sure, but it was like we were supposed to stop here for a while, take a break or something. We never really talked about it but when I saw you, I knew we should stop and that we'd be safe."

Lenny turned to look into Sandy's eyes, dark and deep, offering a sea of understanding. While the machine gurgled and belched, she told her about Jackson and college and her three kids who are grown and gone and as far away as she could convince them to move. She told her about a dream that has somehow slipped away during the years of diapers and pigs and sleeping alone in a bed the size of the Grand Canyon.

Sandy listened, smiling, nodding, thinking the whole time how much she liked this woman with the boots and the fine hair and hands as strong as steel. Before Sandy could tell her how she felt, her turn in the bathroom came. The stove timer beeped and Lenny began mashing potatoes, No one saw that she had quietly taken the phone off the wall and stuffed it into the drawer where she kept towels and hot pads.

"Hail to you, Lenny," J.J. finally said as the women finished their feast and sat with their arms on their bellies and their eyes at half-mast. "This is just the nicest thing you could have done for us."

Lenny put her fork down on her plate, glanced quickly towards Sandy and then away, and told the women how much she admired them, how easy it would be for her to slip out the door and walk with them, how she knew for certain that other women were listening to the same footsteps.

"The minute I heard about you on the radio, I knew something was going to happen," Lenny told them, keeping her eyes on her plate. "You have to keep going, you can't stop yet. Not until you go for days and days and more people hear about you."

The women felt dazed. Janice, J.J. and Susan looked at Lenny as if she had just told them they were all going to die in 30 minutes of some terrible disease. Alice coughed. Chris smiled, knowing exactly what Lenny was talking about. Sandy had not been able to take her eyes off of Lenny since they were standing close together at the washing machine. Gail started coughing from a piece of turkey that only made it halfway down her throat before Lenny made her pronouncement.

"Come on women," Chris said forcefully. "Didn't you think

this would happen?"

"What the hell are you talking about?" Gail responded defensively.

Chris shifted forward and put her hands on either side of her empty plate. "When was the last time you heard of a group of women just getting up from something, a church meeting, or as in our case a drunken evening at the home of a friend, to start walking down a highway?"

The other women had not thought about their decision in quite this way. They had thought about dead babies and rape and heartaches and uncles who shoved their fingers in private places where they shouldn't have, but they have not thought about what the walking might mean to someone else.

"Well, shit," Janice said, as if she has just discovered a pile of gold. "This is just for us, it's our walk."

"No, it's not. " Lenny spoke softly, moving her fingers around the edges of her plate. "Look at me. Apparently you have no idea how many women in the world would love to say, 'Piss off,' and take off hiking."

Sandy smiled, watching Lenny turn her head and lift her eyebrows and lean forward close to the center of the table, and then breathe. She watched Lenny breathe.

"But . . ." stammered Gail. "It still has to be about us. Don't you think? Don't you all think?"

Chris couldn't believe they had come this far in so few miles. While her friends debated the ins and outs of what they were doing, why they were doing it, and what will happen next, she could only remember how she saw them at first. Alice sad and old; J.J. mousy and just as sad; Janice alternately quiet and startling, always second guessing herself; Sandy, wild and bold, and crazy and ready for something, someone, anything new; Gail, always holding something back, afraid of losing something; Susan, in desperate need of a kick in the ass, so beautiful, so in need of a push in the direction that will honor who she truly is. And Mary, just wonderful, happy Mary who is content with the confines society has set, with tradition, with staying safe inside those boundaries.

"What the hell are you smiling about?" Sandy finally asked Chris after the women have decided to just do whatever they want to do.

"Look at us," said Chris, moving her eyes across every face at the table. "It wasn't that long ago that we were talking about Christmas cookies and what a deal there was on lettuce at the grocery store and what the hell are we going to do about Monica Lewinsky?" She laughed mockingly at the ceiling, "How far we have come!"

"Oh God!" Susan suddenly pushed herself from the table, cupping a hand over her mouth and running toward the laundry tub behind the kitchen.

"Oh piss," moaned Sandy. "It's the baby!"

Alice helped Susan at the tub and Sandy told Lenny, never moving her eyes from Lenny's face, about Susan being pregnant and the broken glass and them on the floor and then walking, The women, all of them, even Lenny grew somber, thinking of things horrible and cruel.

Susan recovered quickly and determined not to let a brief puking session keep her from talking and staking out a spot where she could sleep before they began walking again. She has been pregnant before, so she knows she can eat again in a few hours and the food will stay where it belongs. "What a damn nuisance," she told Alice, who was leaning over to wipe the corners of her mouth."Alice, do you hate me for not wanting to have this baby?"

Alice really only hates the parts of herself that she has never been able to forgive, and although she could never in a million years consider having an abortion herself, she understands why Susan would not want to see this pregnancy through.

Alice dabbed softly around Susan's mouth and then rested her hands on Susan's soft face. "No, sweetie, no, I could never hate you. I can see this would be a mistake for you. A costly one, huh?"

Susan nodded and then rested against Alice, who looked as if she could be blown clear to Chicago on a windy day, but is in fact as solid as the white-washed barn in Lenny's yard. Susan cried again, and the two women stood by the laundry tub, each of them thinking at the same moment how lucky they were to know each other, to be in Lenny's kitchen, to be walking through a season wild with possibilities.

Lenny's house was littered with beds. There were bunk beds in her son's room, two double beds in her daughter's room, the Grand Canyon bed in her own room, two couches, and a basement filled with an assortment of sleeping bags and cots and two very funky mattresses for the long-since ended family gatherings that stopped abruptly the last time Jackson forgot to show up for Thanksgiving dinner.

Near midnight, everyone but Chris and Sandy found a place to lie down quickly after dinner, and while Chris escaped to the kitchen to put the phone back on the hook and to call Mary, Sandy followed Lenny from room to room finding extra pillows and talking as if her mouth has been set on fire.

Mary knew Chris would call, and she picked up the phone before the first ring had stopped. Chris sensed Mary was alone, standing by her kitchen window, her paradise.

"Well?" Chris asked. "Are you home now?"

"Don't be an ass," Mary said, half laughing. "Where are you?"

"We are at Lenny Sorensen's house. It's that old farm we always talked about just past where the road turns really quickly.

Nice woman. Sandy is crazy about her. Lenny is a hog farmer and her husband, not surprisingly, is a prick."

Mary laughed as loud and as clear as Chris has ever heard her laugh, and then she took charge. Also something new.

"I called everybody, all the husbands I could find anyway, and it was kind of a hoot," she said. "Lots of stammering so I just cut them off and told them they would simply have to understand."

Chris could see her sitting in her kitchen with the curtains pushed back, dishes on the counter, and her left foot rubbing the back of the 13 year-old black Labrador that refused to die.

"What did Boyce say?"

"Same ole same ole."

"What's that, Mary, what does Boyce say?"

"He says he loves me and he's glad I'm home, and I think he's hoping we'll have wild sex tonight because he took a shower."

"Well, honey, get off the phone."

"No, wait." Mary asked urgently. "Is everyone okay?"

"We are wonderful, just wonderful, except Susan just threw up."

"Listen," Mary said quietly. "I'm going to follow you now and then, you know, I'll stick some food out there, whatever you need. Are you going to keep going?"

Chris told her yes, they are going to keep going, and that the food and water isn't necessary but she can do whatever she wants to do.

"Listen," Mary continued. "I have this idea that I'll just sort of keep tabs on you and maybe try to keep the husbands at bay, but I don't think they are going to say anything to cops or reporters either."

Chris knew her husband Alex wouldn't say anything. He'd be thinking, 'Well, at least I have somewhat of a vague idea where Chris is today.'

"Mary, we'll be fine, what about you?"

"I'm thinking about things. Thinking about my wonderful women friends out there and me not out there. That's fine, I know that, but I still feel bad."

"I think Boyce has a pretty good idea how to make you feel better."

"Should I go screw his brains out?"

"You sound like Sandy now."

"That was bound to happen sooner or later," Mary told her. "You are all a terrible influence on me. Hey Chris, be careful. I think people are starting to go kinda ape about what you're all doing."

Mary added that the radio was running a story about them and that her kids saw something on television. Chris, knowing all about these things, decided not to relay the information about media coverage to the others because her friends already had more than enough to keep their minds occupied.

Later, Chris roamed through the house and discovered everyone fast asleep except Sandy and Lenny, so engrossed in a conversation from Lenny's Grand Canyon bed that they didn't see her peek into the bedroom. She ended up on the couch in the living room.

She could hear Lenny and Sandy whispering in the dark, occasionally shifting their weight but rarely pausing to be still for more than a few seconds, and she wondered what it had been like for Lenny to live all these months alone in this house—waiting, just waiting for the courage to change her life.

Chris smiled as she shifts her own weight, wondering in which century Lenny's couch was built, and then rubbed her aching calf muscles and her whole legs down to her ankles, which are slightly swollen. "I'm going to start working out when this is over. I feel like crap."

Sleep was just a short step away and Chris fell into it, still smiling, thinking to herself that out of all of her life's adventures, this walk might take the blue ribbon. She thought of Mary and Boyce, panting by now like dogs, and then of Alex waiting once again and always for her to come home. "I am home, Alex," she wanted to tell him. "I'm just down the road."

In the morning, the women began arising and roaming through the house before daylight. Lenny had already fed the pigs and scraped the poop out of the three largest pens when she turned to see the women walking back and forth in the kitchen like moving silhouettes. She wondered how she would get along for the rest of the day, the rest of her life without them.

"People," Lenny told herself. "I need to get away from these damn animals and live with people, lots of people. People who can't stand the smell of bacon." Then she laughs out loud, and the sound of her own cackle makes her laugh even louder.

The women dressed and stretched and reconnected, with considerable complaining and exaggerated limping. Susan managed to keep down toast and cereal and to conclude that she could walk to Siberia. Everyone fought for the bathroom, a room they wished they could take apart and carry in pieces throughout their odyssey.

By 7 a.m., before the reporters had even had their first cup of rotten coffee, the women were ready to walk. Their pockets were stuffed with aspirins and a few quarters for phone calls and pieces of fruit that Lenny made them take "just in case" the next meal isn't easy to find.

"I can't believe you aren't worried about anything," Lenny told them, with her shoulder pushed against the front door as she watched them lace their shoes and pull up their clean socks. "If I didn't need the money from the pigs, I'd just go with you right now."

"We know," Gail responded, rising first to open the front door and touching Lenny on the arm. "I believe we'll see you again."

Sandy left last, waiting until her friends were down the road a ways before she made her move. Before she could change her mind, she grabbed Lenny by the waist, pulled her close, wrapped her arms around her back through the center of Lenny's long, dark hair and kissed her.

Lenny was not startled by the softness of Sandy's lips, or the way she eased into her arms and moved her head sideways, by the movement of her own arms around Sandy's shoulders that came to rest in a perfect, solid line across her smooth neck.

When Sandy jumped off the step, rushing to catch up with the women, the sun was poking through the tall evergreen trees at the edge of Lenny's yard. She ran fast and hard and didn't turn when she heard Lenny's solid voice holler, "Be careful, Sandy. See you."

Associated Press April 28, 2002
—Features Syndicate
Wilkins County, Wisconsin

WOMEN WALKERS CREATING MIRACLES

In a section of the country where miracles have always been associated with successful crop rotation, a wet spring, and a bumper crop of corn and wheat, there is a new kind of miracle unfolding.

Seven women who are expected to begin their third day of what local residents are calling "The Pilgrimage" have set this otherwise sedate county on its ear.

When the women left a study class sometime after 10 p.m. two nights ago and began walking down a rural highway, only a handful of people, mostly the women's husbands, took immediate notice. Two days later the entire county, state, and nation are buzzing with stories about the women.

"This spontaneous pilgrimage seems like one of those miracle kind of things that happens in places like Yugoslavia," said Barton Kind, manager of the only Clintonville grocery store. "Nobody around here has ever seen anything like this before."

What people are seeing is a group of women who walk slowly, occasionally speak to each other, but not to anyone outside their group and appear to be in incredibly good spirits—walking. They are simply walking.

"Look at them," said Selby Cannon, a housewife from Abonddale. "They're just walking along, happy as heck, and nobody can stop them. I tell you, what woman in her right mind would not join them for two cents?"

Rev. James McQuade, pastor of St. Patrick's Catholic Church in Granton, said the women could have had some kind of religious experience that promoted them to simply get up and begin walking.

"Such simultaneous fervor has happened before with people who are very spiritual, but I don't know all of these women well enough to know if they are spiritual and have strong feelings about their faith," he said. McQuade said the word "miracle" meant many things to many people, and added that he could never speak for the women or suggest why they were walking.

"Every morning that I get up and my bad leg doesn't hurt, well, to me that's a miracle," said McQuade. "We will never know why they are doing this until we get the chance to ask them, and perhaps it is best to leave them alone, to let them find whatever peace they may be looking for."

That's advice Wilkins County Sheriff Barnes Holden seems to be taking to heart. Barnes has assigned a full-time deputy to follow the women and keep everyone else at least 150 yards away.

"This is just a quiet county, and I figure if these women want to walk on the road, we should just let them and no one should be allowed to bother them," said Holden.

Holden did admit that he made the decision to assign a deputy following a rather lengthy discussion with his wife Selena.

"You have to listen to women," said Holden. "That's something I've always done."

In every store, gas station, or bus stop in this entire county, the "Women Walkers" seem to be the center of the conversation.

Newspaper stories from the one locally published newspaper usually talk about high school graduations, a truck rollover, or the rising Fox River. The women walkers are now the biggest news in a section of the state where life is quiet and predictable.

The husbands of the walkers are keeping as quiet as the walkers themselves. The men have all decided not to speak to members of the media.

"We just don't want to say anything at all," said Tim Johnson, who's wife Joanne is one of the walkers. "Joanne knows I'll be right here when she is finished walking."

When that will be—no one knows for certain. The women spent last night at a remote hog farm and are expected to begin walking again before noon.

In the meantime, business as usual will never be the same.

An entrepreneur has started selling t-shirts that say, "Walk With Me Baby." The t-shirts depict the seven women holding hands and walking on a two-lane highway, with their heads pointing towards the heavens.

—30—

The Women Walker Effect: Rudy

Deputy Rick "Rudy" Rudulski was the kind of guy who was always waiting for a murder that didn't happen, a sink that never clogged, a taxi that never showed up. Rudy's dreams, meager as they might be, never quite materialized.

When Sheriff Holden told him he was being assigned to follow the walkers, he said, "No shit?" loud enough so the other police officers in the room would hear him. Then he slammed his black duty book against the side of his leg to look like he was pissed off.

But Rudy wasn't pissed off, he was so happy he could have flown right out the door and into his squad car. He knew there were reporters hanging around, and that something big might happen out there in the middle of nowhere with those goofy broads steaming up the asphalt.

"This is *it*," he told himself as he cranked the rearview mirror toward himself to check his teeth and the top of his brown wavy hair. "I can tell this is *it*."

The only reason Rudy was even a cop was because he was standing in line to pay a parking ticket when he was handed an application to the state police academy. He realized he was in the wrong line, but filled out the form anyway.

With a decent but undistinguished work history, no dependents, no criminal record (or even the hint of one) and his genetic Polish build that bordered on hulky, Rudy was a shoe-in for one of the two open positions.

Much faster than he had expected, Rudy graduated from the police academy and then found himself driving around the county in a slick uniform. With a gun on his hip, and not a clue as to how in the world he had come to be at the wheel of a squad car that had the biggest engine he had ever seen in his life and perpetual radio chatter about citizen business throughout the state. Rudy was privy to confidential information about everyone from the mayor to the mailman.

When Rudy caught himself dozing during his weekly runs across the county, he would quickly tell himself that he would either be promoted or that this job was just keeping his bills paid until something better came along.

One of the many things Rudy didn't know was that his long-time girlfriend Michelle was about to dump him. His lack of interest in a permanent relationship and his inability to do something "wonderful, magical and brilliant" for her had made her almost physically ill over the seven years of their courtship. Michelle was an attractive, bright, third grade teacher who had passed up more than one dating opportunity to give her 28-year-old beau with a badge another chance.

In fact, this morning as Rudy drove out of the county garage and into the bright spring sunlight, Michelle had already packed up every single thing he had ever given her and placed it in two large cardboard boxes. She was going to dump them on his front step, along with a short but sweet note that told him to "get a life and eat shit."

Michelle also changed her phone number and had already made plans to go to the Dungas Bay Inn for happy hour with her friend Jane, who was so happy Michelle was dumping Rudy that she planned to buy the drinks all night long.

Clueless, Rudy stepped onto the gas just as he pulled out of the garage so he could hear the tires squeal against the edge of the concrete right where the road started. He did that every morning, and every morning the barber across the street flipped him the bird because he was certain some day Rudy was going to come right through his front window in that county cop car.

Rudy's interactions with women left much to be desired. If he had been prone to do something as simple as think about this fact, he would have remembered his mother wiping his face in public when he was a teenager, telling him to stand up straight in front of his buddies and how she always spoke to his father in a tone of voice that sounded like fingernails on a chalkboard. He had lost touch with his sister Joyce after his parents moved to Arizona, and he had never dated much before hooking up with Michelle, which was fairly surprising because he often made more than a few women on the street pause and wonder what he might look like out of his baggy, ill-fitting uniform. Introspection was just one of those things he never quite got around to. What he needed, but didn't know he needed, was a rather large glimpse into the heart of a woman.

As he moved out of the city and towards the stretch of high-way some 16 miles from Granton where he would find the women walkers, Rudy wondered briefly if he'd better start think-ing about what his day might be like out there, but he could barely imagine anything. Rudy's lack of emotional involvement with women gave him a huge disadvantage on this big assign-ment.

Rudy came from a nice family. His mother and father loved him, did everything they could to make certain he knew right from wrong and followed the rules, and provided at least basic direction to his life. Rudy was simply satisfied to stay in his home town, never set a goal and never thought to look around the cor-ner. Nothing inspired him, so goal setting wasn't his forte. He surely wasn't a bad person, just the kind of son who made his mother wear out one rosary after another praying fervently, "Pretty soon now, Rudy will . . ." and right there at the end of the sentence, she could fill in just about anything she wanted to.

Many people could, and in fact do, spend their entire lives living just like Rudy and never think twice about it. Except that way in the back of Rudy's mind, there was a question that needed answering. He couldn't answer it, however, because as yet he didn't know what the question was. He knew he wasn't happy. He always felt like he was in a state of suspended animation, like he was supposed to be somewhere else doing something else, but he had no clue what any of that could be.

Before he drove out into the country, Rudy stopped at the Super America for an extra large cup of black coffee, two chocolate-covered donuts, and a copy of *The Milwaukee Journal Sentinel*. He flirted with Diane the clerk, who saw him just about every morning of her life; told Sam Witgby his rear tire was low; decided to walk around his own car and look at his own tires; then got back into the car, spilled coffee on the passenger seat and rubbed in the stain with the edge of his watch.

"Here we go," he said to absolutely nobody as he wheeled out onto the highway and turned left onto Wittenberg Road.

For the first couple of miles, all Rudy heard was the wind in the back windows, his own breath—steady and even—and one static hum that bleeped from the police radio. The sun was just stretching awake, and Rudy could tell that half of the county was still trying to accept the arrival of morning. He liked these first few minutes of a shift when anything seemed possible, when he had no idea what would happen, when he held the notion, even if misplaced, that this would be the day when something big would happen to him.

Those first thoughts could carry Rudy through the most boring day in the history of the world. He was actually one hell of an optimist, but he never bothered to assess himself that way or to wander into deep and uncharted philosophical waters. If a door fell on top of his head, Rudy would say, "A door fell on my head," and not, "Why did that door fall on my head right here in the middle of the desert when there is not a doorway in sight?"

He let life steer him from one point to the next without ever thinking about what he really wanted to do with his gift of moments. He bought his pick-up truck because it was the first vehicle he saw after he was told the engine in the car his dad had given him could no longer be fixed. His apartment was next door to his brother-in-law's law office, in a fairly rundown and dirty part of town, but Rudy never considered moving. Today as he drove to his assignment, he had no insights into this group of women or their potential to change his life forever.

Just after he passed Grunkees Corner, Rudy began to notice those water bottles that athletes carry lying along the edge of the highway. Sheriff Holden had told him that some people were leaving water and food for the women, and not to disturb anything of that nature because when they were finished, he would send someone to collect it all and take it to the homeless shelter in Harrisburg.

There weren't that many bottles, but it seemed to Rudy as if they were pointing the way for him. "That's cute," he said out loud, wondering if they had water inside of them or juice or maybe something else refreshing.

The bottles reminded him of his mother, because where he grew up there was still a milkman and she used to line up the empty milk bottles down the long, wooden steps at his house. Sometimes she would leave a bag of cookies or a pie or fresh baked rolls near them. Rudy had not bothered to go and see his parents since they retired and moved six years ago. He had a sudden unexpected urge to talk to his mother and tell her something nice. The urge started as a slow thought that gradually took hold of him so fiercely he thought he might cry.

"Jesus," he said, trying to shake himself out of it. "They're just water bottles on the side of the damn road."

When the thought would not leave him, Rudy picked up his

radio and called into the station.

"Hey, Brocter," he said to the dispatcher. "Papa Goose out here chasing the duckies. What's the 10-80? Are they airborne? Crawling? How close am I if I am near Hanson's farm?"

"Rudy," answered Brocter, "Is that you?"

"Yeah, it's me, who the hell do you think it is, the fucking Queen of England?"

"You sound kind of funny."

"Well, it's me, okay?"

"Yeah," said Brocter, still not sure. "What did you want again?"

By now Rudy had actually forgotten why he called in.

"Rudy?"

"Listen, I'm just on this walking thing out here, and I want to know if anyone has seen them yet today, that's all."

"Geez man, are you sick?"

Rudy thought to himself that anyone who hadn't bothered to see his mother for six years must be sick. Now, where that came from he had no idea but he told Brocter, "No," when he really wanted to say "Yes, frickin' absolutely, what's it to you?" Brocter's voice squawked over the radio.

"Nothing yet, but maybe they slept late because they haven't stopped or anything for shit, what was it, two days or something."

"Well okay, then I'll just wait, but if you hear anything, call."

Rudy couldn't eat his other donut after that. He slowed down his cruiser, rolled down the window, and took a whiff of the morning. The spring air filled up his lungs and he held it inside of himself for as long as he could, thinking something strange again. He was picturing what the women looked like as they walked down this very stretch of highway.

He imagined that they didn't walk in a straight line and that they changed positions and that they often looked off to the side of the highway and into the beautiful open fields that most local people take for granted.

"I feel like I'm drunk or something." He put his coffee cup to his nose to see if it smelled funny. "Maybe Brocter's right, and I'm sick or something. Shit."

Rudy knew he was getting close to the walkers when he spotted one of those big television trucks festooned with antennas and parked alongside of a ditch. Ahead of that, two other cars and a group of people were standing in a circle sipping coffee out of styrofoam cups. He had to break the news to them that they had to leave the women alone.

When Rudy got out of the car and his feet touched the highway, he felt as light as a feather. Yet he also felt invincible, tough and strong, like he would do anything to make sure no one bothered a group of women he had never seen before in his life. Rudy felt unusually protective. Maybe this was due to his earlier consideration of his mother and feeling guilty, but he went with the feeling anyway just to see what would happen.

First he went to the television truck, totally forgetting that they had the power to send a vision of him clear across the county so fast it could make your head spin. He reviewed the sheriff's orders and warned them that if they went any closer, he would stop them. He said it in a kind way, softer than he might have on any other day of his life. Then he tipped his hat and walked toward the larger group of people. Rudy gave them a polite notice as well. A remark about the nice day, and then he was back inside of his car and looking at the inside of his palms.

Once when Rudy was 15, he went with his cousin Mark to a fortune teller at the county fair. The woman was so beautiful Rudy got an erection when he looked at her, and he had to pull his jacket down so far the zipper never quite worked the same after that. She looked into his eyes and ran her fingers back and forth across the lines that seemed to swallow up every inch of his hands.

"You a fine boy," she told him in a hokey kind of foreign accent. "Some day, you make a lotta people, women specially, bery, bery happy."

Then she winked at him and told him he would travel and see the world and that he would marry a woman with golden hair and have two big sons.

Sitting in his car now, with the sun barely touching the top of his forehead, Rudy traced the same lines in his hand and wondered at what point in his life he had stopped believing that beautiful woman. Was it when he goofed off his last two years in high school and lost any chance he might have had of getting into a good university? Was it two years after that when he flunked out of a small state college and ended up working at a tape plant eight hours a day where he used a big stick to separate rolls of gray tape that hung in sheets? Was it when he forgot to return Margo Blatten's phone call, Margo being the most beautiful woman he had ever met?

Rudy was fairly dazed and had no idea how long he had been gazing at the palms of his hands. When he looked up the reporters were way up ahead of him on the highway, walking slowly, but at least 150 feet behind what he decided must be the women walkers.

"Oh, piss!" He grabbed for his radio again. "Brocter!" he yelled into the microphone. "The mama ducks are airborne."

"10-4, Big Quacker," responded Brocter, laughing at his own ridiculous joke. Then he waited for Rudy to say something back, but Rudy didn't.

"Rudy? Yo, are you there?"

"Yeah, hey, Brocter, do you think I should walk behind them or drive in my car?"

"What?" Brocter was stunned that a deputy had bothered to ask his opinion.

"They're walking so slowly, it seems stupid to follow them in this big car."

"Well, geez, maybe you should ask them what would bother them the least. It seems like the Sheriff doesn't want them bothered, so you'd better ask them."

"Yeah," said Rudy, shaking his head up and down as if Brocter could actually see him. "Hey, I never thought of that. Thanks, Brocter, that's a great idea."

"Yo," said Brocter, shaking his head the exact same way but in total disbelief at the conversation he was about to end.

"Hey, Brocter," said Rudy.

"What now?"

"Did I ever say thanks for all the shit you do all the time to help me out when I don't know what in the hell to do?"

"No man, you never say jack shit, just like everyone else."

"Well then, thanks Brocter."

Rudy signed off then and flexed both hands in and out, as if the palms needed to be exercised. Then he pushed the magic button on his car that instantly rolled down every window in the squad car. After that, he just sat with his head out of the window, trying with all his might to hear the footsteps of the women walkers.

When he thought he had heard something, just a soft tap like someone might have stumbled and caught a heel that made them drop onto their toes, he inched the car forward slowly. As Rudy moved towards the women, he thought about being happy, really happy. So happy that you couldn't wait to get up in the morning. Then he thought about smelling the wet sagebrush in Arizona, and how his mother would look if she saw him standing at the door. He saw her reaching out her stubby fingers and bringing her hands to his face.

"Still got that mustache?" He imagined she would say this while his father bellowed, "Who the hell is it?" in the background, just loud enough above the television for half the world to hear.

From out of nowhere, these thoughts about different places and people and himself started moving through his head, and for once Rudy knew why. He was elated that he had an answer for at least one of the questions that was floating around inside of him. "The footsteps," he said out loud. "It's those damn footsteps of those women walkers."

As the wind kicked up from the fields, the thoughts kept coming, flooding his mind as if a dam had burst. He thought about working with small children, and coming home at night to just one person. He thought about sleeping outside in a place just like this, where it wasn't crowded and where the dew would settle right onto his face so that he would feel damp and salty when the sun hit him at daybreak. He thought about telling everyone who had ever been nice to him that he was grateful. Asking could he do anything for them. He thought about driving his mother to the rim of the Grand Canyon and buying her one of those pink visors at a gift shop.

Getting out of the car when he was close to the women walkers was not easy. As light as he had felt talking to the reporters, he felt unmovable now, shy and scared. Without taking that one thought any further, he pushed his legs onto the asphalt and came up behind the last walker.

From the back she could have been anybody. Just a short lady wearing jeans that had been washed maybe 500 times and had shrunk to way above her ankles. Her tennis shoes were a K-Mart off brand but they were so clean, Rudy thought she probably hand washed the laces like his mother did when he was a boy, rubbing them with a bar of Fellsnapta soap and then gently placing them on top of the cabinet to dry. This woman had short brown hair, and when she moved one foot in front of the other all the curls in the middle of her head banged together as if they were confused about which way to go.

Rudy didn't want to startle her so he tried to walk heavy and pound his big black boots on the asphalt. This didn't stop her or anyone else, so he leaned over to touch her shoulder.

"Excuse me, madam," he said softly. "I'm Deputy Rudulski, and no one is going to bother you. I just need to ask you one question."

Rudy asked her why she was walking. He did not even know where the question came from. It rose from his throat to his lips and moved out of him without him realizing how the question had formed.

The woman didn't stop, but she turned for just a moment to look into the deputy's eyes. Her eyes were as bright and blue as the ocean Rudy had seen in his *National Geographic*. If he could have jumped right inside of her at that moment, that is exactly what he would have done. Gone swimming right into those blue eyes of the woman with the K-Mart shoes, as if he had planned it for 15 years.

She put up her hand and walked backwards for just a minute or two, and Rudy realized that he would have to stay in his car and follow the walkers. This woman was smiling and he smiled too, and then he stood there in the middle of the road for a long time until the woman popped out of sight over the hill. Then he turned his head to the Southwest, right towards the spot where he was certain the sun would set like a big, beautiful red rubber ball that looked as if it was on fire.

Rudy couldn't take his eyes off the horizon. He was thinking about these women and what must have brought them out here like this. Suddenly that thought, something he would never have bothered to bring to the front of his mind an hour ago, seemed as natural to him as waving his hand in the air.

When he got back into the car, Rudy pulled down the rear view mirror to look into his own eyes. They were dark, and small white lines ran from the corners of his eyes and out towards his ears. "From squinting," he told himself, laughing, just laughing in his police car as the footsteps grew softer and softer until they were gone, and Rudy had to pull ahead slowly to keep up. He had to protect the women, the walkers, and there were other things, hundreds of other things that he had to do.

Deputy Rudulski was still smiling as the women disappeared around the corner just before the Stackowski farm. He fumbled for a piece of paper so he could jot down all the thoughts that were pushing against the inside of his head. Places he wanted to go, the people he wanted to see, experiences he wanted to try jammed up against each other until he thought his eyes would pop out. Then he slowly inched the cruiser forward again, just a few feet at a time.

The Milwaukee Journal, Dec. 14, 1974
Milwaukee, Wisconsin

STREAKER STALKS NEWSPAPER PAGES

by Gina Halkin

Everyone put your ear to the ground and get ready to hear a whole bunch of deceased newspaper editors roll over in their graves.

When the *UWM Post*, the student newspaper at the University of Wisconsin-Milwaukee, ran a full page photo of a streaker in this morning's paper, that's most likely what happened.

The black and white photo caught a rather large man on the bounce as he was running buck naked across the campus outdoor concourse.

The man did have a stocking hat pulled over his face and was wearing track shoes that helped propel him from the end of the concourse and into a waiting and hopefully warm car.

UWM Post Editor Chris Boyer, said people might be surprised to know that the staff did agonize about whether or not they should publish the photo.

"Believe it or not, even though we like to have a good time down here, we are all serious journalists so we debated this issue for hours before we decided to run with it," she reported. "And no, we did not consult administrators on campus, because we are an independent newspaper."

Boyer said she was tipped off about the streaking incident about a week ago and decided to send a photographer to the concourse with a wide angle lens just in case the streaker showed up.

"This year streaking is a big fad, and it hasn't been unusual to be sitting just about anywhere when suddenly a naked person comes running past," said Boyer. "It's happening in a public spot so it's news."

The bi-weekly *Post* prints close to 75,000 papers and is considered the most popular paper on the East Side of Milwaukee.

Assistant Chancellor William Bevens said he saw the paper while he was drinking coffee this morning with his wife, and he almost had a heart attack.

"Ms. Boyer seems to find the most interesting subjects for her newspaper," he said. "What they did is legal, and they are an independent paper, but I would be lying if I said I'm glad they printed the streaker's photo."

When students on campus were asked what they thought about the photo, the most common reactions went like this:

* "Cool!" [literally]
* "Did anyone get his phone number?"
* "I'll never miss another issue of the *UWM Post.*"

"Hey, just a couple of years ago there were veterans protesting all over the place and now we have streakers," said Chad Gromley, a senior majoring in Business. "It's news, man."

Past issues of the *Post* have contained controversial stories about professors and their long ago student work experiences, humorous looks inside locked campus bathrooms, and interviews with female college students working their way through school as prostitutes.

Boyer said a framed copy of the photo will be hanging in the lobby of the newspaper office in case anyone missed the issue.

—30—

The Elegant Gathering: Chris

Oh, for chrissakes. If I had a camera right now, I could take some pictures that would get me enough money to pay off the mortgage. Alice has on a pair of shoes that belong in the Wal-Mart Hall of Fame. I haven't seen shoes like that since 1972. Poor Alice. Her ankles are taking a hell of a beating out here. I can actually see them swelling at this very minute. If we would have thought this through for more than 30 seconds, I could have bought her a pair of Nikes, which is exactly what I will do the minute we stop, that is *if* we stop. But hell, we left the house so damn fast, who thought to bring something serious like tennis shoes that were actually made for walking?

This is the kind of thing our mothers warned us about when they said to make certain we always wore our best underwear if we were going someplace. I've always wondered about that. Did our mothers have one pile of underwear for staying-at-home and another for going out in public? I never saw the staying-at-home pile. My mother did have wonderful underwear, a trait that was definitely not passed on to me.

My God, I used to watch her folding her little white brassieres, now there's an antiquated and formal word—*brassiere*, when was the last time you heard that? Anyway, she folded everything that came out of the washing machine as if she were fondling pieces of cloth that had touched the cheek of Jesus. Socks, hankies, (she ironed the hankies) hell my father's work pants, all my brother's geeky plaid shirts. Folding clothes for my mother was a religious experience and those brassieres, she would fold one cup softly into the other and tuck the straps inside that cup and then lift it onto the pile of her pink underwear as carefully as if she were feeding a sick baby.

My mother looked great in her underwear, too. She worked

for a time as a model after she ran away from home in the late 1940s. One night I caught her trying to burn a bunch of sexy old black and white photos that showed her draped, naked I think, under pieces of silky, see-through lacy satin. My brothers loved to see her run from the bathroom to her bedroom in her panties and bra. Once my father caught them and rapped them upside the head with his slippers. Then he stood there just like them, grinning as my mother ran past him, flipped up her left hip, and slammed the door. Last I heard, just before we hit the road out here, she was still streaking down the halls of the condo in Florida.

Maybe it makes perfect sense that I, Chris Boyer, became her bra-burning daughter from hell. For half of my life, I never even wore underwear. Back in the late '60s and '70s when I was chasing around the world as a journalist, underwear was just one more thing that might weigh me down. It also saved time later in the evening when I was dunking donuts with the guys from all those foreign newspapers who had the most fabulous accents. Well, that was a lifetime ago, and now I own the oldest damn jogging bra in the world and I would give my left tit to have a little support out here on this highway.

I'm the tall, big-boned gal who usually walks towards the back of this small crowd of exceptionally good-looking women. When I turned 40, shit, that was nearly 10 years ago, I stopped dying my hair, let it grow past my shoulders and bought three dozen long cotton skirts so I wouldn't have to shave my legs any longer. Thank heavens I always wear hiking boots too, because this is like the goddamned hike of my life and I've been around this world a time or two. Yes, these big, honking size 10s of mine have been up some pretty sad-ass trails.

Blah, blah, blah. My mind is wandering around like a Prozac-dosed rat. I like to think that I'm the one out here with no problems who simply came along for the ride, but these days of solitude and walking and frying my brains in the sun have taught me that is definitely not true. In just a few days, I am already looking at myself differently and that thought causes me to wonder how in the world these women are dealing with everything that must be clanging around in their heads.

Not that we haven't talked about it. Shit, people think we are out here praying or something and really, we talk all the time, and the night we stayed at that farmhouse was like the slumber party of the year. So we talk about this, about why we came, about when we might stop, about who we will all be when this is over.

Here's what's on my rambling brain as we struggle up a little hill: underwear, bad shoes, what I might have to do next to get one of my pals through this experience. Am I in a drug-induced flashback? I'm the one who came along because she thought it would be fun, and because I worried that I might have to drive one of my pals to the hospital in Milwaukee where women go who forget to take their hormone pills on a regular basis.

Fun at all costs, that's always been my motto and especially if there was something happening that I could write about. But now, this very second—as we are pushing down the highway and our butts are being followed by some goofy cop hanging his head out of the squad car and whistling and about 12 reporters who make me want to vomit—now, I'm wondering if this just might not be the most meaningful thing I have ever done.

I'm pushing 50 these days and definitely not interested in some fucking pre-menopausal "spiritually-moving" experience. I'm the quintessential tough broad who always knows where she's going and where she's been. Everyone thinks Alice is the mom of this bunch but it's me, it's always been me. Here, and pretty much everywhere else I've ever been.

For these women, these pals of mine, this walk or pilgrimage or whatever in the hell the media has taken to calling it by now, is something spiritually moving and life altering. During the past 16 or so months, I have listened to and watched each one of them expose a torturous moment in their lives that has drawn them to this moment. A rape, death, lost love, mental illness, the bumps and dips of life—there is a story of great loss or love or longing that has slowly worked its way loose from each one of their souls.

And oh, my God, how I have relished watching them turn to face themselves in the mirror. The transformations, the relief— the relief has been an amazing portrait of life. Everything that I have done and seen has flashed before my eyes once again just because of them. Because I have witnessed most conceivable human emotions, because they let me witness their march back, and now, finally forward and into something—a place or state of mind or whatever we will get to when we are finished.

I see myself as the great chronicler of life. The journalist who has finally come to this remote area with her man and books and writing instruments to try and touch a quiet side of life that I have ignored all the years of my past. So maybe that is the reason I am here. Maybe I am walking into my own tranquillity here, or bet- ter yet, away from the madness that was my constant companion for 30 years.

I have been to war and witnessed many forms of death and dying. I have traveled the world and slept in huts and crawled through the tunnels of darkness beneath a sagging river on my belly. In my arms, 100 women have wept for the loss of their babies. Men powerful enough to destroy the world have whis- pered into my ear. I have jumped from airplanes and slithered down the side of a burning mountain. Bullets have whizzed through the edges of my hair, and one morning I walked across a valley as wide as all the plains of Kansas to witness, in the quiet of the wilds, the birth of thousands of birds who filled the fields with a frenzy of wicked chanting.

Amidst all this I had no regrets, and I was happy. I chose not to have children whom I could not be there for or watch grow. The man I eventually married kept watch over me like a bright-eyed hawk, and he waited, waited patiently. On the day that I came to him and told him I was ready for this quiet part of my life, he was ready too.

"Take me to the farm now, Alex" I whispered as we drove home towards the apartment for the millionth time from the Chicago airport.

"We'll drive out there tomorrow," he said, trying to maneuver through traffic, all the damned traffic.

"No, now please, I want to go now and I never want to go anyplace else, ever, please."

Alex knew then that I was pleading. I never plead politely, and I was pleading ardently.

"What is it? What happened?"

"Nothing happened, honey. It's time, it's just time to be quiet."

He was quiet himself then, thinking, I know, wondering, I'm certain, if this was really going to happen, if he was finally going to be able to live with this crazy woman he had pursued across several continents for most of his adult life.

"Are you scared?" I asked him before he could say anything else. "Worried that you might not like waking up with me every morning for the next 30 years?"

"Thirty, huh," he grunted. "You're pushing your luck, Cat Lady."

"No more Cat Lady. This is my ninth life. The one I'm sticking with."

It took another 30 minutes for him to believe me. First we pulled up to the apartment and he hopped out, expecting me to follow him. But I didn't. I never went back into that apartment. Ever.

We drove three hours to the farm that very night two years ago. The farm is one of those goofy "hobby farms" where city dwellers retire. It occupies about 45 acres of land on the edge of a huge, *real* farm. Alex had built a house there before we met, adopted several scruffy dogs to fill up the yard, and spent the hours he wasn't working as a marketing specialist on one of those goddamn big lawn tractors. When I moved to the farm, I made him let every piece of land we own go wild.

But I have to admit, I lied about never leaving our quiet retreat again. I occasionally take an out-of-state magazine assignment, though I pretty much spend most of my time writing and on the phone from the farm, talking to people who have yet to come in from the cold, cruel world. I'm working on a biography of obscure writers who died before everyone thought they were supposed to, and I'm trying hard to get up enough courage to work on a novel.

Mostly, Alex and I sit around like a couple of old farts and talk about how wonderful we are and how great our lives have been. He still drives to Chicago three days a week to work on his advertising campaigns, and works the rest of the time out here in heifers-ville.

There have been some days when we don't bother to get dressed, and finally one of us bothers to look up and becomes frightened by what the other person looks like.

"Jesus Christ," I'll mumble. "Alex, you look like hell. How about a shower, big fella? The dogs are scratching at the door."

"They're after you, Christine."

"In your dreams. The dogs love me."

"The dogs?"

"Yeah, the damn dogs. They think I'm Elizabeth Arden."

"These are the same dogs who tried to make it with the garden hose."

"Oh, shut up," I yell, throwing a ragged couch pillow towards his face.

And on it goes until we realize someone is supposed to come over or we need to drive into Granton to get groceries. One of those zippy drives brought me into the lives of these women with the inappropriate shoes. Sandy Balenga was standing on one of those little stools in the produce department, separating a bunch of jalapenos from red chili peppers. I watched her for awhile from over by the red peppers, because I was trying to figure out what in the hell she was looking for down there. Then she dipped forward and fell right into the bin.

"Shit!" she screeched, and I knew that perhaps I had found a soul sister out here in the wilderness. You must know that besides the screech, there was clawing and grabbing and profanities galore.

I yanked her back out of the midst of red pepper hell. "There's pepper juice all over your face."

"Do you like hot peppers?" she asked as the juice ran down her face and dripped onto her sweatshirt.

"As a matter of fact I'm fairly crazy about hot peppers." I wiped off her face with one of those soft, spongy tray liners kept beneath fresh vegetables.

"What in the hell are you looking for?"

"Oh, I dropped one of my priceless bracelets into the bin while I was flicking one of those little fruit flies off my hand," she said, holding out her right hand, adorned with at least 20 bracelets. "The jewelry is a 40's thing, you know, and the one that fell in here is from some old hippie from Montana. That sucker was really special to me."

So that pepper juice bonding (and the profanities) formed

our critical connection. Within about 10 seconds, I was ready to reveal all the deep secrets of my heart. We're talking about periods, sex positions, favorite old rock groups and our need for freedom—in a matter of moments. This quick leap into a new woman friend's arms wasn't as if I had ventured out into the great world of rural friendliness since I'd quit one life for another. I had a hard enough time simply getting out of bed in the morning without a plane ticket in my hand. Worrying about friendship had not been a high priority for me, but Sandy floated out of those peppers and into my life when I didn't even know how badly I needed a friend.

When I left my fast-paced journalist-on-the-go world to try my hand at the contemplative world, I had no idea how quickly I would miss all that human contact. Getting into the silent groove was not as easy or as natural as I had expected, so when Sandy popped into view, I found a wonderful friendship I didn't even know I was looking for.

"Listen," she said that first day, hands on hips, pepper seeds in her ears, "What are you doing tonight?"

"Well, let's see. There's happy hour at five, and then I have to try and convince my husband to make us something to eat, maybe a few hours of work. That's my thrill-filled plan. Why?"

"There's this bunch of women I belong to, we get together on a pretty regular basis to just bitch and moan, share our tribulations. Our husbands think we're studying books or something, but we just use those for props so they don't get pissed that we're having so much fun."

"What the hell," I said brilliantly. "I really don't know anyone else around here."

That night I was amazed at the incredible women who sat and stood and perched around me in Sandy's living room. They all seemed so different and yet so alike. I felt mesmerized just sitting among them. Maybe it had been so long since I'd sat around like that, with women who had real lives, that I was just in a state of shock. Everything felt like normal but yet it was all so odd to me because I had never done things like go to Tupperware parties or baby showers, because I was always catching planes and writing stories on the floors of bathrooms in Nairobi.

"So," J.J. said. "Tell us about yourself, Chris."

That was a question I was used to asking, so that's what I told them. That I was a woman who usually asked the questions but was finally looking for my own answers instead of making someone else do it.

What I remember most about that evening was that all seven of the women listened to me. I could tell from the way that they leaned into each other, touching arms and hands, and legs, that they had genuine affection for each other, too. They were in a way like new lovers who can't seem to get enough of each other and think if they let go or stop touching, the other person will fly right off the chair and disappear.

Suddenly, just sitting there on the edge of Sandy's plastic kitchen chair, I knew I wanted a piece of this action, a plug into this energy. I wanted all those women to love me and to call me and to stop over for a glass of wine and a walk through the woods. And so I said it, right there, moments after I met them.

"I need some friends," I told them honestly. "I've never been in one place long enough to have a real friend or to know what to do with one. Friends. I really need friends."

Well, hells bells, it was like kicking over a lantern and starting the barn on fire. I've never heard so many goddamned "oohs" and "ahhs" in my life.

"According to some people, we're about the friendliest group of people in the world," Gail said as if she were drinking at Cheers. She was straddling a huge bar stool as if she were riding a horse. "We're so good at being friends, we formed this here club just so we could sit around and look at each other."

"Geez," I answered brightly. "Sign me up before you change your minds."

I did sign up, which meant I would just come and hang out with them at their make-believe Bible meetings and for that privilege, although it was never spoken out loud, I knew that I had to turn over the keys to whatever I had inside of my heart.

To say that nothing like this or close to it has ever happened to me is an understatement. It seems fairly bizarre that someone like myself missed the bra-burning era that included women's "consciousness-raising" groups bordering on "touchy-feely" therapy sessions because I was covering the world crisis-of-the-day as a journalist. But, hey, I'm the underwearless wonder, dontcha know. I wrote about those consciousness raising groups, about those years, about that movement but all from a distance as if I were simply peeking in over someone's shoulder, which is exactly what I was really doing.

As the consummate work junkie, I had no time or desire to stop and smell the musk and patchouli. Hell, I wasn't even unhappy because I had no idea what I was missing. But now that I have these women in my life, it's fairly obvious from the damn blisters on my heels that I would walk to hell and back for them.

Oh shit, how I love these women! I have studied their faces, watched them open up and share their deepest secrets, held them as they sobbed into the banana bread, tried to understand the unique qualities that have brought us all together. As we wobble up this road, there isn't one of these women I wouldn't die for, or kill for. These women have become my oasis, and their lives, so different from my own, have turned my own life into a sweet secret that gives me a strength and happiness I have never had before.

I have always felt such simpatico with Alex. I always knew that he was back there, someplace, waiting for me to fall into his arms, and that thought gave me great comfort. Now I have that same comfort, that feeling of perfect purpose, with my women walker compatriots.

I know that as much as they give to me, I also give to them. Where they are wise in friendships and love, I am wise in the ways of the world. It's a magnificent alliance we have forged. I'll trade what I know about a trip across the tundra any day for the chance to have Alice run her fingers through my long gray hair, touch the middle of my back with her other hand and say, "Chris, you're looking a little tired today."

That's what I get and so much more. Even for a writer with all these words, there is so much more. Out here walking like this, I think about every gift these friends have brought me. I think about a night I spent in a hotel room in Alaska, near death from food poisoning after eating some gawd awful bear meat or rotten salmon, and my hand on the phone poised to call for help. Then, rolling on the floor and retching into a garbage can, I realized there was absolutely no one to call except Alex.

I think about the night I spent curled up against the wall of a hut in Baghdad. My coat is pulled over my head and a soldier's helmet, and a pack of Marines are firing out of the windows and praying to God our own guys do not bomb the hell out of us. I had to actually piss in my pants because we could not move, and once after hours and hours of waiting, I remember looking over to see a tiny exposed spot on the neck flesh of a guy named Brad. I wanted to just touch that spot, just wanted to feel something warm and alive and breathing. I would have sold my soul for just a simple touch of flesh-on-flesh there in that one spot.

All those airports and sleeping on the floor and rushing to find a phone and the faces of the world blurred into one questioning smile. People on the end of the phone line asking, "Are you okay?" so quickly and then, "The story, did you get the story?" Which is really what it was always about. Just the goddamned story.

So now I can just walk and look at all the spaces on the necks of the women that I love. My friends, these walkers. These goofy broads who have taken off on this journey with me to point the way when they wonder which way to turn. Tomorrow I am thinking that they will start turning without asking. They will look for the highway that has the most trees and the one that is less traveled because that is the best road to go down, you know, the one that is less traveled.

I told everyone right off the bat that there would be dumbass reporters like myself hot on our tail immediately. Shit, I'm surprised that Gail didn't just call and announce our plans. She was so damned worried about what her husband would say, she almost tried to get us to stop but, ha, there she is right out front with her huge breasts pointing us right down the highway.

The miles and miles I have already traveled have brought me to this new adventure, which is unlike any war zone, mountain climb, or sweaty deadline that I have ever known. It is a rich, poignant, internal journey that has filled me like I have never been filled. I'm right in the middle of it all now, and I'm laughing my ass off because I can't wait to tell Alex that I had the most wonderful trip I have ever been on, and I didn't have to get on a damn airplane.

CHAPTER FOUR

I F IT'S POSSIBLE to not think and talk about everything in the
entire universe, the group of women walking through a remote
section of Wisconsin and wearing an assortment of clothing that
appears to have been shanghaied from a St. Vincent de Paul delivery truck, have definitely not been told this startling fact.

Nor do they know that across the country, thousands of
women are telling their husbands, boyfriends, girlfriends, lovers,
would-be lovers, and just about anyone else who might irritate
them in the next 50 seconds to fuck off. Virtually every daily
newspaper in the free world has carried some story, small or large,
about the seven women who have seemingly thrown caution to
the wind. Just so they can tiptoe through spring as if the rest of
the world does not matter.

Even if they had a moment to stop and think about how their
walk might affect the 52 percent of human beings who share the
same anatomy, the women walking down Highway P—two days

into their walk on a morning filled with high clouds and the promise of 10 hours of sunshine—have focused on issues that do affect all women. They have already spent an hour talking about labor pains, with another 35 minutes devoted to a discussion about how their men and children are getting along, and now as the sun is close to it's peak they are so engrossed in a discussion about the joys of sex past age 40 that they do not even notice the many cars passing them, slowing down and almost stopping when the drivers and passengers finally spot the walkers.

One car does make J.J. pause mid-sentence, because it is yellow and she loves yellow, as she is describing the day she crossed over from good sex to really great sex. J.J. has not noticed that the blue Toyota directly behind her belongs to her but is actually driven by her daughter Jess 99.9 percent of the time. When she hears Jess shout, "Hey Ma," she throws her hand over her mouth just as the word orgasm escapes from the center of her extremely dry lips.

"Don't call me Ma, you know I hate that," J.J. shouts back, as her daughter and three friends roll with her step by step. "What are you doing here?"

"Ma, you're all over the news, and Dad is back, and he brought all his stuff and hey, Ma, we think this is really cool what you're doing."

"Cool? Hey, why aren't you in school and who said you could take the car?"

"Come on Ma, it's lunch break and we just had to get over here and tell you how cool this is."

"Look sweetheart, we're just walking, and it's not something for anyone else but us. Do you understand that?"

"No."

"Well, it's just something we're doing, and someday I'll tell you all about it, but you really shouldn't be out here. Is everything okay at home?"

"Sarah and I cleaned the house yesterday, and we made dinner and I broke up with Jason. He laughed when he heard what you were doing, so I told him to go to hell."

Chris is now looking at J.J. and trying hard not to laugh. J.J. has walked over to her car window but the car and all the women are still moving. The walkers are trying hard not to forget about all the sex stories they want to share once J.J.'s daughter leaves. Before J.J. can register the miracles she has just heard about, Jess keeps talking. She is hanging out of the window, and her best friend Meggie is concentrating so hard on not running over anyone that she looks like she is sitting on something pointy.

"Oh, yeah, I forgot all the guys, you know everyone's husbands and everything. They all got together at Chris's house, and they were there for a long time, and they aren't talking to anyone at all because they have some kinda pact or something. They had so much fun, they're getting together Friday night at our house, and Sarah and I are sleeping over at Pam's house."

"You know, baby, I don't need to hear any of this right now. We were just having a great talk about sex and now we have to start over."

"Mom!"

"Well honey, 17-year-old girls aren't the only people who talk and think about sex."

Inside the car the other three girls snickered, and Jess has put her head in her hands and she is blushing.

"Listen," J.J. tells Jess softly, "don't tell anyone you came out here, and try to find a way to let the others know that we really, really need to be left alone until, well, just alone."

"Mom . . ."

"This isn't about you or your father or anything in the whole world but us, just us. Hey, you know how you feel about the girls in the car with you?"

Jess lifts her head off of her arms, smiles at her mother and reaches her hand out of the car to touch J.J.'s face

"You love those girls don't you, baby?"

"Yes, they're my best friends, and we talk about everything and I just, well, I love them, yes, I love them, Mom."

"See these women here?" J.J. says sweeping her hand out in front of her chest "you know all of them and you know that I love them and they are my friends and that I would do anything for them."

"Mom," Jess says, her voice shaking and hoarse. "Mom, don't you know that you were my first best friend? Don't you know that you taught me how to be a friend, how to stay a friend, how to keep a friend in my heart?"

"Oh, sweetie . . ."

"You're my hero and you are still my best friend, and I'm so proud of you. I know all about you and Dad and how hard things are for you, and that's why, well, that's why I know why you're here. I knew right away. I'm a woman now too, Mom."

Tears the size of her silver loop earrings run down the side of J.J.'s face. Inside of the car, all the girls are sobbing. Chris has stepped to J.J.'s side and put her arm around J.J.'s waist. They are all moving, next to the Toyota ever so slowly, but they have not stopped.

"Oh, baby, I love you so much. Will you do one thing for me, baby? Just one thing?"

"Oh, Ma," Jess says, as she wipes her face on the side of her long-sleeved t-shirt. "Don't make me take Sarah shopping."

"Very funny, you little smartass. I want you to tell your father something."

"I thought you said not to tell anyone."

"This is a special case."

"What?"

"Tell him we are going camping without a tent and tell him the washer is broke."

"What?"

"He'll know what it means."

"Does it have something to do with all that sex you're talking about? I mean the camping part because the washer really is shot."

"You betcha, baby. Now get out of here before I get that cop to haul your rear ends back to school."

As the Toyota pulls away, Jess hangs her head out of the window until she can no longer see her mother and the other walkers. Her hair blows around her face, dancing first one way and then the other until there is a tangled mass of it, suspended over her face, like a long halo. J.J. is quiet, watching as the round face of her oldest daughter gets smaller and smaller and then dips out of sight behind a hill that looks like it is touching the tip of the sky.

"Are you all right?" Chris asks her, as the other women slow and turn their heads to wait for the answer.

"You know that's the best damn talk I've had with that girl in three years. I had no idea she felt that way."

"She's told me," said Susan.

"What?" J.J. is incredulous and startles herself.

"Remember last month when you asked me to take her to Milwaukee? We stopped to eat on the way home, and she told me some of this but she asked me not to tell you, because she was embarrassed."

"Were you drinking?"

"Just one beer at a truck stop."

"Hey, I told you not to give her any beer."

"Wow, you are so ungrateful. I unlock her heart for you and look what it gets me."

The women laugh, and J.J. kisses Susan on the side of the face and grabs her hand and then Alice of all people shouts, "Sex! Girls, we were talking about sex. Let's stick to the subject here."

But the mood has suddenly shifted to friendship, and the women are thinking about each other and about their own mothers. It is warm enough to go without coats and jackets, and Sandy has taken off her shirt, which is dangling from her waist just below the edges of her black jogging bra.

"Did your mothers have friends like us?" Gail asks her friends as they clump just at the edge of the blacktop at the top of the hill where Jess disappeared.

"My mother had wonderful friends," Sandy says without hesitation. "Back then women were together all the time because few of them worked outside the home. There always seemed to be someone at our house, and they would smoke and drink coffee and then like two minutes after 5 p.m. if anyone was there, or really if no one was there, my mother would start to mix up martinis and that would lead into the most interesting discussions."

"Can you remember any of it?" Janice grabs for Sandy's hand and swings it into her own. "My mother had like, no friends, and that's why I'm weird."

"Oh, they talked and they talked about everything and really, I think they were all in love with each other. You know, they spent more time together than they ever did with their husbands."

This stops everyone a little short, and the women begin to think of their grandmothers and their mothers and wonder, some of them for the first time, if such a thing were possible. Before anyone can say anything, Sandy launches into a philosophical discussion about how we learn behavior from our mothers, and that's why it has always been difficult for her to be totally devoted to a husband.

"You can't say you haven't given it a good try," Susan states before she laughs, throwing her head back and cackling at her own joke. "What was it, three husbands? I can hardly imagine after you've been married once even thinking about doing that again."

"Shut up," Sandy bellows back, "you can bet your sweetass I've learned my lesson. From now on, I'm sticking with the advice my mother gave me. Enough of this man shit."

"What advice?" Alice whispers from the end of the line, still a little peeved that they are not talking about sex anymore.

"It wasn't really what she said, it was what she did."

"After her father died she moved in with her best friend."

"Like roommates move in or like lovers move in?"

"I'm certain they were lovers, but their generation was too restrained to do more than act like two matronly old bags. Still, I could tell from the way they took care of each other, their consideration, and the way they always looked into each other's eyes, that their relationship was more than that."

"Wow," said J.J. "So that taught you to be a lesbian or something?"

"No, darling, it taught me to be true to whatever it is that I am."

Feet are sliding then as the women walk down the hill, and Alice suggests that they stop for a break and everyone nods, lost in the thoughts of lessons they have learned from their mothers. They head for the backside of the hill and sprawl on a path of short grass that has somehow managed to dry in the first few hours of warm sunlight.

"You know," Chris says, speaking for every single one of them, "Our mothers really were our first friends, and they really did teach us the value of that female-to-female relationship. Just think about it. What your own daughters see you doing is mostly how they're going to handle their own relationships."

"Can't you see it now," says Susan, rising up on her elbows.

"We are creating an entire generation of hikers."

Susan gets serious quickly and tells everyone a story about her own mother. In 1970 when she was a junior in high school—and her many friends were more important to her than the air she breathed, especially more important than her immediate family—Susan discovered her own mother's high school photo album tucked behind boxes in the hall closet. She looked at all the faded black and white pictures of her mother's friends. All women she had never, ever seen.

"Mom, who are all these women?"

"Oh, Susan, those were all my friends in high school. We did everything together." ·

"But I've never seen any of them. Where are they? What happened to them?"

Susan's mother moved onto the couch next to her, put her arm around her incredulous daughter's shoulders and smiled.

"Sweetheart, I have no idea whatever happened to most of them."

"How could that be?"

"Here's what I know for sure, Susan. I know that if a woman has one good friend, one really good friend in her entire life—someone she can count on, someone she can trust who will be there when times are hard and horrible, even if she must take risks that could hurt her—if a woman has one friend like that, she is a really lucky woman."

Susan can remember every detail of the conversation as if it has just happened. Her mother had worn blue slacks, and her hair was tied up in one of those old, red scarves that she liked to wear on Fridays while she would clean and bake. The radio would always be on in the kitchen, and the entire house, every little nook and cranny, would smell like fresh-baked bread.

"My God," Susan tells her walking friends. "You could have

pushed me right over with a breath of fresh air. I was stunned because, well shit, in high school my friends were my whole world. But I found out later that my mother was right, and when they all left and never helped me, my mother was always there. So there was that one best friend. But she was wrong about the same thing too. She was wrong because of you, because of all of you."

Susan's tears fall into the grass, and Alice, who is sitting next to her, follows each one with her eyes. To her the tears look like melting dew. She moves behind Susan and holds her in her lap like a baby, a small baby girl.

"This is a time, one time, when I need a friend more than anything in the whole world because of this stupid mess I've gotten myself into. My mother should see me now." Susan lifts her eyes up towards Heaven, where she imagines her mother might be watching her. "Good God, what a mess! I must have about six of someone else's friends, but I'm not about to give up any single one of you."

Janice laughs, and Alice tilts her head back and also looks heavenward, thinking to herself that if Annie Marie had lived, she might be kind and open like Susan and that would be wonderful. J.J., Sandy and Chris laugh too, thinking about all the women they know, all the women in the world who would be green with envy to be with them, walking, talking and exploring.

The quiet of the fields surrounds them. The light in the trees and the short, soft grass waves like tiny fingers as cars again begin moving past the women. All the people inside the cars have their heads pointed sideways, wondering what in the world the women could be doing out on the grass.

Alice, who has curled up in a little ball to stretch out her back, lifts her head like a little turtle who has spotted something in the distance. "So what about all the sex everyone but me has been getting for the past 40 years?"

Associated Press, April 29, 2002
—National Release, Feature Follow
Wilkins County, Wisconsin

WALKER'S MOBILIZE NATION'S HEARTS

Reporters following a group of seven women walkers here are betting the farm that the walkers will capture the attention and imagination of women throughout the country.

With the war in Afghanistan cooling it's heels, the economy in a total mess, and people still afraid to travel because of the threat of terrorism, "this phenomena closer to home offers everyone some positive drama," said Jim Slaveny, a *Chicago Sun Times* reporter who has been hiking behind the women. "This is a glimpse into the world of women and what could be better."

Although no one is talking, the women apparently left what is being called a study meeting two nights ago and have been walking ever since.

Spouses, relatives and friends of the women aren't saying much either but just about everyone else, including the female reporters covering the story, have something to say about the apparent pilgrimage.

"There isn't a woman alive who hasn't dreamed of doing this," said Peggy Burns, a feature writer from *The Milwaukee Journal-Sentinel*, who admits she is tempted to step out of her pumps and into her hiking boots to join the women. "These women are on the road to becoming national heroes."

Burns might be on the right road herself. Letters and phone calls have been pouring into Sheriff Barnes

Holden's office in support of the women, and it is no surprise to him that the letter writers are mostly women. Holden said he has received offers of money and cars and food for the women, and one group of women from California has volunteered to help protect the walkers from curious onlookers.

"We haven't ever seen anything like this before but I can tell you my wonderful wife is standing by the door with her own tennis shoes on," he said. "Some days, I'd love to chuck it all and join them myself."

In an era where meeting schedules and excess on every level has men and women running to stay in place, Holden and others who know the women say it's not hard to understand someone wanting to get away from it all.

"Even if they have seen some kind of a vision or something, really, good for them," said Holden. "It's a free country, let's all remember that."

The reporters tailing the walkers have vowed to stick with them, even though Holden has assigned a deputy to keep everyone from getting too close to the walkers.

"I could be covering the Elmwood City Council meeting tonight," said Slaveny. "This is the best assignment I've ever had."

—30—

The Women Walker Effect: Margaret

It took Margaret 18 minutes to inch her bony body to the edge of her hospital bed so she could turn up the small radio that was sitting on the clunky brown stand beside her. Each time she managed to grab a handful of her worn and faded sheets and drag her brittle bones a centimeter or two, she could feel the insides of her legs burn like fire because of the bedsores. When Margaret finally reached the silver volume knob, she said, "Thank you, sweet Jesus." Her soft words echoed off the empty walls, down to the dusty floor, and across the room that Margaret had come to call her cell.

She stretched to turn the radio on, then began to cry.

Breathing, moving, just being alive for another day was a great struggle for Margaret. The simple act of successfully turning on a radio overwhelmed her with joy.

In a life that now consisted of one indignity after another, Margaret found little reason to prolong the last months of her journey on Earth. Urine-filled bed pans, the stench of death, sores in her sides that gnawed at her brittle hip bones, roommates who cried for help in the night. Not one visitor in three years. In her 87 years, life had given her many things and taken away just as many. In her wildest, craziest dreams she never, ever thought she would end up alone in a nursing home with nothing, absolutely nothing to look forward to but the voices that rolled out of the radio.

Margaret had been living at the Wayside Home near Brenton, Ohio, for 759 days and nights. How she came to be in such a place was something she had been trying to remember for almost all of those days. She wanted to piece together her life one last time before she let herself go, before she shed her brittle bones and faltering body parts for something, anything better.

But Margaret was having a hard time remembering. She wanted to line up all the days of her life and file through them, searching for the people and places that she once loved. However, when she tried to focus on something or someone, everything grew foggy, and she could not remember anything—at least not long enough to get a clear vision of whom she once had been.

Of course Margaret knew that the drugs given to her constantly to keep her asleep contributed to her forgetfulness, her inability to connect the past to the present, to even know who she was. Just knowing that gave her the courage to spit the pills into her own urine and crush them with her long fingers until they dissolved and were thrown down the toilet by the sullen, unkind attendants who tended brusquely to her.

She was right about the pills, and after 10 days without them, her mind began to flow at a more even pace and life, her life, came into the clearest focus she'd had for nearly three years. Slowly she began to see things—smiling faces, the tiny hands of a baby, a porch as wide as her cell, and a field, a long field that was filled with blossoming fresh corn one day and then snow covered the next.

Margaret grabbed at the details of the men, women, and children that once again filled up her mind. Mostly her memory was searching for a man and children. Margaret knew there had been children, and she wanted to know what had happened to them. For one quick moment, she had a feeling of great sadness as she saw herself standing alone on that long, rolling porch; yet there was more, much more, and she was determined now that the pills were not inside of her to retrieve these crucial memories.

On the 12th day without the pills but faking her own awake-sleeping behavior that the attendants were used to, Margaret first heard about the women walkers. If she could have, she would have sat up straight in her bed and leaned over to place her ear directly in front of the radio speaker. Against her pillows, she listened intensely to every word of the story about the women.

In her mind's eye, Margaret could see the women. Even as she stared at the fading green wall of her cell, she could see the road they were on and their scuffed up shoes moving them down the highway. Two of them were holding hands and another woman, with long hair that was as gray as winter sky, was laughing so hard and long that Margaret willed her to take a breath.

For the rest of that day, Margaret floated in her own imagination and walked with the women. She felt the wind blowing across the sides of the road and she saw blackbirds chasing each other and a small robin chirping in fright as they passed by. Margaret's feet were as light as the air they walked through, and she felt as if she could walk with them forever. She felt as if the walkers were her friends, and that if she just reached out they would touch her, someone would finally touch her.

By noon Margaret felt famished. From the walking, she told herself as she ate parts of a meal for the first time in months. After lunch when more pills were pushed beyond her paper-thin lips she quickly rolled them up in the corner of her pillowcase. The walkers rested for a while after lunch, and Margaret rested too— eager to return to her own secret world. The walkers were lying in tall grass next to a woods so that the women could go to the bathroom. Then Margaret fell asleep.

While she slept, it came to Margaret that the place where the women walkers were resting was in the field of her old family farm in Wilkins County. This knowledge burst into her mind and flooded her with a layer of peace. It made her smile in her sleep, though no one noticed.

Her matted hair fell in long stands down the sides of her face. The turned-up corners of her mouth, the soft lines in her face, the suddenly pink color that rose in her cheeks, made her look beautiful.

As her dreams continued, she saw her mother, with shoulders as broad and wide as the man's she had called Dah. There were brothers and sisters, so many that Margaret took a deep shocked breath. The world around the farm was a buzz of activity as everyone worked feverishly nonstop. Margaret could feel her feet and hands and the bones in her youthful body long for something as simple as a few moments' rest.

Margaret would never be able to remember everything that passed through her mind during that sleep. She slept for hours, almost the entire day. She slept as the walkers rose and moved down the highway. She slept as the nursing shift changed, and first one and then another attendant cracked open the door to see if she was still breathing.

Indeed Margaret was breathing. Breathing through all the winters, springs, summers and falls of her former life. She breathed through her wedding to a man who caught her eye at the local drugstore and then packed her away to live in a series of hotels and a sleazy boarding house while he tramped through town with his tarnished silverware and chipped china. When he didn't come home one night and then the next, she searched for him. He had fallen drunk under a wagonload of the same corn that her father might be growing, left her a widow with a baby inside of her and nothing of tangible value but a cardboard suitcase.

She came back to Wisconsin and moved into the room off her mother's kitchen, enduring the stares of the brothers and sisters and aunts and uncles who whispered, "We told you so," just loud enough for her to hear. Then another man came for her. He was a farmer too, the son of her father's friend. He took her away from Wisconsin once again to the long porch house in Ohio where she spent all the rest of the days of her life until she came to be in her hospital bed.

Margaret never woke or moved while she slept. While her memories rolled on, the walkers trudged up the hills and through one field to sit by a pond, and then back to the highway. Margaret knew they were there, moving on, and she began to grow comfortable in her sleep, dreaming about the walkers and the life that she had been desperate to remember.

She remembered in her dreams that her new husband had loved her and the baby boy very much. She grew to love him too, with such a fierceness that she thought she might die if she were never to see him again. Their love brought them two more sons, and for years there was a perfect mixture of hard work and happiness as the family grew and the farm flourished.

When the Depression came, they did not go hungry but worked harder and helped as many friends and neighbors and wandering souls as they could. The war that followed is what broke Margaret's heart the first time. Those inconceivable, distant battles snatched the two oldest boys before either of them reached 20 years of age. What Margaret sent off to war were two, strong, handsome men who adored her and promised to be careful, to come back to her and their life on the farm. What came back was a simple pine box for each one of them, medals with purple ribbons, tattered clothes that had once touched the bodies of her baby boys.

When the third boy fell from the top of the barn during haying season, Margaret wondered if she could go on living, if her broken heart would allow her to continue feeling anything. And there was always Raymond walking towards her at the end of the day, with that look in his eye that seemed to say over and over again, "I'm sorry, so sorry, my love," as he peeled off his worn gloves.

The years stored in Margaret's memory marched by while she slept, and when she finally rolled her eyes open, it took her a long time to remember where she was. She smiled as she stirred awake, listening to a light wind push a tall bush against the side of her window. This repetitive sound reminded Margaret of when she'd first heard it, night after night during those first days after she'd come to this place. Now the sound was a comfort, something familiar, to keep her focused as the women were walking and she was remembering.

For the first time, Margaret found she could move a little more easily to turn on the radio. She wanted to hear the latest reports about the walkers even though she already knew where they were going, why they were walking and what would happen to each and every one of them. Margaret knew all about the trials and tears of women and how sometimes you have to simply take a stand and say, "No more. That is the end of all of this."

Feeling grateful with all her new knowledge, Margaret also felt relieved that she could finally fit all the pieces together. She could never remember feeling quite so happy or light. She knew that her body would not respond to the commands she wished to send to it, but her mind was alive and crisp and anxious for what she was going to allow to happen to her next.

When the morning attendant arrived, saying gruffly, "Hello, Mrs. Helgenson," he reached to turn off the radio. She clasped her hand on top of his, feeling for the first time in many, many days what it was like to share the warmth of a human touch. "Please," she said in a clear strong voice, "Please leave the radio on. It comforts me and it's very difficult for me to turn it back on myself."

"Fine," the man growled, his eyes widening slightly at her voice and the firm touch of her fragile tight hands. "I'll leave it on all day if that's what you want."

"That's what I want." As he started to leave, she added, "What is the weather like outside today?"

He cocked his head at her. "You haven't said two words in all these months. What's happening today?"

"I'm just traveling through time." She winked at him.

"Wow," he said nervously. "Well, here's your pills."

"The weather," she asked again. "Tell me about the weather."

"Warm stretch throughout the Midwest," he answered. "Not expected to rain for weeks. Just lots of sun out there."

Oh good, she thought to herself, then it won't rain the entire time the women are out walking. By the time they are finished with their journey, the rain can come and it won't matter. For now, Margaret thought to herself, we need this warm spring weather so we can get to where we need to go.

"Here," the attendant said, pushing the blue pills into her narrow fingers. "Swallow these while I check the bathroom."

"Why, of course." The minute the young man turned his back, she slipped the pill through her hands and watched as they dropped under her arm where she pushed them with what was left of her elbow, just a bone really, next to the other ones.

"Should we change the bed?" he asked her next, hoping she would say no so that he could run outside and have a cigarette.

"Oh, honey no, I think these sheets will be good for a while yet, don't you worry about that."

The fellow nearly ran out of the door then, and although Margaret desperately wanted to stay awake for the news, she was exhausted again and the room swirled. She saw her beloved husband, the one she loved, the man who had showed her how to open her heart, standing so close to her she knew it must be a dream. Raymond talked to her softly, standing close to the window with his arms dangling loose and his eyes lowering from hers and then holding her again in them.

"Margaret," he said lightly, as if saying her name was part of his breath, part of what he did every moment of his existence. "Margaret, I miss you."

Drifting awake and then asleep with her eyes rolling back and her head sideways on her pillow, Margaret had a clear picture of Raymond. She saw him as he looked in his late 60s, 20 years ago, how he looked just before he died. His eyes were set so deep inside of his head that she seemed to get lost gazing into them. Deep lines pushed wide by the prairie winds and the winters in the barn and the pain of all those lost boys ran from the edges of his eyes and into his wide face. Raymond's neck was as thick and brown as the leather gloves that always stuck out of his back pocket, and little gray hairs popped up here and there from the chest Margaret had loved to lie across. "If I could just hear his heart beating, beating, beating one more time," Margaret told herself, hoping God would listen.

In life, Margaret had memorized every line and turn in Raymond's body. She could pick out his footsteps from a crowd, smell him from one end of the manure-filled barn to the next.

"It's getting close, Raymond, isn't it?"

"We'll be together soon, Margaret, so soon now."

While his image faded away, Margaret remembered those last years of her life. She remembered the first signs of blood in the bathroom, and Raymond dropping his head to admit that he had been sick for a long while. The cancer quickly wrapped itself around them tighter and tighter each day, until he was unable to walk or move or to look her in the eye. She washed him and turned him on his creaking bed and at night, when his sleep was wild and he cried out, she climbed in next to him and rocked him back and forth, just as she had rocked their three sons.

After Raymond died, Margaret thought of those months not with bitterness but with gratitude because she had learned a whole new level of love. She learned that after all the pain and suffering and loss of her life, she could go on and she could keep her heart open and unlocked, and that she could love Raymond, her wonderful Raymond even more than she already loved him.

For 20 more years, Margaret lived her life in the same house, walking the same paths through the long rooms, sitting each morning in the chair by the window, wondering mostly how she had managed to outlive everyone.

Now as she tossed and turned in her cell-room bed, Margaret didn't think of all those days alone as lonely days. She had her church and her friends in town, and she had all those years of memories to keep her company from one season to the next. Yet Margaret grew old, and she could tell every day that her mind was shutting down. One morning she woke up on the kitchen floor and realized that she had slipped against the side of the refrigerator and hit her head on the counter.

Not more than a week later, she tried to make a frozen pizza in the oven but she forgot to take the plastic and cardboard wrapping off of it. The house filled with smoke. She stopped driving soon after that, and waited out another year, hiding out mostly in the bedroom she used to share with Raymond. Everything frightened her, and often she would look out the window to see all her babies playing in the corn crib and then she could hear Raymond shouting from the barn to get down and be careful.

In the second year as newspapers and mail piled up on her porch and neighbors finally noticed, her pastor came with the Sheriff. All the rest of those days that followed were lost to Margaret. All the days when someone sold the farm and people from Chicago took away all the pieces of furniture she had polished for years. The days when she was shifted from side to side in this very bed, and all the days when there was no one to pull the weeds from around the graves. No one to say the prayers and to pay for those Masses on the anniversary of those deaths.

By the time Margaret woke up from her last remembering, it was almost time for the last newscast of the afternoon. She grabbed at the thin sheets, pulling herself with one aching lunge just an inch so she could slide her head down the side of the pillow and toward the radio. She heard the women were walking, and she smiled and closed her eyes, listening to a woman announcer on the radio for the first time.

"How many of us have thought about this, ladies? One day you are just fed up and you need a break and you say to yourself, 'I'm just taking a walk and getting out of here.' That's apparently what this group of women from a rural section of southern Wisconsin are doing at this very moment."

As Margaret listened to the progress of the women walkers, she willed them to keep walking and to walk away all the fears and sorrows that had piled up in their hearts. Although she knew it was impossible, she wished that she could be with them, walking away all the heartache that had filled too many nights and days of her own life.

She knew from her vision of them in her dreams that the women had a great deal of affection for each other. As they walked past that old pond and vanished beyond the next hill, Margaret drifted away again. As she focused on the women, and saw her old childhood house in the distance, her mind was filled with the sounds of barking dogs, and her mother's hand warm and soft, and smelling the soap against her face. When Margaret rolled over in her bed, she dreamed of her mother's arms, her wonderful kind arms, and as she slept, her shoulder rested gently on top of the mound of white pills.

United Press International, June 5, 1959
—For National Release.
Washington D.C.

DIVORCE—NEW FABRIC FOR SOCIETY

Government statistics show that by the year 1980, one in every four households will be run by a single parent.

"This might sound like an exaggerated figure and fairly shocking today, but by the year 1980, divorce and single family households will be as common as two-parent families today," said Clement Jenkins from the U.S. Census Bureau.

According to Jenkins, government records show a dramatic increase in the nation's divorce rate, and he said that rate will only continue to climb.

Dr. Martin Gibbons, a psychiatrist at John Hopkins University, said that the long-term effects of divorce on a family are often devastating. He said it's very difficult for a mother to raise a family by herself, and the mother usually ends up with the children while the father leaves the home.

"Divorce is more widely accepted now than it ever has been, and although there is still a great deal of social stigma associated with divorce, that is going to change dramatically," he said. He added that great changes in the legal and social welfare systems in the country will have to be made during the next 20 years to accommodate this huge lifestyle change.

"I hate to be the bearer of bad news, but someday the divorce listings in this very newspaper will be as long as the marriage notices," said Gibbons. "Times are changing."

Today traditional families, with the father working and the mother staying home to raise the children, still outnumber nontraditional families 50 to one. In some states, especially the central United States, those figures are even higher and divorce or separation remains fairly uncommon.

—30—

CHAPTER FIVE

EVERY DAY FOR YEARS and years now, I have started out thinking that I will not make the same mistakes over and over again. I won't yell at the kids. I won't have them leave the house with their heads hanging down and their hands in the air. I won't secretly wish that school lasted for 14 hours, and that a woman with her hair up in a bun will show up to clean the house, cook dinner and do every other thing that I am sick to death of doing. I won't blame Bruce for leaving me with the whole damned mess, bills up the ying-yang, and a heart that is as hollow as the black stump on the back road that runs behind the house.

I used to call my mother on the worst mornings, and even then, I would hold out the phone while she told me the same thing I had already heard a good 4,000 times before.

"Gail Marie Harksman, if I could raise three children by myself and send them all to college, then by God, you can get through this too."

Well, Mother, here's some big news for you. You screwed up big time and that's another thing I keep promising to change blaming you for my own two divorces and a life that seems to have me moving in no particular planned direction.

My life is the one that everyone whispers about at the class reunions. "Oh my gawd!" they all say. "Two divorces, how many affairs, who fathered which kid and she works where?" I've become the *National Inquirer* poster mom of this entire state and every other state I have run from or to.

I don't suppose my parents planned for me to end up this way. When I was a girl before my father took off with just a raincoat, a paper bag with three books, some underwear, and a bunch of junk from the garage, I did what all little girls do. I spent countless hours paging through the wedding album that my mother kept on the table next to the fireplace, imagining what it would be like to marry my own father.

That album was for me the most beautiful and wonderful thing that I had ever seen. My father wore a dark blue tuxedo that was just a bit too big that he had borrowed from his friend in the show band. My mother wore my grandmother's dress that fanned out like the feathers on the back of a peacock. I never ever remember seeing her look happy like she did in those photos. Often, when I was older, I would spend hours and hours watching her eyes for any sign of happiness, for some glimmer of hope or joy, for anything that might confirm for me that happiness does not have to disappear from a life.

My father did say good-bye to me, and even though I was only seven years old, I can remember everything he said, how he stood, the way he raised the side of his hand to my face and let it rest there the entire time he talked to me.

I remember looking out the window to see lilac bushes

swaying against the side of the yellow siding of the house where we lived in Detroit. My mother was sleeping off one of her headaches, and my brother and sister were in their rooms pretending to do homework but really hiding from my mother.

I was in the living room, and I watched my father pull into the driveway from work but he never got out of the car. He just sat there, and I wondered if I should go out and get him. I don't know if he saw me watching him but finally he got up, swung both of his long legs out of the car, paused a moment, and then pulled his legs back inside.

I suppose I knew then, as suddenly he jumped out of the car and rushed into the garage. When he came into the house, he had a paper bag in his hand and he looked startled to see me. Then quite to my surprise, he came forward and knelt down in front of me as if he was making a marriage proposal.

My father's eyes were so dark, they looked as if they had been set into the back of his head. His hair was longer than the other dads I knew; it hung down across one eye, especially late in the day when all the hair oil had disappeared or been rubbed off by his soft, fine hands. He had a way of tilting his head to the right when he was serious, and he was serious just about all the time.

"Gail, do you know I love you?"

"Yes, Daddy."

"My princess," he said, smiling just a little. "Now give me a big kiss."

I never asked him about the paper bag or why he was whispering or why he just turned on his heel and left the house.

I ran to the window, saw him backing up without ever looking around to see if I was there, then I watched the Buick's tail lights disappear. I sat there and sat there until finally the phone rang. Then I could hear my mother upstairs, yelling like my father was still in the house.

Nothing was ever the same after that, and my mother kept telling us that our life was better without him. I could never understand this because all we did was yell and cry and look out the windows, hoping he would come back. My brother got in all kinds of trouble, but finally settled down when a note came in the mail from our father. My brother stood right there and read it. Big tears rolled out of his 15-year-old eyes, and then he ripped the note into pieces. After that he was like the perfect son.

I know now from my own life that my mother tried as best as she could, though it was never quite enough. She went back to work right away, telling us we couldn't count on our father or anyone (any man is really what she meant to say) to ever take care of us again. Her working meant that she wasn't around so much, and that was good for us. When she was there, she yelled at us as if it was our fault that her husband and our father had left.

I always got home before my brother and sister during those first years, and I loved being in the house alone. My mother made a big point of telling me that it was against the law for me to be seven years old and home alone, so I would literally run into the house, lock the door, crawl on my hands and knees into the kitchen so no one driving by could see me, grab something to eat and then crawl up the steps to my bedroom like an old, tired dog.

This is what I loved the most: locking the door, turning on the light on my dresser even if it was sunny out, grabbing my books, pulling my dress over my head, then slipping into the cool cotton sheets to read before everything was loud and crazy again. For just that hour, I was everywhere in the world but really just inside of my own strange life. Mostly I was with Nancy Drew chasing down bad guys, standing on the seashore with the wind in my face and my beautiful hand resting against my forehead. My God, how I loved those Nancy Drew books.

For Christmas that first year after my father left, I hoped and prayed for a set of my own Nancy Drew books. "Just even one, Mama," I begged. We were by no means poor after he left, but there was never anything extra. Mother let us all know that Christmas was not going to be much because of him. My sister and brother didn't bother to ask for anything, but I was still young and hopeful, thinking the world was full of happy endings.

There were presents under the tree on Christmas morning. My sister was so shocked to see the sweater she had been drooling over at Dobbyn's Department Store that she burst into tears. My brother, who actually ended up becoming a scientist, got one of those chemistry kits that helps young boys explode chemicals and put holes in basement ceilings across the nation. And me? I got two sets of hard bound Nancy Drew books. There were three books in each set, more words for me to pour over than I could ever have dreamed. When I unwrapped them, I was so overcome with emotion that I pushed them against my chest, hugging them like a baby doll, making certain that the sharp edges that pressed against my soft skin were real and not just something imagined. Then I cried and cried until my mother left the room.

She was so funny that way. Acting all the time like breathing was a burden, making certain that we knew everything was hard and difficult, proving every day that she was sacrificing every single thing she wanted so that we could eat and stay together as a family. Then she would do something like get us each what we wanted for Christmas and throw us totally off balance. I have a constant vision of her sitting in her brocade chair with the big claw feet, smoking Salem cigarettes, her feet crossed at the ankles, her hair pushed to the side with a big gold barrette, waiting for us to discover how much she loved us.

This time in my childhood was all so confusing for me, especially because my father never came back to see us. He stayed in Detroit, kept his same job, moved into an apartment, and sent "just a little" money, according to my Mother, each month. There would be an occasional note, and my brother told me that my father came to see him at school three times. But I never saw him again. Never.

By the time I was jumping into puberty, I hated my father. I had come to realize that my mother and I were bound together as women and because of that, I had to share in her sorrow, in her anger and in her pain. After all those years of not understanding my mother, some bright light went on when I turned 14. I vowed that I would never marry, never let a man tell me what to do.

For the rest of my at-home years, my mother became my hero and I adored her. Around this period of time, she told me that my father had married the woman he was having an affair with when he left us. She was his secretary. This was big news to me. I thought he left because my mother had headaches, three children and a relentless need to treat him like an old shoe. I was old enough to be angry about what he had done. I saw him as just another man who abandoned his family. This great family shame only fueled my desire to treat men the way I thought my father had treated my mother, and to try hard to pick the men who would treat me the same way.

Eventually mother did her own dating. She was and still is fairly beautiful. She always wore stylish clothes and hasn't gone up a dress size since eighth grade. She probably could have married a movie star or anyone she wanted. Why she chose my father remains a mystery to me. Love? I often asked myself. More likely lust, although I knew she wasn't pregnant when they married. Generally the love-versus-lust question is one my mother and I leave unanswered. But I've often imagined my parents having sex in his old office downtown; maybe this is because it is something I've done myself in more than one office.

After a time, it seemed as if every guy in town, married and unmarried, became a suitor for Mother. To me, they seemed an endless parade of losers walking in the front door and out the back door. A bunch of men no one else wanted. I had no idea where they all came from, but I was fairly relieved when mother would come home after each date and say, "Well, that was a waste of time." Some of these men were clearly smitten with her as she continued to look glamorous in spite of all the anguish that filtered out through her skin.

One guy, Harry Rasmussen, went so far as to ask Mother to marry him. I watched all this from the kitchen. We had one of those swinging doors that you could push forward and then it would swing back into place. Once all my front teeth were knocked loose when my brother slammed that damn door right against my face. This time I knelt right by the crack of the door, pushed it open so I could peek into the part of the living room where they were sitting, and listened as if my life depended on hearing every word.

Harry was actually the best of them. He sold cars in Wasburn, and his wife had been killed driving one of them. He had two daughters who were mostly grown. What I liked was that he slicked his hair back just like my father. My mother went out with him a lot, and she was always smiling when she came home. They went dancing and drinking and dining, and it would have been just fine with my mother to keep going like that until she died. Alas, Harry fell in love with her. You could see it the minute he walked into the room and saw her. His eyes went droopy, and he would slide up to her and try to put his arms around her, on her, near her. Anything to draw her close.

That night they were sitting on the couch having some kind of drink, maybe vodka gimlets, my mother loved vodka gimlets. I didn't know he was going to ask her to marry him, I was just watching to see if there was anything I could pick up in case anyone ever asked me out on a date.

Right in the middle of a conversation about the new restaurant on the lake with the big picture windows, he set his glass down on top of the little white napkin. I could tell that his hand was shaking. "Oh boy," I remember whispering to myself. "Here comes something."

Harry got down on one knee in front of her and pulled a little box out of his suit pocket. This was like being at the movies for me. Even though I pretended to hate boys and had decided I was going to be a single career woman, I dreamed constantly about true love. Truth is, I still do. Anyway, Harry said, "I don't think this is sudden, Beth, because I know you know that I love you." He gulped, "Would you marry me?"

The next few seconds seemed like an eternity. My mother uncrossed her legs, and then she did something that was not like her at all and made me realize that she was probably in love with him. She leaned forward, put her hand behind Harry's neck, and kissed him on the lips for a long, long time. Then she took a large sip of her gimlet, ran her fingers across her face and said, "Harry, I can't marry you. I can't marry anyone. I'm sorry."

Harry became a statue. He did not move or blink. I watched my mother's face and realized that after my father, she would never let herself fall into the marriage trap again. Just imagine Harry in the middle of this sad mess. I kind of liked him too, but I know my mother must have been thinking, "Well, hell, how long will this one stay?" I suppose she was right to say no but now, just today really, I think about how happy she might have been. Harry's girls had been nice to me, and the house would have filled up with other voices, and my mother and Harry could have had a million vodka gimlets and giggled every night for the rest of their lives.

Harry never came back, and I found out from Marcie

Strumpa at school that he married some woman who had three boys, and they were always driving around in a big new car. I saw them several times, and I would imagine myself riding behind him, with the sun glistening off of his bald head. I always had my beautiful, silk, hand-painted, mauve scarf wrapped around my neck when I had this fantasy thought, and I would dream that my scarf was whipping and cracking in the wind just as all my dumb-ass classmates came out of the school to see me dipping by in a big honking car.

School was tough after my parents split up. I was the only kid in my entire school who had divorced parents. The odds of this happening are extremely slim, I know, but there I was day after day with everyone pointing at me. My friends tried hard to be nice but they were probably thinking, "How pathetic." And I was pathetic, moping around as if I had leukemia or some terrible disease that had rendered me permanently unhappy. For a long time, I basked in the fame of being from a one-parent household. After awhile, that got old and the kids weren't so nice anymore and I was simply picked on.

My mother is right about her raising us all by herself and managing to get us into college, and help us with apartments and cars and relationships. I suspect now that because I was so young when my family fell apart, I was the one who took it the hardest. My sister Claudia ended up marrying a doctor, someone she met while she was in nursing school, and I think she is serious when she says she is happy. My brother Jonathan, the scientist, works for a huge chemical producing company in their research department.

Here comes the best part. Jonathan is gay. This, according to my mother, is totally my father's fault because he was not at home to be a role model. My brother and I are fairly close, and we joke about this all the time. "Mom's the one who made me gay," he likes to joke. "Remember how she always told me I was a sissy when I cried? Well Gail, she was right."

This revelation about her only son caused a wonderfully memorable scene at our house. Dishes flew. Chairs dropped. Glasses broke. When he told her to stop asking about his dates because his dates were all men, I was still in college. She called me home to hold her hand and help her put the house back together after her scene over a long weekend while she pondered what had gone wrong with Jonathan.

"Oh hell, Mother, is it so wrong to love someone, man or woman, dog or donut? Would you feel better if he had come home to tell you he was an ax murderer?"

"It makes me want to vomit and throw more dishes and rip the lights off of the walls and damn it, Gail, it seems unnatural." Mother said all of this with her hands waving wildly, fists clenched, eyes on fire.

"According to whom?"

"How about the rest of the world, and me. Do you mean you think it's okay?"

"For godssake, Mother. He's happy. He is not physically attracted to women. He's a brilliant scientist. Think about it."

"I can't accept it. Homosexuality, this idea of being queer, oh Jesus, Gail, it goes against everything I believe in."

"Look at us, Mother. You're divorced and have turned away every decent man since Daddy left, I'm so screwed up I can barely think straight, while Jon is successful, he's got someone to love him, hold him, be there for him. His boyfriend is sweet and generous. It's fairly obvious to me that not only is Jon onto something here, but he's a hell of a lot more together, sane and whole than we are at this moment in our lives."

Mother never got over the idea of Jon, her queer son, being real and satisfied. When I think about how she hangs on to events and conversations from the past, I wonder if she's not still feeling bad about the time she fell off of her bike when she was a little girl. So the deal is that I never got over my mother, which is fairly ridiculous considering that I am a grown woman with two children, two ex-husbands, and I possess all the tools I need to straighten out myself and my life. I've just never been able to take effective steps towards doing that.

I haven't really been the worst mother in the world. For one thing, I don't believe in dragging my children through all of my moaning and idiotic behavior. Being involved in healthy relationships yourself is hard when your mother is changing men like some people change socks. I figure at this point, if I can straighten up my act, I can pretty much make up for lost time. My kids have learned how to be tough, and I've been honest with them. There have been plenty of good times. To be perfectly honest, I have been thinking about crawling on all fours back to their father.

Bruce brought a sense of stability into my life that would have been in my life all along, I think, if my father hadn't abandoned us, except Bruce left too, but that was because I made him. He never wanted to leave; he loves me, and he's crazy about the kids. The kids are crazy about him too, even though they aren't his natural children. Bruce took to fatherhood as if he had been searching for it his entire life. My God, you should have seen his face the day we got married, it was as if he was receiving Christmas and every other wonderful holiday all at once.

He grabbed me just after we said our vows, I'll never forget this, and he was crying. He said that he was marrying the kids too, and that he loved them and would never hurt them.

"I'm not like anyone else," he pleaded ardently. "Gail, it's going to be okay now, you can just let go of everything."

People who know him and who think I'm a few bricks short of a load, also think I don't deserve to have a man like this even be in the same room with me. I guess I pretty much agree with them, and that's part of the reason why it's been so hard for me to find and to deal with happiness.

One of my many problems is that I have a hard time apologizing. It's as if the words won't come out of my mouth because my brain can't comprehend such a statement. I have been trying for months and months now to figure out how to do this. So many months I am fairly exhausted from fighting who I am, from working, from raising the kids, and from years of self-doubt. That is, until all this walking started.

If only I would have known I would feel this good, this confident, this humbled, I would have been walking every day of my life. J.J. says it's not the actual walking that makes me feel this way. The other night when we stayed at Lenny's house out on the hog farm, it was like one big huge slumber party, and we all talked so much about how we felt. It turned into a massive therapy session. But better than that because no one was getting paid to help us solve our problems, and we were all there because we love each other so much and understand each other. That's the key word here, everyone *understands* everyone else because of this woman thing, and if they don't understand, they sure as hell try hard.

One of the ideas expressed as we talked came from Joanne—she thinks it's the simple act of doing something where you can put all your energy into just one focused effort like now, with the walking. Except I feel as if my energy is reaching out and bouncing off of everybody else and then when it springs back to me, I feel more powerful then I ever have in my life. I want so much to make something in my life work, to maintain the courage I seem to be hoarding up, to go on and finally be happy.

What I am thinking about mostly is Bruce. I know he is with the kids, and that last night he crawled into our bed and buried his face in my pillow to smell where my head has touched. That is just how he is, and how he thinks. When I imagine him lying there with his one foot out of the covers as if it is too hot, I get an ache in my chest that makes me want to take a deep breath. This ache is love. My God, I love Bruce so much, so damn, damn much, like I have never loved anyone before.

I wish my mother could be walking with us now. She could limp along, and we would all help her get beyond whatever it is that has never allowed her to let herself fall, just fall, so someone else can catch her. Maybe this walk might purge her own soul of all that black dust she has let settle into her pumping veins. She is living all alone in an apartment with a bunch of other old sour women, and when I fix this thing with Bruce, I hope he will help me go get her and bring her back here so she can live with us. I am fairly determined that she will not die with a puckered face, and that she will be able to rock the kids by the window before they are too big to sit on her lap.

Alice thinks we could walk forever if we put our minds to it. I can hear her up there muttering, "Walk, walk, walk," under her breath, like a stuck record. She has the kindest face I have ever seen and when I look at her, because she is older, I think that my mother could have the same expression if she would only let herself. Alice has her own row to hoe, and we know about her sad life, but these last few days I have seen a transformation in her where the lines in her face have loosened up and her eyes began to glimmer. She even steps lightly as if there are mounds of air and light under her old tennis shoes.

Walking forever wouldn't be my choice, but I know we will walk for awhile because we are still not there yet. When we get there, I think we will all know at once. These things just happen, just like when we all moved out of Susan's door with the same unspoken idea to walk, and stopping at that hog farm, and meeting that old man on the highway in the middle of the night. I think if we were to try and choreograph a Broadway play right now that we could do it. With all these women, these friends, these people I love around me, I have never felt so powerful or so certain of myself and where it is I need to go.

Yet even with all of that, I'm really not ready yet. I have all these good things to think about and lots of plans to form in my mind. I could be really honest now, which is my goal anyway, and tell you how I am planning and thinking and aching to make love with Bruce. That is what really keeps me moving every second of the day.

I think when we do make love, the sex, the emotion, every single touch will be like nothing else I have ever felt because of what I will be able to admit to him, and mostly to myself, about how it is fine to love someone so much, so damned much. I am dreaming of lying down with him in a field like the one just beyond the big house we saw late yesterday. When I saw this field, my heart pounded. I saw a big tree where I would spread a blanket and bring him down to my breast and kiss him. I would kiss Bruce everywhere and come up for a breath now and again, only to whisper, "I'm sorry" and then, "I love you."

Bruce will laugh at me, and he will cup his hands around my face, making a perfect frame out of it. He will forgive me like he already has 100 times, and when he looks in my eyes and clear inside of me, I know he will see finally that I do love him with all of my heart and that I will never make him leave again. We'll strip naked and roll clear to hell and back right through every field in Wisconsin.

I told everyone what I was thinking about, and this morning I am getting winks from my sweet women friends. I wink back and smile too, and then I am back to Bruce and it seems that the further I walk, the less I can remember about the bad things and my years of mistakes. Then I know why Alice says we could walk forever, only I am hoping it won't be that long. I have already been to forever, and I want to stay in this place of power and hope —pushing forward, my arms full, my heart flying in a direction that can only be called happiness.

Chapter Six

Tabor's pond wasn't much more than an overfilled puddle. It ran from one edge of a clearing—a massive low spot—to the other, and when spring was at it's peak, so was the pond. Geese flying south through Illinois often stopped for a drink or a nibble of corn but rarely, unless it was a terribly wet spring, the pond would all but disappear.

Janice jumped for joy when she saw the speck of water from the highway. She loved water. Loved to touch it, see it, take off her shoes and run into it any way she could. Most of her life, Janice had fought what she considered to be primal urges to strip naked and hop into water wherever she happened to be. Her singular heroine was Katherine Hepburn, who swam in the permanently cold Atlantic ocean almost every morning of her life.

"Come on!" Janice yelped as she veered from the highway and ran toward the pond. "Oh, water, water!" her pals heard her yell as she disappeared from sight into the low land.

"Holy shit," said Sandy. "Did anyone else know about this?"

"At least she still has her clothes on," Susan answered. "I've known Janice longer than any of you, and I tell you this is one of the most interesting attractions I have ever seen in my life."

"Attractions?" asked J. J. pushing down the hill with the rest of the women.

"Yeah. Attractions," continued Susan. "Janice and water. She's nuts about it. Growing up, she would jump into the river or any of the lakes around here or something like this dumpy old pond at the drop of a hat. I'm sure her children were all conceived in water."

"Oh baby," Chris said with a sexy edge to her voice. "Now you're talkin'."

"Once," continued Susan, "when we were still in high school, she actually chopped a hole in the ice down on Ranker's Beach so she could get in the water."

"You're kidding?" said Gail. "This woman has it bad." Gail shook her head.

"You don't know the half of it," Susan sighed, then laughed as she sauntered down the hill.

Beyond the pond was an old farm that looked as if it had been abandoned for years. Every single one of the women looked over the decrepit farm buildings, as if wondering with one mind who had once lived in this place. They could see bent clothesline poles weeded-over, flower beds that ran in a circle out from the side of the house, and strips of colored cloth that had been hung on top of old wooden bird feeders.

The women knew when they saw those things that a sister had once lived there, a woman of the wilds who loved her place, who loved to watch those bird house streamers dancing in the wind, who probably walked through the long, rolling grass in the yard holding the hands of her children and wondered what could possibly be happening beyond the small territory of her own life.

As they followed Janice from the edge of the highway to the lip of the shallow pond, they questioned why the farm windows were boarded up and wondered out loud what had happened to the woman who must have lived there.

"What do you think?" Chris asked first, already forming a story in her mind about the hardship and rigors of living on a farm.

"Oh," Alice said quietly. "You know, Chris, life on a farm. The depression. Young sons killed under falling wagons . . ."

"Stop," shouted Chris, putting her hands over her ears. "Jesus."

"It's all true." Alice continued anyway as the women moved to a clump of trees that kissed the edge of the water. "We each have our little tragedies, but you know women back then had tons of hardships and years of loss. Whoever lived on this piece of land, heavens, just think about it and the stories my own mother and grandmother told me."

Alice started remembering with a vengeance. Stories of early frost, long harsh winters, and burning the dead babies. Watching from the window as the smoke from those fires drifted first one way and then another, as if the ashes of the infants' souls did not want to leave the very place they had been conceived.

"Once," she said, closing her eyes to form a picture in her mind of what she was about to tell, "I was working with my grandmother Lucille in the kitchen. It was snowing, and we were chopping vegetables—carrots, radishes, anything from the root cellar. Grandma turned to check the stove fire. When she looked away, her hand instinctively kept cutting and she sliced her own finger off."

"What did you do?" Gail imagined what the bloody scene must have looked like.

"I was horrified and screamed, but we were alone and there wasn't much to do," Alice responded. "My grandma ripped a piece of material right out of her own skirt and tied up her finger, and then she made me get down Grandpa's whiskey bottle, and she took a swallow."

"And?"

"She sat on the floor and I cleaned everything up, went out to the pump for more water, and washed the blood off those vegetables since that was all we had to eat."

Alice smiled then as the women stared at her, lost in their own gruesome perceptions.

"Well," laughed Alice. "My grandma kept on drinking and drinking, and after awhile, I think she was glad she cut her finger off. She picked up the finger with a big wooden spoon, and we took it outside and buried it near where we always plant the tomato plants."

"What?"

"Grandma was more than a little tipsy then, and she put the finger in the ground like she was planting seeds. The ground was frozen and we had to kick at it to get it loose. Grandma laid the finger in a little wedge we'd dug and then covered it over with the frozen chunks of dirt. She'd pointed that finger towards the West, and then she looked into my eyes and told me I was supposed to get the hell off the farm and follow the direction of that finger just as soon as I could."

J.J. said, "You didn't listen, did you?"

"No, I fell in love with Chester pretty quick, pretty darn quick."

Alice told more stories, and there was a whisper of early afternoon wind that blew across the empty fields, and the sounds of toes dipping in and dipping out of the water. The disgusting echoes of cars roaring past on the highway sounded as if a convoy was stalking the women walkers.

Janice took off her pants and waded into the water just far enough so it lapped around her thighs. She stood with her hands on her hips, her head tipped back, trying with all of her being not to slide under the water and swim into its friendly blackness.

"This is ecstasy," Janice told herself, edging just a bit further into the shallow blackness of the pond. Her toes ploughed through the mud, and the tips of her fingers caressed the top of the water. It was physically and mentally impossible for her to think of anything else but the water and her place in it. Impossible to hear Alice talking about eating grass and shooting the dogs, and the women ripping apart their own undergarments to replace their children's rotten clothes.

Her friends could think of nothing but those things, and when Alice got to the part about all her dead brothers and sisters, about her own dead baby, she stopped. Alice stopped because she said she didn't want to talk about that anymore.

"Let's just enjoy this time here now," Alice said. "Look at Janice. I think she's heading for nirvana."

Alice looked around from one woman to the next, wanting to say, "That's fine, isn't it?" The women looked into her eyes, needing to see that Alice wasn't sad anymore and that whatever they felt about her life's journey was as fine as the day that was ticking away around them.

And Alice knew, from a glance at these girlfriends who had spared her years of anguish, that life could begin again in a flash, in a second, before a heart beats twice.

"It's time now," Alice told herself, pushing her hand to her own beating heart. "Time now to watch the horizon for something new."

The horizon had indeed changed rapidly in these 100 hours since the women had looked into each others' eyes in Susan's kitchen, shifted their weight toward the front door, and walked out into the night. Just hours since they had turned away from years of wondering and trying and aching. Only hours since the spring air seemed too cold for wading in shallow farm ponds.

In a world where every nuance, where a shift of the hand or a turn of the head can mean something so significant that it can alter a whole life, the women might appear nonchalant to at least 49 percent of the world. But their unspoken words bound them together as if they had learned to communicate in a secret language, the one shared by many women over many years, in many lands.

Alice unexpectedly stripped off her pants, smiling as if she had been caught doing something she absolutely loved doing but knew was incredibly wrong. The other women watched her with something akin to awe because they knew that Alice had lived most of her life in quiet acceptance.

Before Alice could finish pulling down her brown polyester slacks, the others followed suit: J.J., Chris, Sandy, Gail and Susan were fumbling with their zippers and buttons and metal hooks as if they had just been propositioned by a sex Goddess for middle-aged women. There were no second thoughts about stretch marks and rolling layers of skin and veins that glittered in the sunlight. If it had been a month later, when the sun would turn the pond into a hot mudhole, the women would have stripped naked and pounced in the pond like dolphins.

The water was cold at first but then an electrifying numbness worked its way up their ankles and into the large bones of their legs with a kind of pain that made them all feel glad to be alive.

"Shit, it's cold!" yelled Sandy. "But it feels kinda good in a sick sort of way."

"Hey Janice," said J.J., "doesn't this make you want to pee?"

"All the time, but who cares? The only time I really feel

beautiful and thin is when I'm in water. It makes me feel free."

"I know what you mean," said Gail, pushing her hands in small circles on the surface of the water. "When I swim, I just love to lie on my back and watch the sky. It always makes me feel as if I could stretch out my hands and become a part of the atmosphere that was designed for feathers, birds, sailing leaves."

"That's it," said Janice, watching as her friends glided around her, smiling. "You know some people eat, some read, some drink, some—excuse me Susan, some screw around. Me? I can just fill up the wading pool and be happy as hell."

"Do you and Paul have a waterbed?" Chris asked.

"But of course."

"You should move to a lake, Janice," Gail suggested.

"Wouldn't that be great—to just look out and see the water and to take out a canoe whenever you want or dive off the end of your own pier?"

"Can't afford the property taxes, sugar," Janice mused. "I just put in one of those create-your-own-environment tapes of crashing waves, and then I make-believe I'm sitting on some island or at the edge of my favorite lake in northern Wisconsin."

An hour passed as the women stood in the water, turning their heads towards each other and shifting their conversation from water to walking and then back again to their families and all the people who might be wondering what in the hell they were doing standing in a pond half naked during the middle of the day.

There were no ringing phones near the pond or places to hurry off to. The women briefly considered chopping down trees to build a shelter or moving into the abandoned farm house and working the land, but Alice glared at them and held up her hand with one finger pointing down as if it had been chopped off.

"No indoor plumbing," Susan said, pointing to her stomach. When the cold water did finally make half of them want to go to the bathroom, the women left the pond one by one and dried off their legs in the sun before they put their clothes back on.

"Alice, do you think it was easier to bear things back then?" Susan asked, motioning her head toward the old farmhouse. "I mean, women had babies and kept on working in the field and then made dinner and got up and did the same thing all over again the next day. As bad as it was, it seems to me that was about as good as it was going to get."

"Maybe things were simpler back then," Alice said, resting her hands on her knees and bending into her words. "People found joy in simple ways, you know, like this, like putting their feet in the water and by having conversations that were meaningful and by being thankful that somehow they had managed to make it through another day."

Susan shrugged, and her eyes reverted to the sagging fence in front of the farmhouse. "I feel like an ass to be whining about being pregnant and having a failed marriage and never being able to bring myself to do anything about it."

Alice patted her arm. "Sometimes it takes a long, long time to figure out how to be happy. Seems to me that it might never be too late, though."

"Alice, do you think you'll be happy again?"

This question brings all the whispering women to silence and everyone looked at Alice as though they want to scoop her up and carry her to a rocking chair. Alice herself isn't sure what to say so she is quiet, but only for a moment.

"I'm tired of not being happy, really tired. You know, just walking out here like this makes me realize I have missed a lifetime of moving, relationships, experiences, of doing, of being happy," Alice says, looking out across the tops of the trees and into the afternoon sky that is as blue as one of Janice's oceans. "I think it's okay to be sad, to hurt and to miss and to even hate, hate isn't that horrible if it makes you do something that might change what made you hate. But really, a woman shouldn't be my age and not have stripped half naked and jumped into a pond in spring-time."

The women smile, and they know in their hearts that Alice is thanking them for walking with her, for stopping at the pond, and for moving somewhere, anywhere except where they have all been. Some of them see Alice running for School Board President or burning all of her clothes and starting over the minute she gets back home. Chris sees her on a world cruise exploring some jungle with her son and making certain that Chester has enough to eat back at the hotel room.

Alice doesn't see herself anywhere yet. She is taking every-thing just one step at a time and that's fine with her as long as she continues to move, continues to walk away from what is behind her now and what she thinks should have been behind her a long time ago.

"Oh girls," she half-whispers because she is crying softly. "I'm just having the greatest time."

"Alice . . ." Sandy reaches from the log so she can touch Alice on the cheek. "You know we love you so much."

"Oh, you don't have to tell me, Sandy. I know you girls love me, you're the best."

There are now about one million other things everyone wants to say, but there is also all the time in the world to say it now, so there is a shuffle of shoes swishing through the grass. Gail pulls Susan up to her feet and asks if anyone is starving to death. They all stretch their necks to the side to take a last look at the aban-doned farmhouse.

At the top of the hill, the highway is quiet because all the cars and reporters have dashed way to the end of the road looking for them, terrified that the women have slipped away and they will lose their story of the month and have to go back to covering boring routine community meetings and re-writing press releases that make them want to gag. A laugh passes from one walker to the next when Chris tells them they need to pick highways with lots of taverns on them so the reporters have something to do when they stop at the next pond.

In seconds the women reclaim the highway, feeling comfortable and joyous once again to be walking. It is their purpose now, this group of intimate friends, to be walking and to say whatever comes to mind as they put one foot in front of the other. Normal routines having been abandoned, and the women have the sudden freedom to think of the unusual, to contemplate those parts of their lives so often left untouched, the unhurried textures of emotions that need to be massaged back to life.

Before they have walked a quarter mile, they spot a green Coleman picnic jug with a note taped to it that has been placed neatly alongside a highway sign. Janice immediately recognizes Mary's handwriting. The women gather round the jug of juice as if they have just found the first Easter basket of the season.

"I bet you are down by the pond with Janice," reads Mary's note. "I can't stop long because I don't want those goddamn reporters to see me. Carry this jug just around the bend and go down the hill. I've left you some lunch. Your husbands are drinking beer together at Alex's house—I think he's trying to keep them calm. Hey, I'm not there but I'm with ya. Love, Mary (The Good Girl)."

Lunch is chicken and potato salad and carrot sticks that they can tell Mary has peeled and cut with precision. At the bottom of the bag are two bottles of wine, the same kind they had been drinking at Susan's house the day they left. Also a note urging them not to do anything else brash when they finish drinking the wine.

"Like what else could we do?" asks J.J., who is sitting with her head lifted toward the sun and her arms wrapped around her legs.

"Any ideas?"

"Ravage and pillage."

"Been there, done that."

"Nothing."

"Ditto."

"Walk to the nearest airport and really escape?"

"Not what it's cracked up to be."

"Guess we keep walking then," Chris proclaims, rising after the last of the food has disappeared. " But I have a funny feeling there isn't enough wine in this basket."

"That's fine," Alice says, stretching out her legs just like a runner before she rises. "We'll just all have to go to the bathroom again if we drink too much. Come on girls, we have miles to go before we sleep."

The women leave Mary's lunch on the hill and because no one has a pen or pencil, J.J. simply turns it upside down, picks eight dandelions, and sets the yellow weeds all in a row on top of the empty container. She touches the flowers one by one, kisses her fingers, and then turns to join her friends who are already back on the highway with their arms pumping and their heads moving up and down as if they are all listening to the same song.

Associated Press, April 29, 1999
Wilkins County, Wisconsin

NUMBER OF WALKERS INCREASES— SUPPORT GROWING

If the seven women who have been walking through the rolling Wisconsin hills here were looking for solitude, they may be in trouble.

The women walkers, an assortment of local women wearing everything from t-shirts and jeans to baseball hats and a scarf, have attracted enough local, state, regional, and national attention to scare off the local birds.

While the County Sheriff here is keeping everyone away from the walkers, it's becoming more and more obvious that the group has hit a national raw nerve.

Reports are circulating that women in at least seven other states have begun similar walks in rural areas not unlike this remote county.

Janet Secumb, Regional Director of the Wisconsin Chapter of the National Organization for Women (NOW), said she thinks women across the country are energized just thinking about supporting the walkers. She said women are being called to action to walk for their own reasons and to show some solidarity for women everywhere.

"We're all too busy and caught up in following our schedules," said Secumb, who threw her cell phone in her car trunk while she was talking to one reporter. "Taking off, just leaving, hey, doesn't that sound good to everyone?"

Secumb said she has also been notified by the national NOW office that phone calls asking about new memberships have doubled since news of the walkers started making national headlines. She said women are perhaps thinking about what they gave up to have it all.

"We all have our own ideas about why they are doing this and why we would all like to do it ourselves," stated Secumb. "Pick a reason—personal sorrow, world peace, the need for quiet, reconciliation, the hand of another female—it's a very attractive proposition."

At last count about 45 people, mostly women, were trailing behind the walkers, who continue to follow their own agenda.

—30—

The Women Walker Effect: Claudia

Claudia Bandoulin was pissed. She sure as hell didn't mind being assigned to follow the story about the Wonder Women who were on a goddamned walk out in the middle of nowhere, but she couldn't believe they had assigned Bob Gilbert as her cameraman.

"What the hell is wrong with you?" Claudia shouted at her editor two seconds after she slammed his door hard enough to stress crack the frame.

The editor winced, squeezed his eyelids shut and prayed aloud that Claudia wouldn't smack his desk. How could such a beautiful woman, the most sought after broadcast journalist in Chicago be so . . .

"Now Claudia," he began timidly, for this was not Claudia's first assault on his office. "You know Bob's the best guy we have available."

"He's a pig, Burt. You know this is a women's story, for chrisssake, Bob may try and hump any one of them."

Poor Burt wanted to get inside of his overflowing desk drawer. In all the years he had been working at the Chicago-based CBS affiliate, he had never met anyone like Claudia, and he still had no idea how to handle her outbursts. Audiences loved Claudia, with her 'young Diane Sawyer' look that was just sexy enough to make every man, woman and young adolescent drool with passion and envy. Worse for Burt, she was just good enough to make all the stations who didn't have her under contract wish they did. He couldn't say she wasn't tough, or lacked any creativity or didn't bag good stories. When a group of union guys got out of hand at a local protest, she beat the living hell out of two of them who tried to jump her while she was on-air. After that episode, Burt would have gladly given up half his inflated salary to keep her at the station for the rest of her life.

"Look," Burt finally said, opening up his hands as if he were about to catch a basketball. "Just get down there, and as soon as someone gets back from other assignments, I'll have them switch places with Bob."

"Shit, Burt, give me Jenny for this one. It might be a way for the walkers to open up to us if they are flaming feminists. An all-woman broadcast crew. They will love it."

"Claudia, this story is getting bigger by the minute and that's why I want you on it and Bob. Jenny is working on the story about last week's train crash. Come on, a bunch of housewives packing it in to hit the road. We could make some hay with this, baby. I've already called New York, and they want to see the piece tonight for possible national coverage."

Claudia took her hands off the top of Burt's desk and looked out of the big window behind him that revealed the entire news-room. At least 50 times during the past three years, she had wanted to throw Burt and everything in his office right through this window. "Burt, if he even looks sideways at me, 'accidentally' bumps into my breasts with his arms, or tries to interfere with these women or my story, I'm going to kill the son-of-a-bitch."

Actually, Burt would have loved that great story for the early edition. He rose up out of his chair, looked into Claudia's beautiful brown eyes and said, "Okay. Do what you have to do, babe."

Bob the Swine Man was waiting at her desk, his hands in his pockets. Rocking back and forth on his heels, his eyes as big as his wide angle lens, he greeted her. "Hey, baby, how much of my time do you need?"

"Don't call me baby," Claudia shot back. "In fact, don't call me anything. Go wait in the fucking car. I'll be down in 15 minutes. Clear out the back seat because that's where I'm sitting."

Mr. Bob now rocked in silence, his eyes starting on Claudia's face, then roaming down her body. Eventually with a smirk, he propelled himself forward and disappeared around the corner whistling. "Shit," Claudia muttered as she grabbed her briefcase and hollered over to the production assistant for video news clips on the walkers. "What do you have, Paula?"

A small woman all but leapt over three desks to get to her. "I think you'll like this one," Paula said nudging close to her. "A few stations are already out there in Wisconsin, but from what I've seen, they're covering the story in a pretty bland way. Just the usual, 'The women are headed West' kind of thing."

"Do you have any background on the women?"

"Not much, but someone said Chris Boyer might be with the group."

"You're kidding!"

"No, though external sources are rare as hen's teeth on this one. There's like a local conspiracy to protect these women. Kinda cool in a way."

Claudia ignored Paula's unprofessional admiration. "My God, Chris Boyer was one of my heroines. She's the reason I got into this business to begin with. No one else was ever like her. Amazing."

"Here," Paula said, sticking papers into a file and pushing it into Claudia's briefcase. "Just read this on the way down there and call me if you need anything else. I bet you'll have some ideas by the time Bob is wiping the drool off the steering wheel."

"Hey, thanks Paula, can you get me the office shotgun so I can kill Bob on the way?"

"Don't be too hard on him," laughed Paula. "He's just in love with you like the rest of us."

Claudia grabbed the suitcase she always kept packed just in case she had to jet off to an impeachment hearing, impending war or a breaking news story about loose women. Then she logged out on the assignment board, and finally, without acknowledging

Bob's existence, settled into the back seat of the cheap Chevrolet for their ride to Wilkins County, Wisconsin.

Claudia had seen several of the wire stories on the women walkers and she had to admit that from the get-go, she thought this was a terrific story. She could personally name about 5,000 women who would be perfectly happy to pick up and take off with not so much as a change of underwear. Once, just a year ago, Claudia had actually called in sick seven days in a row from a small hotel near Salt Lake City because of the breathtaking view of the Wasatch Mountain Range. She had just finished contract negotiations, knew for the first time how much she was actually worth, and she was certain no one would say a word about her brief retreat.

Heading north into Wisconsin, Claudia took a few minutes to look out the window, avoiding the persistent gaze of Bob the Swineman. She thought about the women pounding down this country highway. She knew that Chris Boyer had all but disappeared from the news scene several years ago, into the occasional guest editor's contribution. Now she recalled that Chris lived near where the women were walking. When Claudia was a broadcast journalism student at Marquette University, Chris Boyer had been constantly used as an example of the career journalist willing to give up everything to get the story. There were pictures of her hanging all over the campus newspaper office, and Claudia had won the Chris Boyer Award for Investigative Journalism. Ironically, Claudia didn't have to reach far to understand why Chris would want to chuck the life of constant deadlines, complete loss of privacy, and unbelievable competitiveness that had Claudia constantly wondering if the world of journalism was worth it.

"Christ," she told herself. "I haven't had a normal relationship in three years, the one man who might have lasted couldn't handle knowing everyone in Illinois was lusting after me, and the only way is up or out. No wonder Boyer got the hell out."

Up in the front seat, Swineman fondled the radio as he tried to figure out how he was going to get Claudia to calm down long enough so he could say more than five words to her. "Claudia," he finally interjected, but she cut him short. "What?" She didn't even look up at him. "Never mind," he said, fixing the radio on a brain-mashing death dirge by Metallica.

It proved fairly easy to find the road where the women walkers were staging their escape. Bob spotted another television station's antenna about a mile away, sticking into the air like a sore you-know-what and breaking up what would have been a beautiful blue, spring sky. "Damn," he said as he piloted the car around a corner, and a horde of about 200 people lined up on the highway came into view. "They're broadcasting live," he said out loud, hoping Claudia might offer some kind of response. "All this for a bunch of women."

Claudia muttered into her notebook, "That took about 14 seconds." She got out of the car while it was still rolling to a stop. She stood quietly at the side of the highway for a few minutes, just gazing off into the fields, noticing the line of trees that looked as if they surrounded someone's piece of property. Rocks piled almost intentionally around a fence that ran from the road and then disappeared beyond a quick dip in the field.

Bob was already pushing his way through a crowd, shaking his head at those gawkers gazing down the highway as if the Second Coming was impending. Claudia had decided to approach the story from the women's point of view. She wanted to see what they were seeing, understand where they had come from and where they might end up. This kind of thinking, she knew already, would get her into trouble. Burt would want something fast and dirty, and she already wanted to spend way too many days trying to find out every possible angle she could about the women. He'd want to know what they did for a living, the last time they had sex, if they slept on their sides, where they bought their underwear—just the facts. Claudia was wondering about their lost loves, missing dreams, what they had all left behind.

Before she could reconcile those contradictions, Claudia felt Swineman at her heels. He was such a throwback that she almost laughed every time she saw him. Twice-divorced, an avid reader of *Soldier of Fortune* magazine, and part owner of a shot-and-beer bar, Bob the Swineman, thought Claudia, was one small-dick-big-compensating-ego-asshole totally beyond saving.

"Well," he said quickly. "There's shit here to shoot. Some asshole sheriff won't let anyone near the women, and there's a deputy on the other side keeping people away from them. To get through, that leaves us, like I said, shit. Now what?"

Claudia said calmly, "Why don't you get some crowd shots and let me talk to a few people. I want you to scan the horizon too, let's show our happy viewers how beautiful the Wisconsin scenery can be."

"Thrilling choice," Bob sneered, kicking the toe of his black boots into the gravel.

"Maybe we'll get lucky and someone will pull a gun. "

"Really? Did you hear something?"

"Bob, get a grip. I'm kidding. This is what we call a 'human interest story'. If you need some blood, go poke out your eye."

"Ah, Claudia, don't get me all excited like that."

"Look, Bob, we might be here for awhile. Let's just do the best job we can and try to be decent to each other. How's that for a novel idea?"

Bob let his eyes roam to her breasts. "Like I said, there is shit to shoot here. What the hell are we going to do?"

Whatever they did, Claudia was determined that their

coverage would be different from the reporters now standing in the rows of old cornstalks and almost whispering about these seven mysterious women who had abandoned their safe world for "life on the road." Claudia knew there was more to it than that. One thing that she had learned from Chris Boyer was to always try to connect to a story on a human level. When she was beyond the eyes of the newsroom, Claudia could unveil a heart she rarely shared with journalist colleagues.

"Bob," she said suddenly and softly. "Run into town and book us a couple of rooms at whatever fleabag hotel you can find. I'm going to slip into the backseat while your little head is turned and change my clothes."

Mr. Swineman didn't say a word but managed to shake his head up and down while he clenched his right fist into a tight ball. He was already thinking about her, the hottest, sexiest woman he had ever seen, climbing into the backseat and removing her silk blouse and then those long, dark slacks that covered up legs as shapely as a marathon runner's. The fantasy made him weak-kneed and definitely aroused.

"Bobbie," said Claudia, putting her hands on his shoulders and turning him away from the car, "You stand here and think about driving into town, and I'll be right out."

Thanking her brilliant mother for everything she had remembered to keep in her little suitcase, Claudia quickly transformed herself from a high-powered reporter in broadcast drag into what she guessed was the local fashion in about two minutes.

Claudia's mother told her to always wear clean underwear, and she also taught her to be ready for any damn thing that came along. That's why she had a jogging suit, tennis shoes, a small backpack, and everything from a toothbrush to a few tampons in that magical suitcase. She slid out of the Chevy. "Bye Bob, get me a queen bed."

"Uh huh." As Bob turned the car around, adjusting the rearview mirror so he could watch Claudia as long as possible, she turned away from him and called Paula on the cell phone she had slipped into her front pocket.

"Paula, corn city reporting in here."

"Did you kill Bob yet?"

"No, I called a truce and just sent him packing to get a hotel room. Wanna bet he claims there was only one room left?"

"Oh God," Paula moaned.

"Listen, Paula, this is weird down here. The cops have the women sealed off on the highway and the other networks are filing those cornfield pieces, just like you told me."

"So what are you thinking?"

"I'm not sure yet, but there's definitely something happening here, Paula. It feels like more than just a bunch of goofball females walking on a road."

Paula was quiet for a minute, and Claudia could see her sitting on a stool next to a computer with her free hand wrapped around her head. Claudia liked Paula, she was one of the few people in the newsroom whom she trusted. They often had dinner together and talked about the rest of life that happens outside of all the heartache and sorrow they brought to life on the television screen. She considered them friends. Claudia also knew Paula was in love with her, and she was on the brink of asking her out on a date. That would drive Mr. Swineman and every other man on the face of Earth into a deep depression.

"Claudia?" Paula said her name like a question, feeling through the phone, through the vibrations in her friend's voice that something was up.

"Paula, don't ask me much right now. I've got about an hour to figure this out before Bob shows up back here with his penis wrapped around his camera lens. I'm not sure what I'm going to do yet. I'm just not sure."

For a second Paula could see Claudia standing out there on the highway with the wind blowing her hair around her face. She knew Claudia would have one hand on her hip, legs apart, her shoulders squared to the world. Paula had always thought that Claudia was a fish out of water in the broadcast business, but she also knew she was so damned good at what she did, nothing really mattered. Claudia, she knew, would be good and successful at whatever she decided to do.

"Hey sweetie, remember the time we saw that Sundance movie about the photographer in New York who was messed up on drugs and was just like, so close, so close to getting back out there and then she blew it?"

"Yeah, I know, don't blow it," Claudia said, not really sure if she knew where anything, including the conversation was headed. "Hey, I'm just trying to figure out where to go with this story. I don't think this is some life-altering situation here, but geez, just thinking about these women and what they're doing, well, it makes me want to just say piss on it and join them."

"And?"

"Come on, Paula. We've talked about this. Shit, last week we were all but headed to the airport for Bora Bora so we could find a couple of 20-year-old well hung boys or just be with each other. I'm thinking, Paula, that being with each other would have been the best choice and that too many women make the wrong choice and never follow their heart."

"What are you saying?"

"I'm saying who the hell doesn't want to walk down a highway and keep going. Why the hell didn't we get on the plane and just go? Everyone is so goddamned afraid, and here's a bunch of women about whom we know absolutely nothing, but they just did what the rest of us only dream about."

"So these women have like, real balls?"

"Yes, really big balls."

"So?"

"I don't know the next part yet except I keep thinking about all those women I do stories about who get pregnant or raped or shot or beat up, and then that's it. Their lives turn into little piles of shit."

Paula got up from her stool and moved quickly into the broom closet so no one could hear her. She looked left and then right, then closed the door, slid down its backside and sat in the dark, hugging her knees, touching the phone as if it was the soft skin of her friend's face.

"Claudia, did Bob give you a joint?"

"No, I'm sure he's saving that for the big night he's busy planning right now back at the hotel."

"Listen," Paula said, slipping into her producer persona. "Before we decide what to do, why don't you do some interviews. Get your bearings. Who's hanging around there? Can you get to the cop? Fish around a little bit, and then call me back before you rip off your bra and run through the cornfields."

Claudia laughed, and then searched through a group of women who stood in a clump gazing down the empty highway. Before she said good-bye to Paula, she focused in on a 40-ish woman in hiking boots who was hopping from one foot to the next and thumping her long fingers against the side of her leg.

The woman was clearly agitated, and Claudia thought about flinging herself on top of her to make her stop moving and sliding and twitching. Finally, she sucked in her breath and walked up to her, trying to decide on a good interview line.

"Hi," Claudia said, touching the woman on her right arm.

The woman startled and then turned to put both of her hands on Claudia's shoulders. Her eyes were dark, and red veins popped out from their centers as if she had been crying. Before Claudia could see anything else, the woman pulled them both together and embraced her.

"Oh my gosh," the woman whispered in her ear. "You scared me so much."

"I'm sorry," Claudia said, wondering instinctively what she could do to make the woman feel better. "Are you okay?"

"Yeah, yeah, I'm just like, don't you want to just get out there and walk too?"

Then she added, "You look kinda familiar."

"Well," Claudia said, "I'm a reporter. CBS out of Chicago."

The woman stopped for a moment and looked into Claudia's brown eyes as if she were searching for something she had lost just a minute ago. "Thank God they sent a woman."

"Do you know any of the women?"

"Is this on the record or whatever where you might use it?"

"I don't know yet."

"What do you mean?" The woman inched closer to Claudia and looked again into her eyes.

"Just between us?"

"That's what I asked."

"I'm thinking how great it would be just to chuck it all and go off with them."

The woman leapt forward then, sweeping Claudia off her feet and lifting her into the air as if she were nothing more than a wisp of cornstalks. Claudia was amazed at how strong the woman was, how she pushed her towards the sky with an ease that made her think she had some kind of physical job, like log rolling or lifting entire buildings off of their foundations.

"Who are you?" Claudia asked as her feet touched the ground.

"I'm a friend of a woman they stayed with the other night.

She called me and told me she thought it was wonderful what they were doing, and I laughed at her. But you know, I only did that because I was scared. The minute I heard about this, I wanted to go too, and I thought the world would laugh at me."

Claudia wondered if she could have it both ways. Could she just walk off with this woman she didn't know, and throw her objectivity out the window on such an important story? Could she go and be one of them and still do her job? Could she just say "fuck it" and not worry?

"What's your name?" Claudia asked her.

"Sue."

"Sue, I'm Claudia and what the hell are we going to do?"

Sue put her head down and started moving around again and that's when Claudia understood that Sue was scared to make the step. In a flash, she could see Sue always with someone, never alone, always waiting for someone else to go first.

"Hey, Sue, what are you leaving back here if we do this?"

"A couple of kids who can take care of themselves and a husband who loves me but kind of forgets he does. That's it, plus lots of empty spaces and things I've never done and, geez, I can't believe I'm even telling you this.

"I could talk to Lenny, my friend who runs the hog farm, like this for hours but out here like this, you know, living kinda in the middle of nowhere, there aren't that many of us."

"Well, shit," Claudia sighed as she put her arm around Sue's shoulder, thinking about all the times she wanted to reach out and touch someone she was interviewing but never did. "Have you thought how you can get past the cop?"

"Wait," said Sue, pushing herself away but not letting go of Claudia's arm. "What about you? What are you leaving?"

Claudia laughed louder than she expected to. She thought of the condo she had never bothered to decorate, all the stories in her tickler file that she hadn't finished, she thought about Paula crouched in the video storage closet and how she really was in love with her too, and about how this could either be the dumbest thing she ever did or the only thing she ever did that made any sense.

"Not a hell of a lot, really," she finally said.

"Will you get fired or something?"

"It could go either way, you know. They could shit-can me in about 10 minutes or they could turn this into something big and make me part of it. What do you think?"

Sue tilted her head towards the sky. Claudia looked up too and moved her eyes back and forth across the tops of the trees.

"Do you hear the geese?" Sue asked.

"Yeah, but where are they?"

"The sound is a little fast, you should always look back, or forward I suppose, depending on what you hear."

"That's pretty damn funny, Sue."

"That's the kind of stuff I know from living out here in the country. I know about migrating birds and how to load the rear end of a pickup so you don't screw up the shocks and the alignment. I wouldn't know a news story from a horse's ass."

Claudia laughed so hard she thought she might tip backwards, and the laughing made her wonder when she had ever had so much fun. "You might know better than you think, Sue."

Sue looked at her, really looked at Claudia and saw how extraordinarily beautiful she was. Perfect hair and perfect eyes, features that looked as if they had been designed by an artist. She also saw uncertainty crossing through eyes that most likely were usually sure of every single thought that was processed behind them. In those eyes, Sue saw for a moment, just a speck of the woman she had once been, and this remembering moved her to do something that was extraordinary.

Claudia poked her own toes into the dirt and remembered that Chris Boyer was up on the highway someplace striding through the afternoon in pretty much the same way she had stormed through life. Her usually certain mind swarmed with confusion, and it was only Sue's arm, dragging her from the toes of her feet that made her realize she was moving forward.

Sue pushed her way through the crowd, side-stepped around a police car and one of those big plastic orange water jugs, whispered something into the ear of the policeman who was standing with his arms resting on the hood of his car and then took Claudia by the hand and started walking down the highway.

Claudia matched her steps and turned around once to see the ugly Chevrolet glide to a stop right where she had been standing while she talked with Sue. Try as she might, Claudia just didn't have the heart to wave good-bye to the Swineman.

Wilkins County News, March 5, 1968
Granton, Wisconsin

PROM COURT MEMBER SETS RECORD

The 1968 Madison High School prom court has been selected, and Mary Jean Michlienski has set a new school record by being a prom court member two years in a row.

Mary Jean, a senior who plans to attend Harrisburg Junior College next year and major in Home Economics, said she feels as if she's living in a dream.

"I'm really excited about this honor and it means a lot to me," said Mary Jean, who will be designing and making her own dress for the dance.

Mary Jean is a member of the cheerleading squad, National Honor Society, Yearbook staff, and was also a member of the High School's 1968 homecoming court.

Prom activities will begin on Friday afternoon in the high school cafeteria when the girls on prom court host a community tea.

—30—

The Elegant Gathering: Mary

There's a wedding photo of Boyce and me hanging on the wall that is just next to the closet in our bedroom. I swear to God, I look at that picture about 10 times a day and every single time I see my wedding gown, and Boyce in a tuxedo, I could just about faint.

Lots of women find it highly ridiculous that someone can fall in love in high school, stay married and then stay in love. Well, I have to admit right off the bat that it is unusual and that makes me a bit strange myself. But, I'm the one who has screwed up the statistics about young marriage and women who only sleep with one man, and although I admit I've never been 100 percent certain that I don't have a screw loose myself, I do know it's all damn right to be happy.

Oh cripes, I have to say that I have never felt so torn in my entire life as I did the other night when I left my friends out there on the highway. But I have never been one to steer away from what I feel in my heart and because those woman are real friends, really, the best friends I have ever had in my life, I know that they understand me and that leaving them like that will be okay.

I suppose many people would call me loony for walking away from something that looks like it's turning into an adventure of a lifetime, but I think it's just as loony to have to apologize for being happy with something so simple.

So I'm the one who has never been raped or divorced or had an affair with my brother-in-law's uncle's cousin, although he did try, but he probably just did it because I looked so happy. I'm Mary Jean Michlienski Valkeen, the ex-prom queen who married the guy down the street, had three kids, honest-to-God sold Tupperware, candles, and then those expensive baskets and went on to attain possible great fame as the woman who took food to the women walkers but left them before they could turn around twice.

Although really, I'm not all that simple and even though I didn't go to college or do drugs in the 60s and sleep with the entire football team or fall in love, well physical love anyway, with someone of the same sex, that doesn't mean that I'm not really that much different than everyone else out there. And I know that I'm not alone either. Well, I might be alone in the women walkers group but those are exceptional women.

When I got home the other night after Boyce picked me up at the truck stop, I went in to kiss the boys and then checked the house quick. Then, while Boyce flopped back into bed, mumbling, "What in the hell was that all about?" I slipped into the bathroom and spent such a long time looking at myself in the mirror that my feet fell asleep and my hands are still stiff because of how I was leaning up against the side of the vanity.

What I saw in that mirror wasn't startling because I have been watching myself push towards my 48th year for the 47 years in front of that. It's not like I woke up one morning and saw that my hips had spread, and the muscles in the sides of my breasts had taken a nose dive, and the lines around my mouth had suddenly turned into relatives of the Grand Canyon. I have seen this body of mine changing now for quite a long time. So I ran my fingers over the lines around my eyes and around my flabby chin and over those little hairs down there that seem to grow into monsters overnight. I looked and I looked at the gray hairs that never seem to quite make it when Denise does my roots, and when I looked way, way back inside of my eyes, I saw how I started to be and never diverted from that path even though I had more than one chance.

In the beginning, I am standing in the high school halls knowing with all my heart that whoever I am going to marry is inside of the building with me at just the same moment. It is a sure feeling, as sure as love itself or knowing the sun will be right up there again the next morning.

Jackie, with her long hair and dark face, is standing over me and I am telling her the secrets of my soul. "He's here," I tell her, leaning so the weight of my own body and the weight of my words can be supported by the metal locker. "I'm not sure yet who it is but I know he's here."

"Come on, Mary, that just sounds so, well, it sounds pretty stupid. You've got your whole life ahead of you and everything, and marriage, well, it sounds silly thinking of it now."

"I don't care," I respond with just as much certainty. "I know this is what I'm meant to do and so what difference does it make?"

"Don't you want to go places and don't you just get sick of always having to make sure that you have a boyfriend?"

I'm thinking down there on the floor. Thinking of Mike, and Scott, and Jim, and this boy named Shawn who transferred in from another school last Fall, and how he picked me to be his girl-friend first and how that's all that mattered.

"It's not just the need so much," I try hard to explain to her. "It's more like what if I miss the one that I'm supposed to marry."

"Oh shit," said Jackie, swearing with a bit of a flare because we were just in the process of thinking it was cool to swear. "That sounds even more stupid."

Then I'm stuck. Trying to think of a way to tell someone that I've known since the time I was a little girl what my life was going to be like. Jackie is ready to take on the world and has been accepted to the University of Wisconsin where she plans on living in a house with males and females. She wants to be an anthropol-ogist and has not worn a bra since the first day of second semes-ter. In her mind, she is a woman who knows what she wants and I am a fairly useless hunk of female parts because I'm "much simpler." How can I make her understand something so foreign? How can I tell her that it's okay for some of us to do just the exact opposite of what she wants to do?

"Look, I've tried to think like you but it's like trying to get Mr. Hobsin to change the style of clothes that he wears. My God, he's worn the same shirt every Tuesday since we were freshmen. You know what you want and really, I know what I want. I would think for a liberated mind that would be enough."

"Don't you wonder what you might miss?" Jackie asks with her hands moving up and down as if they are the wings of a bird. "Like how could you think that you could sleep with just one guy and know all about sex? What about seeing the world? What about anything? You know I just don't get this whole thing about you."

Jackie's eyes are popping out while she talks, and I am at a loss to explain myself to her any more than I already have. So I give up. I just sit on the floor and raise my shoulders up about two inches, and there is a little wall of silence that builds higher and higher between us. Finally Jackie says, "Oh brother," and then turns to walk down the hall.

I can't quite get up just because she has left. My mind is storming around inside of my head, and I am at a loss to think of another way to relate my 17-year-old feelings to someone who thinks I'm as dumb as a toad. So I agree with Jackie and try to think how it must seem to someone like her to even want to know someone like me.

"Addicted to my dreams," I say out loud, forming the words and then running them over my lips so slowly I can almost feel the consonants sticking to the insides of my gums. "I'm addicted to my dreams."

Not many years later when I heard that Jackie had indeed tried every single thing that she had ever talked about and was now living on some island with a bunch of people who were studying some kind of dried up old bugs who maybe, maybe not, had some medical use, I laughed out loud at a very inappropriate moment.

Boyce was just about to do the magical number to me and his little penis was not happy when I laughed so loud the entire moment fell apart.

"Honey, what's this all about?" he groaned as I continued to laugh as if I'd been struck by the funniest damn thing I had ever heard.

"Oh, I'm sorry."

"What is it?" He rose up on one elbow, massaging my right breast, hopeful I'm sure, that he could get back to where he had just been.

"Well, I was thinking about high school and Jackie and how I always thought I was addicted to my own dreams and how really, she was too, maybe everybody was."

"Oh," he sighed, rolling over and placing the pillow on top of his head. "Is this the 'What I did and didn't do' crap all over again?"

"It's not crap," I said moving my fingers over his cute little rear end. "It's just that they also picked on me because I wanted to marry you and they were just as set on doing what they wanted to do."

Boyce and I had conversations like this on and off for a good 20 years or more, but most of them didn't end up in me becoming hysterical. Although there had been times when I really was hysterical and continued to think that something might be wrong with me because I didn't want to do what most of the other women in my generation were doing.

"Addicted to dreams, huh?" Boyce rolled over, flinging his leg across my hips so we were lying side by side, connected in almost every possible manner. "Do women ever stop going on like this?"

Well, I suppose now that women never stop going on about things that are important because of what we are made of and how we feel, and I can honestly say that leaving the women walkers might have been one of those great defining moments for me. In many ways it would have been so much easier for me to stay with them. After all, they are my friends and I know all these things about each one of them, and I know how important it is for them to do this. Honest to God, yesterday when I took them some food I was thinking that I might actually run into a trail of tears and blood and guts, all the other garbage of life they are hopefully leaving on the side of the road.

Now what I would like to leave on the side of the road is how I have always felt like I had to explain myself to everyone, especially women, who might think its nuts not to want more than what they have always had. So, really, the simple act of me coming back home is my big statement, not that I expect to ever really have to stop explaining who I am. It's just that I don't give a damn as much anymore.

You see, I did find Boyce before I had even left high school, except I was wrong about him being in the same high school. He lived about a half a mile away from me and attended a private Catholic school near Kenosha, and I ran him off the road one night while I was driving home from cheerleading practice. I don't care what anyone else says, that's a pretty cool way to meet your future husband.

He was running along the highway and I could tell from a few blocks away that he was cute. When I got close, something made me swerve—I have no idea what, ha, maybe it was Cupid! He jumped into the ditch. When I leapt from the car, which by the way kept on going without me and ended up in the same ditch, I saw that he really was gorgeous and although I didn't quite know that he was "the one" at that exact moment, I had a pretty good idea.

The rest is all pretty predictable. We married when he was a sophomore in college. I worked full-time to help him through college and then graduate school. We had three boys; I worked at a bunch of part-time jobs and took my role as mother-wife-homemaker seriously. I never slept with another man, and unless Boyce is a lying dog, we've both been faithful and happy since the day we were married.

Have I been attracted to other men? God yes. I have at least imagined myself with 10 men that I can name just off the top of my head and at least 10 more who have come on to me and whispered in my ear and slammed me against the side of a few walls—mostly when I was a bit younger. But like I tell Boyce, if sex with someone else is any better than what I'm already getting, then it would kill me anyway.

Once about five years ago, I did let another man kiss me. I have no idea why this guy was so smitten with me, but then again it could be the tequila we were drinking at Boyce's summer office party. I think the man's name was Greg or Craig, and he was some consultant they had brought in to help with a big renovation project that was going on in the office, and hey, I was the prom queen once and almost twice so maybe I looked pretty damn hot that summer.

Craig was a cutie and while the rest of the party goers gathered round to play some of those stupid games they always set up at these parties, we stayed in the bar and talked. Was I flirting? Maybe. I occasionally put my hand on his arm and when I bent down to scratch my leg, I suppose he could look right into the heart of my cleavage. I don't actually think I was doing anything different than I normally do, except sitting in a bar with some good-looking man who happened not to be my husband.

Finally, when I got up to go to the john, he must have followed me. There's a little hall at the country club and then you can either turn right to go to the bathrooms or left into the coat closet. When I came out of the bathroom, I heard him whisper to me and I went into the coat closet. He promptly grabbed me, pushed me up against the full length of his body where I quickly realized he had a rather large hard on, and then he kissed me.

Well, my God, I kissed him back and was a little weak in the knees but when he started to pull down the strap of my dress, I quickly came to my senses.

"Hey," I said, slapping the heck out of his hand. "Get your hand out of there."

"Don't you want me to do this?" He sounded so smug that I slapped him again.

"What?"

"Listen," I said, pushing him away and wiping my mouth off with the side of my hand at the same time. "What the hell are you doing?"

"I kissed you and you kissed me back."

"Yes, I remember that part and it was a mistake. I'm sorry."

"I'm not," he said, stepping back towards me.

Then I had to explain myself all over again to him, a man, of all creatures. It was a variation of the same story I had been repeating since I was 17 and had revealed myself to Sandy. I was married, had three kids, was happy. The whole deal.

"So why did you kiss me?"

"You know what, I have absolutely no idea but I'm not used to drinking margaritas at one o'clock in the afternoon. Usually I'm brushing sand out of some kid's hair or hauling a car full of sweaty boys to baseball practice. Necking with strangers in a dark closet usually isn't at the top of my list of things to do in July."

He was a gentleman then and apologized, told me that if I

dared, I should tell my husband what happened because he thought I was pretty hot looking and he'd have me in a minute.

"Go on," I said, finally smiling and pushing him as we walked back into the bar.

That night I told Boyce what had happened; he promptly threw me down on the bed and made love to me as if he had just been released from prison. I think it was his way of saying that old Craigie had good taste. When I told him I was sorry, he didn't much care and added that it was probably the booze because by 2:30 p.m., the boss's 65-year-old wife was looking pretty good to him.

My life hasn't been perfect. Honestly, there have been a few times when I have wondered about my interesting choices. I would be a few bricks short of a load if that never happened to me. Who doesn't have nights when they sit up long after the house is quiet, looking out into the darkness and wondering if the path they have chosen is the right one.

The nights that were the worst for me were right after one of the boys had been born, not so much the first one, because I had no clue about what I was about to get into and I was pretty young, but later, that's when I wondered the most.

We have a couple of acres of land that is now all filled up with everything from forts and piles of junk and a couple of old cars to grass and weeds that we have never bothered to trim or prune. But when Shawn and Jake were babies, there was nothing out there but hours of darkness.

Boyce put a rocking chair for me right in front of the big window that looks into the backyard, and that's where I would sit and nurse the boys at night. When it was warm enough, I would open up the long window next to the wall and listen for the sounds of the night world to whirl around me. All those nights sitting in the chair, I felt as if I had been given something magical because it was always so quiet and calm. For those minutes I often felt great threads of peace and happiness running through my veins.

That's where I also cried and wondered why in the hell I hadn't run off to some island with someone. I would rock and cry and rock and cry. Sometimes the tears would fall right onto the face of one of the babies, and they would blink and get this "What the hell was that?" look on their face. Then I would brush away the tear and turn my head a little bit so they wouldn't be upset by the aquatic break in their drinking routine.

During those dark nights I tried to imagine myself not being myself. I would see me being single and living in some apartment building and driving off to work each day in a little sports car. Although try as I might, I could never think of what it was I would exactly be doing. It would be such a false picture of why and what I am that I just couldn't hold onto the idea very long.

Even now, when it's one of those rare nights or days when I might be home alone, I pull that old chair over to the window and just sit there rocking, rocking, rocking. Sometimes I grab a pillow off the couch and I make believe one of the boys is a baby again. Is this ridiculous? It doesn't matter because those are the times when I know that my choices have been good ones. I think about what I might have traded to be someone else. Could I have given up a minute or an hour with a warm baby pushed against my breast? I don't think so. Not ever.

Boyce and I have had our differences too, but come on, fighting over the purchase of a car or truck and where to go on summer vacation isn't my idea of a life-altering trauma. Boyce has always been a wonderful father, a fabulous lover, a friend to me through every little phase and question in my life, and I can't imagine that in this whole world there would have been another man like him for me.

Sometimes he was actually too nice, suggesting about a

million times that I should to college and that we could afford it, and wouldn't I always wonder what else I could have accomplished?

I would tell him, "I could do and be anything. I could do what you do or manage a restaurant or be a psychologist, but I want to be a homemaker and a wife."

I did run the PTA fund-raiser, learn how to rewire the washing machine, cart kids from one event to the next until I wore out three sets of tires, dance on our new wooden deck in my underwear when the kids were at camp for seven days in a row, make dinner for five almost every night of my life, know that when I shifted to the right side in bed, Boyce would roll right behind me, look forward to the sound of his car hitting the gravel five nights a week, stand at the bedroom window stark naked at midnight while Boyce brushed my hair and told me that he had just talked to Shawn about masturbation, listened for the sounds of the shower at 5:45 a.m. during track season, spray painted all of Grandma's old wicker furniture dark green, baked cookies for all the neighbors every Valentine's day, and smiled a million smiles upon hearing something as simple as the dishwasher kicking in after I finally figured out how to use the timer.

Looking in this mirror lately while the walkers are out on the road, seems to give me a flash of the past. I understand that something as simple as turning away from the walk has affirmed everything that I have done and everything that I am. I know I could have stayed with my friends, plodded on with them through all the miles that they have already wracked up, but that's not where my heart feels comfortable. Leaving to me was as powerful as anything I could have done with all the rest of the days and nights of my life.

I thought it was interesting that Chris was the first one who perceived my thinking and my ultimate decision. When they get back, I will tell her exactly what I was thinking about when she stopped me and looked into my eyes. My thoughts were not on Boyce or the boys or the singular moments that have created the heart of my life. I was fixated on my girlfriends—my girlfriends. The courage that we all gathered from each other was what gave me the strength to leave them.

Some of them, like Alice, I have known for many years. I have watched as a heartache or a tragedy or a sadness has etched itself into each of them so deeply that it seems impossible that anything will ever be the same. We have been open books to each other, and that process has been a joy to me.

As I watched them limping down the highway, touching hands and talking softly; I knew that as much of a part of me as they have all become, what I still needed more than anything was to be true to myself and my own heart. Their strength is really what made me weep that night. I have such an admiration for them, for what they have been through, for what they are facing by walking that I almost, just almost feel inadequate.

To be true to them, to myself, to the very reasons why we all do whatever it is that we do—that's why I am here and about to hop into bed with Boyce. That is why tomorrow morning, I will make those women walker friends of mine lunch, why I will sit the boys down one at a time and talk to them about making certain any woman in their life is a real woman and does whatever in the hell she wants to do.

"Like your mother," is what I will say. "Just like your own mother."

CHAPTER SEVEN

J UST AFTER DARK there always seems to be a line of light that
laces itself across the bottom of the horizon. Gail is sitting in
the big wicker chair, her arm extended, and she is tracing the line
with her outstretched arm as if she is an artist. The women follow
her hand from north to south, watching for the spaces that are
blotted out by rolling hills and trees and a silo that juts out miles
away like a tall building.

"It's so beautiful out here," she says. "Have you ever seen anything or really felt anything so peaceful?"

The women have wandered outside of Jack and Audrey's
Champshire Hills Bed and Breakfast for a glass of dark, red wine
that Jack said will make their dinner settle gently into their stomachs, "Like everything in there is being tucked into bed." Jack and
Audrey have closed down their inn to let the women have a night
of peace and rest. They have been perfect hosts: serving dinner,
not intruding, smiling gently, whispering occasionally about what

a marvelous thing it is to get out and do something that you have always wanted to do.

"Jack and I left everything behind in Chicago to own and operate our own Bed and Breakfast," Audrey told the women. "We both worked there, we were so busy that one time we didn't even seen each other for eight days."

The couple move together in the kitchen like dancers. She pushes, he pulls, he cuts. She stirs and taste-tests. He shakes the spices. It is clear that they have found their own magic inside of this old farmhouse, which once housed a thriving brood of German immigrants who danced and sang and ate and drank until they dropped to the floor in this same kitchen.

"Once a week," Jack tells them proudly, "we spend an entire day in bed. We read and talk, we work on the books, and we plan what we are going to do the following week." Then he blushes. "You know there are lots of things that can happen when a man and woman stay in bed all day."

The women are fairly astounded by Jack and Audrey's generosity, and Janice keeps knocking her fingers against something wooden to make certain that they have not all been struck dead by a cattle truck and ended up in a glorious limbo.

After dinner, Jack and Audrey give them all jackets and blankets and usher them out onto the long porch with two decanters of the red wine. In the kitchen, they begin closing doors and putting away dishes and eventually the light goes out. The women hear a soft "Goodnight," and then the walkers are alone with the lines on the horizon and a hope that they can make the night last forever.

There is a long wooden couch that has been stacked with deep cushions, a wicker chair where Gail sits, a long bench with a backrest that is curved to fit perfectly between shoulder blades. Although it is cool in the dusky moments, the women have pushed themselves hip to hip with blankets on their laps; their feet are covered in wool slippers that Audrey says she washes special for all the guests so they can enjoy being out on the porch.

Everyone sighs and sips and shifts in their seats. Somewhere far away, a dog barks and then another dog answers. The quiet of the place and the moment is astonishing, and Janice turns her head slowly to look from one of her friends to the next. She can feel her heart beating under all the layers of clothes and the blankets, and she knows that she has never felt more alive, more sane, more happy than this moment with her friends.

"I have something, right now, I really want to tell you about," she announces, moving her gaze to the dark sky. "I've never told anyone this story, but here, sitting with all of you and thinking about where we are and what we have done and what's happened to each of us, has reminded me of something that happened before, a miracle really. Just like this, and it also seemed like a miracle to me."

Janice's friends know about Janice and her struggles, about her quest to still her mind and to erase all the thoughts that created a world filled with shadows, dark hands, images bent against the frame of her liquid mind. They know how remarkable it is that Janice is with them, that she has raised a family, that she has come out on the other side of that liquid world with a smile on her face.

Everyone bends forward to see her face, which is now hidden in the shadows of the night-filled porch.

"This is really a beautiful story for once," she says, moving her eyes again over their faces before she begins to speak. "Stay with me on this, it's got a tough start. But the ending is exactly like this time right now, right this very moment."

Janice begins her story in 1981 when she is wandering the streets of Oak Park near Chicago. Her babies are at home with her mother-in-law who thinks Janice has gone on a shopping trip to the city. The truth is, Janice is only a few miles from her house. She is looking for a place to stop the car near the train so she can throw herself on the tracks. Janice wants to die. She can no longer stand to live with all those voices inside of her mind, who shout in her ears, "Kill yourself. You are worthless. Throw yourself on the train tracks, Janice." Too many overwhelming voices and faces, and she knows the medicine doesn't work, and she is afraid of what she might do to the babies or to Paul but not afraid of what she might do to herself.

Janice finds a parking spot about six blocks from the train station. She hopes for a big roaring train coming by within the hour and gives herself enough time to park and walk to the tracks.

The smell of fall leaves and the trees blinking shades of red remind Janice that it is Fall. Fall means walking to the river and wool sweaters and leaving the window open at night so she could snuggle under the heavy blankets. She remembers that before the babies when she had to stop taking the medicine, that she loved Fall.

Two blocks into her walk with her head bowed and a look of agony on her face, Janice stumbles into a man who has stepped outside of a small store, a name she can't even remember, to shake out a red and black checked rug. He waves the rug up and down like a grandmother on a spring cleaning frenzy. Somehow she steps wrong and the man shakes the rug into her, almost knocking her over.

With a pronounced lisp he tells Janice he is sorry at least seven times before Janice can bring herself to look into his eyes. Miraculously he sees into her—where she is headed and why.

"Please," he entreats, stepping back so he doesn't frighten her. "Please, come in for just a minute." He sweeps one hand toward the door of his shop.

Janice doesn't want to go in, but this man is like a magnet. He has on a green apron and there is a rich, sweet smell coming from him. Without saying a word, Janice follows him up the three concrete steps and into his store. She does not notice that he flips around the OPEN sign so it says CLOSED. He shuts the door and slips the latch over the handle.

The tea store is a world unlike any Janice has ever seen, smelled or touched. Inside the door, caught in a web of spicy scents, beautiful glass containers, and walls covered with colored gauze sheets, she cannot seem to move. To her left is an antique stove that is glowing with heat, and Janice is astounded to think the kind man has built an actual fire inside of the store. A copper teapot whistles lightly and fills the air near her with the scents of cinnamon and nutmeg. The store is no bigger than her own living room but Janice thinks it would take her years to see everything that the man has displayed and hung and placed perfectly on rows and rows of shelves that are made of old barn wood.

Six tables form the heart of the tea shop, and each small table is painted a different color—bright yellow, pink, orange, turquoise, black, red—all bold and brilliant with not one chair matching. The tables are set with a variety of teacups and teapots that astound Janice with their shapes and colors. "Works of art," she thinks to herself as her eyes pass over a hand-formed clay pot, one made of stainless steel in the shape of a man's hat, and another made from clear glass and poised with a handle bent in a graceful S and a spout long and straight, pointing directly at her. The cups are mismatched sets that somehow seem to blend into a gathering of fine and attractive settings. A short, bright blue cup littered with daisies, a clear thick-rimmed glass that looks more like a delicate beer glass, one petite cup that would fit perfectly in the hand of a Barbie doll, another a delicately molded cushion of clay that seems to float on the edge of a wide white saucer—all so beautiful, all so perfect. Janice feels as if she has been invited to a private and very intimate banquet.

She takes a step forward and is drawn again like a magnet to rows and rows of clear glass jars that are filled with tea leaves. A coffee aficionado all of her life, Janice cannot imagine that the teas could be so different in color—greens and blacks in more than a dozen shades—and so glorious in size. Then the smells flood her nose: a blend of earth and water and the way her mother's warm kitchen smelled when she baked on Friday afternoons.

Janice finally takes a step forward towards the shelves lined with glass tea jars that customers dip tiny silver spoons into when they purchase the leaves. She raises her hand to touch the labels and the words, the names of the teas sing songs to her heart. *Japanese Chrysanthemum Flowers. Rooibos Ruby Tuesday. Mist on the Gorges. Soft Jasmine Pearls. Jade in the Clouds.* These names roll off her tongue as she whispers them to herself and they are so beautiful and fine, like the tea leaves themselves, that Jancie begins to cry. Her tears are just as beautiful and fine, and compelled by tea. "Tea," she says out loud, laughing just a bit because she has never seen or thought of tea as beautiful before.

Her hand stops at a tea dictionary that has been posted every few feet along the rows of tea. Janice feels as if she is touching a Bible, something holy, something remarkable. "Autumnal Tea," she reads, "A term applied to India and Formosa teas, meaning teas touched with cool weather." Janice learns that a garden mark is the mark put on tea chests by the estate to identify its particular product and that well-twisted tea indicates a full wither. "Wither," she says to herself, reading that this means the tea has dried sufficiently to capture its intended flavor.

This knowledge moves her in ways that she finds intoxicating. Janice feels light headed as she opens a tea marked

"Mountains in the Clouds" and fingers the dark leaves that will open up like a woman's heart if you touch it the right way. She wants to inhale Mountain in the Clouds and let the leaves drift through her soul. "Communion," Janice thinks. "It would be like communion."

When she raises her hand a good five minutes later, the man catches her eyes and smiles at her. Janice is not embarrassed because she now sees that this man is brilliant and that he knows about flavor and spice and the winds of the world that turn leaves ripe and make tea that can make grown women weep.

"Go ahead, sit down there for just a second while I get the water going," the man tells her. "Oh, I've got something new here, a beautiful and very rare tea that I have been dying to try myself. Can I have a cup with you?"

"Sure," Janice answers. "Please."

Janice doesn't think about leaving, which surprises her. She has fallen in love with the low lights, the slanted chairs, smells at once foreign and friendly.

"This tea," the man says, as he pours water and crinkles packages, "is an amber Oolong with a most complex flavor and I've heard it leaves a wonderful aftertaste."

The man goes on and tells her a remarkable story about another tea called *Ceylon Silver Needles Special*. Janice cannot move when he speaks. "That tea is from Sri Lanka, and I have talked with women who have been lucky enough to pick the tea leaves," he says. "There are but four days in spring when this tea can be picked, and the women who are selected to pick the tea are considered worthy of a great honor. The aroma of this rare tea leaves a taste that is clear, fresh, invigorating—like spring itself— and the tea can be infused at least five times, often more, which is most remarkable."

When the man stops speaking, he closes his eyes, and Janice

imagines that he is thinking of the tea as it makes its journey from a foreign country, across the ocean and to his shop in middle America. "It is all glorious," he finally says. "It is a gift from heaven, I know it is—a rare and fine thing of beauty." He talks with reverence of teas that Janice never knew existed.

No one that Janice knows has ever talked about tea this way. She has no idea what he is saying. A tisanes? What the hell is a tisanes? Janice knows Lipton and Folger's and she knows a bit about Jack Daniels, too. So she sits and waits and looks out the window, never wondering why no one has come into the tea store.

It takes 10 minutes for the man to brew the Oolong tea, and Janice is a little curious about what he is doing. In those minutes, her mind narrows and she thinks about her babies. She doesn't want to think about them but the warm room and the quiet and this man, who seems so kind, all make her think about her babies. Janice loves her children, she loved them dearly even before they came into the world and even though she had to stop taking the medicine so they wouldn't be sick when they were born. It almost killed Janice to have them. She was crazy mad, and they took her away so many times she thought she would never come back. But those babies, she is thinking now about how very much she loves them.

"Tea is like magic for the soul. You know, most people have no idea about tea—how to brew it and what it can do for your health, for every part of your body."

"Oh," Janice manages to say. "Really."

"Most people pour boiling water onto the tea. The water should be not warmer than 180 degrees, and so you should let it sit for a little while after the boil. Then pour it, the tea must rest because it has just had a very tough journey, you know, for at least seven minutes."

Janice has never heard a man talk about tea as if he is in love with it. This man could be a priest, Janice thinks, distributing Holy Communion. His voice is solemn, and when she turns she can see him standing behind the counter with his hands folded while the tea is resting. He looks as if he is praying at an altar.

The man continues to talk about tea and China and how sometimes the rain can ruin the tea crops and how he often doesn't know what exact teas he is going to get until the shipment arrives. His voice must be like the tea, Janice thinks, soft and pleasurable. Gradually she is forgetting about the train.

To herself Janice thinks she should be saying something but she can barely breathe. She thinks maybe this man is an angel. *Maybe he is trying to stop me or maybe he's just a nice guy but lonely who wants to make me some tea.*

There's no way for Janice to know that this tea store is one of the most popular places in the Chicago area. She doesn't know that people from around the world order tea from this man, and that chefs from Paris have called him to ask about recipes for cooking with tea or serving the perfect tea with a buttery croissant. She doesn't know that this man's father escaped from China, from all those fields where the tea grows, and that he could only take one child. He took this man when he was a little boy, the same age as her oldest child is now.

The man is finally finished brewing the tea, and now Janice sits with her hands folded like she does in church.

"May I join you?"

"Oh, yes, it's your store and everything. Sit down. Please."

The tea is in a small glass cup that has a tiny handle. The man tells Janice that tea needs to be sipped like fine wine and kept warm in a pot. "That is why the cups, the best cups, are usually no bigger than the fist of a young child." The man places the cup on a saucer that cradles it not unlike a mother who brushes the crumbs off her daughter's beautiful face. Janice thinks it's beautiful to see the clear glass and the amber shade of smoky tea floating within it. When she touches the handle of the glass, she is surprised that the little handle is not warm. The man, who is watching her, smiles and says, "That's why I like these glasses."

She waits then for the man to say something else. There are little drops of water along the rim of the glass, and she wants to touch one and hold it to her lips but she waits. Finally the man tells her it is fine now to take a sip, but she waits and lets him move his hands to his glass first.

Janice doesn't use the handle, instead she places her hands around the glass and lifts it very slowly off the saucer. The glass is warm, and she can feel that heat move pleasantly into her hands and up towards her wrists. Then she moves the glass higher and higher until it touches her lips, and she looks down into the glass and sees out the bottom of the amber tea onto the wooden table, a kaleidoscope of grains and dark curves.

The temperature of the tea is so perfect that Janice wants to hold it in her mouth. She tastes a sensation of fruit and a lighter flavor, something musky like the earth and the rivers and trees.

Janice closes her eyes while these feelings cascade through her mouth and wake up all her senses. It is hard for her to know if the tea is real or if it's the voices, but she thinks it's the tea and that the entire world is talking to her. When she swallows, the tea moves down her throat yet doesn't seem to leave her mouth. She whisks her tongue across her teeth, to the side of her cheeks, to the roof of her mouth and everything is warm and soft and she is flooded with happiness. Janice begins to cry as she raises the glass to her lips again. The tears are unlike anything that Janice can remember. Deliberate and warm, the tears seem to caress her face in a way that feels like the hands of the tiniest woman in the world. They fall slowly, and she thinks there are about 16 tears, one for every year that she has been so ill.

The man continues smiling at Janice. He says, "Magnificent," and then continues to watch her as he sips his own tea.

In the quiet of that tea shop, Janice thinks she can hear the beating hearts of her own children, then Paul's footsteps, the wind outside of her living room. She closes her eyes, and she can see what her children will look like when they are grown, how her hair will grow grey and curve behind her ears, and how the trees behind the garage will grow to cover the entire backyard.

"Oh, my God," she finally says. "Oh, my God."

"You like it?"

"Oh, yes, I like it very much. You are so kind to share this tea with me."

"Tea is happiness, you know."

Janice is so happy that she feels as if she could cry and cry, but she is only able to smile and to lift the glass again and again. She then asks for another glass of the amber tea, a tea she can only describe as amazing.

When she has finished the second glass, the man rises and takes her glass away and moves back behind the counter. Janice can't seem to move. She waits for whatever is going to happen next. The man comes back with a small glass bottle filled with tea leaves.

"This is for you," he tells her, smiling, touching her hand for a second.

"What is this?"

The man smiles. He bows before he tells her, folding his hands again, moving like an Apostle.

"The tea we have just had is called *The Elegant Gathering of White Snows.*"

When Janice finishes her story and looks around again, she sees that Chris, Gail, Alice, J.J., Susan and Sandy are weeping. Their blankets have fallen to the floor, and they are sitting with empty glasses on the edges of their seats.

"Oh my good God in heaven," Gail manages to say. "That is the most beautiful story I have ever heard. Janice, my God, how could you keep that to yourself all these years?"

"I'm pissed," said Susan without rancor. "I've known you longer than anyone, Janice, I had no idea."

"Well, the killing myself part is really no big deal because for years I thought about it all the time, although I can tell you that I never quite came as close as that day. But that wasn't why I wanted to share this with you."

By now the moon has risen, just a speck of bold white, beginning- of-the-month moon. Behind the moon, there is a sea of darkness, surrounding everything. Jack and Audrey are in their bedroom, reading with little lights that are hooked above their beds, and there is only the sound of the women's voices.

"That was a wonderful story," J.J. says. "Did you ever go back to the tea shop?"

"Oh, no I couldn't, I was afraid I had made the whole thing up and I couldn't ever think about that possibility. But I saved the tea. I still have it. It's in my jewelry box. Paul thinks its dope. "

Sandy slips her arm around Janice's shoulder, rests her head on Janice's neck. This touch makes Janice think of the tea and what she really, really wants to tell the women.

"I've waited all these years, since that day, to feel as I did in the tea store. Now, here, this evening and yesterday and all the days since we left Susan's house, I have been feeling it. This, and every moment that we are together and loving each other and sharing and just being here, this is that same feeling."

Each woman said it then, the words moving from their throats, across their tongues and lips, into the chilly night air. "The Elegant Gathering of the White Snows." The words were heavenly and sweet and as rich with truth as the deep and ever darkening sky.

Associated Press, April 30, 1999
Wilkins County, Wisconsin
Editors Note—This continuing story has been pegged
for front page status. Local follow-ups will come in 30
minutes. This has become a priority one story.

WALKER'S SURGE INTO NATIONAL AND INTERNATIONAL HEADLINES

There's a good chance the seven women who are into the
fifth day of their pilgrimage through the backroads of this
rural part of the state have no idea they have caused a
national uproar.

Friends and relatives of the walkers and the walkers
themselves have refused to talk to media representatives.
The women continue to walk, occasionally stop for food
that is left out for them on the side of the road, and they
are apparently spending lots of time talking.

—30—

The Women Walker Effect: Mitzie

Mitzie Rogula picked up the *Hill County News* about 15 seconds after the paper plopped onto her chipped concrete doorstep. She shuffled past the door frame in her ratty slippers, as if arthritis was nipping at every bone in her small body. For a 60-year-old woman who should be just an inch or two past her prime, Mitzie looked as much like hell as a woman could look.

She had stopped getting her hair dyed three years ago. To call the minute round mass sitting over her long face one specific color would be pushing it. "It's kind of a reddish, blackish, brownish, grayish color," her only friend in the world Karen told her. Karen was being kind, of course, because Mitzie would have been wise to shave everything off, wear a stocking hat for a few months and start over. What she needed was an Xtreme Makeover.

These days there was no such thing as lipstick or eyeliner or makeup of any kind in Mitzie's house. Delicate worry bags had formed under her eyes. Mitzie likened them to Barbie doll flour sacks, when she bothered to look into the mirror and see them stacking up under her bloodshot eyes. Her skin was dry from the frigid, constant winds that blew every single day of the year in Northern Montana.

She sure wasn't having a problem in the weight department. Mitzie was so thin she had taken to using a short piece of rope from her long-abandoned camping gear to hold up an old pair of jeans that she wore six out of the seven days a week.

The top half of her body was usually covered with an old t-shirt, a red and black checkered flannel shirt that only had three buttons left on it, or a Mickey Mouse sweatshirt that had been ripped open at the throat.

Without fail Mitzie wore her pink slippers, those little slip-on kind that make clip clop sounds like a galloping horse when the rubber bottoms hit the floor. Mitzie had other shoes, but she just never bothered to wear anything but her pinks. Once, about a month ago, she was standing in front of the frozen food section in Albertson's Grocery Store and when she stepped back to focus on the frozen waffles, she got a glimpse of her own reflection in the big glass freezer door. Most people might cry or run from the store if they got a good look at their decomposing self like that, but Mitzie just looked and then looked harder as if she was trying to find something inside of that hunk of glass. Then she turned away without making a sound and headed for the frozen pizzas.

Mitzie had been smoking Salem's since just about a week before she started menstruating and wearing a brassiere with several inches of padding. While quitting had never entered Mitzie's mind, these days she smoked pretty much the way she had been living for the past 15 years or so, half-heartedly.

Once Mitzie had lived life with a whole heart, but that was long before her husband George was transferred to the United States Air Force base that was close to the middle of nowhere in Havre, Montana. Outsiders often called this part of Montana "The Armpit of the World." It wasn't the isolation, the loss of a job she loved, the fact that her children refused to move with her and bunked with their aunt and uncle for two years until they went off to college, that turned her heart. It was George's drinking.

On this particular day when she bent down to snatch up the newspaper, George was beginning his 78th day at a detox center down in Great Falls. Actually, this day was the 78th day of George's 11th stay at a series of treatment centers spanning from North Dakota to the bowels of the Rocky Mountains. George had seen the inside of every padded room in five states and from the looks of things, he would probably be trying out what California had to offer by early summer.

On her last visit to see him in Great Falls, before she could

197

bother to sit down on the edge of his rather comfortable bed in a room that was nicer than any hotel Mitzie had ever stayed at in her entire life, George pushed the door shut and asked her, "Did you bring me anything to drink?"

George loved to drink more than anything. He loved the way the whiskey or the gin or whatever he could get his hands on seemed to anchor his thoughts and feelings to the world. Once he had loved Mitzie like that too, but that was just for a little while before the kids were born, before the family moved to Montana, before every single moment of his life was centered on when and how he was going to get his next drink.

The saddest part was Mitzie loved George long after he stopped loving her. She gave up every single thing she ever loved or owned or wanted to try and help George. She hauled his sorry ass out of every bar and saloon from Canada to Wyoming. She packed him food, checked his car for booze bottles, worked with the counselors at the Air Base, never bothered once to think about what she needed throughout all of this—turning herself inside out because she thought it was the right thing to do to help her husband.

One Monday morning she woke up and found George lying naked on the living room floor with two women. Mitzie stood in the kitchen, poured herself a cup of coffee and for a few minutes thought about pouring lighter fluid on the three of them and then flinging her cigarette towards the heap. George's flaccid little penis was crunched up in one of the woman's hands, and Mitzie stood quietly in her green plaid bathrobe, stirring her coffee with a long silver spoon. She imagined what the penis would look like just as it caught on fire.

That was the last time Mitzie ever had what she would consider a positive thought.

Lucky for George she called the MPs at the Air Base instead

of getting the lighter fluid, and then she let herself drift back into the body of this woman who was now bending down to pick up the newspaper.

The lady across the street, who was certain that any day now Mitzie was going to jump off the roof or paint the house bright orange, was shocked as hell to see Mitzie get her newspaper for the forth day in a row. Last month the poor newspaper boy had finally picked up 30 newspapers in his father's van because Mitzie had not bothered to move any of them off the cracked sidewalk that was used by absolutely no one but the paperboy. So when Mitzie appeared at her door, grabbed the paper as if she was hungry enough to eat it, and then waved, my God she waved, the poor neighbor could hardly believe it.

Mitzie saw what she wanted right on the front page and stood there on the step in the little veil of morning sunlight, dropping the inserts which were promptly blown into the evergreen trees by those damned Montana winds. She did not lift her eyes from the paper until she had read every single word about the women walkers.

For three days now, Mitzie had been mesmerized by the stories in the newspaper about the women. She found out about the walkers by chance when she pulled in for gas on the way to the grocery store and accidentally hit the radio ON button. Otherwise, Mitzie would never have heard about the group of women in Wisconsin who were walking, just walking, on some Wisconsin country roads.

Mitzie's daughter Elizabeth lived in Wisconsin, but that's not what grabbed her about the story. The one thing that Mitzie had wanted to do in her entire life was to go to California and stand on the beach and watch the sun set on the other side of the world. Up until about five years ago when she gave up on every single thing in her life, especially George, Mitzie had actually believed that she was still going to make it to California. Now Mitzie was worn down. She was tired and she was hopeless and she didn't know what in the hell to do about it. Except the walkers were making her dream of California again.

She pretty much figured there was little she could do for George anymore. She knew he had a terrible disease that was eating him up from the inside out, but George didn't want to change anything about his drinking disease. She had given George 39 years of her life, and the one last thing that she knew for certain was that if she gave George even another second, it would kill her.

Not that there was much left living inside of Mitzie. There was just one tiny spark. The spark that made her walk away from George for the last time, and then the same spark, just a tiny bit bigger, that made her read the newspaper three and then four days in a row. Mitzie could not stop thinking about those damned women on the highway. From what she read in the paper, she figured they weren't fancy or stuck up or anything. She knew they were just normal, normal like she used to be, and right away she also knew they were riddled with heartache. But strong enough to turn their backs on the whole damned mess.

This day, after Mitzie waved to the big old fat lady across the street, she went right into the kitchen, set the newspaper on the table and started opening cabinet doors until she found an old but really good bottle of Tanquery gin. It was 9:34 a.m., early enough in spring for several piles of snow to be standing at the edges of the house, but warm enough to open up a window and smell the earth warming slowly in the sun

Mitzie had always loved having an occasional drink with her cigarettes in the evening. When the kids were in bed and George was on night duty, she spent an hour sipping on one drink, maybe two, and thinking about her day, about the next day, and about that trip to California. But when George started to drink and then never quit, she stopped drinking altogether and although she missed the little evening rituals that she had built up around her drinking time, she simply couldn't bring herself to enjoy the taste of liquor, or any other pleasures for that matter.

For an hour Mitzie worked at the kitchen table. Her pen moved across a long yellow tablet, she sipped her drink, rose once to refill it, and then kept on working. After 20 minutes she got up for a phone book and paged through it, touching the pages gently, as if they might disappear if she moved them too quickly, writing down an occasional phone number, holding her glass to the light to see how many ice cubes she had left, turning her head to look around at what was left of her kitchen, and then bending her head back to her paper.

At 10:45 a.m., Mitzie put her glass on the counter and walked into the living room to get the portable phone, which normally she used about once a week to call her kids. Her friend Karen called her about as often, and those goofy telemarketers got through once in awhile but that was about it. Back in the kitchen she scooted to the edge of her chair, stretched her legs as far back as they would go and she began dialing the numbers on her list.

Mitzie was surprised that it took her less than 30 minutes to line everything up. Mostly, that's because it was a spring day in Havre and everyone was waiting around for something to happen, and on this day what was happening was Mitzie. Everything fell into place so nicely she almost felt like having a third drink. Instead she put the glass in her freezer for later, grabbed her purse and walked right out of the door in her classic pink slippers.

Bank manager Jack Sprangers ushered her into his office. He opened his eyes in a wide frightened manner that made it seem as if he had just gotten caught in someone's headlights, and indicated a chair for Mitzie that was in reaching distance of his desk.

"Do you mind if I ask why you want to do all of this now?"

Jack asked, as he began passing sets of documents towards her.

"Don't worry so much, Jack," Mitzie said softly, never looking up from the paperwork. "You've been so helpful to get this all lined up for me. I've just been meaning to take care of these things for such a long time now, and well, it's spring, isn't it?"

"It sure is, Mitzie," he agreed. "You know, you've made a real hunk of money with all those investments, especially the money your parents left you."

"What money?" Mitzie asked in all sincerity, since George hadn't bothered to reveal her inheritance to her.

"Well, in the past, let's see here now, 16 years I think it's been since this account was transferred here, and not counting the 19 times George took money out, let's see, its still going to net you about $260,000. Then there are the stocks George apparently forgot about, his retirement funds, the house, and oh, two other accounts that we rolled over when you quit working before you moved here."

Mitzie was trying really hard not to pee in her pants, but the gin had kind of given her a hazy, what-the-hell kind of feeling, and she managed to act as if she had known all of this information for more than the past minute.

"So, Jack, are you going to get your cut on all of this?"

"Oh yes, Mitzie, I've already pulled out my share, and let's see, the grand total, including the retirement—"

Mitzie cut him off then, her mind raging, her kidneys squeezing. Now that she had so goddamn much money, maybe she'd leave some for George to drink up after all.

"Listen," she said. "Let's leave the retirement and the house in George's name for now."

"But, you do know you have his Power-of-Attorney?"

"Yes, but this will do for now, Jack. This will do just fine."

When Mitzie walked out of the First National Bank in downtown Havre, Montana at 11:31 a.m., she had ten grand in cash and a cashier's check for the balance on a half a million dollars in an envelope that she jammed into the side of her purse, right next to a ball of Kleenex and a sock that had been there for three years. All she could think about, as she turned the corner and walked into Betty's Beauty Bazaar was the women walkers and whether or not they had gotten anything good to eat for breakfast.

Kileen, Junanita and Merle almost died with delight when Mitzie walked in and announced that she wanted the most expensive, grandest makeover they had ever given anyone in their entire lives. Good thing for Mitzie that the gals had just renovated the place, adding everything from a makeup booth to a little spa where one of the girls from the junior college worked part-time providing full body massages and coordinating the color of your fingernails to the color of your eyes.

Mitzie didn't think twice about stripping naked and getting into a purple spandex jumpsuit that the gals had just ordered from a ritzy place out in California. The beauty specialists went to work on Mitzie with such enthusiasm they were too busy to ask her why she was changing her entire appearance. Right at the beginning, Merle asked Mitzie if she cared about the length or color of her hair.

"Well, I've been thinking a nice deep red would look pretty hot," Mitzie said.

"Oh, my Gawd," yipped Merle. "That's exactly what I was going to suggest!"

"Short is good too," Mitzie added. "The shorter the better. That's been my motto with men, by the way."

Everyone cackled. "Oh, Mitzie. Where have you been hiding, dear girl?"

"Sweethearts, it's a long story, a very damned long story."

That was the end of anything resembling a conversation as

scissors flew and Kileen, the coloring expert of the world, mixed up the dyes and poor Junanita, pissed that she had to cut Justine Ann Blackman's hair, didn't get to help much with Mitzie's but constantly got in her two cents worth. "Not so short on the sides," she piped up, and "For her eyes, let's try that new shade of purple."

It was nearly 3 p.m. when Merle spun Mitzie around in her salon chair so she came face to face with her new self in the mirror.

"Good Lord," said Mitzie, squinting to make certain that she was actually seeing what she was seeing. "You gals, this is just fabulous."

In a matter of hours, Mitzie had been transformed into a hip-looking grandmother with short red hair, makeup that accentuated her high cheekbones, and her dark eyes appeared almost luminous under the purple eye shadow and freshly tweezed brows. Mitzie sat in the chair for several silent minutes before she could move, and when she stood up, she really liked how the jumpsuit made her look.

"Can I just buy the jumpsuit too?"

"Well, sure, sugar," Junanita said. "Looks like it was made for ya."

The bill for the makeover came to $213, including the jumpsuit, and Mitzie wrote out a check for $350 and told the gals to split the tip. The three women had been working in Havre for over 20 years, and the biggest tip any of them had ever received was ten bucks. They watched with their mouths hanging open as Mitzie gathered up her old clothes, dropped them into the garbage can and then shuffled out the door looking like at least a half a million bucks in her new spandex jumpsuit.

During her New Day Dawning outing, Mitzie had been so engrossed in starting her new life that she had forgotten to smoke one cigarette. By the time she realized it had been four hours since her last smoke, she also realized she was going to quit. Later she would be glad because the smell of smoke would remind her of the smell of a bar and that would remind her of the smell of George, who always smelled like a bar.

Shopping for new clothes was much quicker than getting the makeover because Mitzie decided she only needed a few things. She picked up one of those little jogging suits that had fringe on the pockets and fit like a hot glove, a pair of baggy carpenter jeans, two blouses that were cut lower than anything she had ever worn in her life, six pairs of black bikini underwear that made her swoon just a bit as she remembered a scene from a Kathleen Turner movie she'd seen months ago where black underwear was a definite theme, a six-pack of brightly-colored socks and a pair of solid leather clogs that she wore to the checkout counter. Back in the shoe department she had taken off her slippers, tucked them under a display stand that looked as if it hadn't been moved in 25 years, and walked to the checkout counter like a little Geisha because she wasn't strong enough to pull apart the plastic tag that held the shoes together.

By 4:15 p.m. she had whipped through the new department store downtown and purchased three suitcases, a road atlas, three best selling novels, and a bottle of Escape, a scent Karen had once worn.

Mitzie wanted to stop at the grocery store, but the van was going to be at her house at 4:30 p.m., and she didn't want to miss it. Three guys from the Purple Heart furniture donation center pulled in right behind her, jumped out, smiling and followed her right into the house, with their arms dangling and just itching to lift.

"Listen," she told them as she threw her packages on the kitchen table. "Follow me from room to room and I'll tell you what I want you to take."

As it turned out, what she wanted to donate was pretty much everything. The furniture was good for nothing, the books, dishes and knickknacks were now meaningless to Mitzie, and she sure as hell wasn't going to need or use anything that was in the garage. She ended up leaving all the furniture in her bedroom, just in case George came back before his next detox. She also kept a small box of letters and photographs of the kids, a dresser that was her mother's, a set of tall beer glasses that she had always loved, a big oak mirror that her Uncle Paul had given to her as a wedding gift and a stack of old coins.

While the men hauled tables and boxes and lamps through the house, Mitzie carefully emptied out the kitchen cabinets and made herself a little keepsake box that included several pieces of ratty Tupperware, her grandma's worn wooden spoon set, two old spice canisters, and a few odds and ends that had always made her happy when she cooked meals for the family that had all but disappeared during the last 20 years.

By 8:30 p.m., the men had packed up her entire home, another lifetime really, into their truck. Mitzie stood by the kitchen door, hands on her hips, and could barely believe that the house was almost empty.

"You're done already?"

"The house isn't that big, ma'am," answered the wiry short guy.

Before the truck had backed out of the driveway, Mitzie had mixed herself up a gin and tonic and called Karen. She asked Karen to come over right away and to pick up a pizza she'd just ordered from Malivika's.

Mitzie should have been ready to catch the pizza when Karen opened the door and got her first look at the new Mitzie. She'd already forgotten that she now had red hair and real clothes and a new face. Karen stopped dead still on the concrete step when she saw her friend and dropped the pizza, right side up, thank heavens. Mitzie could only smile.

"What's happening?" Karen made it only a few steps into the house. Mitzie retrieved the pizza and squashed a napkin into the collar of her jumpsuit.

"It's those walkers."

"What walkers?"

"You know, those women in Wisconsin who are out there walking."

She pushed a napkin into Karen's hand. "Come in, I'm starving. Here, put the pizza on the table. Do you want some gin?"

"Gin?"

"It's good for you."

"Fine. Put a lot in my glass." Karen kept looking at the empty rooms as she sank down into one of the best chairs left in the house.

"Karen, I'm leaving Havre. You'd better drink up and I'll pour you another one."

Finally Karen was able to focus on her friend without her mouth hanging open.

"Mitzie, you look absolutely wonderful. Is this what you used to look like or something?"

"Oh sweetie, I don't think I ever looked this good before. This is what I look like now, and the way I'm feeling, I think that I'm only going to get better."

"I guess the gin helps with that, because I'm feeling better myself."

Karen raised her glass to Mitzie and smiled, thinking about how much she loved her friend. "Tell me, Mitzie, tell me about the walkers and you and what in the world is going on around here."

Mitzie told Karen about George and that she had decided not

to divorce him because he would probably be dead anyway within a year or so. She showed her the check that was in her purse, and mostly for one hour and then another, she told her about the women walkers and how they had inspired her to stop living in a dead zone.

"I can't save George anymore," Mitzie said, swishing her glass around in little circles so the last of the ice cubes almost popped out the sides, and looking into the eyes of her friend. "I guess I never could. He's gone and he's been gone for a long time and frankly, I don't think he deserved me all these years. Not that I was smart or anything to even stick with him, but I never had the courage to do anything else."

Karen wrapped her fingers around her glass, one of the beer mugs since everything else was packed, and she couldn't stop looking at Mitzie.

"You know, Karen, staying with George was really the easy thing to do all these years. I knew a long time ago that nothing would come of all my trying to help him but it was just simpler, much simpler to plod along."

This was a rare night in Havre when the wind had decided to take a break. Mitzie left the kitchen window open just a crack all day and even though the night was as chilly as winter in most of the rest of the world, she couldn't bring herself to shut the window. Tonight Mitzie wanted to feel as much of everything as she could.

"Aren't you scared?" Karen tipped back the rest of her drink.

"Oh, gosh, no, I'm excited as hell, but I'm embarrassed and ashamed for not having been a better role model for my daughter."

"She's turned out just fine, Mitzie. She knew that you loved her, and you've always been here for her."

"Maybe but I could have been more. So much more."

Mitzie hoped she would have the time to set things straight.

As she walked Karen through what was left of her house and fished around until she found her a key to the back door, she asked her only friend in the world to keep an eye on the house and to come back and get what was left of Mitzie's things and keep them in her basement.

When the two women went back into the kitchen, Mitzie ran her finger down the lines she had written on the yellow pad of paper until she came to the very last word.

"That's it," she said throwing her ice cubes down the sink and setting the glass back into the freezer.

Karen stood by the table, and as much as she wanted to cry, she just couldn't bring herself to do it because Mitzie looked so damned happy. And quite foxy too.

"Mitzie, I'll miss you, miss the lights on in the kitchen and the sound of those God-awful slippers, and those days when we just drove around the hills."

It had been years since Mitzie had held anyone for more than a second or felt what it was like to have someone put their arms around her, and when she hugged her friend Karen under the kitchen light, she wanted to cry too.

"Karen, I'm going to send a ticket real soon for you to come and spend some time with me because I'll miss you too, honey. Will you come? Will you come visit me?"

"Of course I'll come, Mitzie," Karen whispered into her friend's ear, just along the edge of what used to be her mixed up hairline. "Where you going? You never told me."

Mitzie pulled back from Karen just far enough so she could look into her eyes, but not far enough so they would let go of each other. Then she sucked in a huge dose of the cool kitchen air and smiled at the thought of a long, winding highway.

"I'm going to California, sweetie, I'm finally going to California."

The Milwaukee Sentinel
Court Files
June 23, 1969
Divorce Proceedings—Third Circuit Court
Sandra Jean Brims Plohinski and Dean John Plohinski.

The Milwaukee Sentinel
Court Files
December 14, 1973
Divorce Proceedings—Third Circuit Court
Sandra Jean Plohinski Barnes and Paul Stephen Barnes

Wilkins County News
County Courthouse Records
January 15 to February 15, 1989
Sandra Jean Plohinski Barnes Balenga and Robert Balenga

The Elegant Gathering: Sandy

People always want to know about the sex part.

"Sandy," they ask me, just a little breathless as if they are about to come themselves, "What do two women do in bed?"

My usual response: "What the hell kind of question is that?" You would think that a woman of the world such as myself, married three times, mother of two, a flaming liberal with an axe and about 49 other things to grind, would not take offense when someone dares to ask me what I actually do when I make love with a person of the same sex. Is this so hard to figure out? Isn't there a movie they can rent or some magical part of their imagination they can tap into to answer this astounding question?

I suspect people are curious about same-sex relationships because they have either imagined it themselves or tried it more than a few times and need a little expert advice. But I am definitely not an expert at relationships—physical, emotional, or spiritual.

Actually, I've done such a piss-poor job of figuring out who it is that I am that I find it surprising anyone in the entire world would actually consider for more than 10 seconds anything that I have to say. The sex question is a curiosity thing, I suppose; people look at me and try to imagine me without my clothes on, which is really something to see, believe me, in some kind of sexually-exotic position with another woman. I am certain they would be disappointed to realize the simplistic beauty of making love with another woman is not as complicated as they might think. It is soft and giving and glorious—an act as natural as breathing.

Walking out here in the country, in the sunshine and this unbelievable weather with these fabulous women—is putting everything in perspective. All these hours of solitude and talking and sharing is not unlike walking naked and knowing that no one is going to laugh or say anything foolish when they see you so exposed, see you for exactly who and what you are.

For me, Sandy Plohinski Barnes Balenga, clarifying moments have come far and few between. It took me so damn long to figure out who I am, who I really am, that it was almost too late to do anything about it. Now, this very moment, as the world has narrowed and all of us can focus on just ourselves, these intimate encounters, the closeness of whatever it is we want to talk about and share, it feels amazingly wonderful to be alive and to just be me.

Beyond this group of women who have looked inside of my heart and soul, the other people who think they know me, who would say that I am brazen and sex-crazed and wild and the kind of woman who would try, and probably has tried anything—those people, they only know half of the story. My life has been and continues to be a wild ride into the unknown. I have filled up one half of myself with enough heartaches to choke a horse, I have tried desperately to be someone I am not, and somehow in all this craziness I have come to be exactly where I belong. I will be the first to admit the journey, the goddamned journey, has not been picture perfect.

This whole thing about sexuality and liberation has been so blown out of proportion, it's very hard to remember back when the world really was not so damn crazy. I was so happy when that sex study was released by a group of female doctors and psychologists, beginning of 1999 I think, that talked about how most of the world is really in deep shit when it comes to having satisfying sex. The book was a kind of in-your-face updated version of Seymour Fisher's *The Female Orgasm* that was published in 1973. Well, what a shock! But not to me—because while it's rumored that I have had physical relationships with half of the free world and about one third of the rest of society, the sex itself was almost never why I rolled into all those sets of interlocking arms and legs. Now that we know most of the world is lying not only about how much sex but about the quality of sex they're having, maybe we can move onto more focus on emotions and affection.

My story is really not so different than many of the other 53-year-old women who seem to be wandering around the continent in a daze. I came from a wonderful open-minded family. My mother was a liberated Bohemian who could have gone either way sexually but married my father, whom she adored, instead of running off to a wildly liberal life in New York with the rest of her friends, who were writing poetry and sleeping with each other. My mother was college-educated and graduated from the University of Chicago, which was more than a miracle for a woman of the 1930s, and she has always been the most important person in my life. It really has nothing to do with the fact that she now lives with another woman, and they are not just roommates, but it's because she is sincere, kind, brilliant, and because she has never stopped loving me.

My own children, two grown men now, have managed to sail through life with complete competence. The oldest boy, Damien, has no memory of his father, Dean, who simply disappeared from our lives and has not acknowledged his son's existence in almost three decades. My youngest son, Joshua, chose to live with his father, something that almost broke my heart, but he remains as much a part of my life as does his older brother. Somehow—probably because my mother was always there to help me, and my sons act more like her than me—they have chosen to ignore my faults, my exotic and erratic behavior, my inability to stay with any partner for longer than, well, in some instances a night or two. I consider it a mark of success that they accept me no matter what I do, and for that I am proud of whatever part I had in making them so open minded and accepting. I believe such traits are anchors of the soul.

My mother, Anne, was incredibly open with me, partly because I was an only child and she raised me to be more like a friend than a daughter, but also because she truly believed that is how children should be raised. She told me everything, and I do mean everything, about her life. My mother slept with three men before she married my father, sluttish behavior to say the least in the 1940s. She smoked marijuana in her college dormitory and anywhere else she could, and she believed, even from an early age, that it was fine for women to love each other. When she met my father, she had already had an affair with a married woman. However, with her sexual liberalism still intact, she bumped into my father, a banker of all things, in the lobby of a shoe store and that fateful meeting ended anything wild and crazy for her— except raising me, of course.

Imagine how pissed off she was when I got pregnant about 15 seconds before high school graduation. Oh Christ, I was so stupid, and I chose the most idiotic male in the world to help create my first child. I wasn't in love with him, but I felt like it was time to see what sex was all about. Dean, who had been professing his love to me repeatedly for three years, happened to be handy. I could have done anything, had an abortion, not married him, run off to Cincinnati, but in another fairly stupid move we got married, moved to Kansas where he had already been accepted into Kansas State University, and tried hard for about three months to act like this was how life was supposed to be.

I left him when Damien was less than a year old, and moved back in with my parents. My mother loved that, my father wanted to kill Dean, and I just wanted to enroll in one of Wisconsin's universities and get in on some of the college action myself. I was not a very nice person after that for quite a long time. I was swept up into the Sixties life as if I had been lit on fire. I discovered birth control, cheap drugs and a liberated lifestyle that allowed me to remain in a daze for a good four years. While the rest of the world tried to explain away their sinful behavior by saying they were trying to find themselves, I didn't much give a rat's ass about that. I was just having a great time.

While Damien was learning how to walk and talk and count, I was spreading my legs and watching ceiling fans in every dormitory, frat house, back seat and front yard in Madison, Wisconsin. I owe my mother so much for not only being patient during those years, but for giving Damien the same foundation of love and support that she gave to me. My first choice for finding myself seemed to be giving myself away—and I thank the Goddesses every day that my mother was there. It wasn't until years later, when Damien was a young man and I had come back to the land of the living, he told me he was almost eight years old before he realized that I was actually his mother instead of Grandma.

In the summer of 1966 when I was 20 years old, I slipped out of the house one night and didn't come back for four months. I had managed to reach my senior year in college—and following a particularly ugly demonstration on the steps of the Wisconsin State Capitol building—I met up with a group of six hippies who were headed for California and invited me to join them.

We left at dawn, because someone in the group supposedly had received a message from a supreme being that we would have good luck if we left just as the sun rose over Lake Mendota. That gave me just enough time to slip into my room, grab my diaphragm, three t-shirts, a jacket and $50. I never bothered to say good-bye to my baby, never walked into his room to see him curled around his blankets and the big teddy bear that was always with him when he slept. I never ran my fingers across his forehead and put my lips to his before I walked off into the night with my hippie consorts.

In Vernal, Utah, I did manage to write my mother a note and tell her that I was headed to California and would be back before school started. One July morning from a dirty wayside in Montana, I sat and scribbled a postcard to her and this is the only clear, solid, retained memory I have from those months on the road. I'm certain that we must have been someplace close to Havre when I scribbled around the edges of that ratty postcard. Perpetually stoned and horny, I straddled a long bench, looked at a rolling set of hills that were most likely the Bear Paw mountains and wrote, "Mom . . . the sky is my pillow . . . my heart stretches so far . . . I can feel you . . . caressing my son, my heart, these souls of my life . . . I'll be back . . . the journey is the destination."

Thirty-three years later, that postcard is still taped to my refrigerator. A glimpse of it pauses me every time I look at it, and I think about wasted moments, about the necessity of self-discovery, about making certain that all the lights in my own heart and life stay tuned to the proper frequency. I meandered many miles those summer months. I tripped through Haight-Ashbury with the rest of the world, sat on a San Francisco hillside and watched sailboats parading out to sea. I fell in love at least 15 or 16 times. Sometimes the entire experience seems like a mirage.

I did come home at the end of summer, but I didn't come home alone. I brought along a new husband and I was expecting a baby. How ironic that a young woman who paddled against every tradition invented by our society would end up embracing motherhood and marriage—the backbones of what our male-dominated society designed to keep women in check.

If my mother had been the kind to say, "I told you so," I'm sure she would have told me that I had really screwed up royally. But she didn't, and not a day has gone by during the past 30 years when I have not thanked the She-God I have come to worship in thanksgiving for allowing me the good fortune of being hauled from Anne's fine womb.

My second husband Paul turned out to be a hell of a lot better human being than I deserved. He was crazy in love with me, excited about being a father, and he actually had a college degree, which meant he could get a real job and support us. I loved him too, in a goofy sort of way, and to this day our time together remains one of the best memories in my life. We moved into a small apartment in Madison, and he took a job at the engineering firm where he still works today. He threw himself into fatherhood and domestic life as if his trip to California had been nothing more than a sad mistake.

My mother helped with Damien, and although I gave birth to Joshua a month before graduation, I somehow managed to get a diploma and a degree in social work, which had been a passion of mine since I did the Helping Hands badge in Girl Scouts. When I walked through the graduation line not far from the steps of the State Capitol where I had started my California hippie adventure, my life seemed a paradox to me.

After that I tried really hard to do what everyone thought I was supposed to do. Paul worked and I stayed home and shit, I really tried hard to make everyone happy and to be a good mother and follow all the rules but I was so goddamned miserable I made the rest of the people around me miserable too. What was it? Why couldn't I be happy? I had no idea. I just knew that what I was doing, the kind of routine and stifling life that I was leading, the lies that had begun to spill from my mouth, all of those things were drying me out from one cell to the next. I had fallen into the deep, dark hole of tradition, of social norm. Taking care of children and punching the time clock and paying the bills had turned me into the very person I had rallied against becoming for the first 20 years of my life. I had stopped thinking. I had stopped listening to the inner voices in my soul that were crying for me to be who I really was—a wild, free, non-traditional woman.

This realization made my decision to leave seem natural and normal. This time when I left I didn't disappear in the dark. I took the boys to my mother's house and told her that I had to leave again for a while. She put the boys down for a nap, and then took me into her bedroom and made me lie down on the bed. She tucked my head into her shoulder and held me for the longest time without saying anything. Then she started to talk.

"If you don't go, if you don't leave now, you will regret it for the rest of your life, like I have regretted it," she told me as I stopped breathing, stopped crying, stopped the beating of my own wild heart.

"As much as I love you and as much as I love your father, I should have never lived like this either," she told me. "We fall into these patterns of traditional behavior because they are comfortable and because so many people are counting on us and because a tiny part of us is scared we may not make it. There are so many things I never finished, so many places I never saw, so many things I turned my back on."

I was astounded. As much as I thought I knew my mother, knew who she was and what she was made of, I had absolutely no idea.

"Like what, Mom?"

"Sandra, you are very much like me. Your heart, the shape of your soul, the way you can get lost in the world . . . oh Lord, you are truly my daughter."

"Mom . . .?"

She hugged me hard again. "That woman I told you about, the one that I was with when I met your father. Do you remember that story?"

"Yes."

"I've never stopped loving her, Sandra. Never ever stopped

loving her."

I wasn't sure then exactly what that meant or had to do with my leaving but within moments, I shuttled out the door and drove to Milwaukee. I checked into a no-name hotel and found a job with the county in about 15 seconds. I came back right away for the boys. Paul had sensed my restlessness for months and was ready for me to be who I needed to be. I settled into an apartment on the funky East Side of Milwaukee. It was the first time in my life that I was really alone and really away from my mother.

Our lives settled into a routine then, one that gave me no time to think. I worked and took care of the boys, and then went back to work the next day and did it all over again. When Joshua was six, Paul asked for a divorce and he wanted custody of the boys. By then I had come to realize the joys and sacrifices that gave me title to the word *mother*, and I was devastated to think that I might lose the boys. But Joshua wanted to be with his daddy.

I could have died then. I could have taken some pills or flung myself off of the top of my apartment building. But Paul, bless his goddamned little heart, saved me. He figured out that I could transfer to the Madison County office, he helped me buy a condo; eventually we worked out an arrangement that ended up not being much different than life in Milwaukee. Through all of this, I kept my life in a constant holding pattern—never daring to feel, never daring to try again, never wanting to listen to what my mother had been trying to tell me for the past 30 years.

By 1982, the boys were well on their way to being grown, and my life in Madison had settled into a fairly secure routine. Paul had drifted into another relationship, and I was very happy for him. Although I had bedded and dated numerous men, there was absolutely nothing serious in my life except my work and my sons. Then I met Sarah.

Sarah Jorgenson was a Madison civil rights attorney. She first contacted me about a woman in town who was in desperate need of help. I agreed to meet her one hazy, early afternoon, the temperature just cold enough to require a jacket, the day felt one minute warm and the next freezing cold. Perhaps that should have alerted my inner senses to the possibilities that lurked just ahead of me. Sarah rose when I walked into the coffee shop, recognizing me from a photo that had recently been in the newspaper about my work on a state legislative committee. She slipped lightly through a crowd of college students and grasped my hand as if we had known each other our entire lives. I had never, ever seen anyone so beautiful.

Physically, Sarah was a wisp of a woman who wore her black hair pulled tight to the sides and then long in the back. For someone with such naturally dark hair, it was shocking to see eyes as blue as a summer sky and skin just about the color of the wheat that grew less than a mile outside Madison. What I loved about her from that first second was the way she moved. She was sure of herself, confident of everyone around her, certain that what she knew and felt and touched were real and true.

I was 36 that year, and Sarah was a year older. Unlike me, she had never married, unless you can count her extreme devotion to her profession. She had never given birth to a child, never spent years trying to find herself. Until I met Sarah, I had never been certain of anything in my life, yet when I looked into her eyes and she touched my hand that very first time, I was never more sure of anything.

Sarah and I did not become lovers right away. It was not anything that I ever expected to have happen. But when it did, on a summer night after a wild day in court, it seemed as natural as breathing. Sarah had called me as a witness in an abuse case, and she did a marvelous job of making the suspect look as guilty as if he had committed the crime right there in the courtroom.

We had become nearly inseparable, Sarah and I. Working on cases, eating out, sharing books, calling each other 12 times a day, solving the social ills of the world one sad person at a time. It had never entered my mind that I was already in love with Sarah. My sons were busy preparing for adulthood, and I was overly involved in my own professional world.

The evening following Sarah's wonderful performance in court, we celebrated our one small victory over a quick dinner and a not- so-quick few bottles of wine. I was lying on the couch, playing with the back of her hair as she sat on the floor and looked through a stack of legal files. Sarah never stopped working. The stereo was on, it was my favorite time of day—when light faded as the entire world dipped into the arms of the night and shadows began to form outside the window. Just then, Sarah placed her hands on the side of the couch, lifted herself off the floor and bent over to kiss me.

She offered a long kiss, and I remember thinking that if I could, I would swallow her right inside of myself. No one had ever tried to kiss me like that, I had never let anyone kiss me like that. Her hair swept against the side of my arm, and I raised my hands to her face. I followed the pull of her arm, and by full nightfall we ended up in a tangled mass of legs and clothes and skin and fingers dancing lightly everywhere between the sheets on my old wooden bed.

If I could have chosen a moment to die, it would have been right there with Sarah. Sarah with her legs wrapped around my hips, her mouth moving from one breast to the next, her fingers sliding everywhere at once, and everything about her soft and warm. The countless times when I had let others touch me and hold me and rock me into orgasm had never moved me like this. For the first time in my life, I cried while I made love.

I kept on crying, tears of unspeakable joy because Sarah and I were barely clothed or apart for more than a few hours following that evening, later that night, the following morning on the bed, on the floor, in the shower. We spent three entire days together, never left my apartment, called out for food and talked and touched in a marathon that I wanted to last the rest of my life.

It didn't take me long to realize that Sarah was the first person I had really loved, and the intense longing and lust that captivated every single fiber of my being made me weep for joy and in realization of all that I had missed with all the others that had come before her. Sarah, I was wise enough to realize, could have been either a man or woman, but Sarah, the woman, came into my life just then, and she loved me in a way I know for certain that no one had ever loved me before. I was suddenly alive and sure and so incredibly happy I could barely breathe. I also came to know that a woman's love for another woman is what made our relationship move me, center me, bring me home. I had always been attracted to women but I had ignored what could have been permanent feelings because, in spite of my Bohemian mother, I was so programmed to the social standards of society that I refused to listen to my own heart.

Sarah moved in with me right away, sold her own condo, packed up every single thing she had bothered to accumulate in between her legal cases and personal causes, and from the beginning our relationship was no secret. My mother knew, the boys knew, Paul knew, pretty much the entire world knew, and they all seemed just as happy about us as we did. To say that my life was suddenly perfect then would be as true as anything. I was floating, and for the first time since I was a little girl, there were no questions in my heart.

During those years with Sarah, I had a friend who before she finally found the right medication—lived her life in total fear that any second something brutal and tragic was going to happen to her. She would get into the car with me and say, "Sandy, we could be hit by the next car that drives through here," or "What if this is the last time we'll ever see each other?" Even with Sarah in my life, I continued to be a "live for the moment" kind of woman, and I thought how sad for my friend that she couldn't enjoy a simple moment without worrying. If only I could have known how true this friend's fears were.

Although my life was far from horrible and most of my mistakes and sorrows were surely caused by no one but myself, I never dreamed after I met Sarah that I would ever be unhappy again. I never dreamed that after 11 magical years with her, my entire life would come to a dead end and that I would have to start all over again.

Sarah and I were on our way to a gourmet tea store to get our monthy stash of our favorite drinks—what we called "our medicine." We were lucky enough to have sustained that lustful, physical, "gotta-have-you" part of our relationship, and we were holding hands that day in May. I really don't remember most of what happened next and for that I will always be grateful, but what they told me later, just after Sarah's fingers slipped through mine and they pulled her out of the car already dead, was that a drunk driver barreled into us at 50 m.p.h. smashing directly into Sarah's door and killing her instantly.

In the accident, I suffered broken windshield glass embedded in my face, up and down my arms, and one large hunk that totally changed my hairline. My left leg was broken, one rib punched a hole in my lung, and the only thing that saved my left hand was the fact that it had been holding Sarah's hand when we were hit.

It took me days to wake up from that mess, to my mother, slipping softly from her chair and with tears streaming down her face, putting her beautiful long hands on my lips and telling me that Sarah had been killed. "Oh baby," she said as her own tears dripped onto my face and ran down my neck. "I'm so sorry, so sorry."

Sorrow consumed me in much the same way that Sarah's love had consumed me. Her memorial service was held in my hospital room, and I kept her ashes in an urn that sat on the air conditioner by my bed. I wanted to die, I willed myself to die, I cursed everyone and everything that tried to keep my spirit in the land of the living. I refused to believe for weeks and weeks that Sarah was not going to come through the hospital door and slip under the sheets with me and place her lips against that one private spot at the corner of my eye.

My recovery was slow and incredibly painful. My mother took me home and let me wallow in my misery for one and then two months. When I could walk again, when I had the last of my plastic sugeries, when it was time to either move forward or simply stop living, my mother took me on a long drive into the country. She stopped at a spot where we could look out over the Fox River and miles of rolling hills in Frank Lloyd Wright country. She placed her hand on my arm, and then slowly took a long, silver chain from around her neck. She had worn this chain ever since I can remember.

"Betsy gave me this."

"You've always worn this chain, Mom, but I had no idea it was from Betsy."

"Put it on."

"It's yours."

"I don't need it anymore, sweetheart. You wear it."

"Mom?"

"Sarah won't come back, you know that, but she gave you so much, she's still here. You'll always love her, you'll always have her love inside of you, and you have to realize that you'll never get over this. The rest of your life, every moment that you breathe, you will remember her."

The chain in my hand was warm from my mother's neck, and I moved it from one hand to the next, not daring to put it on. I knew I had to decide right then what I was going to do. I held the chain up to the light and saw little places where all the years of wearing had caused the metal to become as thin as fine thread.

"How do you ever feel good again, Mom? It feels all the time like a knife is moving up and down inside my stomach and cutting right through my heart. I was just so goddamned happy for the first time in my life."

"Remembering helps. You think of something wonderful that Sarah did, the way she touched you, the way you felt as if you could tell her anything and it would be okay. It's true too, what they say about time. It helps. The ache will never leave, and I know it's hard to imagine now but you will love again. You will do that because she taught you how to love."

"What ever happened to Betsy? Did you ever see her again?"

My mother looked out the car window then, away from me for the first time in weeks. She pushed her fingers through her hair and then let her hands drop slowly into her lap, forming a perfect circle, the fingertips touching.

"No, I never saw her again."

I took the chain then and set it on the top of her fingers. It slid down into the palm of her hand where it came to rest, where her fingers closed over it just as she closed her eyes.

"Oh Christ, Mother, all those years when I was trying to find something, someone and then it finally happens and then it's gone. You keep this chain. You've already given me way more than I deserve. I know Sarah is still here, and I have you, and it's time I kick myself in the ass and get on with living."

Mother looked into my eyes, and a veil of sadness moved across her face. It was a visible pain that made her entire body shudder.

"It won't happen like that. It will hurt you for a long, long time. I can't tell you how many times a day I think of your father, how little things like the way you tip your head make me see him all over again. There's Betsy too, such a long time ago for me, but she's in my heart, always in my heart."

I was only kidding myself that day with the idea that I could simply say my life was going to move forward, and I could live and be happy again without Sarah. I eventually moved back into my house in Madison, though every single thing that I saw and touched brought my love for her right back to life again. As much as I already admired my mother, my feelings for her took on a whole new level of respect. She had truly loved my father and Betsy both, lost them both, and somehow managed to find love again. By God, she was a heroine to me.

Eventually my body healed, leaving me with a few kinky scars and some aches and pains that kick in every time the wind shifts. The progress of my heart has been an entirely different matter. While I gradually inched my way back to the gnarly wild person I have always been, it has been close to impossible for me to open myself up from the inside out again.

Two years after Sarah's death, I had a quick and quiet affair with a man from my office. The thought of another woman, loving me and touching me like Sarah had seemed unimaginable, but after my passionate love for Sarah, it was obvious that a man would never be able to satisfy me again. It was the last time a man ever touched me.

Those who keep track of me will want to know about my third marriage that often pops up when people look at me and try to imagine all this kinky sex I supposedly had. Three years after

Sarah's death, I married my dear friend Robert, an old man really, whom I had befriended twenty years earlier when he was one of my clients at Walworth County Social Services. Robert was a sweet man who never married before our nuptial, when he was seventy-one years old. When we met, Robert wanted to make certain that his few material assets went to someone who had cared about him, and I was the only person he could think of who had been a significant part of his life. He also didn't want to die as a single man because he said his mother would be pissed off when he saw her again in what he called heaven.

Robert had come into my life following a fall that took out his left hip. While I transitioned him from the hospital to a nursing home, we talked about his life as an English teacher, his lost dreams of writing the great American novel , and how sad he was that he never had any children. He had a brilliant mind, a kind heart, and he wanted to leave his money to help me put the boys through college. I could not say no when he asked me to marry him. It was his last wish.

One of Sarah's associates married us about a week before Bob died of cancer—fifty-five years of smoking will do that. I held his hand while he took his last breath, which included a smile and a thank you that made his last moments gracious and sweet, and that managed to open up a small fresh spot in my wounded heart.

I moved to Granton three years ago when a position opened up in Wilkins County, mostly because there would be less of a chance I would run into ghosts of my past life in Madison. I really didn't know anyone in my area, but I gradually let my heart come to rest in the hands of all these women, my friends, who have managed to talk me through every bad day I have had since I started this new phase of my life. My mother, who is having the time of her life with her new mate, Margaret. She is convinced that soon, very soon I will meet someone, another woman who will fill me and touch me and make me happy again.

It's been close to impossible for me to totally move forward since the accident. I know before that can happen, I need to release my own heart, I need to fling my remaining seeds of sorrow into a higher wind.

My mother is right. There will be a woman in my life again, but first there are the rest of these miles to walk and the rest of my seeds to scatter. This walking now is for Sarah, for what she taught me. And it is for my mother, who held my hand throughout this incredible journey. And it is for me, finally, at last, forever and ever to have the courage to follow my heart.

Chapter Eight

THE FIRST DAY OF MAY has ushered in clouds as tall as the Empire State Building and a wildly dark horizon that is forcing back an endless succession of clouds the color of the turquoise stones Sandy wears in rings on half of her fingers.

Yet no one is worried about the weather, and Alice—who can tell time, test the wellness of meat, and talk to people in France via the arthritic bones in her body—says with all certainty, "It ain't gonna rain." When the women decide suddenly to turn south on a picturesque lane that crosses through the middle of the county, she adds, "Besides, why people worry about the weather has always puzzled me. What in the name of the good Lord can we do about it anyway?"

The women are scattered across the width of Pembury Lane, and now that their sore ankles and calf muscles have adapted to the daily rigors of walking, they are moving at a pace never before seen on this tree-lined lane. None of the women has ever been particularly athletic, and this is the day they may realize that perhaps they have missed the boat when it comes to exercise.

"Can you imagine how great we would feel if we had decent shoes and equipment?" Janice asks this as she kicks her beat up Wal-Mart tennies into the air.

"Lots of that junk you read about is nothing more than marketing hype and entirely bogus," Chris says.

"You have on Nike's, Chris, so what in the hell are you talking about?" Sandy snorts.

"I got these for 25 bucks, for your information. What I'm talking about is top-of-the-line stuff that all the kids covet. If you walk around in flip flops your entire life, there probably is a good chance your arches will drop and your ankles will slump and your toes will curl under before you're 50. Come on, did you ever spend $150 for a friggin' pair of tennis shoes?"

Alice, who thinks expensive is a big meal at Pizza Hut, can't help but laugh at her friends. She is wearing a pair of black oxfords with a fake leather and canvas middle and hard rubber soles that she purchased six years ago out of a *McCall's* magazine for $19.95. "These babies have taken me around this county about 56 times, you know. Now that we are all used to this walking, I think we'd be pretty smart cookies to keep it up the rest of our lives."

Everyone, even Susan who continues to vomit twice a day, agrees that the walking has made them stronger. No one has mentioned stopping, but the women agree that when the time comes, they will most likely add walking to their meetings once they go back home.

"If we are ever allowed to get together again," laughs J.J., who has imagined walking until she ends up in a foreign country, hopefully someplace warm with tall, booze-filled glasses and men who wear tight shorts and smile with their bright teeth.

The women have grown accustomed to being constant companions. They have talked about men in war, about babies and sex and weather, and how to place the chicken in the bottom of the pan with just a little garlic. They have grown comfortable touching each other and holding hands and walking with arms around waists and shoulders. At the Bed and Breakfast where they paired up in double beds, they all slept like sisters who have shared sheets and space for years and do not flinch when an arm flops across a breast or a leg pushes in at the back of a knee, or one sister rolls into the back of the other looking for a spot that is warmer than the edge of the bed.

There is a fine rhythm now to their walking that could be set to music—a back and forth kind of stroll that picks up and slows down when someone stops to tie a shoe or needs to sit on a log for a short rest.

Because their lives have been filled with the needs and wants of the rest of the world, of their husbands and babies and mothers and fathers and lovers, the women have sucked in the silence of the Wilkins County countryside as if they are inhaling the most pure air that ever floated close to Earth.

Sometimes they walk with their eyes closed, leaning against each other and listening for nothing but the sound of the shoes and the birds that are as curious as all the human onlookers and the wind whipping through the beautiful pines. Once when Alice started to whistle just like her grandma, it made Gail cry because she remembered that same sound from a time ago when her own grandfather worked down in his basement workshop.

Each one of the women has talked about how the walking has forced something up through the soles of her feet, into her stomach, then to the heart, past the throat and right to the lips. These women who have always loved women have grown to love each other in a deeper way and have never felt so unbelievably content.

"I believe I could tell you that I murdered 12 children and 12 adults and then ate their clothing, and you would want me to talk about why I did that as we sat and held hands," Chris observed the day before as they were sipping lemonade that someone had left for them at the side of the road.

"Well, honey," J.J. said, "12 might be pushing it just a bit far."

"She's right, though," Susan said. "My god, look at us. I'm knocked up, some of us have screwed up royally, we all have some secret tragedy yet here we are, sipping lemonade as if we've just finished a round of bridge and had some brownies."

"I hope you don't find this too amazing," Sandy said. "Women are like this, you know. If any of you had any sense, you'd dump your men and jump on my bandwagon with me."

"Dears, dears," Alice said forcefully, "some men, so I've heard, especially the sons of women like us, can be good girlfriends too. But I don't know, it just isn't the same talking with a man about menstrual cycles, making love with a woman, and stretch marks, now is it?"

"It's a stretch, Alice baby, it's one long goddamn stretch," Chris sighed.

In three hours, the women walk seven miles, and Alice grins when the sky opens up and the sun comes back out. Susan has walked ahead, and when the women catch up to her, she stands just off the highway in front of three paper bags and a box of papers that are covered with a big plastic garbage bag.

"What is it?" J.J. asks.

"Well, lunch for one thing and it looks like a bunch of letters, notes and things," Alice says, examining the bag.

As they carry the bags of food and the letters over to the base of a big oak tree, the walkers quickly discover everything from a tablecloth and napkins to ham sandwiches, drinks, and carrots and celery all cut up in neat little lines.

"Good Lord, we have lots of guardian angels," Alice says, spreading out the food and drinks. "Girls, grab those letters and let's eat."

Susan, clutching the mail in her hands, starts reading first. She sits at the edge of the tablecloth, unable to move or eat as she begins reading out loud:

> "Dear Ladies—My husband and I have been watching you on television every night, and we want you to know that we think you are a bunch of sick lezbeens and you are all going to go to hell. Women who leave their children and husbands deserve to be punished. We both believe you'll be damned for what you are doing."

The women all stop eating and look at Susan as if a snake the size of New Hampshire has crawled right out of her mouth and spoken French.

"Holy shit," says Sandy. "What the hell is that all about?"

"It's probably from my mother," Janice comments with a smile.

"Keep reading," Chris encourages. "This is cool."

Susan opens another letter.

> "To the Walkers: I have wanted to take off like you are doing for the past 23 years. My husband is a jackass, but he has all the money in his name. This morning when I listened to the radio and heard that you are still going, I got the idea to sell the car, the stereo, anything I can get my hands on while Joe is at work. If you ever get this, I will be on my way back to New York. I should never have left. Thank you for giving me this inspiration. Your fan, Bernice P."

"That's one for one. Keep reading, for crissakes, how many are there?" Sandy wonders.

"About 30 or so. The postmarks are from all over the world. This is unreal." Running her finger over a line of odd signed stamps, Susan adds, "Listen to this one."

"You don't need to know my name but every single one of you knows who I am, and I think you are all fucking nuts. Some day you will pay for this, and I hope you get this letter so you know that someone who lives near you hates your guts. My now ex-girlfriend is out there looking for you, and if you find her you can have her."

"Hey," shouts Susan as she drops one letter into the pile and picks up another, like she's rummaging in a bingo cage, "I guess my husband has turned up. I had no idea he was still living in this county. Oh wait, listen to this one. This will make you all jump up and down.

"To the women who are walking: My father doesn't know I am writing this but I was wondering when you get done if you could help me. I am only in eighth grade but my father, who is very conservative, says he won't let me go to college because all the students take drugs and have crazy sex. He wants me to go to this Bible school in Waukesha and be a missionary, and I have straight A's and want to be a doctor. If you could do anything to help me, because my mother does whatever he says, I would really appreciate it. My name is Amanda Brocklet and my phone number is 980-648-9543."

"Sounds like a new client to me," said Sandy.

"I had no idea so many people would be thinking about us like this," concluded Alice, as she fingered some of the letters and tried to read without her glasses.

"I tried to tell you this would happen," said Chris. "People love this kind of shit, and it's spring and we had a long winter, and no matter what the rest of the world says there are still a lot of pissed off, unhappy, women out there."

Susan starts passing around the letters, and the women stretch out, exchange notes, and marvel at what a fine storm they have whirled up. Susan holds the last letter in her hand for a long time, until Janice sees that she is crying. "What's wrong, Susan?"

She wipes tears from her nose with her fingertips, and then shares the letter:

"Dear Friends—It is never easy to do something different. I know that what you are doing took a lot of
courage, and you need to know that there are many,
many of us out here who understand perfectly what you
are doing and why you are doing it. I am a 39-year-old
woman, who is dying of cancer. Every day that I am alive
and am able to touch the fingers of my little son, look
into the eyes of my husband, and watch the beautiful
trees outside of my window, every day is a gift to me.
Now you are a gift to me also. I think of you all day out
there walking, talking, sharing secrets and working
through your troubles. I am encouraged by your courage.
Part of my heart is out there with you, and if you could,
would you please say a prayer for me as I say a prayer for
you each morning. Love, Your Friend, Patty Gulinsky—
Room 45—Mercy Medical Center."

There is a moment of silence as Susan sets the letter down in her lap gently, as if it may break in half if she makes a sudden movement. Alice waits for a few seconds and then rises up and extends her hands out from her sides. The women look up at her, and then they all get up and join hands.

The women form a perfect, unbroken circle. Above them the sky has cleared, there is only one cloud, and it is drifting away in the high fast-moving spring air. The tablecloth is littered with half-eaten sandwiches and letters, twisted and placed right where the women have dropped them.

"Dear Lord," Alice whispers with her head bowed and her eyes closed. "Please give our friend Patty the strength to know that she is not alone. Guide her through her days of pain, gently whisper in her ear when she thinks she can no longer go on, let her know that every minute, every second, she is in our hearts and she is walking here with us. Lord, please do not let Patty suffer, please help her to let go when the time comes. Please let her know that her son will be loved, and that you will be waiting for her. Thank you too, Lord, for blessing us with the gifts of friendship and love as we walk and talk and share. Thank you for lifting our sorrows and lightening our load. Thank you for keeping us safe, and for showing us that we are not alone. Stay with us, Lord, and please, stay with Patty."

When she finishes, Alice slips Patty's letter into the front of her jacket and gently gathers up the rest of the notes and places them inside of the paper bag. The women are all crying, imagining Patty in her bed with a quilt draped over the side, pictures of rainbows from her son hanging on the edge of her table, and an IV drip attached to her arm.

"That's the shits," says Chris, bending to stuff the rest of the food under the plastic. "That was really nice, Alice, your beautiful prayer. Thank you."

The sun shifts a few inches higher as everyone moves to sip a drink, finish a sandwich, or pick up the rest of lunch, though no one is very hungry now. The women can hear an occasional car beyond the trees; and that sound, the rushing and movement, makes them all think of the world that is still waiting for them.

"Sometimes," begins Susan, "I think about never going back, about walking to some clinic and taking care of my situation, and then I see myself walking and walking and never stopping. I guess I'm a little bit scared of ending up like Patty or falling back into the same rut where I've been for so many years."

"Oh Susan," Gail says, moving to stand in front of her. "I think going back is going to be great. You won't ever really want to go back and be the same way you were before this. I just think you aren't ready to go back yet. We are still walking, you know."

"It's just that when I think of everything we have all done and been through, it makes me tired. Then I think of all those women, like the ones who wrote these notes, can you even believe that? All those women who are watching us and looking to us for inspiration."

Sandy stands up, puts her hands on her hips, sways a bit, dipping her head into the wind so the gray ends of her hair whip around her face like lightening bolts.

"This is how I see it. First of all, we are out here for ourselves. We all know each other well enough to know that we all had something or someone to walk away from, or to step over. You can't take that away from us. This is like one very large moving therapy session. We all know we can't keep walking forever, we can't stay wrapped up in each others' arms like this the rest of our lives. We are all too smart to really want to do that, even you, Susan. We're also having one hell of a lot of fun, we're together, we love each other, and if someone like Patty or that little girl can find hope in our personal choice to walk, that's just a bonus. But it's not a responsibility."

"What about those other jerks?" queries J.J.

"Oh hell, that couple and everyone else who thinks we are perverts or nutso would just find something else to be pissed off about if it wasn't us. Come on, we all know 100 people like that. They point their fingers and roll their eyes and shame the world while they live in a little box. That's just not our responsibility."

Alice drifts over to Susan and puts her left arm around Susan's waist. Chris shifts her weight from one foot to the other, looking for a moment like a runner who is stretching before a big race. "We all need to know, we should know that this isn't going to end when the walk is over," she says. "We still have the rest of our lives, and that includes a hell of a lot of meetings and parties and maybe walks in other places once we regroup. I think this is one hell of a beginning. I have to tell you all, I haven't felt this damn good in years. This is for us, Susan, and if someone else gets something good or bad out of the whole thing, well, that's pretty damn okay too."

"You're right, Chris," Susan agrees. "I just need, you know, I need to take care of myself, and there's still so much to think about."

Alice, like a little light beaming out from behind Susan, says, "That's why we are still walking, dear. I, for one, have to figure out a few more things myself, and you know what else? We never finished hearing all those stories about sex the other day."

There's a wave of laughter that escalates into movement that carries the women back to the highway. Behind them, out of sight, the rest of the world is poised to see where they will go next. "Will they sleep outside? Will someone else take them in? Are they eating? What are their husbands thinking? And the kids . . . what about the kids?"

The walkers, who have worried about everything from floor wax and soccer shoes to hormone replacement therapy and the size of their boobs, have chosen to notice at that moment the way the clouds have circled at the edge of the horizon. In this moment, they don't care about car payments, retirement, relatives, the Christmas party, college tuition for the last two kids, or the fact that their husbands no longer have any hair on the top of their heads. The women moan as the clouds and their spirits lift.

They begin to describe to each other a pitcher of frosty martinis with blue cheese stuffed olives like those served at Eddie Martini's in Milwaukee, the thin spicy pizza at Balistreri's in Wauwatosa, and steak the size of Zena's or Robert Redford's beautiful left thigh.

Some of them are dreaming about a big, tall man with strong hands and hips that fan out in layers of muscles just above his big cock, who can rub their aching calves and that lower part of their back that has not been pain-free since 1973. Some of them are dreaming about a woman with magic eyes, pendulous breasts and hands that dance. The martinis, the man, the Amazon, and then that steak snuggled next to baked potatoes—it all sends each woman into her own fantasy.

Gail thinks a few bottles of merlot, maybe something from Chilé, would be good with the steak, and she says she loves those big Brandy Alexanders after a meal like that. "Lots of thick ice cream and an excess of brandy and then some nutmeg sprinkled on top of the drink to make your tongue curl up like a slinky cobra," she muses.

Alice can't get off the sex thing, saying "a good screw" for the first time in her life, forming the words like a naughty teenager. The women discuss their fantasies with such fervor that miles pass them and they barely realize they are walking.

Alice listens intently, taking mental notes like this is the day before the biggest test of her life. J.J. has always had the hots for a guy she met on a train trip once a long time ago on the way to meet her sister in San Francisco. They had a drink together, flirted like crazy, and she has always regretted not going into his sleeping car and screwing his brains out as the train rolled through the tall, penis-like Wastach mountains of Utah. Janice relates that she fell in love with one of her doctors about 10 years ago. She describes him as a goofy-looking guy, yet with the kindest face she has ever seen. His shoes were always untied, his hair was a grizzly mess. But whenever he talked with her, she got the urge to slam him down right on his office floor because the desk would be just too small.

Chris, who has slept with almost as many men as Sandy, manages to shock her friends by telling them she had a mad crush on a National Public Radio correspondent who shared her room in Beirut. The correspondent was a woman, and although they did some wild necking, the entire process was always cut short, literally, by bombs dropping.

Sandy picks Olivia Newton John as her secret, wild sex fantasy and that cracks everyone up. No, she says, she had a girlfriend for a long time, long before she had breast cancer and broke up with her husband. The woman is sexy and beautiful, "and she could sing while she took off my clothes."

Gail claims to have a hard time picking just one fantasy lover, "Damn, it's not fair." She finally settles upon a tall, older man with gray hair, dark eyebrows, and a voice deep and buttery that made her wet just to hear him. He is a dear friend's uncle, a happily married man who would never, ever think about touching her. "But god, what a man!" she says, and this was 25 years ago.

Susan has a hard time even mentioning the word sex these days. She's thinking about becoming a nun, except for the problematic vow of celibacy, but all right, she has someone in mind. But her fantasy is more of a conglomerate – a man with the best qualities of all the guys she would love to claim for wild sex. He has a long blonde ponytail tied in a rubber band, no hair on his chest or back; he's probably a professional athlete who has made a lot of money and roams the country just looking for women to seduce. He has dark eyes, and teeth that are so white they glow in the dark. His hands are full of calluses."When he caresses me," she describes, "especially on the face, I want to kiss his fingers and place my own hands over all the tiny marks and nicks that have scarred his hands." Susan can't seem to stop, and the women begin to understand why she has had a hard time getting rid of her sorry-ass lover. "When he drops his pants," she says slowly, panting just a little, "his penis pops out erect, and it's the most beautiful goddamned penis I have ever seen in my life."

Alice thinks Susan should stop talking, but she can't quite bring herself to suggest that. Most of the women have almost stopped walking and seem to be just shuffling along the highway, as if sucked wholly into Susan's Big Penis Amusement Park Fantasy. Susan has her eyes closed, and she has her hand on the back of Gail's shirt, and she is in that damn bedroom and Fantasy Guy is putting his hands on her breasts because he thinks that's what women like. She can barely stand to look at him because he is so beautiful. When he bends to kiss her mouth, Susan tilts her head back as if she is doing just that, and J.J. and Chris and Alice also part their lips, take a breath and wait for, wait for…they wait for this guy to run his hands down Susan's stomach and hips and legs, where he will move them apart and then inch his way from the bottom of the bed and then into her, right into her, slowly, slowly because he is so blessedly endowed.

Finally Susan opens her eyes and smiles, and the women breathe again. Alice says, "Geez, I was just thinking about Paul Newman because he is so beautiful, and he's had the same wife all these years, and he's, well, geez, he's so beautiful that I would love to just have him kiss me once, just once. Well, okay, maybe just a bit more, if Chester was dead or wanted to watch or something!"

As everyone laughs, a car goes by. A fellow rolls down his window, tells them his wife said it's okay if they want to sleep out in the trailer tonight on his property. His wife cleaned the trailer all out, and he has to go clear to Iowa to check on some chickens, but their property is the next place over the hill——two miles——there will be supper too.

The women are still laughing, wired enough by wild sex talk to make another two miles. They say yes, yes they will stop because they need a break. When the wind picks up, the man shifts the Buick into drive again and dips his hat out the window. Only Sandy has the gall to say, "You women are getting to me. Even that guy looks pretty damn good."

Associated Press, May 2, 2002
Wilkins County, Wisconsin

WISCONSIN WALKERS ARE GIVING THE WORLD A CHANCE TO PAUSE

Spring could very well turn to summer before the seven now world famous women walkers decide to end their backroads pilgrimage—a simple journey that has ignited people from one end of the country to the other.

This beautiful farm country is only quiet these days where the women happen to be walking. The rest of the county is pretty much on fire because of the national and now international publicity the women have been receiving.

The women remain unidentified, but sources say they include one journalist, a social worker, housewife, one grandmother, and a secretary, who seem to have no exact destination in mind, and that is one aspect of the adventure that seems to appeal to a broad range of other women.

"Half of the world is running from one spot to the next, while these gals are doing something we all dream of doing," said Cecelia Mackums, who traveled to a police roadblock to show support for the women. "God bless 'em all and I wish I could join them."

Mackums, like many of the women who show up each morning near the highway where walkers may pass, says she knows most of them personally but refuses to reveal any additional information.

Husbands, friends, and relatives of the women have also refused to provide further details about the walkers, saying only, "We respect what they need to do."

243

While some experts think the women are protesting, perhaps against unkind circumstances in their own lives, others see the walkers as a symbol of this country's desire to slow down and put their own lives in perspective.

One woman who shows up near the walkers' roadblock each morning said she has not only quit her job because of the walkers, but she's decided to travel by bus from one end of the United States to the next.

"I don't know what took me so long," said the woman, who refused to give her name but smiled as she spoke. "I've been wanting to do this my entire life, and when I heard about these women, I decided I was just finally going to get on with it."

While the walkers have inspired at least this woman to change her life, they continue to march along these Wisconsin country roads seemingly oblivious to who is watching them and holding a collective breath.

"We're all having fun," said the sheriff's deputy Rudulski who has been assigned to assure safe passage for the walkers. "This seems like it's something really important to them and it's my job to give them the space to do what they need to do."

—30—

The Women Walker Effect: Jane

Jane was beginning to think there was some major conspiracy going on or something. For five days in a row, her entire routine had been the same as always. Get up, eat a bowl of Raisin Bran, let the cat out, shower, dress, get the cat back in, drive five miles to work, punch in at the time clock and walk through her office door. Work, work, work, all day long. Answer the phone, type up the records, file the records, lunch at noon, usually some fruit or maybe a salad from the cafeteria. Work some more, home by 6:15 p.m., dinner, television, and then once in awhile, Katherine or Michael would come over. But most of the time, she was alone.

All that was fine except for one darn thing. For the last five mornings when she got to work, her desk seemed to be just like she left it the night before. Her pen would be by the telephone, a pad next to the edge of the stack of papers, her coffee cup sitting on top of her box of Girl Scout sandwich cookies. But after she would check the fax machine in the back room and sort the messages, by the time she got back to her own office there would be a neatly clipped newspaper article sitting right in the middle of her desk.

Every article was a story about those women walkers in Wisconsin, and while Jane had to admit it was a really neat story, she couldn't figure out where the newspaper clipping had come from because there wasn't anyone else around. Gloria, the shipping clerk, was always in the back warehouse—unless she sneaked in the side door, which was possible, but unlikely. Mark and the other guys were always hunkered around the coffee and donuts that Bruce brought in every day of the week.

The first day, finding the article was a singular strange occurrence. But by the third—and then the forth and fifth days—Jane was really spooked by the whole thing. The articles were from the

Austin Daily News, and they were trimmed right to the edge. Jane could almost feel where someone's hands had touched the edges of the newsprint.

Each day as she discovered the articles on her desk, Jane would look around her office really fast and then tiptoe to the hallway, but she never saw the person obsessed with newsprint. She had absolutely no idea how those darned clippings got on her desk. She was certain no one knew about her, certain no one would really care. But who was doing this?

From the first day and the first article, Jane could feel a little nudge next to her heart when she saw the word Wisconsin. Oh Lord, it had been such a long time, and she thought she had done such a good job for the last 12 years of avoiding everything and anything that might remind her of the place she had come from.

On this morning, the fifth morning, Jane knew that someone was trying to tell her something. She sat at her desk for a good 15 minutes fingering the latest article, this one recounting the geography of the walk to date, what the women looked like, how they acted and why this strange journey was attracting so much attention. The articles, the women, the way the stories showed up on her desk—everything had her mind swirling because she was a Wisconsin woman herself and she had lots to remember.

She was thinking about how green Wisconsin always was in late spring, just about this time, and about how she would go with her cousins down to the Wisconsin River. They would all wade into the frigid water on a dare. Someone, never the same cousin, always jumped in first and splashed everyone else until the entire gang forgot about the cold water, the frigid winds and feet and fingers that quickly went numb.

Jane thought about campfires in the forest, and she remembered from way back when she was about 11. She and her cousins Mary and Sharon sat talking for hours and roasted an entire bag of marshmallows, then hunted through the edge of the dark trees for more wood to keep the fire burning.

Greg, the assistant manager of Big Wheel Tires, came in then to see if he had any messages in the big basket that sat at the edge of Jane's neat desk.

"What's up?" he asked.

"Oh," Jane said, startled that someone had interrupted her thoughts.

"I haven't seen anything for you yet, Greg."

"Whatchya readin'?"

"It's a newspaper article about those women in Wisconsin."

"Oh yeah, I heard about them on the radio. What the heck is that all about anyways, Jane? Do ya think those babes had some bad bananas or something?"

"Greg, Greg, Greg. Could this explain why none of your wives ever stayed very long?"

"Hey, it wasn't me, ya know."

"Okay. The women are just walking, Greg, like when you and Steve go down to that rodeo for a week each year. It's the same thing. This is their rodeo." Jane knew Greg could relate to this explanation, and anything beyond that would float right over his head. She knew he would never understand why women needed to move, to change, to experience, to share, to be with other women. She waited for his predictable response.

"Well, it's goofy ta me, is all. Wisconsin, too. Where the heck is Wisconsin?"

"Oh Greg, it's a long ways away from here, really, really far."

When he left, Jane didn't move. She knew Wilkins County was down south, not close to where she grew up in Prairie du Chein, Wisconsin. When she closed her eyes she could see the rolling hills and tractors and trees, mostly those big old oaks dotting the horizon and then usually one or two, standing alone in a big field where the farmers plowed around it and sat to have their lunch, and where there would be a big pile of rocks right by the tree that the pioneers had collected.

Jane touched the words on the newspaper with her index finger, and she imagined the women walking, maybe she even knew some of them. Imagined them walking and holding hands and stopping along the side of the road to rest. If Jane missed anything in Wisconsin, it was those times when she had so many friends and they would go so many places and share so many things. Jane had loved her friends and they had loved her but now, sitting in the tire store, she started to cry. This sudden burst of emotion startled her more than the recent appearance of the newspaper articles.

Jane forced herself to get up and go to the restroom. She washed her face, wondering as she checked to see if her eye shadow was okay, when those lines coming off the edges of her eyes had become so long. She straightened her hair and pulled down the edges of her green jacket. Back at her desk, Jane folded the newspaper article into a palm-sized square and slipped it into the top section of her purse. Then she started on the summer publicity sheets that advertisers were already worried about putting into their system.

All day long, she did a pretty good job of forgetting about Wisconsin and those walkers, distracting herself with projects she had been putting off for weeks. At lunch Jane decided to leave the office, something which she rarely did. Instead of eating, she walked around the block and sat on a little concrete bench that was in front of the fountain over by the library. No one recognized her. No one said, "Hello, Jane, do you mind if I sit down?" She was all alone on the bench until 12:30 p.m., time for Gloria to have her lunch.

The afternoon was a blur, because the Ford salesman went

nuts in the outer office and needed to have about 16 tires mounted yesterday. Jane handled him in a calm manner, and caught Greg winking at her as she got the guy to smile and sit down and accept a ride back to his own office.

Jane stayed late that night to finish all the paperwork so she could have a fresh start in the morning. She hated coming in to yesterday's work, and now that she was pushing 40 herself, she could understand what Gloria had been talking about when she said getting up every morning wasn't always easy. Jane stayed up too late each night, watching television because she knew she wouldn't be able to sleep when she went to bed anyway.

That night Jane stopped at the small corner deli, Fratanno's, near her apartment complex. She bought a little pizza with the works, even anchovies, and then turned and grabbed a six pack of beer out of the cooler. Usually she would just eat at home—soup or maybe some eggs, or sometimes she would cook a small piece of meat out on the little barbecue grill she kept on her wooden patio—but this night, pizza had sounded just right.

There were no messages on her answering machine, particularly no word from Michael, who hadn't called her in 10 days. The cat was happy to squeeze out the front door when she checked her empty mailbox. In her one bedroom apartment, she turned on the radio and then the oven, slipped out of her work clothes and into sweat pants and an old jogging bra because it was warm but not too warm, then finally sat on the couch.

The long coffee table was now filled with the unfolded newspaper clippings from her purse, and when she added the one from today, the entire top of the table was covered. Certain words seemed to stand out in the newsprint like *Wisconsin* and *women* and *support*. Jane sat with her elbows on her knees and her hands on her face so her fingers stretched all the way to her eyes. She reread each article, scooting forward to touch the edge of the table while she read the one at the far edge.

The bell on the oven went off and Jane jumped up, took out the pizza and let it sit for a minute while she popped the tab on a beer. Her uncles had always loved to drink beer as they sat around outside in those dorky old lawn chairs that always had strips of plastic missing. They would fill up one of those old metal tubs with water from the hose and put all the beer, always in bottles, right in the tub, and they would sit in a circle and talk about the war, and work, and their wives, popping off beer caps and looking each other in the eye, which they usually didn't do unless they were drinking lots and lots of beer.

Jane started to cry again after that, and she let the tears come as she cut up the pizza and stood at the kitchen counter for the first bite. She decided to go outside, even though she didn't know why, and filled up her plastic wash pan with cold water and put two more beers into it and then set the pan out on the patio. Then she grabbed the pizza and sat on her lone chair, looking right into the side of the apartment building that was next door. The lawn between her apartment building and the one across this small patch of dying grass was empty. There wasn't anyone watching her from a window. No one waved. It was endless emptiness. Nothing. No one. This made Jane cry some more as she felt a growing ache of loneliness rise from her stomach and into her throat.

Jane continued to cry while she ate. She finished the entire pizza and was into the third beer when she heard the phone ring. She jumped off her chair and grabbed the phone on the counter just in time to hear a sound, like a person finishing a cough maybe? Then there was a click. "Shoot," she said, wiping her eyes and heading back to the chair.

Jane hardly ever drank anymore, and the third beer was making her head spin. The Texas sky was as dark as it was going to get.

There were a few spring stars to the north, the same stars, Jane figured, that the women in Wisconsin might be seeing at this exact same time.

Jane lifted her legs, still fairly firm and slender, over the top of her chair and returned to the living room to scoop up the newspaper articles. When she plopped back into the lawn chair, she put all the articles into a pile and then set them on her chest, right on top of her heart. She took a big swallow of the beer and let her mind go back to Wisconsin again, like she had that morning at work. In the Texas night with the cold beer cuddled in her right hand and Wisconsin on her heart, Jane began to remember for the first time in many years. She remembered, and she smiled and closed her eyes, and nothing she saw was as horrible as she had pretended all this time.

In her family kitchen, Jane is 20 again, her hands are on her hips and around her everything is familiar from her childhood. The kitchen window has a crack in the bottom that her father has been going to fix for 16 years; the long wooden table has scratches and lines and one big crack in it where her brother Jonathan stuck that big cleaver the night her parents went square dancing.

The kitchen is also littered with her mother's "stuff." This includes coupons and boxes and stacks of newspapers that she will never, ever read in her entire life. Loaves of bread wrapped in plastic with twisties on the end are lined up against the back of the counter, and there is a little china dish filled with rings, bracelets and single earrings that have lost their partners. There are always dishes in the sink and a slab of meat thawing on the counter for dinner.

Jane cannot see herself, but she is beautiful. Her hair is down to her waist, and she has skin the color of the milky white sky, and those legs, so long and slender, for a girl who is not really tall. It is Fall, and there is a nip of winter in Wisconsin. The popular wardrobe style in 1979 is jeans and sweaters and for Jane, cowboy boots—always a pair of cowboy boots since she has been a girl and dreaming of horses and cowboys and the West. Oh the West, the mountains and deserts and horses and spaces. The West.

"Mom, you can't stop me," Jane shouts, and her mother raises her hands to her ears and is trying so hard not to shout back at her only daughter.

"Janey, this is so foolish to throw something like this away, there's just a few months left. In spring, you will be done, can't you stay and finish?"

"I hate it. I hate school and everyone there, and it's just too damned stupid."

"Please don't swear in here, Janey. Don't swear."

"Let's face it, Mother, you are the one who wanted to go to college, and you should go up there and finish and get the diploma, not me. I never wanted to go. You made me go."

Her mother cries then. She is a big woman, almost as wide as the space between the counter and the refrigerator, and Jane hates her for that and for every other thing she can possibly think of.

"Look, it's not my fault you got married and had three kids and never leave the damned kitchen, and that you eat and are fat."

The level of Jane's cruelty astounds her mother, and she lifts her head from her hands to look at a daughter whom she no longer knows. Her heart has fallen into her stomach, and Jane's mother feels as if she is going to be sick.

"Sweetheart, please don't do this. Please, oh please."

Jane hates her mother, even as she knows her hatred is misplaced. For this is the very mother who has always been here and helped her and loved her and encouraged her to do something, to see the world and to read and travel and to give herself a chance. The mother who has worked a night job at J.C. Penney's for six years so she can help Jane with college tuition. The mother who comes home with ankles the size of grapefruits and then eats to make herself feel better for all the dreams she had that have   evaporated.

Jane can't stand it any longer. She can't stand her brothers who remind her of that damned high school, and her father who sits around drinking coffee and poking his finger into her waist, whom she hasn't seen touch or kiss her mother in, when was the last time anyway? Jane can't stand Wisconsin and the dumbass boyfriends who only try to screw her brains out and never listen to her stories about where she wants to go. She hates every single thing in her life except this idea, to get out, to just get out.

For Jane, there isn't much thinking left to do after that. The bags have been in the car for weeks, since she dropped out of college and never told her mother and father, since she slept in that bed with Matt for six months to get the money from what she would have spent on the dorm room, since she called that guy at the ranch and said she would be there in early September. Her mother cannot move from the kitchen. Her feet are glued to the floor, and she knows in her heart that something horrible is happening, yet there isn't one thing she can do to stop it. She hears Jane run upstairs, she hears the drawers, she knows Jane is looking for money and the little box of jewelry. She's seen that brochure from the ranch under the stack of old t-shirts.

Jane doesn't bother to say another word as she flies out of the house. She doesn't look back or wave either. Janey doesn't see that her mother is slowly falling to the floor and wrapping her arms around her own shoulders. She doesn't see her mother's heart breaking, and she is way too young to know about anguish and loss and suffering and dreams that can turn into nightmares.

In those first few minutes driving away, never cranking back the mirror to look at the house or the river or that spot where she sat with her cousins, Jane only knows she is doing the right thing.

She thinks about this all the way to Colorado, where she almost dies with delight the first time she sees the mountains—first as tiny dots against the horizon, and then as a growing vision of snow and light and darkness that leave her breathless and driving faster and faster as she approaches the sloping foothills until she realizes she is going 110 mph and the car hood is shaking. She stops thinking about those wonders when she sees that she has to live in a rat-infested cabin with no indoor plumbing, and that the ranch manager will never let her tend the horses, and that her job will always be to work in the kitchen.

In a year, there is another ranch and all the men who have never noticed that it is no longer 1856 and that women can do whatever they want. Jane has managed to send home one postcard without a return address and when she leaves Colorado, she does not know that her mother is right behind her, looking for her only daughter, and she misses finding her by a single mile.

Jane drives South to Arizona, where she waitresses and then works part-time at a drugstore because she blows her car engine, and she has no skills that will get her a job paying more than $5 a hour. In Arizona there is a guy she thinks she loves, but then she doesn't and suddenly it has been five years since she has been in Wisconsin. One Christmas she calls her mother and says she is okay but not coming back, and someday she might call again and "No, I'm not telling you where I am."

In 1985 Jane gets up and looks around at the walls of her trailer. She looks in the mirror to find she's a young woman who still doesn't own a horse or live on a ranch, and she is so tired from working all the nowhere jobs and going nowhere. Once again, she puts all her things in the car and leaves. This time there is no one to argue with because she is alone in the trailer, and her few friends won't care. She drives away without calling in to say anything to anybody, with a total of $678 and a car that is as many years old as all the years it has been since she left Wisconsin.

This time Jane lands in Texas because in the back of her mind, she identifies this state as a world filled with ranches and cowboys. In all this time, Janey does not let her heart soften. She doesn't know that her mother has finished college and lost 75 pounds and that her father's heart is not so good but he will be okay if he retires early. She doesn't know that her mother also finishes a Master's Degree and is now a counselor at the clinic in Prairie du Chein, where she helps 19-year-old girls, and some much younger, who want to run away.

She doesn't know that her father has taken a cooking class and remodeled the kitchen. Her brothers are gone, and the house is big but Janey doesn't know that her parents will never sell it because they think she could come back and then what? What would she do if they weren't there?

Jane isn't aware that her cousins Mary and Sharon pray for her and still cry when they talk about her, and then say it isn't too late. Janey could come back and they would all be together. She doesn't know that even with all these changes, some things are still the same. Her uncles, all but Uncle Tommy who died that Halloween night three years ago, still come over and her father cooks and they have a few beers, but not like before.

Once when Jane's brother Bill, the one who is the cop up there in Door County, called in some favors and found his sister's phone number at the small gas station that Janey was managing, he didn't know that Janey was just about ready to leave the little Texas town and move to Austin. So Bill missed her by 14 hours. Then his wife had a baby, and he never tried to find his lost sister again. Never again.

In Austin, things were better for Jane. She met more men, including Carlton, who wanted to marry her. Carlton hired her to manage his jewelry store, but Janey didn't love him, and she had always told herself that she would never settle. Sometime, she knew, she would fall deeply in love with a man as wild as all those miles and miles of open space she has seen. Maybe this man of her dreams would be a rancher, so she would finally get her horses and make love in the blooming sagebrush, not caring about anything but that specific moment and the way her entire body smoldered against the warm sand, and how she opened herself up—to this man and to the world beneath her.

When Janey took the job at the tire store, the biggest franchise in the whole state, life definitely seemed to change direction for her. She was too busy at first to go out much, because the last business manager had failed to do things like record sales and check inventory. She met a few people, but no one she wanted to know better.

Eventually her life took on a routine, and there were no more wild nights and crazy lovers and driving to a new town in the middle of the night. There was, in fact, absolutely nothing new, and Jane was holding herself in place as the rest of the world moved. Back in Wisconsin, her mother discovered yoga and took her father to France, where she made love to him right out in the open in the middle of the day on a grassy ledge near a long river with a name they could not pronounce.

While her parents were making love in France, Janey was neatly and efficiently filing tire order forms into her newly organized system and thinking about how Greg always bothered her at work, and nothing else. Jane was thinking of nothing else.

Then another year passed, and she met her lover Michael. The sex was just this side of marginal but Michael was mysterious, he wore cowboy boots, and he made her laugh and forget how mundane and simple her life had become. Then those articles just this week, those articles began appearing on her desk and Jane felt herself moving forward to a place that she could remember as being directly behind her.

When Jane opened her eyes after all that remembering, she was no longer crying but thirsty as hell, really thirsty. She carried the beige plastic bucket into the kitchen and dumped out the warm water that had settled in the bottom. She filled up the bucket with cold tap water and then dumped every single ice cube on top of the last three beer bottles. Her memories had sparked something. She slipped into her bedroom and exchanged her sweat pants for her little red running shorts, then grabbed a pad of paper and went back outside.

Jane was done traveling down memory lane. Now she was going to do something. She made herself a list because that was how she worked these days. She had just finished a book about organization and graphing, and that's what got her to making a list. When she finished writing, she cracked open another beer, and then she called the only real friend that she knew would help her. Katherine had been in her weight-lifting class, and the women had bonded over coffee and the major decision that weight lifting was not for them.

"Katherine, I need some help."

"Who is this?"

"Oh come on. It's Jane. You know, the geeky office manger with no life."

"Are you drinking? You never drink. Are you drinking?"

"I'm having a few beers, that's all. But Katherine, something's happened to me."

"Jane, you are scaring me."

"Well, get ready for the rest of this then."

"What?"

"I told you about those articles, right. You know, articles about those women walking in Wisconsin?"

"Yes, isn't that something? What's that all about, do you

think?"

"That's where I'm from."

"Wisconsin?"

"Yes, that's where my family is, and I haven't been back there in 20 years, 20 damn years, Katherine."

"Jane, do you want me to come over there?"

"No, no. I just need a little help. Not much, just a little help."

Katherine said she would take care of the cat, who knows for how long, does it really matter? There wasn't much in the refrigerator, and the way Jane had everything organized at work, the place could run without her for a year and they probably wouldn't even notice that she was gone.

Jane almost fainted when a really cute limo driver knocked on her door four hours later. He was late, but not late enough for Jane to catch the next plane to Chicago. She expected some old fart of a driver, not a hunky-looking guy who smiled when he saw her in those tight jeans and a blouse that was open three buttons down and showed the top of her firm breasts.

When the plane lifted off the runway, Jane never thought about the fact that she was pushing 40 herself and had never even been on an airplane. She watched the lights of Austin glitter for a few minutes and then disappear into a thin layer of light clouds that seemed to float with her all the way to Chicago.

Her first plan was to fly on to Madison, which was just a bit closer to Prairie du Chein than Milwaukee. But just after 6 a.m., while she was having a Bloody Mary in the O'Hare VIP lounge with the very pilot who had flown her plane, she decided to fly into Milwaukee and rent a car. That way, she could drive out to Wilkins County, which was really sort of on the way.

Milwaukee was unrecognizable to Jane as the plane circled over Lake Michigan and passed all the city rooftops. She remembered it as an ugly, old city where nothing happened and where people never changed and always did the same old things day after day, year after year. Life seemed to be hopping in this city she hadn't seen for 20 years. In the airport terminal, where Janey had to whip out a blazer to keep warm, she was astonished to see camera crews racing all over the place. "It's the women walkers," she said to herself. "They are bringing us all in here."

By 10 a.m., when Jane had pounded down three cups of coffee and wiggled her car out of the lot at the airport, it was already 60 degrees. She flipped her blazer into the backseat, checked her teeth in the mirror, and headed out of the airport.

Not far from the terminal, less than two miles, Jane decided suddenly that going to find the women was ridiculous. She was certain they didn't want to be bothered, and even more certain that it would be fairly pointless to stand and watch them if she could even get close enough to see them.

Instead she swung the car around right in front of a Seven Eleven and scooted back to I-94, the freeway that traveled north. The road that would take her home. Just to see. Just to say she was sorry.

Jane smiled as familiar landmarks clicked by her car. She set the cruise control at 70 mph and flipped on the radio. She started to sing because she was certain, after all these years, that she knew the way home. Thirty miles out of Milwaukee, where the subdivisions had given way to long fields and stands of trees that were as green as the hills along the Mississippi, Janey reached down and pulled off her silver-tipped cowboy boots, one at a time. She put them on the seat next to her and then she kept driving, barefoot and singing at the top of her lungs with the window down and those buttons on her blouse flapping against the top of her beating heart.

Newsweek, June 12, 1989
—Features Syndicate

DEPRESSION—THE HIDDEN KILLER

Janice Simmons was a little girl when it started. Days of mood swings and anger and sadness that seemed to zip by "under a dark, dark cloud." The inner turmoil never went away. Janice is now a young woman, a woman who has survived three suicide attempts, a broken marriage, and institutionalization—finding out nearly 24 years later that she suffers from a severe form of depression. Medical professionals now say her depression is treatable and more common than the rest of the world can imagine.

"If we knew then what we know now, many lives could have been saved and many women like Janice could have led much different lives," said Dr. Bernard Calhoon with the Mayo Clinic in Rochester, Minnesota. "This depression is a disease, no one asks for it, but for years we have treated it like it's a form of leprosy."

Calhoon and other psychiatric specialists agree that the misunderstood illnesses of the mind are often hidden by men and women who try to deal with their problems alone because they don't think anyone will understand.

"It's also no secret that people are fearful of someone with mental illness," said Dr. Susan Ellis, with the New York Psychological Institute. "We can see a broken leg or cancer and we understand that, but when a person is depressed or on the brink of some horrible mental episode, we tend to treat that illness entirely different."

It hasn't been that many years since anyone who had

a mental problem was simply locked away at places with names like the Territorial Insane Asylum.

"In many ways, society's means for dealing with mental illnesses of all forms has not changed much in the past 50 years," said Ellis, who has conducted numerous studies with new drugs that are now giving hope to millions of people suffering from severe depression throughout the country. "We have the drugs, and now we need to open up the minds in the rest of the world."

Today, thanks to research, new drugs and public awareness campaigns, life for people with severe depression no longer has a bleak future.

"There are still things to learn, but we have saved lives and there is hope," said Calhoon. "People such as Janice Simmons can get their lives back, and that's a miracle of science."

The Elegant Gathering: Janice

There was a time not so many years ago when I could not even imagine an adventure like this. Not so many years ago when my idea to fling myself in front of the train was interrupted by that Elegant Gathering of the White Snows. Not so many years ago at all when my life was a charade of locked doors and window shades that were never lifted and lives, so many lives, that were covered in shadows, waiting, and then waiting some more for me to shift my weight and get on with it, just get on with it all.

I think my mother knew long before I did. Long before she held me in her wide hands and called out my name for the very first time, whispering "Sweet baby girl, my beautiful baby girl, little Janice, what have I done, what have I done?"

Now that I have come across my own mountains and settled into life as it was meant to be in the first place, I can't help this feeling of overwhelming sadness for what life must have been like for my mother. Although the medical world of her 1930s and 40s chose to deal with mental illness by mostly ignoring it, my mother was a bright, beautiful woman who knew that if she let anyone know about her dark, secret world, very possibly the tiny fragments of her life that gave her light and hope would be torn from her. They would carry her away if they knew what she was really thinking, take her away from me.

Before she died, when she knew that I was going to make it and live and enjoy life in a way that she was never able to, my mother and I finally talked about that part of our lives. About the dark nights and days, about the uncontrollable urge to surrender to the great well of sadness that was always licking at our heels.

In a cruel twist of fate, my mother found out just months after her medication finally offered her mind some hope, that she had breast cancer. My only solace in the nights and days of the few months that I took care of her was that I could finally do something for her. My mother, because she knew exactly how I felt, had taken care of me and the girls and Paul for so many years I am ashamed to remember them all.

It was my mother's physical illness that finally brought me to my knees at her bedside. We both knew on that cool summer morning that there weren't many days left for her. We both knew that within hours she might slip away into that dark place where you go before you cross over.

For months and months, I had watched my mother fall another inch or two away from me, grinding in pain, first on her couch, then in her bed, then back at the hospital and then back to her own bed. My parents had both chosen a new hospice program because my mother wanted to die at home. And really, after a certain point, there wasn't a damn thing traditional medicine could do to help her except keep her doped up to control the pain, which was something both my father and I demanded. My own depression was under control by then, just six years ago, and after all the years that I had spent crying, I found it a miracle that I could lie on her bathroom floor and cry for 30 minutes straight without stopping. One part of me was glad that I could manage to dig so deep inside of myself, in all those scary and sick places. The rest of me, most of me, was overcome with a grief that defies description.

Throughout the 16 years when my depression had been rifling through my life full speed ahead, there had only been my mother to understand and hold me. Only my mother who would know, without me saying a word—when I showed up at her door with the girls in my arms, dark circles under my eyes, and the smell of gin on my breath—that I was caught up again. Only my mother, who would take the girls and tuck them into my old double bed and put on the teapot and then hold me like a baby on the couch while I cried and cried. She was able to hold me back from the edge, from the damned dark edge.

I thought I was prepared for everything after that. I thought because I had managed to climb out of my own hole that I could handle everything for once in my life with grace and elegance and with all my wits about me. But that was before I knew my mother was dying and that she needed me as much as I needed her.

That morning when we talked, the last time we ever spoke to each other using words and not just our eyes, was one of those cool summer mornings for which Wisconsin is famous. It was early June, and it should have been at least mildly hot by then, but spring that year would not relinquish its hold on our part of the world. That morning I was firm about making certain my father went to see his pals for a while downtown at the coffee shop. After I had organized my mother's medication for the day, I popped open her bedroom window just a crack to let in a wisp of fresh air. I knew she liked that, and that throughout her entire life she had always slept with the window open.

My mother turned toward the window when she felt the cool air move across her bed. She closed her eyes and looked as if she was drinking in something fine and wonderful. "Come here, sweetie," she said as I watched her open her eyes and look at me. I sat on her bed, brushed her hair back from her forehead and then leaned down to kiss her on the lips.

"It's spring out there yet, Mom, and I thought you might like a little air."

"Thank you, Janice. What day is it?"

"It's Friday, Mom, the first Friday in June."

"Is Paul gone now?"

"No, he's been working the local trucking runs for awhile now and the girls love it. After all these years they're sick of me, and he lets them get away with murder."

My mother was thinking. I watched her shift her eyes, and then she lifted her hand and put it on top of mine.

"For so long now I've wanted to tell you how sorry I am about the depression and all."

"Mom . . ."

"No, please honey, listen for just a minute because I know there isn't much time left. I know that and I have to say this."

"Okay, Mom, okay."

"When you were born, I was so scared. I knew there was a chance that you would have what I have because I had read and read and talked to doctors, so I knew that you might end up sick like I was. Oh Janice, I'm so sorry about what I passed on to you, so sorry. I've always wanted to tell you how sorry I am."

"Mom, *I'm* not sorry. You saved me. You really saved me all those days and nights and through everything, you were always there. You never abandoned me. To never have known you and for you to have never known me, that would be so much worse."

"Janice, it's okay now, isn't it? You're going to make it now, aren't you, sweetheart?"

"Oh, Mom, it's not going to be easy without you, but I'm going to be fine and the girls are fine. You taught me how to be such a good mother. That's something I've always wanted to tell you. Thanks for showing me how to do that. How to love so much and sacrifice and mostly how to hang on and never give up."

My mother somehow managed to raise both of her hands and place them around my face. I could feel little pockets of warmness where she touched me, and I placed my own hands over hers. Then I laid down on the bed next to her, tucked my arm under her neck and held her against me while the birds sang and the phone rang and the few hours that she had left ticked away.

The months following my mother's funeral were not easy. I waited and waited for time to heal me, but I could tell time for me was going to be years and years. I was doing pretty well, working part-time, shuffling the girls around to all their activities, making certain that Paul knew I still loved him. Then my father called one day and said he was ready to clean out my mother's things. "Would you please come?"

This was not so long ago. Five years ago is not so long ago now that I am way past 40. It was long enough though for me to have been on medicine, finally the right dose of antidepressant, for me to gain enough years that I often felt perfectly normal, as if I would even know what that was like. Mostly I could tell I was doing good because I was happy, and only sad when I thought about normal things that make people sad, like the death of your only mother.

My father was a mess that day I got to his house. He was pacing in the kitchen, and he had boxes lined up on the kitchen table. He told me he wasn't sure he could even touch Mother's clothing.

"Janice, I think this is too hard for me," he said, standing with his head bowed and his arms dangling at his sides.

"Daddy," I moved to him, placing my hands around his stooped shoulders and pressing my face against his. "It will be fine," I lied, "You just go out today, call Ralph and go to lunch, and then go hang out at his house. I'll call you when I'm done."

My father is a kind man who put up with two raving lunatics for most of his life. I owed him almost as much as I owed my mother, and when he left quickly, I stood in the kitchen with my stomach in knots, trying hard to stay balanced, trying to make certain that my old demons would not reawaken in the midst of all the memories I was about to touch.

Since my mother's death, my father had been unable to sleep in their bedroom so their room was filled with her things, and her smell. Everything that I saw when I went into the room was a painful reminder of the woman who had been my lifeline since the day I was born. After a year, her cotton bathrobe was still hanging behind the door, and when I turned to grab it, I buried my head inside of it and smelled the soft scent. Then I wept, thinking perhaps I could get it out of the way and get on with my horrible task. That did help, though I cried on and off during the next four hours anyway.

I filled the boxes my father had collected with her clothes, one with underwear, another with sweaters, socks, and so many shoes I started to laugh when I remembered how my mother loved new shoes more than anything. There were 24 pairs in all, lined up on the floor of her closet, just as she had left them so many months ago.

My father had instructed me to take apart the entire bedroom. He had decided to paint it and use it as a guest room, so I took all the pictures off the wall, the ones of mostly me at various stages of my life as an only child. This is what my mother looked at, I thought, all those days when she was unable to do anything but lie here and remember. Me in those little brown and white shoes. Me with my head tipped to the side and standing by my first two wheeler. Me, hands on hips, tongue wagging at the camera. Me graduating from high school, then the wedding, then the babies. My mother centered her life around me. Always me.

I saved her jewelry box for last and decided to scrounge through my father's refrigerator for a beer while I sat on the bed and picked through the necklaces and pins and earrings. I kept some of the pieces for the girls, the ones that I remember my mother wearing. I kept her high school ring, some gold earrings and a long gold chain that I vaguely remember playing with one of those long nights when Mother helped me keep those terrible dark thoughts at bay.

There was one particularly terrible time when I was pregnant the first time, and unable to take medication or drink or do any single thing at all to try and keep myself sane. My mother knew how terrible it was for me then, because even though her depression was a much milder form than mine, she too had suffered through pregnancy. I knew because of what she told me before she died that she was full of guilt.

Those months and months of waiting for the baby to come were by far the worst days of my life. Often, I would simply leave, especially if Paul was gone, and go to a hotel alone. My mother always knew where I was and I knew where she was. All I did was watch television and click my fingers against each other, counting endlessly to try and keep my mind on one thing.

Twice my mother had the hospital come and get me because she was afraid that I might hurt myself. I was only violent a few times, and it must have been terrifying for my mother to see me that way. What I found at the bottom of her jewelry box showed me how frightened she had been, and it is the reason why I am thinking every minute that there are still many things I need to forget and forgive. That is why I am walking, walking so hard and so fast that I wonder why we have not reached the river that separates the United States from Mexico.

The bundle of papers I found in the bottom of her jewelry box were scraps of menus, little notepad papers, receipts and other paper odds and ends about four inches thick—put together, one could call them a journal or a diary. When I found them, I had no idea what they were at first, and I set down my beer and began rifling through the stack.

"Dec. 12, 1956 . . . Today my little baby is just two months old and when I look into her eyes I try to see deep, deep into her mind. Is there anything there? Will she get it too? Will my little baby girl, so beautiful, be overcome with the darkness?"

"Oh, my God!" That's what I said to myself over and over when I read the papers, some of them ragged where my mother's fingers might have touched them a thousand times. I put my fingers there and when I closed my eyes, I could see her crouched over some table in a cafe, a cigarette in her left hand burning to the tip as she wrote her heart out.

"Jan. 24, 1963...Today little Janice has been sitting all day just staring out the window. Now I know, I know for sure that she sees horrible things. I tried to go to her and hold her, but she pushed me away and cried and cried. Finally she came to me and said, 'Mama, I feel so sad, I just feel so sad.'"

I dared not read many more of these notes from my mother because I could not remember any of the things that she was talking about, and there was no way in hell I wanted to remember.

My severe depression bordered on every other mental disease known to man. One step south, and I could have been a flying mongoose. Another step east, and I could manifest 13 different people inside of my brain. By the time I discovered my mother's diary, I already considered myself to be lucky. Lucky to be alive, to be better, to be able to function and to recognize colors and the beauty in the smile of my own babies, and in all the sunsets and sunrises that blew past my house.

But I also know, and will always live with the fact that every day of my life is a gift that might be taken away. My mind remains constantly crammed with "what ifs." What if my chemistry shifts, and the current medicine no longer works? What if I'm struck by a car and go into a coma where I can sense everything but can't speak, and they take away the medicine and leave me there inside of myself like a trapped rat? What if my daughters—who are absolutely fine and healthy and mentally alert—develop this same disease in five years or when they have their own babies? What if Paul is finally sickened by the thought of living with a crazy woman who may dip over the edge at any minute?

And Paul, what about Paul? Paul who was gone lots and lots

but who always came back and looked into my eyes as if he had just realized he loved me? What about Paul who still has the long and lean muscles of the 18-year-old boy/man I fell in love with? Paul, who bakes bread and built me a flower garden in the shape of a heart, who takes his extra money to buy me a $12 bottle of wine instead of the new things he needs for the truck? This is the man who can turn me on by simply lifting his pant leg. When he steps into the shower each morning and I watch him moving through that clear glass I made him install, one look at his lean body and the water is enough to make me want to dive on him through the shower door.

I used to wonder if maybe it wasn't a secret blessing that we are doomed to this middle class life, because he loves to drive his truck. He has a degree in accounting from the University of Michigan, but chose to follow his heart and become a truck driver. Sometimes I think maybe the truck that took him away so much before he switched to local routes, maybe that truck saved us because he never saw everything.

Maybe if Paul would have seen me pounding my head on the table and locking the girls out of the bedroom and crawling on my hands and knees through the living room because I was afraid if I got up I would fling myself off the balcony, maybe if Paul saw all that over and over again, he would have had a hard time remembering why he loved me.

Not that he didn't see enough. Paul saw and heard plenty. He held me too, and walked the girls for mile after mile in the old stroller while I tried to figure out how in the hell I was going to make it through the next five minutes. He listened to me tell him at least 5,000 times that he would be much better off without me, and that he should just take the girls and leave "or better yet, I'll leave and you keep the house." He always stopped me at the door, even when I scratched his face and drew blood. Still he held me, firmly but gently and then carried me to the bedroom, where he would pull back the covers and put me in the sheets and get in beside me. There we lay, him holding me while I cried and cried. Hours later, when the girls got up and I couldn't move, Paul made me dinner and breakfast and called in sick. This happened more than I want to admit.

It has taken me so long, so damned long to think that I even deserve to be loved by a man like Paul. Yesterday Chris was telling me what a shit she had been to her husband who followed her from one end of the world to the next, often rescuing her from the arms of vicious men and circumstances. She told me that men like Paul and Alex surely know a good thing when they see it, and we talked for such a long time about being able to forgive yourself, just forgive yourself for things you had no choice about.

"Paul is still there," she told me. "He's crazy about you. Do you see the way he looks at you when you do something exotic like walk out the goddamned door? Lord, girl, he knew that under all that crazy shit there was Janice. Janice the woman he fell in love with all those years ago. Love, baby. That's what real love is all about."

I hear that, I know that in my heart, but then I think about my mother and all the guilt that weighed her down all those years. Actually the stress probably gave her the cancer that killed her. I don't want that to happen to me. I don't want to watch my life crumble ever again, and I don't want my daughters to find notes about my sadness when they are rummaging through my underwear drawers after I have died.

They both know, though. They know about severe depression, and although they claim they only have good memories of staying at grandma's while Mama "went off," they know the truth because I decided there was no sense in hiding what could become a reality from them. So we have read books and talked to doctors, and sometimes I see them watching me with their eyes narrowed and such a serious look on their faces, as if they are wondering if I am going to go off the deep end at any moment.

Some of our discussions have been quite magical. Like the time Mattie and I were sitting in front of the fake gas fireplace Paul built for us as a Christmas gift. Mattie wanted to know what it was like those times when I couldn't recall my name or where I lived or that I had anything wonderful like her in my life. Cassie and Paul were out getting a pizza, and Mattie and I had hot chocolate. We were sitting right in front of the fireplace, holding hands, shoulders pushed into each other, talking—just like my mother and I used to do.

"Mom, what did you see those times, you know, when it was so crazy inside of your mind?"

"Mostly it was just this overwhelming feeling of sadness. I could look at you or you sister or dad, all people whom I love so much, and I would see or feel nothing wonderful and good. Only this terrible, terrible feeling that I was ruining everything and there was no hope."

Mattie grew quiet, and I saw her 14-year-old wheels turning, and she was squeezing my hand so hard I thought she might bruise me.

"Was it hard to stay, Mom, did you just want to go away and leave us?"

"Lots of times, sweetie. I thought you might be better off without me, and I prayed, and your grandma, oh your grandma, she always stood by me and kept you safe. She made it easier for me to stay. Otherwise, yes, I might have left and who knows what would have happened?"

"We read about this homeless lady in Social Studies and then we saw a film about her. She had a family and a good job, but she was schizophrenic and she couldn't find the right medicine. She ended up living in a box in New York. That made me so sad,

Mom. I thought about you and about how weird my life would be without you and everything."

"Honey, so many people loved me and helped me. Your daddy, he always loved me even when he knew I was sick, and he helped me. And you and your sister. I knew that no matter what I did, you would love me too, just like I'll always love you."

"Mom, if you ever get sick again and because you know, because Grandma isn't here any more, well, I'll take care of you. I can do everything like she did, and make sure you are safe and everything. Just so you know, Mom, just don't go away, even if I'm mean and act like a teenager. Don't ever go away, Mom."

That talk with Mattie would have made my own mother so proud and happy. If she could have seen how bright and happy and sensitive the girls have turned out, she would know that every single painful thing that we went through was worth it. She would know that her spirit and her heart and her caring and never giving up have helped create an entire generation of young women who will change the world.

That is what I believe with all my heart. Even when the girls act like little jackasses and throw stuff out their bedroom doors and pout because I won't let them do stupid things like rent a hotel room the night of prom or drive to Fort Lauderdale for Easter break, even then I know that they have hearts as strong as their grandmother's. They will always love me, and if they had to, they would hold me back from that dark abyss.

But there is still so much to put behind me, and I have to sort out what to save and what to throw away. There may be a time when I will be able to read all those notes my mother kept. Chris seems to think I should use them to write something to help other people. She thinks I have undersold my abilities with my English degree by working part-time at a video store. She wants me to get a teacher's certificate and work with high school kids, and maybe

I'll be able to do that when I figure out how to get beyond the same guilt that consumed my mother.

Every day out here walking on the road is like a new beginning for me. Every moment that I can look to one side and see my friends and then look up and see this blue spring sky watching over us. Sometimes, like that night at the Bed and Breakfast where we talked about The Elegant Gathering of the White Snows and we all cried and said what a wonderful thing this was to just be doing to make us all feel better and to do it with people who care, at times like that I have to shake my head because I can almost feel my mother.

I can also smell that soapy scent of hers, and I can feel her hands touching against my face. The way she studied me when she thought I was not looking still makes my heart skip to a fine rhythm that must be the music from her own heart. I can see her eyes filled with such kindness and love for me that it is as if she is right here with me on this great walking adventure.

If she is here, if she is still watching out for me and the girls and Paul, I would want her to know that I have never been finer, that I am onto something glorious, and that I am ready to try a few new things in my life.

I'm betting that my mother could look into my eyes and see that my soul is healing, and because she held onto me with such fierceness, she saved my life.

With every step I take out here, I seem to feel lighter, seem to see more light, seem to feel a strong pulse of life beating through me. I think this light has the chance to overtake any darkness that might try to sneak up on me.

Maybe when I am finished, and my mother knows that she is here inside of my beating heart, maybe she will finally fly free herself and rest quietly. She will know that she was wonderful and made me wonderful too, and whole and happy.

CHAPTER NINE

G AIL PUSHED HER LEG against the side of J.J. and tossed a huge
oak log into a campfire that was already the size of a small
barn. "Oh man," she said, lifting her head towards the rising
flames. "I haven't had this much fun since Girl Scout camp."

Not suprisingly, Chris had a different memory of Girl Scout
camp. She quickly launched into a story about losing her virginity on the floor on an old platform tent with an assistant cook.
According to Chris, this young stud had the perfect recipe for
making his customers happy campers. A huge scar that launched
at her right hip and moved into the upper part of her thigh was
definite proof of her positive first night of lust and love.

"The tent floor?"

"Yeah, you remember those big old wooden tent floors and
that smell of moldy canvas and the assistant cook? My gawd, did-
n't anyone have guys at camp who worked in the kitchen or as the
handyman?"

The women had gathered up a huge pile of wood from the miles of trees surrounding them. Mary set them up on her brother-in-law's uncle's farm, with sleeping bags and shiny blue tarps spread out under this seventh starry night in a row. Coolers of beer and wine called to them seductively. Everyone agreed that Mary deciding not to walk was doing wonders for their appetites. Still, they missed her at the campfire and when they talked for hours into the night.

"It was hard to tell the girls from the guys at our camp, especially if they were counselors," quipped Sandy, relating back to the story about the night Chris lost her virginity to the naughty cook. "If I only would have known then what I know now, I wouldn't have bothered trying to seduce that little twit stable boy. There were plenty of attractive girls now that I think about it. They were all most likely sleeping with each other."

"The tent floor," begs Alice. "Let's get back to the tent floor."

"The cook was young but very beautiful, and he had me fooled if he was a virgin himself. I think he was crazy about me."

"Oh sure, he liked you," laughed Susan. "Have your breasts always been this large?"

"I remember that he liked me and that's what I'm stickin' to, you smartass."

"Go ahead, lie to yourself, but just finish the story."

"The sex wasn't anything really spectacular, like all the great sex that followed many years later, but from what I've heard from you ladies, it could have been a hell of a lot worse. We got into some heavy petting on his bunk bed, rolled onto the floor, and when I flipped off my jeans, he got a little too excited and tried to drag me right onto him. This chunk of wood from the old floor lodged itself right inside half my body."

"Geez, didn't that sort of put a kink on the moment?"

"Actually, he bent over me, his long hair fell across my large breasts and the way he touched me as he pulled out the splinter was so erotic I almost didn't wait for him."

"Chris, that's about the sweetest story you ever told us," moaned Janice. "Of course every single story you do tell us has something to do with blood or guts or gunfire, so you should have known way back then about your exciting destiny."

The camp stories from everyone flew like bullets then. Stories of burning down buildings; the summer the lifeguard got pregnant and someone finally had to sit her down and get her to a doctor; the next year when the entire van load of female counselors drove into town. They picked up every single man they could get their hands on, and partied until the sun came up.

Alice hauled out the marshmallows and lined up little pieces of chocolate on top of graham crackers. When the women huddled around the fire to make s'mores, Alice said that she was glad they were camping one last time because she had never been to camp.

"Well, Alice, we ain't driving into town to pick up guys tonight," said Sandy. "So you'd better keep your little hands on that stick there."

"What did you mean by calling this the last time camping, Alice?" asked J.J.

Alice lifted her eyes, and in the light of the campfire she looked so incredibly beautiful that J.J. wanted to lean through the flames and touch her face. Her gray hair framed her face, and her wide eyes were glowing in the light of the campfire.

"Well, it's almost time to stop, you know."

Susan stood up then, shifted her weight from one foot to the other and then walked around the fire. She stopped behind Alice and rested her hands on Alice's shoulders until she grounded herself in the cool earth. Then she slowly pushed the hair out of her eyes.

"It's me," she said softly into the crackling wood. "I need to get to a doctor and get on with everything. I'm not sure I want to wait much longer, and Alice, Alice is starting to have a little problem with her knees. All those years of pulling weeds out of the garden, huh Alice?"

Alice smiled but she didn't turn around. She covered the top of Susan's hand with her own.

Chris looked up and saw that Alice and Susan looked more like mother and daughter than simple friends who loved each other. Alice cocked her head to the right just a tiny bit when she talked, and so did Susan. Both women were not very tall, and Chris often wondered if their short bones rubbed against each other as they walked mile after mile. She knew that Alice would go to the doctor with Susan, and then take her home and sit with her through the night. She also knew that for the rest of their lives, Susan would be the daughter that Alice lost.

"It's going to be better than you think," Chris finally said, breaking the silence. "When, Susan? Tomorrow, the next day, how much longer?"

Susan sighed, looking relieved to have said what she needed to say.

"I don't even know what day it is. I can walk a little more, it's just that I'm scared, and I don't want to wait to have an abortion. I feel strong about this, and if I wait, I don't know. I just don't know."

When some sparks cracked and flew out of the fire, Sandy jumped to mash them with her feet, then walked over to Susan and kissed her on the check. "Two more nights? Can you handle tonight and then just a little more walking and then one final night?"

Susan nodded in agreement, and Alice shifted her weight, and then Gail jumped up and started passing out beer, hugging each one of her friends as she handed them a drink. "I love you," she whispered six times. J.J. suggested that they forge a plan for leaving the following day.

The stars shifted then, and the brilliant spring sky looked like a dark, singular blanket that had been placed in just the perfect spot, miles above the campfire over a small Wisconsin forest where the whispers of a group of women were lifted high into the night air. Whispers filled with bonds of love and abandoned sorrow, and the hopes and wishes of these women with the courage to plow ahead through the challenges of their lives into the destinies they would fashion beyond that point. Whispers that spoke of love and loss and of circling hearts within the hot fire of friendship. Whispers that floated onto thousands of window ledges where other women were waiting for permission, for the moment when they could rise up through the dark and begin walking themselves. The whispers floated through Wilkins County and out across the Great Plains and through cornfields that were just beginning to rise up above the ankles of all the farming women.

Those women cranked their necks into the night air as they walked towards the barns, and saw the flickering lights jumping back and forth between the windy whispers. These farming women who rarely rested, stopped suddenly and felt a breeze, as warm and comforting as the hot baths they dreamed about, float through their bones. The women smiled and they walked on and they felt a push at their hearts that would stay with them for a long time.

The whispers glided across the mountains that separate the East from the West, and all the women who were poised with their heads towards the hills—those women felt the last of the day's sun change from hot to cold in just a moment, in just the time it takes to blink. All those mountain women who often forget in their busy days to look West before Aspen glow, before the bright orange sun blazes a mellow, moody light on the rocky cliffs, all those women were suddenly unable to keep their eyes off the mountains. They stood quietly with their hands dangling at their sides, and watched as their day melted quickly into night. They took in breath-tiny particles of the whispers, and they felt stronger and eager to stand alone and think about the joys and sorrows of life and all the possibilities that can straddle a hungry soul.

Near the oceans and the green, lush forests along the coast for hundreds of miles, all the women who were driving home from work and picking up their children from soccer practice and dance lessons and science club, all those women were amazed when out of nowhere a warm, lusty breeze—like a lover's urgent whisper—made them stick their hands out of their car windows. These women separated their fingers and let the powerful wind move inside of their skin and into the muscles and fibers and molecules that formed their hearts and souls and every ounce of them. When the whisper of a breeze stopped as suddenly as it began, the women who had felt it gained a sudden charge of life and love. Those women smiled, and they knew that whatever they made happen next in their lives would be amazing.

The whispers picked up strength then, and floated from one country to the next, dipping down here and there when a woman stood alone or seemed frightened or unsure of which direction to turn. The whispers breezed across China and into the mountains, where beautiful women stood holding baskets full of the green leaves of a tea called The Elegant Gathering of the White Snows. As these women gathered the leaves, they stopped suddenly, every single one of them, when they felt something as warm as a burning fire push across their sweaty faces. They looked from one side of the mountain to the other. They raised their eyes toward the heavens, and then they looked at each other. They were moved to tears just to know that someone else, another woman, had felt the moving wind, the whisper of this warm breeze. They cried, yet their tears were warm and soothing, and the women who were gathering the tea leaves would always remember how the warm wind stilled their hearts and made them happy for those moments on the beautiful, steep mountain.

In all the other countries, in the places where women were watching their own babies die and where sons and daughters would disappear and in all the places where soldiers carried guns and the world was always dark, even in those places there was a hint of a breeze that night. Women felt they could look up and catch the eye of a female neighbor or another woman who was headed toward the river. Without a word or a gesture, they would smile and laugh and circle their arms around each other, touching hands and hearts. In a second and then another two or three, when the whisper had moved on and the pop of a gun or the crack of another heartbreak would bring them back, they would always remember the whisper and how that woman on the street held her to her breast and felt so warm and so alive.

The force of the whisper was unknown in Wisconsin, where the women had joined their energies to create a night of love and laughter. They looked into each other's eyes, and they felt a love and tenderness as strong and enduring as any love they had or would ever know. They saw lines reaching out from the corners of each other's eyes, and they knew exactly where the tears of their friends had fallen and where they had landed. Those women walkers held hands and shared drinks and sometimes they kissed each other and felt the warm softness that can only be found on another woman's lips. Once in awhile, one of the women would turn her head away from her friends and look into the dark night sky just to make certain that everything was real, that it really was a spring night and that everyone was actually sitting right there by the roaring fire in the middle of nowhere.

The women knew who would get up first to go to the bathroom, and who would want to lie down before the conversations had slid to a sleepy halt. They knew who would be up first cooking breakfast, and who would roll into them when the temperature dipped and there was no other way to get warm. Each one of them knew who would have the hardest time when the walking stopped, and who would be the woman to make certain that they all stayed in touch and kept their ears to the ground and their hearts right.

Sandy could look into J.J.'s eyes and see every misstep and every single regret in her life. In a flash, Alice who had a life like none of them, could pull each one of them to her chest and hold them with such a powerful force that they could feel her beating heart. They would know that if nothing else worked, if they took a step back, Alice would love them.

The women, like all the women who hear whispers, could talk for hours without saying a word. They could sit across from each other at a campfire or at a restaurant or walking down a highway and move their eyes and dip their heads in such a way that they could read the interior chapters of each other's minds. The unspoken words could carry them through a lifetime, past every heartache.

The hard part for all of them would be stretching out the next hours, remembering every footstep, every breath, every moment that they could claim for themselves and no one else. The way the sun skipped across Susan's hair as she walked sideways, and the way Janice always talked with her hands moving and shouting with her fingers spread apart. The moments when Gail would close her eyes and put her hand on Sandy's shoulder and walk like that, without looking for one mile and then another, thinking the whole time of each step as if she had never walked before.

They would all think of Mary, watching over them like a hovering bird from just the right distance, and they planned over and over what they would tell her, especially how much they missed her.

All of them watched the flames dancing and each one thought how intoxicating the fire was, how it told its own story and consumed itself to keep going—just like them. When the coals were fanned out in clumps, the women all pushed in another foot and held out their hands, and they would remember that circle of fingers touching, hovering above a flaming banner of wood.

There were at least 100 stories yet to tell, and who would go next? That was the question always, and what would they save for next time? Would there be anything left?

Alice told them about taking a bath in the barn while Chester held a lamp above her, watching for 30 minutes as she washed her face, her arms, her breasts, her small legs. "If I could do that again," Alice told her friends, "I would make Chester put the lamp on the box and take off all of his clothes. Then I would get on top of him, all wet and soapy, and I would make love to him until he howled."

"Alice," said Chris, placing a hand across her friend's wrist like a doctor checking for a pulse, "You can still do that! You don't ever have to wait for anything again."

"But the barn is gone now," said Alice in all seriousness.

"I can get you a barn," laughed Chris, who had almost always believed that anything and everything is possible. "I can get you a barn and a tub and I can bring you Chester, Alice. You can count on me."

"Oh, do you think?" said Alice. "I have thought about that so many times. I can't even believe I am telling you this but Chris, could you really find me a barn?"

"Honey, I'd build it myself if I had to. I'll get you a barn. You can bet on that."

Everyone closed their eyes and imagined Alice as a young and beautiful woman in love with a clumsy man who could never bring himself to tell his wife the secrets of his heart. They watched Alice drop her skirt and roll off her stockings and dip first one foot and then the other into the tub of steaming water. They watched as Alice ran her hand down her arm and across her beautiful breasts and then down, down into the water.

"Alice," said Susan. "You are still a very beautiful woman."

"Thank you, sweetheart. I've never quite felt this beautiful in my whole life."

Then Janice talked about how she was ready to rest her heart, finally and forever in one place. "I'm tired of all this ridiculous shit that I've put Tim and the girls through. Pretty damned tired," she told her friends as she swigged down her fourth beer. "You know what, I'm also getting a little bit crocked out here, and I feel great."

The women laughed, and the laughter rolled from one mouth to the next, as if in the end there had just been one laugh and one mouth and one woman sitting beside a fire in the middle of the rolling Wisconsin hills.

Sandy didn't need to say it, because everyone already knew, but she did anyway. She said she had developed a severe case of the hots for Lenny Sorensen and for the first time since she had lost the true love of her life, she felt as if she might be able to love again. "The minute I saw her, standing out there like that on the lawn, my entire world pretty much dropped to a spot that lingers just below my belly button. My fingers tingled, my breasts tilted sideways, I had this sudden desire to lie down right there and shout, 'Take me!' I kissed her, you know."

"You're kidding!" Chris hated not to know something.

"Where the hell was I?"

"Not looking."

"So what's the plan? How are you going to make this work?"

"Perfectly. I'm going to make this work perfectly, and I'm going to do anything, whatever it takes in my world to make something happen. I've been so fucking lonely and needy and wanting and desirous."

"All those other women in your life?"

"Just helping me fill in the blanks. I care about them all. I do. But I need someone who grabs my heart, makes me bend over with wanting, who can look into my soul and see who I am and what forms the craters of my life. It also helps if this woman happens to have breasts that call out my name and an ass that looks as if it was made to fit the contours of my hands."

The instantaneous laughter is a bullet, ricocheting from one woman to the next. Susan alters the mood when she begins talking about the abortion and knowing there are hundreds of couples who would raise the baby, but the pregnancy would kill her, it would just kill her.

"I just can't have this baby. Physically and mentally. I'm old and tired and I need to start over. Right now. Not in a few months. I have to do it now."

"Susan. We'll rent a big van and all go with you, honey," said Janice. "This is your decision, and I think it's the right one. This is your life, your body, and by god, we're going to help you make it all work. Would you like us to beat the shit out of the baby's father?"

Susan told them it was a waste of perfectly good energy to want to kill someone so weak and helpless. She suggested more beer, and when they discovered that the beer was gone, the women moved to the wine, which they knew would prove to be a costly mistake in the morning, yet they forged on recklessly.

Wonderful Mary had included brand new wine glasses and bags of snacks, and if it were not for the blazing fire and the fact that they were not on Susan's floor, the women could have been anywhere, anywhere at all.

Within an hour, Alice crawled into her sleeping bag and then Susan joined her. Chris and Janice talked for another hour about collaborating on a magazine article about depression, and Janice agreed that if she shared her story, if she talked personally on a level that would expose her years of hell and heartache, maybe someone else might be spared even a day of the same misery.

"It's not the same if you don't use your real name, but sometimes people can't handle that. You'd have to ask Tim and the girls how they feel," said Chris. "You'd have to be sure."

"They would want me to do what I could to help someone else, that's what I think," Janice said. "They would also know that whatever I do, it's my decision, a choice for me."

Janice thought for a moment, added that her mother would know that with survival comes a kind of debt, a debt that needs to be repaid. "It's a cosmic thing. I've made it, and if I can help someone else make it, then something good, even something better, will come right back to me. Is that too goofy?"

"Look out, here comes the old 60s cosmic justice theory that has never been proven wrong by me. Even when I tell someone to fuck off, I usually get the same thing back. You'd think I would learn."

"It's tough to balance how you feel inside sometimes with doing what you think needs to be done."

"Well, I haven't killed anyone yet, and I've wanted to do that about 600 times, so I guess I'm more in control than I think."

As the night wore on Sandy, Gail and J.J. lingered the longest by the fire. They tossed log after log into the flames, sitting in the silence, watching the wood burn itself out until another log brought it back to life. The three women sat close, wrapped their arms around each other, held hands, waited in the cold while they took turns shuffling off to nature's bathroom in the trees.

"It's not so bad to love women, is it?" Sandy asked, rhetorically.

"I've never felt bad about all the pain and suffering we end up going through because of all the other good stuff," said J.J. "To be totally accepted and loved and to know someone will be there for you no matter what happens is an absolutely perfect feeling."

"I think we all have the potential of loving a woman like you do, Sandy," Gail said, turning to look Sandy in the eyes. "Maybe this next generation of women who have been even more free with their affections and emotions than we have, maybe they will even be more honest."

Sandy rolled onto her left hip and pushed her legs out in front of her, thinking the whole time how fine it felt to be talking about her favorite subject. "Women can find such comfort in each other, it's a shame all this sexual bullshit even got started. Some of the times when I was the saddest in my life, all I wanted was to just have someone hold me. Usually I didn't want that someone to be a man, because he was usually the reason why I was so goddamned sad to begin with. Not that I was perfect or anything, but women are so much less self-centered and open and caring and sensitive. What was I thinking?"

J.J. reminisced. "But remember before we started telling people to eat shit, remember how people laughed about things like how we could go to the bathroom in front of each other and sleep in the same bed and how we always seemed to know how the other woman felt, remember how it really changed how we treated each other?" She smiled and stared at the fire. "My god, is there anything better than lying in bed with a friend and talking and feeling her warm legs next to yours and just knowing from the center of your being that you are safe and loved. That the world could spin away and those feelings of closeness and safety would not change?"

The conversation eventually drifted away into the mechanics of male and female personalities. The stars eventually shifted, and the sky grew light where it touched the horizon.

"What's that?" Gail asked. "Is all that light from the city?"

"It's the entire world, thousands and thousands of people looking for us with flashlights," Sandy declared.

The women laughed, and Gail rose up to make certain that everyone who was sleeping was covered up. She threw two more logs on the fire and stood in the growing light, looking like a strong and brilliant light herself.

"You know we are the only ones who have been looking for ourselves," she said, her voice a small echo above the snapping wood. "I suppose we'll look back on this and say we could have done this sooner and saved ourselves years of anguish over all our problems. But really, it's like love or sex, or knowing anything . . . it just can't happen until the stars are lined up properly and everything."

"You mean like three months ago or last year, we could never have done this, but a week ago, that was the perfect time?" asked J.J.

"Yeah," said Gail, shrugging against the wind that cut into her back. "Yeah, it was just the right time."

"But you know maybe now we can make any time the right time," suggested Sandy. "Even me, the ballsy bitch. It's been hard these last few years for me to do what I knew I needed to do, but now I feel strong and healed and ready to reclaim everything I let slip away."

"She'll be ready, too," said Gail, pointing in the direction of Lenny's house. "The stars are going to be lined up just perfectly for the rest of our lives."

J.J. jumped up and pushed her hands out to the side. She smiled and patted Sandy on the shoulder. "Hell, if those stars aren't lined up just the way we like'm, we'll shove the little bastards right where we think they should go."

The women rolled into their own sleeping bags, tucked their jackets under their heads for pillows and watched the fire dance and dance, until their eyes closed and there was the simple hum of quiet bodies, even breaths and the embers burning slowly into the earth.

In the last few hours before dawn, the women walkers didn't feel the whisper of another wind roll over them. They didn't know in those sleepy hours that their hearts beat in unison, and that when one of them sighed, the rest of them felt a reciprocal push of air. They didn't know that their breaths mingled with the breaths of millions of women, and that their souls would be entwined in those whispers forever.

All their dreams were soft, gentle and beautiful; when the fire burned away into the ground and there was nothing but a warm glow in the dirt, all of the women were warm. They rolled and wiggled deep into their sleeping bags. If they could have floated above themselves, they would have seen a perfect circle of connecting arms and ends of bags. They would have seen one finger reaching for another, and a long strand of hair touching the opposite side of someone else's face. They would have seen boots and shoes that looked as if they were moving in that same circle, and a tangle of sweaters, and in the center, the very heart of the circle, they would have seen a glowing ember that would always be warm, a tiny knot of heat that would never burn out.

Associated Press, May 2, 2002
Wilkins County, Wisconsin
Alert—Changing Status

OFFICIALS HOBBLING PROTECTION FOR WOMEN WALKERS

The seven women who have been trudging silently through this scenic portion of America's dairyland while causing a national uproar had better get moving.

County officials have decided that they can no longer keep back huge crowds gathering each morning at a roadblock to show support for the walkers.

Ironically, a group of men have filed a request with the County Clerk's office here asking for the county highways and roads to be reopened immediately.

"These women are out there walking around like queens, and it's not right to keep the rest of the world from using the roads," said Bruce Guilden, a spokesman for the group of men. "It's time for everyone to go home."

Women across the country and throughout the world seem to identify with the walkers and have gathered to form similar walks, as well as showing support for the Wisconsin walkers. Those women initiated their pilgrimage one week ago, but have not disclosed the exact reason for taking to the road on foot.

Sheriff Barnes Holden said if it was up to him, he'd let the women walk indefinitely, but he's been ordered to remove roadblocks that have kept back everyone except local residents.

"There will be hell to pay at my own house because

of this," said Barnes. "Anyone who doesn't understand this just needs to go talk to their wife, or sister, or just about any woman they happen to meet on the street."

When the barricades do come down, one thing is certain: the women walkers will forever have changed the history of this rural community. If women across the world are to be believed, they've also ignited more than a few hearts.

"Women give strength and love to everything they see and touch," said Victoria Bramling, a Detroit woman who flew to Wisconsin to offer support for the seven walkers. "These women have said to all of us that's it's right to follow your heart, and we all owe them so much for that."

—30—

The Women Walker Effect: Cynthia

Cynthia kept her eyes closed for the longest time. Although the small room was dark, she wasn't ready for what she might see. For what she wanted to see, for the picture of herself that might appear in front of her and change everything.

She had double-locked the door of this borrowed room, sneaking softly up the back steps of the university building in the English department that she had been told would be virtually abandoned at this time of day. At 4:15 a.m. Cynthia had slipped from her own room, past all the closed and silent doors and out into a morning that still held a touch of winter. Unaccustomed to being out so early, Cynthia was immediately enthralled with the quiet of that hour, with the hands of darkness that rose up to greet her. She walked, almost ran, down the sidewalk and began the thirteen-block journey to the university.

In the time it took her to do that, Cynthia saw only one car, a dark green taxi, and not another human being. "Oh," she said to herself. "There are so many colors out here, it looks like a rainbow."

Cynthia noticed every single thing she saw on her quick journey. She saw the way the early shadows played tricks on her eyes and lingered just long enough to make her wonder if it was late or early Winter, or Fall. She noticed a man sitting in the last house on the left side of the highway, drinking what she supposed was a cup of coffee. He was all alone, looking out into his dark backyard.

There were no animals about, no other people walking, just the quiet sounds of her feet moving quickly, like the practiced steps of an early morning jogger. When Cynthia got to the large building, the second building on that side of campus, she walked to the back door. She had to walk through a dimly lighted path that was almost buried by a thick grove of evergreen trees. She never thought of the danger that might be there and would have been astonished if someone lurking there had jumped her. Cynthia never thought anything bad could happen to her.

The back door was propped open with a wad of yellow note pad. Cynthia smiled to think of her friend rolling up the paper from her own thick tablet and sticking it in the door, way past midnight, past the time when the night janitors and the security guard would be there.

This is the friend who had been her second secret. A woman who worked at the University and who had simply stopped her once in passing to ask about the time, and then followed her from one place to the next until she would sit and share something to drink with her. Cynthia had never had a friend like this before, had never dared to let someone become so close to her. It took two years for Cynthia to tell her friend, Carolyn, her real secret. One afternoon when the two of them sat for hours on a bench, they talked and talked, and then Cynthia turned to her new friend and looked into her eyes. That's when she knew, because of the soft glow she saw there and the light. She knew that her friend would not harm her or laugh or look away if she shared the secret.

Less than a week ago, Carolyn had asked Cynthia if she had seen the articles in the newspaper about the women walking in Wisconsin. Cynthia, who never listened to a radio or watched television and rarely bothered to pick up a newspaper, had not heard about those women.

However, she did reveal to Carolyn, "I'm from Wisconsin. There were 12 kids in my family, and my mother, I can remember only how tired she was all of the time."

"Twelve children," said Carolyn, trying hard not to swear because she had promised Cynthia that she would not do that. "Your mother had twelve children?"

"Well, really she had 16 children, but she lost two others through miscarriages and two died just after birth. Imagine that, after all that work."

"Imagine it!" said her friend. "Some of us find the thought of all those children and no birth control and a woman who, well, we just find it disgusting."

"Oh," Cynthia said, amused by Carolyn's outlook. "I suppose it was a different world, even though that wasn't so long ago."

"Cynthia, were you the baby, the last girl?"

"I was born when my mother was 47 years old. Imagine that now," Cynthia shared, nodding as she spoke.

"Cynthia, how old are you now? "

"I'm 39 years old, and my mother would be 86 now, but she's been dead for a long time."

"*Well, shit,*" Carolyn said to herself, "*of course, she's dead. Judas Priest, what in the hell were they all thinking!*" Carolyn, a clinical psychologist and part-time professor, desperately wanted to take Cynthia to her apartment and treat her to a long hot bath in a gallon of lavender essence. She wanted to take her to a salon and then shopping, and she hoped and prayed that she could do that someday. For now, just a few words, a few well planned words would have to do.

So the women sat on the bench out near the university library, and Carolyn told Cynthia about the walkers in Wisconsin. She described how they had simply started their own pilgrimage. Carolyn had a feeling that Cynthia could well understand a woman or a man in search of something miraculous and wonderful, and she was right.

Cynthia turned her head, and then she asked to see the newspaper articles. While Cynthia read, Carolyn closed her eyes and let her mind wander to her favorite beach where she could picture her new friend lying in the sun. Carolyn finally turned and touched Cynthia lightly on the arm, and when Cynthia smiled and her eyes lit up, Carolyn wanted to jump off the chair and yell something like, "Holy shit, she's alive!"

"What do you think of this, Carolyn. You're a woman of the world and smart, and this is your field, Psychology, isn't it?"

"It's a great story, Cynthia, a beautiful story really. I'm thinking that these women all had something to forget or work out, that they are great friends, and they are out there walking with nothing to bother them or nothing to be in charge of except each other. I'm thinking that some powerful communication, healing, problem solving and just some beautiful togetherness must be going on."

"Oh," said Cynthia, sounding to Carolyn like a little girl who really doesn't quite understand what's being explained to her.

Carolyn in all her worldliness, with her bountiful practice and research and teaching appointment, had never met anyone like Cynthia. Most of her clients were women, most of them career women sick with guilt and mothers who lacked the desire to have sex or do anything except sleep when they had five extra minutes, along with a large number of middle-aged women who needed someone to say, "Hey, it's okay to fly to Bermuda and leave your husband and change jobs and hack off your hair." Many of her clients were also women who loved women but who had no idea how to embrace their emerging lesbian identities. Never, ever before in her 21 years of clinical practice had Carolyn met a semi-cloistered Catholic nun who appeared to be walking through life like a half-hearted zombie.

It took about 14 seconds for Carolyn to become completely enchanted with Cynthia. Although Cynthia wore extremely traditional dark skirts and white blouses, there was really no way to tell that she was a nun and that she spent half her day praying in that convent not far from campus and the other half working at the monastery bakery. What she saw immediately with her trained eye and with the kind heart that had taken her into a profession where she could help and heal, was the soul of a woman who had yet to learn how to live.

For months Carolyn had pursued a relationship with Cynthia. She had come to look forward to their chance meetings, which she actually planned with great effort once she figured out Cynthia's routine. She quickly became captivated by her new friend's sincerity, by her devotion, by the simplicity that marked every hour of her day. Inside of her own hectic heart, Carolyn was also smart enough to know that she could learn many, many things from Sister Cynthia that were not obvious on the surface.

She told absolutely no one of her new relationship. Carolyn guarded her new friend like a treasure, and she had dipped into her own basket of faith to help guide where she might go with Cynthia and what might happen in the precious moments they spent together.

In the months that the two women had spent talking in the cafeteria, empty classrooms, or on the steps of the library, both of them had inched closer and closer to each other. As much as Carolyn wanted to help Cynthia learn about life and choices and blending one part of one's life with another, she also wanted to simply rest her spinning head on Cynthia's shoulder and have her talk about the arc of light that always flooded her bare bedroom when she knelt for her hours of prayer.

"It's a soft light that seems to be constant and unchanging, no matter what time of year it is," Cynthia had explained. "Because my contact with the rest of the world has been so limited, I've. . . well, the truth is . . . I've come to look at that light as a friend, as a place to draw warmth. Sometimes I try and put my arms around the light as it comes in the window."

"Cynthia, that's very beautiful."

"I feel bad telling you these things, but there is so much in the world that I've always wondered about, so much I don't even know about."

"You can ask me anything. Anything you want. I'll do whatever I can to help you."

Carolyn kept that promise in her heart, and after a year of meeting with Cynthia, she also began touching her – to introduce her to the affection of adult friends. First touching her on the hand, then the arm, and twice she reached out and almost, almost touched her on the face. Finally, Carolyn grabbed her friend's hand and raised it to her face, closed her eyes, and let her warm, soft fingers brush against her cheeks, across her eyes, over her forehead.

"It's all right to touch people," Carolyn said. "Friends can touch each other, it's a way to express how you feel, Cynthia. It's no different than touching the light that comes in through your window."

Back in her office, Carolyn poured over books about cloistered nuns. She pulled 50 articles off the Internet that dealt with girls who had gone from strict family homes and directly into convents. Then she confided in her own husband, a man with a heart that equaled hers. She told him all she wanted to do was to give Cynthia a glimpse of the world. She wanted to give her a choice, a choice she knew Cynthia had never had.

"Come here," her husband beckoned, holding out his arms, toward his beautiful wife.

"What do you think? " she asked him.

"I think you have to do what you have always done. You have to follow your heart. It seems as if your heart has landed this time on Sister Cynthia's sleeve."

"She can be who she wants, but she seems to be searching. There's something she wants to tell me, and she asks me questions about unbelievable things like flying in airplanes and computers. My God, honey, she's never even touched a computer."

"That's not so bad, you know," he smiled. "She's had a pretty simple life, but that doesn't mean it hasn't been just as fulfilling as yours, does it?"

"That's what scares me," Carolyn told him. "I don't want to change her, just show her, that's all. She should know."

"Then show her," he said. "Show her whatever you want."

Carolyn took a chance with the newspaper articles, and when Cynthia told her immediately about her mother and her family and how she was simply sent one day to the convent when she was 12 years old, Carolyn knew that she had struck gold. She would find her way into the heart of this woman, who had worked her way into Carolyn's own heart.

That first day when the articles about the walkers appeared in the newspaper, Carolyn, with all her years of training and expertise, almost blew it by shouting out, "Cynthia, what's your heart's desire? What do you dream about behind those doors and in the dark of the night?"

For sure, Carolyn and Cynthia were as opposite on the surface as two women can be: Cynthia in her plain clothes and self-cut hair with no make-up and barely a smile to hint at any emotions, Carolyn with the gorgeous hazel eyes and a runner's lean body, who had traveled the world and loved and been loved by quite a list of fellow humans.

But Carolyn, as wise as she was wonderful, knew women shared many things. She knew that Cynthia could dream and that she could love. She knew that even in a life so secluded and cautious, anything could happen. She knew that absolutely nothing could suppress a longing for touch and desire and that need to find out, to just find out what would happen if only, if only . . .

Carolyn was just as struck by the women walkers as was Sister

Cynthia. For years she had been recommending a particular exercise to her clients: to place whatever it is they felt they needed to get rid of into a bag and throw it off the highest bridge they could find. She was a great believer in the therapeutic value of performing some significant act to signal that a person had changed their life and moved into a new place. Although she knew absolutely nothing about the women in Wisconsin, Carolyn was certain that in a way, she also knew everything about them. She had already made dozens of copies of the newspaper stories to share with her clients.

After Cynthia read the first article, she asked Carolyn at their next meeting if there were new stories about the women, and then it was impossible for Carolyn to suppress a smile.

"What's so funny?" Cynthia asked.

"I had a feeling you'd like this story, and I'm glad I was right. That's all."

"I'm so curious about them, what they are doing, where they are staying. It's been in my mind since we talked yesterday. Well, honestly, this morning when I was supposed to be praying, that's all I could think of, just them."

"Praying for me doesn't always have to be saying words. I think that when I have a wonderful thought about someone or feel them inside of my heart, that's just as much of a prayer."

"I feel the same way."

"It's a beautiful thing to think of someone you love and to wish them well and to imagine positive and perfect things for them."

"I've never thought of things like that before, and most of the time I'm alone or with just a handful of other people, and we rarely talk."

Carolyn knew there was a fine line between friendship and her work as a therapist. So, she had to stop then, take in a breath, and force herself to relax. She had already imagined hundreds of times what Cynthia's life must have been like. What it had been like for a little girl to grow up without a mother, without someone to hold her tight against the world. She had to be careful, so careful.

She had to hold back her barely controllable desire to lift Cynthia off the ground and hold her like a baby. In fact, some days Carolyn could barely stop herself from kidnapping Cynthia and moving her into the guest room, hiring out a sex surrogate, and then taking a year long sabbatical to show Cynthia the world, the entire world.

Finding the right words was always such a crucial endeavor for Carolyn that she had developed a unique way of slowly raising her hands from her sides, to her stomach, and then outward, just a few degrees at a time, until they were up to her eyes and her hands were open. By this time, whomever she was working with would be concentrating on her hands and not realizing that Carolyn had been searching for the perfect words.

"Listen," she said softly, raising her hand first to her waist. "There is nothing wrong with wanting something different than what we have, with thinking and wondering about what something might feel like, with trying out that desire. That's why we are here, Cynthia, that's why God gave us all these choices and places to see and people to meet and love."

Cynthia looked off into the sky, thinking about the walkers then, and she said out of all the things that she had often thought about, about all the things that she didn't even know existed, about all the people she had passed on the street without ever actually seeing, there was one thing, one thing that had been stuck in her mind since she was a little girl.

"Do you want to tell me about it?"

"I'm not used to this, you know, but you have been so kind

to me. I can tell that you are a person with a pure heart of gold."

"I would never hurt you, Cynthia, you know that. People come to me all the time with their secrets and their problems. It's been my gift from God to try and help those people, to lead them towards their own happiness."

"Sometimes," whispered Cynthia, "Sometimes, I feel so silly, and it's embarrassing to live in a world that you know so little about."

"It's also wonderful to be so sincere and trusting and accepting of what you have been given, Cynthia. Where we both are, right now, right this minute, there is nothing wrong with that. This is who we are and that's okay with me."

When Cynthia raised her head, there were tears running down her face and her lower lip was trembling. Carolyn put her arm around Cynthia's shoulders and held her right hand. Then she waited.

"It's such a simple thing, you know, such a simple thing when you consider other lives. But I have thought about this every day since I was nine years old."

Carolyn listened, afraid to move, afraid to breathe, afraid that if she bent a finger, something in the universe would change direction and stop her friend from opening up her heart.

"The night my mother was so ill ended up being the last time I ever saw her," Cynthia told her. "My brothers and sisters had decided not to tell me that she was ill. In fact, it was months and months after her death before I even knew that my mother had died. No one told me, no one told me anything."

Cynthia's mother was strong enough that night in 1969 to do something she had never done before. She came into the kitchen, took Cynthia by the arm and said they were going into the city. Cynthia was startled by the news because the city meant Milwaukee, and it was so far to where they were going.

"To see the dance," her mother told her. "We are going to see the dance."

Cynthia had been born with dance in her soul. The sound of a whistling teapot could make her hips sway and her feet tap, and her heart sing. Cynthia danced through the first nine years of her life, singing and humming and jumping off the porch as if she had been lit on fire.

She picked up magazines, just hoping for a glimpse of someone dancing. When her sisters went to the high school dances, she begged them for every detail, for every single piece of information that she could get. "What were they doing? What was the music like? What did you do?" These talks, of course, were small noises in the night because their parents were so strict. They did not even know the girls had dropped out of the windows after supper and skipped through the trees to the waiting cars.

Riding 50 miles to the city, Cynthia remembered how her mother sat straight up in the front seat while her father drove, turning every now and then to look into her eyes. In Milwaukee, it seemed as if her father knew just where to go. He dropped them in front of the Pfister Hotel and then drove away without talking. Inside the building was a small theater. People were everywhere laughing, drinking, touching. Cynthia had never seen so much life swirling in one place, and she had wanted to stay there in the lobby for the rest of her life.

The dance was surely the most remarkable event in Cynthia's life, and 30 years later she could remember every costume, every movement, every expression as if she were describing something that was taking place while she was talking.

"In one of the dances, a modern piece, the women and men were barely dressed and they blended together like a wave – moving and flowing. It was magical to see everything that I had imagined, the movement, the beautiful bodies, the music, so loud and perfect. The men and women, they were so alive. I was mesmerized by every single thing that I saw."

Cynthia said there was another set where the dances performed to music from the 1950s. She said when they did the jitterbug, with hips swaying and women being pulled behind their partner's legs and thrown into the air, that several people from the audience jumped up and started dancing. "It was as if they had been taken over by the music and couldn't help themselves. That was the same way I felt, the same way I always feel when I hear music."

Carolyn cried as Cynthia told the story of that night of dance. Her tears fell into Cynthia's oddly-shaped hair and must have rolled into her scalp but Cynthia never said a word. She only talked on, describing the legs and arms of the dancers and how some of the women wore costumes that showed their breasts, but it didn't in anyway seem scandalous, just beautiful. She looked once to see that her mother was sitting with her eyes closed.

"We never talked that entire evening. My mother never said one word to me, and then suddenly, like Cinderella, my father appeared at the door. We got in the car and rode home. The next morning my father drove me to the train, and that was the end of that part of my life."

So it was the dancing, Carolyn told herself, smiling because it was about the last thing she would ever have guessed. Cynthia wanted to dance, and by God, Carolyn was going to help her do it.

"Cynthia," she said forming an idea even as she spoke. "Do you want to dance?"

"Oh, very much. I have danced and danced in my mind for many years but to actually do it, to have that chance, oh, can you imagine?"

"I can do more than imagine. I can make it happen for you.

Do you want me to, should I do it?"

"Yes, oh please, yes."

It was easy for Carolyn to get the key to the small recital room, to slip the janitor a $20 bill and to whisper in the ear of the security guard whose wife happened to be one of her old patients. Easy to call her friend in the Art Department and find a costume, made from a fabric wispy and thin that might have been used in a 1969 production.

The hard part was not going herself, not standing close in the next room while Sister Cynthia crept up the steps and launched herself into the room with no windows and the soundproof walls. But she did it—she arranged everything, and while Cynthia was walking through the streets that early morning, Carolyn was sitting by her kitchen window gazing out onto the dark and grinning wide with their secret.

Sister Carolyn stepped inside the room so lightly it looked as if she was walking on a bed of soft grass. She moved her hands across the wall until she found the light switch. When she turned it on, her breath disappeared, sucked away into the heavens.

"Oh my," she said out loud. "This is it, this is it."

Before her lay a room surrounded by glittering mirrors bathed in a soft, warm light. The wooden floor was fitted with state-of-the art springs that made it seem as if she was walking on air. There was a piano tucked into the corner, and in the middle of the dance floor she noticed something special.

Cynthia bolted the door and paused with her head bowed before she skimmed across the floor. She saw the costume, the same blues and greens that she remembered from a hundred years ago. With it was a tape recorder, and then she saw a dozen roses spread on a beautiful silver tray with a note that read:

"Dear Friend,

To dance is to sing

is to pray
is to be alive
is to see your soul
as it was truly meant to be seen . . .
after this, when you have landed . . .
I will be here
to help you
to be your friend
for whatever whenever whoever
comes next . . .
Congratulations on your first recital . . .

Your Forever Friend,
Carolyn

Sister Cynthia stopped for just a moment and held the note to her heart. She spun around in a circle, nudged her foot against the roses, first one and then another, until she had touched every flower. Then she bent down and lifted the outfit so it was eye level.

"Oh, it's so beautiful, just like I remember it. Oh."

The next step was perhaps the hardest. To lift off her blouse and drop her skirt and to look into a mirror where she could see her entire naked body for the first time in 25 years. Cynthia did it quickly before she could change her mind. She flipped off her blouse with the worn collar and the missing button and stretched her arms back to release her bra. When it dropped to the floor, she pulled down her nylons and unhinged her skirt. Next came her underpants, until she rose with her eyes closed.

Slowly, slowly, she opened them to see the skin of herself and a body that still looked as if it had been born to dance. There were no stretch marks, and her breasts were firm and high and exactly

305

perfect for a woman who was meant to fly. There were no veins or lines in her legs, no scars from knee or ankle surgery, no tattoos— just the soft untouched lines of a woman who would take the breath away from anyone who was lucky enough to see her this way.

Cynthia turned once and saw that her rear end did not bounce and that her waist tapered in a narrow line, just like that one dancer she had seen. She wanted to touch her own breasts, her legs, the soft part of her stomach and she almost did, but she stopped and ran her hands from her head to her shoulders and along her entire body, just an inch away from her own skin, until she reached the floor with her palms down, not even realizing that most women are not limber enough to do this.

Then Cynthia smiled and pulled on the costume, a body suit with streamers and a skirt designed to sway and move with just the slightest hint of the dancer's movement. She did not recognize herself when she looked up, but imagined what it would be like to grow her hair black and long, the way it always appeared in her dreams, running down her back and touching just below her breasts when she leaned forward.

Cynthia had no idea in that moment how incredibly beautiful she was. She had no idea that the world could be hers, and that she could go anywhere or do anything or be anyone. She only knew that it made her chest heave to see herself like this and that she would never, ever be the same after these revealing, sacred moments.

When she clicked on the tape recorder, the music was something she had never heard before. Jazz, maybe? With a guitar and a saxophone that whirled in an exotic and sensual tone that involuntarily made her feet move and her hips rotate.

First Cynthia laid on the floor, feeling the cool wood under her buttocks and on her bare arms and legs. She rotated her head at her neck and began moving—first one shoulder and then the next, then her elbows and lower arms and then her hands, her hips, her knees and legs until she was dancing, dancing, while lying on the floor. Without willing it to happen, without knowing that she was actually doing it, Cynthia rose from the floor and opened her eyes.

She saw for the first time in 30 years that she had grown into a woman and that she was a dancer. She was a dancer.

While the morning simmered in its beginnings and while Carolyn rolled off her right hip, dressed, and prepared to walk herself to that dance studio, Sister Cynthia danced. She placed her hands on the mirrors and she looked into her own eyes and she glided across the floor and then backstepped, with the music, always with the music, until she saw herself from a distance and could not have recognized even her own eyes, her own smile.

She danced while Carolyn kissed her husband good-bye and then dropped her son at orchestra practice and found a place to park in front of the recital hall building. She danced for an hour, and then another hour. Pools of sweat soaked through the silky costume material and then fell in wild drops onto the floor.

Out in her car, Carolyn saw the first student crossing the grassy field that separated the recital hall from the engineering department. She knew the secret she shared with Cynthia had come to fruition, and with a sigh of contentment, she walked into the dance building.

Even through the soundproof walls, she could hear the music. She stopped at the door, resting her head on her hand and her hand on the door for just a minute. Then she knocked. Before Sister Carolyn skidded over to the door, knowing full well who had come, she stopped and prayed. She offered a thank you prayer to the God she loved and to the walkers, to the Wisconsin walkers.

Then Cynthia opened the door, welcomed Carolyn into the music, and then both of them were dancing, dancing, dancing.

New Woman Magazine, June 23, 1997
Editor's note—For full story and accompanying sidebars,
check *New Woman* website.

FORGET TRADITION—WOMEN ARE DESIGNING "NEW" LIVES

By Rebecca Monley

The female customers in St. Mary's Bordeaux, a chic
New York wine bar, were not talking about their promo-
tions, the latest fashions from the West Side, who got
married during the Christmas holidays, or where their
stock portfolios were hovering last Friday night. The conversation was more serious than that. "Sex in the City"
this was not. Definitely not.

"I don't care if I ever get married," said Tracy Brenks,
a investment banker from Manhattan who is 37, has
never been married, and says she's happy, fulfilled and
unwilling to settle – for anything. "I like to give people
who gasp when I say I don't care about getting married
what I call The Three-Minute Test. Quick, in three minutes give me the names of three or four happily married
couples. I rarely find anyone who can identify more than
couple number one."

Brenks and her pals at St. Mary's may be on to something. The test is a killer, and Suzanne Hamlin, 41, a
news writer for New Wisdom Magazine and a regular at
the bar's Friday "women only" nights, says she made a
decision when she was in her 20s to stay single and be
and do what she wants. Hamlin is also a mother who says
the rules society laid out for everyone to follow centuries
ago need not be followed.

"How dare anyone tell me that I have to get married and live in a house in the suburbs and be and look like everyone else," said Hamlin. "I have a full life, fabulous friends, a family and I have a career that keeps me abreast of what is happening all over the world. If everyone learned to be happy alone before they rush out to grab onto someone else, the world would be a very amazing place."

Brenks and Hamlin are not alone in their views about how to live life, but Dr. Lynn Evans, a clinical psychologist with the Women's Medical Center in Los Angeles, said being true to who you are is no easier now than it was when our mothers' were watching June Cleaver prepare dinner for Ward, Wally and the Beave.

"Even with all the strides we have taken as women and even with all the choices that are now available to women—that doesn't mean living how you want to live is going to be easy," said Evans. "For example, it takes great courage for a married woman to divorce and decide to live her life as a lesbian, or for a single woman to decide to have a baby without a life partner, or for a woman to simply declare that she is staying single because she wants to stay single."

While Evans and other relationship experts, including Dr. Kathrine Harris, a psychiatrist and author of "What Did You Say I Can't Do?" agree that times have changed, they also agree that society still outlines a fairly conventional lifestyle that has not altered much during the past few decades.

"Women are living a variety of lifestyles throughout this country and the world, but that doesn't mean it's easy or simple," said Harris. "It's damned hard to follow your heart, to wake up every morning and know that you are true to who you are, and to not tremble when you think of what you might face when you open your door."

But Harris said it's women like Corissa Sanchez, 36, a secretary from Santa Fe, New Mexico who are helping to shatter the rules and regulations of life that seem to have been authored in the Dark Ages. Sanchez, the mother of two, married twice, divorced twice, remained single for five years and is now in a long-term relationship with another woman. She said her family at first disowned her for divorcing, then again for being involved with a woman, but now they have changed their minds.

"We don't all find out who we are the day we turn 22 or 26," said Sanchez, who also runs a domestic violence program, teaches homeless men how to read, and is attending graduate school. "I am not the same woman I was 20 years ago, and I won't be the same woman I am now in 10 years, or even in a month."

—30—

The Elegant Gathering: Susan

There were times, just days ago, when I would stand in front of the mirror in the tiny bathroom just off the kitchen, push my hips against the side of the counter and look into my own eyes— wondering just who in the world I was looking at. Knowing in that same instant that somehow, somewhere along the road of my life I have lost myself. I have misplaced my soul, my heart, the entire direction of my being.

Truth be told, I am so embarrassed and sad that I am pregnant and that I have let all those years of my life slip away that it would be so easy for me to run away and hide and never come back. Thankfully my friends have held me up and carried me across my own kitchen floor to these glorious days on the road. They have really saved me by giving me hope and unconditional love. Now, it's my turn, my turn to put my life back together.

I really don't know what happened to me. I don't know why I married the wrong man, and then never had the courage to leave. I don't know why I picked up with another man just because he was good in bed. I could guess at all these answers, and in the end my decisions would all come back to me, and that is the only truth I know for sure. Whatever has happened to me has been my own doing.

This baby that I had no business creating has brought me to this decision and the true test of what I really need to do with my life. Is it too late? Is it ever too late for any of us to start over and try again? My life is a question, or it has been a question, and the end to all of that feels so close. As close as anything I have ever held to my heart.

Still there is no clear moment in my head after all these days of thinking and walking and talking that I know for sure where my heart scattered.

I suppose now, now that I know about the world and about sorrow, about the fact that not all of us can control who and how we love, I suppose I could have known even then that I was marrying a man who would always be looking over his shoulder for something or someone better.

God almighty, we were young. I was 19 and John was barely 20, and we were both desperate for something. We thought that must have been each other. We had been friends all through grade school and high school, and then into those first few years of college. Friends, but not close enough even then. "I just need you," he told me over and over again. "Please, please marry me."

John never did say that he loved me but in my heart, my unwise and young and very tender heart, I had loved him for forever. So I said yes, and we literally got up from the floor of his apartment and walked downtown and got married. It took about 20 minutes. Then as quick as you can close a door or turn a page or change directions on a highway, the course of my own life was moved in a way that I could never have imagined all those years ago.

The story is much simpler than it might seem now. Now that I have turned down a different road and then again onto this highway that has seemed like heaven to me this past week. It has been hard, especially this last day or so, to think that something like this, this walking and talking and these precious moments, was always there for the having . . . always right outside my door, and I never once thought to grab it up and run for the hills. But I have learned in these days to stop lingering on what could have been and to simply head for what I need now.

What's whacked is that John did love me, and I'm sure in his own perverted way, he probably still does love me. Mostly because we are connected by our children, by the son and daughter who came so quickly I barely had time to stop and recall how they were conceived. Some of my friends laugh when I say that at least John was a good father. They laugh because he was in and out of our lives so much they can't imagine how it worked, and how my children ended up with college scholarships and goals in their lives.

Some of that came from me, which is hard to believe and absolutely hilarious at this very minute. I just had this conversation with Sandy last night as we sat by the fire and watched the stars come out, one by one, popping into view like fireworks. Each one a bigger surprise than the next one.

"That's the funny part," Sandy said. "That your kids have survived all of this and are doing so well in school. I suppose it says something about John that he helps them and they have a relationship."

"Yeah, but then there is me."

"Well, think about it. Here you are, just a young woman really, pregnant, recently unemployed, a missing husband, and you are on the lam with a bunch of broads who could all be committed."

"It does sound pretty ridiculous, doesn't it?"

"Well, my God, in some countries they would take you away, and we'd never see you again."

"I'd put up a hell of a fight."

"That's what you should have done years ago, honey."

"But I couldn't. I had those kids, and I always thought of that old joke when the minister asks the 90-year-old couple why they are getting a divorce after all those years and the woman says, 'We were waiting for the kids to die.'"

"What about you, though? Didn't you have a right to something?"

"Not then. But now they're grown, it's my turn. That's what I think. Now I can do something about the rest of my life. Before this, really, how strange this sounds, but I didn't want or need anything else."

Sandy turned away then because I know our lives have not been that dissimilar. I know that she has done some of the same things, and that she has been in her own holding pattern.

"I tried," I said softly, putting my hand across her warm back. "That's how I got pregnant. I tried to carve out some little piece of happiness. For me that obviously meant a piece of ass and look where that got me."

Sandy turned back towards me. Her eyes were soft and kind, and she pulled me against her shoulder.

"People get pissed off when you talk about a baby as being an accident. But some babies are accidents, and I know you will have to deal with all of that in your own time and in your own inimitable 'Susan' sort of way. But it wasn't wrong to find some comfort in his arms. People get so whacked out about sex. Sex can just be sex. People do it all the time. Half the women in the world who are screwing right now are for sure not doing it out of love."

"Next time, next time I'm going to pick someone with a bigger penis, though," I said, smiling, waiting for her reaction.

"Oh, that's my girl! How about two men at once? Or hey, how about two men, a dog, four chickens and I'll come too."

"You get the chickens and you are on."

It felt so wonderful to laugh, to make fun of our ridiculous predicaments, the troubles we have caused ourselves. I know I can't erase all those years behind me and really, I wouldn't want to. I could have made better choices, could have changed the course of my life a long time ago, but I didn't. And really, it wasn't all horrible.

For a time, John and I did live like what half the world would consider a normal couple. We both continued to go to school, and I must have gotten pregnant about the third time we had sex. I stayed in school, and John actually worked three jobs so that we could both try and finish our degrees. But that's also how he discovered the power of his little penis. I'm certain he started fooling around when I was pregnant the first time, because the young girl he worked with at the restaurant started calling the house on a regular basis, constantly drove past our apartment, and left things like her underwear and bra in our car.

That was just the beginning. Then the baby came, and John was crazy about Erin. He finished school and started working, and I have no idea about the others, how many there might have been because those were the years of kids and John anchoring his career track and me taking three years of night classes to become an RN.

People drift apart all the time. We were so young when we married, and I cannot say that it was a ridiculous thing to marry a friend, to have two teriffic children, to stay around month after month when the man I married traveled and screwed his way from one end of the country to the next. Most of the time it was enough for me to pull open the refrigerator and find food, to see my children sleeping in their beds at night, to know that someone would pay the light bill.

One Christmas, maybe nine years ago, John staggered in way too late for him to even offer up an excuse about work or meetings or the guys from the club. Maybe it was because of the holidays, or maybe I was exhausted from that year's round of the flu and bronchitis, or maybe my part-time job at the nursing home had me thinking about all those old people who were dying in my arms week after week. But I waited up for him and without knowing it, we came to a crossroads in our relationship that night.

I saw changes in John more clearly than ever before. He had filled out during those years. His wavy brown hair had been trimmed back, his eyes had deepened and darkened. His once thin face had filled in, and it was obvious that he had been spending time working out when he should have been selling computer programs. Some people might be shocked to think that I wanted to make love to him one last time, wanted to lie next to the father of my semi-abandoned children, the man who had all but deserted me and who had most likely slept with numerous other women.

Believe me, he was surprised too when I met him at the door, slipped my hand through his arm, and asked him to come upstairs with me. His puzzled look was almost as entertaining as the sex that followed. Of course I made him shower off the scent of whomever he had been with the last few hours, and of course it was not easy for this almost middle-aged man to strike up his own fire after what he must have just gone through. But he put up a hell of a front.

In the end, the last time I ever touched or made love to my husband was also the night I asked him to leave and never come back. I rolled off of him, swept a sheet off the top of the pile of bed covers and then pulled my knees up to my chest. "John, I think you should just leave now. We can sort out everything else down the road a bit."

"What?" Astonished, he rose up on his elbows.

"You're rarely here, you have girlfriends all over the place, the kids will be out of high school in a few years. Really John, we should both get on with our separate lives."

"But, I . . . the kids and . . ."

"We don't have to get divorced, but I will need money right now. The deal is, you don't need us, John, you haven't really needed me for at least, what, 17 years or so?"

John slumped back, totally deflated, as if he had been stuck with a large pin. I couldn't even imagine what was going through his mind, because at that point I had absolutely no idea how his mind worked.

"John" I said quietly. "It doesn't have to be such a big deal. I'll just tell the kids we're separated, and things will pretty much go on the way they have been."

"What about you?"

"Me?"

"Yeah, you. What will you do?"

"I'll do what I've been doing since the day I married you. I'll take care of the kids and the house and the bills. Then I'll go to work for a few hours, I'll get up and do the same thing all over again."

Unfortunately the getting on with my life never quite seemed to happen. John didn't really ever move out, but he hopped from one friend's house to the next and managed to spend some nights when he was in town on the living room couch. The kids didn't seem to care that we were sort of separated because they had never seen us together much anyway. As the rest of the world and the people around me headed in one direction or another, I pretty much stood right there treading water.

One year quickly slipped into another, then and there never seemed time enough for me to conceive what I wanted or where I should be or what would happen when the kids left for school, or just left. I barely looked at myself in the mirror, had absolutely no idea that anyone at all would find me attractive, and when Don slipped into my life and made a pass at me, I simply fell into his arms because it felt good to have someone touch me.

Don would rent a hotel room or show up when the kids were off on some overnighter. I didn't love him but I was grateful for the chance to have someone hold me, even if he was an old fart with a bit of a belly. He wasn't unkind, but he really wasn't much of anything else either.

Maybe someone dropped something on my head when I was sleeping or slipped some kind of complacency drug into my oatmeal, because now that I have all these huge life decisions to make, I'm kind of pissed off at myself. What in the world was I thinking anyway? To shuffle through life like I have been shuffling with one leg up in the air and the other not knowing exactly where in the hell it should plant itself.

It's this walking, I think. This walking has made me see things and feel things and think of things that I have ignored or denied. And these women, Lord, they inspire me. They inspire me to take action and to know that it's okay to continue on. As Sandy would say, "to grab life right by the crotch."

Not everyone could understand a woman like me, could understand that having an abortion is the right decision to make. Could I even have imagined this a month ago, a year ago, that night when John and I sat on his apartment floor and looked into each other's eyes? Of course not. I would never have been able to travel to this point in my life, to this dangerous stop, to the junction where decisions are so final and lasting.

This is the real hard part for me. This abortion business. The struggle between heart, soul, mind and body. I knew right away. Before I took the test from the drugstore. Before I went to the clinic. Before I missed the first period since I had my last baby 20 years ago. That is when the terror set in. That is when I slumped to the floor of the bathroom and cried until my stomach cramped up, and there simply were no more tears.

I cried for my own stupidity, for the decision I knew I had to make, for the frightening changes that were suddenly spread out in front of me in bright, living color.

Perhaps there are 16-year-old girls, or other mothers, or rape victims who do not linger over this decision. Perhaps they can simply pick up the phone or drive to the clinic. Maybe not. Then again maybe they agonize and cry and imagine what her face might look like. Maybe they can feel her tiny hands reaching for her lips or that smell, that wonderful soft, clean, gentle smell of a baby's skin. Maybe they have dreamed about a different life, a life with a baby and a yard and the sounds of a happy child running up the hall and into the bedroom. Maybe they have seen a friend slip into the baby's room at night and kneel by the side of the crib just to see and hear and touch and listen to the ins and outs of a baby's breath.

There's a chance they have dreamed about those lazy mornings when the babies, who are just walking, climb into your bed and Velcro themselves to your sides. The wisps of hair on your face, and that reflex of your breasts moving towards them and your arms circling their heads and your fingers on their cheeks when they fall back to sleep, so safe and warm in your arms.

Maybe they think of what might be. They think of a life with singing in the kitchen and doors that open to a patio, and a refrigerator that is filled with everything you need just that minute to bake a pie. They think of Friday nights by the fireplace and a child's tears dripping into your hands and then that taste of tears as you kiss away all the sadness.

Those feelings of pure love could just center around that moment of birth. The release of life force that drops from your womb and into the hands of the rest of the world. Those seconds, one . . . two . . . three when your bottom rips and there is a pull that makes you wonder if your stomach has landed on your feet. When the pain sears through your back and along your spine and into your throat so there is no way, absolutely no way in hell you cannot scream, and you hope and pray in that three seconds that someone will slit your throat.

But then maybe they think about what comes next. The baby, covered in blood and mucus and screaming to fill her lungs with air. Maybe they are thinking of that baby who is laid on your stomach and who searches and searches for your breasts, for that purple nipple, until she can find it. And before that, just before that she hears you say, "Oh my beautiful, beautiful, baby . . ." When she hears that, she looks for your face, your eyes, for the source of the voice that has carried her from one month to the next. She knows you. The baby knows your voice and your face and the feel of your skin from the inside out. Just that sound, your voice, makes her stop crying because she knows from deep inside of her soul that you will take care of her and love her and make everything safe and right.

That isn't all, though. That is never all. There is the magic rush of creation that swirls and swirls around you for the rest of the day. Until you can sleep and remember how to sit and wipe the blood off of everything when you forget to get the pads. There is the thought that down the hall is your baby, a piece of your soul, someone with your smile and your crooked nose and beautiful ankles. There is all of that and a lifetime of mothering and caring and wondering every single second of the day if everything is fine, if you will make it through another day and that night too, and what about tomorrow?

An abortion. An abortion. An abortion. How can anyone else understand? This decision, this seemingly reasonable choice in my life at this time. Thank God for this choice, or someone, thank all those women who marched and who went down the back alleys. Thank the women who wrote the letters and who showed the men, all those men who'd always made to the decisions for the women. Thank those men who listened and who saw the little girl who was 12-years-old who had been raped by her uncle and had been ripped and torn from one end to the other. Thank those women who did all that, and who showed those men and the world that how dare anyone, any man, any person tell us what we can and can't do with our bodies.

A choice is really the gift I have now. I have chosen and I will go through with my choice because, well there are 43 reasons now. And it is only me, only Susan Paderson, who can say that this baby inside of me is a mistake. Only Susan Paderson who can say that it is impossible, that giving birth again would kill me, that it cannot happen.

I know now what I needed for so long, that what my life was truly missing was this flow of womanhood that has surrounded me on this walk and for these few short years when I have met with Mary, J.J., Chris, Janice, Sandy, Gail and Alice, oh my wonderful Alice.

Alice, who has held me like no one has ever held me and who has shown me the power of personal forgiveness. Alice, of all people, who said she will drive me first thing, right away when we get back, and who will come and stay with me for a few days. Alice who knows so well about the anguish of loss and regret. Can I ever thank her? Can I ever be for her what she is for me?

Beyond this day and the next and to the day after that, I really don't know what will happen to me. Chris thinks I should sell the house and buy one of those new condos close to her. She thinks I should move into administration and develop some hospice programs for people in this area. She thinks that until I divorce John, that I will go and be and do absolutely nothing.

Finally I know she is right. If I can see anything these days, it is a clear picture of how I have abandoned myself. Given and sacrificed and handed away one thing after another of my spirit until I have left myself standing thirsty in this self-created desert of a life.

And John? Well, hell, it's not John's fault I was so stupid and so willing and so eager to wash his socks and help him find his next appointment on that big map. I do know that in a year, I will be down the road and moving on, and that he will be heading in the same direction and perhaps that is his penance.

Already, it seems like 100 years ago since I dropped that glass, that single glass, one of what, three I think, that is left from the set my Auntie Cheezda gave me just after our wedding. Would we even be here without that glass? Without me being pregnant? Without the wailing and moaning that took place on my kitchen floor?

Oh, I have a new idea! As soon as we get back, I am going to ask everyone over, and we are going to smash those last two glasses, the other ones from my wedding set. Maybe I can line them up on the fence by the garbage cans, and we can take turns shooting at them with the pellet gun.

We'll break those glasses, and then I'll get the hell out of there. I'll be able to turn to these friends of mine, these women that I love and say, "It's just a glass. Not the end of the world. The beginning, maybe."

CHAPTER TEN

THE LAST DAY WAS A GIFT. An early morning mist, lifting slowly from the dark hollow of trees, left shadows of light that Janice immediately likened to streaks of grace pouring from the sky. The immense quiet caused each of the women to lie still, listening only to the sighs of each other's breath, a leg swishing across the bottom of a sleeping bag, a zipper rattling against the rocky earth, even heartbeats pounding.

The birds had been flying for hours by the time the women kicked out of their bags. At first the quiet continued, and everyone was afraid to speak, until Gail stood and stretched her hands towards the sun and said everyone was acting like a morning-after lover.

"Remember those mornings?" she asked, dropping her hands into a practiced yoga stance. "Wondering if that was it and should you make breakfast, or put on clothes, or act as if nothing happened?"

"Some of us still have mornings like that," said Sandy.

"Speak for yourself." Alice rocked from one leg to the other to push blood through them so she wouldn't drop over when she stood up.

"My God, does anyone feel as wonderful as I do?" Gail asked. "Does anyone know with as much certainty that this isn't the end of anything? We've done something powerful and beautiful, and we can keep doing anything from now on, whatever in the hell we want."

"I'm a little scared," said Susan.

"Just the change jitters," Chris offered wryly. "Change is always a bit frightening. You know now that you are not alone. That's pretty powerful right there."

"Everything is different, I have to admit that," Susan concluded, standing and twisting from front to back, unwinding, moving her hands in small circles. "I don't feel powerless, which is something brand new for me."

Alice threw small sticks of wood onto the dead bed of coals, bending at the waist and then blowing with all of her might to start a morning fire.

"Coffee," she called out as she worked. "Once we all have coffee, I have an idea of something we could do before Mary shows up."

"What?" J.J. asked.

"Just wait, come help me get this thing going and then I'll tell you."

"My God, what would we have done if Mary hadn't been Mary and done all of this for us?" asked Janice. "Everything would have been different."

"That's the beauty," Chris said. "Each one of us has been and done what we needed to do. For Mary, that meant something totally different, which is really great. Don't you think?"

Sandy moved to grab some large pieces of wood. "When you think about it, Mary had more guts than the rest of us. Let's make Mary the president of our little club."

"Ha!" laughed Alice, moving toward the cooler to see what was left for breakfast. "If you don't show up, you get to be in charge the next time."

"The next time," yelled J.J. "Hey, I like the sound of that."

The plan for the day was simple. The women wanted to linger until early afternoon by their fire, talking, eating and protecting the last few minutes of their adventure. Then Mary would simply show up with her uncle's huge van to transport everyone home. There was the chance that no one would ever even know who they were or how they had left or why they had done what they needed to do.

"Oh right," Chris told them. "And elephants will fly out my ass at high noon. Don't you think half the world already knows who we are? Reporters probably know our bra sizes and when we started menstruating, by now."

"Do you think?"

"Well, of course I think. That's what I used to do for a living. Screw up people's lives who made terrible mistakes. Look through their garbage. Find out their favorite sex position. Interview their grief-stricken mothers and fathers. Get the dirt from their college roommates."

"They're in for a treat when they try to track down all my old roommates and lovers," hooted Sandy.

"Really?" Alice asked. "I don't think it will be that bad because of what Mary said, you know, how all the people we know aren't saying anything."

"Does the name Linda Tripp ring a bell?"

"Yes," answered Gail. "But our walk isn't bad, Chris, this is something good, and although it's different, it's not like we hurt

325

anyone. In fact, it's really just the opposite of that. We've helped each other."

"Sure," Chris said. "But not everyone thinks that way."

"But, really, who gives a shit?" Sandy finally asked. "Do we really care if someone had tried for a peek into our underwear drawers, or found out that we've screwed up and needed to do this to feel better, and now each one of us has gained something powerful and wonderful?"

"Oh hell, of course not," Chris said. "Of course not."

There had already been crying and tears and talk about the realities of life, and endings and beginnings, and the miraculous way we are able to recall and remember and close our eyes to transcend time and space and whatever else might be in the way of getting back to a place or person of light and warmth. As the moon and sun traded places above them, several women continued to share sacred moments, about experiences that they had frozen in time and could recall in exact detail, about people they had loved, who still crossed through their minds and whispered in their ears and made that glorious spot just below their pubic bones burn and ache and tremble. They said for something to be over didn't mean it really had to end.

All the women were wise enough to know that it is impossible to linger forever in one favorite place or one comfortable position. But they were also wise enough to know it is possible to cherish forever a sense of all the details, a part of the total memory, to rekindle the essence of a time and place when the spirit needs it most. To see a color and remember a day on the lake. To eat pasta and think of that girl who touched your face that summer afternoon, or that strange time when you let a man drive you home when you had a flat tire and kiss you and touch your breasts right in front of your apartment door when you didn't even know his name. That day too, when a solitary wind felt like a tornado and pushed you back into the house and the phone rang and it was your mother crying and asking you to come right then, that instant.

There were a hundred memories and a thousand losses, and then the brilliant fact that what mattered most was the very second in which they stood and breathed and looked from sky to earth and from face to face together. To take this one moment they all agreed, was the magic of life, and the bottom line of every single thing they had been walking towards.

"It's clear now," Alice told them in the dark. "As clear as anything, and I suppose it's up to us to keep this all alive. To not let what we have gained slip through our hands again, ever again."

After Alice spoke, the women cried. They cried for the lost babies and the men and women who had managed to snip off a piece of their souls, for the dark clouds of life that had snagged their emotions, for the mistakes, and the time they had wasted with the thinking and anger and sorrow that could have been placed somewhere, anywhere else. The time when they could have been under a bright light or walking, yes, walking toward something new.

By the time Alice pushed the coffee off the small metal grate, the intoxicating smell of it had everyone standing mute, waiting for their cup of comfort.

"Why does everything taste so wonderful when you're outside?" asked J.J.

"I think it's because your senses are heightened," said Gail. "You don't have the distractions of walls, telephones, chemicals that float out of the pressed wall boards, things like that."

"And we've been walking so much, we just get hungrier."

"Well, breakfast isn't much more than roadkill this morning, girls." Alice passed out funky brown donuts and bananas. "But we can have 23 pots of coffee if we want to."

The women ate crouched by the fire, turning to watch the sun climb by inches, from one level of the horizon to the next, thinking about just what they saw in that moment, what they felt at that moment and looking carefully into each others' eyes—as if they wanted to make certain they were really seeing another person.

Finally Alice put another pot of coffee onto the grate, shuffled wood across the sides of the fire, kicked down some ashes with her cheap tennis shoes, and then pulled a handful of stones from her pocket.

"Okay," she said softly, moving back from the fire to stand away from the heat. "Okay then."

Alice jiggled the stones in her hand, moving them back and forth with her other hand, touching them gently with the tips of her fingers. Everyone waited, wondering what in the world she was about to say and do.

"Here's what I have been thinking," she said, raising her face to sweep her eyes across the faces of all her friends. Alice told them that she knew each one of them had something or someone that they needed to get beyond in their lives. She told them that was surely true of herself as well. "What I did was to think about my own self, you know, and the loss of my baby and what it did to the rest of my life. Well, the rest of my life up until now that is. The day we were walking and I realized what I had given up to mourn, to hold that loss so close inside of me for so many years, the very second I released myself, I looked down and I saw this beautiful stone right on the highway."

Alice held up a stone the size of a quarter that was flecked with tiny pieces of black and red. When she moved her hand up and down, the stone glittered. "So what I did after that was to keep this stone in my pocket, to hold it and feel it as my touchstone for a new beginning. When I think of the steps before this stone, I see darkness, and when I think of the steps after I found the stone, I see brightness and clear skies, and everything is better, so much better."

"Alice, that's lovely." Susan reached out to touch Alice's arm. "Very lovely."

"So finding this stone made me feel so good that I looked at all of you, and each time I saw a stone that I thought you could use, that would be something that you could touch and hold in your hand and remember, well, I picked up that stone. I put it in my other pocket and saved it for you. For the end of our walk, for now."

Everyone was quiet, looking at Alice, gentle, small, perfect Alice, in amazement.

"What a great idea," Sandy said. "Maybe we could have them polished and make necklaces or bracelets with them."

"But first," Alice said, lowering her eyes towards the ground. "First, I want you to come up here one at a time, and I want you to say something about what we have done and what you have given away or left behind."

Everyone understood at once this ritual was like receiving a diploma.

The stones filled up Alice's entire hand, and she moved them gently from one palm to the other, waiting for someone to come and get their stone. Susan jumped up first and moved to Alice, kissing her on the lips, pushing the hair from her eyes, draping her arm around Alice's shoulder. "There are no secrets here." She moved her hand across her stomach. "And although I could take responsibility for initiating this pilgrimage, I think it could have been any one of us. For me, it's not just the baby and my husband and what I have or haven't done. This is just my time now, my time to put one part of my life behind me and to start again. It's finally time to just be happy, and I think that's true for all of us.

So Alice, will you just go with me right away, then it can all start for me, really start?"

"Absolutely, sweetheart," Alice said, picking out a stone that was pure white and round on the edges and not much bigger than the nail on Susan's pinkie finger. "Here's your stone now. You can use it right away."

J.J. moved over to Alice next, smiling, hands on her hips, her feet spread apart. "I just feel so strong all of a sudden," she said. "It's time to let go of what happened to me, time to tell my girls, time to forgive my mother and to just move on with my life, like all of you. That's really what this is all about for me anyway."

Alice handed her a brown stone that would look brilliant when it was polished. J.J. held it in her hand, closed her fingers over it and said she was sure the hard parts were over, that what was left to do was easy and she was going to keep walking—every day, every chance she got for the rest of her life.

Chris cleared her throat before her speech, then said the walk had given her the bonds of friendship, staying in one place, having a family of women friends to delight in, to hold, to call, to count on, to help erase all those years of loneliness and travel and sidestepping her own feelings. "This feels sacred to me," she said, clasping her fingers over her stone as if she were receiving a gift from heaven. "My realization, what I've felt happened, is a mingling of our hearts, souls, and minds to have been here and done all of this together. I will be grateful to each and every one of you for the rest of my life."

"My goodness," Gail whispered next. "It's so wonderful to feel this much, to know that it's okay to love and to hold on and to feel safe and happy. I wish I could stop crying now, because there is so much I could say, but mostly know that I can simply surrender and lie in Bruce's arms and love him completely. Oh, that feels so right and good to me knowing that you will all be out there too. It's so overwhelming, so beautiful to me."

Alice slipped a stone into Gail's hand that was the largest of those she'd collected. Chipped on one edge, but still beautiful and solid. Gail moved it along the palm of her hand and then kissed Alice, holding her for a long time, until Janice stood up and placed her hands on Alice's face.

"I am not foolish enough to think that every day I have from this moment on will be clear and that my mind will suddenly line up the way it is supposed to," Janice said. She dropped her hands, palms out, open to the sky and the air and the sunlight. "But I know more than ever that whatever happens, I will be able to make it through and to stop thinking of myself and my mind and all those years as wasted or my fault. There is so much good, so much to try for, so much more in this world to see."

Alice placed an oval black stone into Janice's hand. When Janice opened her eyes to look at it, she saw the color and she laughed.

"Oh Alice, it's perfect, just perfect." Then she kissed Alice too.

Sandy wanted her stone before she spoke. "I can feel it already," she said, holding out her hand and immediately taking the stone with the green edges and gray center and the tiniest hint of blue to her lips and kissing it.

"It's so damn easy when we get hurt to shut ourselves off, isn't it? To think that nothing will ever be the same, and that it's impossible to go on and be happy again. The truth is that once we love someone and they become a part of us, nothing, even death, can stop our love for them. But also you can love again and take that other love and use it in so many ways, so many positive ways."

Sandy stopped for a minute, brought her stone down to look at it, and then closed her eyes so she could finish.

"The people who love us would only want us all to be happy, would want us to love whomever we wanted to love, and would tell us that running off like this or running naked down Main Street—all of that is just okie dokie if it will make us feel better. It's the lingering in the painful past and indecision that will kill us, the goddamned lingering. And what I think is that we should all keep walking, and stay connected and just keep moving."

Alice had one stone left. An odd-shaped piece of quartz that looked as if it had fallen off the moon. She held it up just above the side of the fire, saying it was for Mary.

In an hour when Mary rolled up, screeching the tires of the old van and almost sliding into the slanted ditch, the women couldn't wait to give Mary her perfect stone.

She strolled over, hands in her parka pockets, a smile on her face, and gave each one of her friends a hug. "All ready?" she asked.

They were. The women rolled up sleeping bags and carried the cooler to the car and picked up every scrap of paper or food that had been dropped while they camped.

Before they turned to get into the van, each one of them dipped her head toward the sun, which floated seductively in the late morning haze. Each one of them took in a huge cleansing breath. The air moved down their throats into their lungs, through their bloodstream past their hearts, and into their very souls. This last saved breath from the walking, pumped through each of them—solid, eternal, ever present.

EPILOGUE

W HEN THE WOMEN WALKERS quietly slipped past the Wilkins County roadblock and were dropped one by one back at their homes, the world refused to forget about them. Women's walking groups sprang up from New York to California, and women's clinics throughout the country reported a surge of interest in women's wellness. Studies about the long-term effects of exercise and natural remedies were immediately commissioned by numerous national and international healthcare groups.

Women's study and sharing groups that were so incredibly popular in the late 1960s and early 70s formed once again in all types of communities in the United States. Women gathered in church basements, library conference rooms, and in each other's homes to share their feelings, what they wanted out of life, what they could do to get back on track. They encouraged hope in each other for making the world a better place for all humanity. Women who had not held hands with their girlfriends since childhood no longer cared if anyone saw them sitting on the park bench with their arms around each other while the kids played soccer.

The National Organization for Women's (NOW) membership roster swelled, and new committees that focused on education, health and getting more women elected to national and state office actually had to turn people away. A new political caucus, Women United, was formed by women on the political committees, and put money behind six candidates for President of the United States. By the year 2003, such political fervor had doubled the number of women in the U.S. House and Senate. In a dozen major U.S. cities, a female mayor was elected for the first time.

In Wilkins County, the women walkers were never openly identified, although everyone in the county knew exactly who they were. When they went into grocery stores, people would discretely touch their elbows and say things like, "Thank you," and "What an inspiration!" The women, while not shocked by what they read in newspapers and magazines about their adventure, were completely overwhelmed by the number of lives they had touched. They only knew their own lives changed in many ways because they had the courage to walk out of Susan's front door.

Alice and Chester spent several months in counseling, where they both dealt openly with the death of their baby daughter Annie Marie, and the loss of their own relationship. Within six months of the first counseling session, Alice moved back into Chester's bedroom. With a few suggestions from Sandy, the couple returned to romance and sex that Alice proclaimed "better than ever." Alice also flew to her son's home and without even asking Chester, purchased a small trailer at the edge of a national forest. She informed her husband they would spend several months each year there so they could have time with their grandchildren. Chester took up daily walking and lost 15 lbs; he surprised Alice with a Valentine's cruise through the Panama Canal. They renewed their marriage vows on the ship, made love in six different locations, and signed up for a hiking tour of Costa Rica the following spring.

J.J. told both her daughters and her husband about being raped when she was in high school. Her husband reacted with the same loving, caring, and sincere attitude that had made J.J. fall in love with him to begin with. When J.J. saw the effect her story had on her own daughters, she approached their high school and began one-on-one counseling sessions with young girls who had also been raped. A guidance counselor at the school arranged to have J.J. attend a series of university classes, where she received grief counseling certification. J.J. loved her school experiences so much that she decided to return to college and work on an advanced degree in counseling. For her Master's Thesis, she is currently developing and modifying a program to help in recovery from date rape that is now being tested in six Midwest high schools.

Chris Boyer decided that she really did miss traveling and writing about world issues. She convinced her husband to slow his work pace even more and made a pact with him that she would never leave the country without him. She now travels and writes exclusively for *Ms., The Women's Legislative Agenda* and *NOW—Women Alive*. She refuses to be gone from Wisconsin or her friends for more than a month at a time. She also started work on a novel, *I Lit Myself on Fire*, works two days a month at the Wilkins County Women's Shelter, which she helped start with the money from her first book and where all of the women in her walking group also volunteer.

Within about 35 minutes of finishing her walk, Sandy drove back to Lenny Sorensen's pig farm. Within about another 15 minutes, both of them ended up in Lenny's down-filled bed. Lenny sold her farm in less than 30 days, enrolled in the University of Wisconsin-Milwaukee, where she finished her engineering degree and promptly received about 21 job offers. The two women purchased a 20-acre piece of land adjacent to Chris's property, where they built a home that has a great room more than large enough to accommodate the bimonthly women's meetings and all of their children, who visit and can't wait to stay with aunties Len and Sandy.

Gail rushed back into the arms of her husband, never bothered to take a shower, and drove him right to the spot where she had imagined making love to him and then did just that - for about 24 hours straight. She also made Bruce fly with her to Las Vegas, where they were married again in the Little Chapel of the King on Elvis Presley Blvd. Gail drank four margarita's and sang at a small casino and made $123 in tips. She also took a trip with her mother to Paris, where they reconciled, and where she convinced her mother to buy a condo near her so they could spend more time together.

Susan had her abortion. Alice, of course, went with her, and then helped for several weeks while Susan filed for divorce, put her house on the market, and applied for a new job in Administration at Northwestern Mutual Life Insurance, with more pay. Susan also enrolled in graduate school at Marquette University, where she finished her Master's Degree and then took another job at Wilkins Memorial Hospital. She is now in charge of the newly-formed Women's Health Center where non-traditional forms of medicine, including meditation, yoga, acupuncture and herbal treatments are offered. She is also in the midst of a glorious affair with a wealthy, good looking, single orthopedic surgeon who will do anything in the world for her. The surgeon is a woman, and she is not married to anyone else.

Mary was so inspired by her friend's ability to pick up and do whatever they wanted that she quickly ordered her husband to obtain a conditional use permit for the craft store she had always wanted to build on the edge of her property. Much to her husband's dismay, she called the store The Menstrual Hut. Within just a few weeks, women crafters from a six-state area discovered her unique candles, needlework, and the pottery that she was creating on her old wheel that had been in the storage shed since two weeks following her high school graduation. Oprah Winfrey, whose mother lives in Wisconsin, actually brought her mother to the store, and then had Mary on a show featuring women who do their own thing and don't give a damn what anyone else thinks.

Janice immersed herself in learning all she could about herbal remedies and preventative medicine after she came back from the walking adventure. She became an expert in the use of phytochemicals as a way to better mental and physical health. With a loan from Chris and her husband, she opened a spa and health center in a Milwaukee suburb that includes a small tea store that showcases Chinese teas. In particular, The Elegant Gathering of White Snows. Within six months, the spa became so popular that Paul built an addition, and is planning to retire early from his trucking job in order to help manage the new business.

The eight women continue to meet on a regular basis, share their hearts and lives, and have booked a suite of rooms in Tahiti next spring to celebrate the third anniversary of their walk. The women walkers who have daughters also talk constantly about the women's groups their own daughters have formed now in Nevada, Minnesota, London, at the Wilkins County High School and on every other Thursday in J.J.'s living room.

Other Titles Available from Spinsters Ink Books

The Magister, Sally Miller Gearhart $14.00
Martha Moody, Susan Stinson $10.95
Modern Daughters and the Outlaw West, Melissa Kwasny . $9.95
Mother Journeys: Feminists Write About Mothering,
Sheldon, Reddy, Roth $15.95
Night Diving, Michelene Esposito $14.00
Nin, Cass Dalglish $12.00
No Matter What, Mary Saracino $9.95
Ordinary Justice, Trudy Labovitz $12.00
The Other Side of Silence, Joan M. Drury $9.95
The Racket, Anita Mason $12.95
Ransacking the Closet, Yvonne Zipter $9.95
Report for Murder, V. L. McDermid $10.95
Roberts' Rules of Lesbian Break-ups, Shelly Roberts $5.95
Roberts' Rules of Lesbian Dating, Shelly Roberts $5.95
Roberts' Rules of Lesbian Living, Shelly Roberts $5.95
Silent Words, Joan M. Drury $10.95
The Solitary Twist, Elizabeth Pincus $9.95
Sugar Land, Joni Rogers $12.00
They Wrote the Book: Thirteen Women Mystery Writers Tell All,
edited by Helen Windrath $12.00
Those Jordan Girls, Joan M. Drury $12.00
Trees Call for What They Need, Melissa Kwasny $9.95
Turnip Blues, Helen Campbell $10.95
The Two-Bit Tango, Elizabeth Pincus $9.95
Vital Ties, Karen Kringle. $10.95
Voices of the Soft-bellied Warrior, Mary Saracino $14.00
Wanderground, Sally Miller Gearhart $12.95
The Well-Heeled Murders, Cherry Hartman $10.95
Why Can't Sharon Kowalski Come Home?
Thompson & Andrzejewski $12.95
A Woman Determined, Jean Swallow $10.95
The Yellow Cathedral, Anita Mason $14.00

Spinsters titles are available at your local booksellers or by mail order through Spinsters Ink Books. Call 1-800-301-6860 to place an order today. A free catalog is available upon request. See also www.spinsters-ink.com. Please include $2.00 for the first title ordered and 50¢ for every title thereafter. All credit cards accepted.

Spinsters Ink Books

Spinsters Ink Books is one of the oldest feminist publishing houses in the world. It was founded in upstate New York in 1978, and today is an imprint of Hovis Publishing Company, Inc. in Denver, Colorado.

The noun "spinster" means a woman who spins. The definition of the verb "spin" is to whirl and twirl, to revert, to spin on one's heels, to turn everything upside down. Spinsters Ink books do just that—take women's "yarns" (stories, tales) and enable readers to see the world through the other end of the telescope. Spinsters Ink authors move readers off their comfort zones just a bit, pushing the camel through the eye of the needle. These are thinking books for thinking readers.

Spinsters Ink fiction and non-fiction titles deal with significant issues in women's lives from a feminist perspective. They not only name these crucial issues but—more importantly—encourage change and growth. We are committed to publishing works by women writing from the periphery: fat women, Jewish women, lesbians, old women, immigrant women, poor women, rural women, women examining classism, women of color, women with disabilities, women who are writing books that help make the best in our lives more possible.

Spinsters Ink Books
P. O. Box 22005
Denver, CO 80222
USA

Phone: 303-761-5552   Fax: 303-761-5284

E-mail: spinster@spinsters-ink.com
Web site: http://www.spinsters-ink.com

KRIS RADISH is a nationally syndi-
cated columnist, author, journalist
and Pulitzer Prize finalist. Her liberal
political and humor columns appear in
newspapers throughout the United States
and she is the author of the true crime
book *Run, Bambi, Run* (Penquin Books).
She is also the author of the psychology
book, *Birth Order Plus* (Adams Media—
Spring 2002) and her travel writing has
appeared in magazines such as "Midwest Living," "Better Homes
and Gardens," and "Islands."

Radish, a Livingston Awards finalist, has been a working journalist for 25 years and has taught communications courses at two
major universities. She has appeared on television programs in the
United States and Canada, most recently on MSNBC's
"Headliners and Legends," and has received numerous writing
awards.